The Perfect Wreck

"Old Ironsides" and HMS Java:
A Story of 1812

Nonfiction by Steven E. Maffeo

Most Secret and Confidential:
Intelligence in the Age of Nelson

Seize, Burn, or Sink:
The Thoughts and Words of
Admiral Lord Horatio Nelson

The Perfect Wreck
"Old Ironsides" and HMS Java: A Story of 1812

BY

Steven E. Maffeo

Fireship Press
www.FireshipPress.com

ISBN: 978-1-61179-151-8

BISAC Subject Headings:
    FIC014000 FICTION / Historical
    FIC032000 FICTION / War & Military
    HIS036040 HISTORY / United States / 19th Century

This book was edited and produced by Jessica Knauss of Fireship Press

Cover painting: "USS *Constitution* vs. HMS *Java*"
Copyright © by Patrick O'Brien
www.PatrickOBrienStudio.com

Address all correspondence to:
Fireship Press, LLC
P.O. Box 68412
Tucson, AZ 85737

Or visit our website at:
www.FireshipPress.com

1.0

To the Memory of

June Augusta Miller Maffeo

1925 - 2006

Pardon this digression; but the thought of former days brings all my Mother into my heart, which shows itself in my eyes.

> — *Vice Adm. Horatio, Lord Nelson, R.N.*

CONTENTS

To the Reader

This is the true story of the battle between the famous USS *Constitution* ("*Old Ironsides*"), and HMS *Java*, in late 1812. It's told from the viewpoints of the officers and men whose story it is. It's also a narrative of the preceding four months when both of these ships, their captains, and their crews took infinite pains in preparation for their two diverse missions—missions which then took each of them thousands of miles in adventurous blue-water sailing.

I conceived this book as nonfiction, having studied at length a vast treasure of primary-source documents. But it soon occurred to me that it would be more effective with a slight fictional treatment. I thus endeavored to mix solid reporting with novelistic description in a scenic, dramatic fashion—fleshing out the story, filling in the blanks, and adding context and depth. I've tried to add color and texture beyond what those documents present, and communicate information using tools of the fiction writer while maintaining allegiance to fact. This kind of thing has been a goal of such authors as Stephen Crane and Michael Shaara in dealing with military history, and though I don't presume any similar stature, it's been my goal as well.

Many—not all, but many—of the conversations are drawn from the principals' journals and letters, and I assure you that the sequence of events is accurate, the events are confirmed, and every named individual really existed. As Shaara wrote, in *The Killer Angels*, in the crafting of the tale "I have not consciously changed any fact ... I have not knowingly violated the action." I *have* tried to entertain you with an incredible sea story, while simultaneously handing you solid, unequivocal history.

STEVE MAFFEO
Colorado Springs, CO
March, 2011

When history and fiction intertwine, the reader may well like to know how far the recorded facts have suffered from the embrace. In this book I have . . . historical frigate-actions, and when I describe them I keep strictly to the contemporary accounts, to the official letters on service, the courts-martial on the officers who lost their ships, the newspapers and magazines of the time, to . . . contemporary naval historians, of course, and to the biographies and memoirs of those who took part.

It seems to me that where the Royal Navy and indeed the infant United States Navy are concerned, there is very little point in trying to improve the record since the plain, unadorned facts speak for themselves with the emphasis of a broadside.

— Patrick O'Brian
The Fortune of War

~ 1812 ~

The second war between Great Britain and the United States—what would later bear several titles, including the *Second War of American Independence*, the *Anglo-American War*, and the *War of 1812*—began on the eighteenth of June.

The conduct of the Government of Great Britain presents a series of acts hostile to the United States as an independent and neutral nation. British cruisers have been in the continued practice of violating the American flag on the great highway of nations, and of seizing and carrying off persons sailing under it... .British cruisers have been in the practice also of violating the rights and the peace of our coasts. They hover over and harass our entering and departing commerce... .and have wantonly spilt American blood within the sanctuary of our territorial jurisdiction... .Against this crying enormity, which Great Britain would be so prompt to avenge if committed against herself, the United States have in vain exhausted remonstrances and expostulations.

— James Madison, President of the United States

Our Navy is so Lilliputian that Gulliver might bury it in the deep by making water on it.

— John Adams, former President of the United States

England shall not be driven from the proud pre-eminence, which the blood and treasure of her sons have attained for her among nations, by a piece of red, white, and blue-striped bunting flying at the mastheads of a few fir-built frigates, manned by a handful of bastards and outlaws.

— *The Evening Star* (London)

In our navymen I have the utmost confidence, but when I reflect on the overwhelming force of our enemy my heart swells almost to bursting, and all the consolation I have is that, in falling, they will fall nobly.

— Paul Hamilton, U.S. Secretary of the Navy

The Americans will be found to be a different sort of enemy by sea than the French. They possess nautical knowledge, with equal enterprise to ourselves. They will be found attempting deeds which a Frenchman would never think of.

— The Statesman (London)

An English frigate, rated 38 guns, should undoubtedly... cope successfully with a 44-gun ship of any nation.

— The Naval Chronicle (London)

I will ask any man, whether, if two years ago, in the contemplation of a war with the United States of America, it had been prophesied to him, that after six months of hostilities, the only maritime trophies to be gained in the contest, would be on the side of the United States, and that our only consolation that we had not been conquered by land, he would not have treated such a prediction as an insult to the might, the grandeur, and the character of this country?

It never entered into my mind that the mighty naval power of England would be allowed to sit idle while our commerce was swept from the surface of the Atlantic... .It cannot be too deeply felt that the sacred spell of the invincibility of the British Navy was broken by these unfortunate captures.

— George Canning, Member of Parliament

The size and force of the American frigates, with the great number of men they carry, were made known to government long before any difference took place between the two countries. Why, therefore, did they not provide against the chance of our ships falling a prey to the enemy, from inferiority of force?

— The Naval Chronicle (London)

Government appear to be—at last—making a serious effort to get the better of the American navy, which might as well have been made before.

— Gen. Sir Arthur Wellesley,
Marquess of Wellington

It is not merely that an English frigate has been taken, after what we are free to confess may be called a brave resistance, but it has been taken by a new enemy, an enemy unaccustomed to such triumphs and likely to be rendered insolent and confident by them. He must be a weak politician who does not see how important the first triumph is in giving a tone and character to the war.

... there are commanders in the English navy who would a thousand times have rather gone down with their colours flying than have set their brother officers so fatal an example.

— *The London Times*

The Americans have had the satisfaction of proving their courage—they have brought us to speak of them with respect.

— Augustus John Foster
former British Ambassador to the United States

THE MAJOR PLAYERS

United States Navy
(On Board The USS Constitution Unless Otherwise Noted)

Isaac Hull, Commodore, age 39
William Bainbridge, Commodore, age 38
Stephen Decatur, Commodore, age 33 (USS *United States*)
David Porter, Captain, age 32 (USS *Essex*)
James Lawrence, Master Commandant, age 31 (USS *Hornet*)
Amos Binney, Navy Agent (Charlestown Navy Yard)
Charles Morris, First Lieutenant, age 28
George Parker, First Lieutenant, age unknown
Beekman Verplanck Hoffman, Second Lieutenant, age 23
John Templar Shubrick, Third Lieutenant, age 24
Charles W. Morgan, Fourth Lieutenant, age 22
John Cushing Aylwin, Fifth Lieutenant, age 34
John Nichols, Sailing Master, age 31
Amos Alexander Evans, Surgeon, age 27
Peter Adams, Boatswain
William L. Gordon, Midshipman
Henry Gilliam, Midshipman
Adrian Peters, Sergeant, U.S. Marine Corps
Asa Curtis, Able Seaman

Royal Navy
(On Board HMS Java Unless Otherwise Noted)

Sir Richard Hussey Bickerton, Admiral, age 53
(Commander-in-Chief, Portsmouth)
James Richard Dacres, Captain, age 24 (HMS *Guerrière*)
John Surman Carden, Captain, age 41 (HMS *Macedonian*)
Henry Lambert, Captain, age 28
J. W. P. Marshall, Master & Commander, age 27 (Supernumerary)
Henry Ducie Chads, First Lieutenant, age 24
William Allen Herringham, Second Lieutenant, age 22
George Buchanan, Third Lieutenant
Christopher D'Oyley Aplin, Lieutenant (Supernumerary)

James Sanders, Lieutenant (Supernumerary)
Robert Mercer, First Lieutenant, Royal Marines
Batty Robinson, Sailing Master
James Humble, Boatswain
Thomas Armstrong, Gunner
James Kennedy, Carpenter
T. C. Jones, Surgeon
William Falls, Assistant Surgeon
Matthew Capponi, Assistant Surgeon (Supernumerary)
John "Barbecue" Smith, Cook
Charles Speedy, Petty Officer
Benjamin Pauling, Second-class Boy (Supernumerary)
George Herue, Third-class Boy (Supernumerary)

British Army
(Supernumeraries onboard HMS Java)

Thomas Hislop, Lieutenant General, age 48
Thomas Walker, Major
John T. Wood, Captain

PROLOGUE

SINGAPORE HARBOR 1845

Singapore Harbor
Malay Peninsula
1°17' N 103°51' E
Wednesday, February 5th, 1845
9:45 a.m.

"Hip... hip... hip..." The oars of the gig bit the water in perfect time to the coxswain's cadence. A British naval ensign fluttered behind the coxswain at the boat's stern. The ensign, and the hat ribbons of the boat's crew—gold letters on black which spelled out "H.M.S. Cambrian"—signified that the gig belonged to a senior officer.

The boat neared the large three-masted warship which had dropped single anchor at the mouth of the Singapore River the previous day. The blue-and-gold-clad officer seated next to the coxswain ordered a halt.

"Ease all," barked the coxswain. The gig gently rose and fell on the calm water. The officer impassively studied the ship while the men rested on their oars. His eye told him that the ship was far from new. In fact, it was very much of an older era. Perhaps 180 feet in length and around 50 feet across the beam, her sides were pierced for about 50 guns. Her masts stood tall and straight with yards, sails, and rigging ship-shape and even Bristol fashion. As that thought crossed his mind he smiled, for the English seaport of Bristol had very little to do with the Stars and Stripes of the United States, which drooped from the old ship's spanker gaff in the light Malaysian breeze.

Beneath the seamanlike appearance of the masts, however, the ship looked decidedly unseamanlike, almost decrepit, as well as old. A faded chronology of past paints competed on her sides which accentuated her secondhand appearance. The whole dismal

1

appearance was further degraded by a considerable amount of rust that streamed down the ship's sides, mostly noticeable from the fore-, main-, and mizzenchains, joined by similar discoloration from the multiple pins, bolts, and other iron fittings in the hull. Lastly, her figurehead, which depicted a white-haired gentleman in formal attire, was a shoddy and disheveled mass of peeling paint and salt-scoured wood.

On the whole, the poor old ship was a scruffy, squalid mess—unprofessional, unseamanlike, and certainly un-naval; a pitiful display, a shadow of what she surely once had been. Moreover, the U.S. consul at Singapore, Joseph Balestier, had been on board the day before. He had later reported to the captain of the port that over 150 of the crew were down with dysentery, and that the commanding officer himself was bedridden.

Eyebrows slightly raised, the officer in the boat gave a nod. "Give way," the coxswain growled. The oarsmen resumed their routine—push-lower-pull-raise-push-lower-pull-raise—and the gig glided forward.

"The boat, ahoy!" came the piercing hail from the old warship's quarterdeck.

"*Cambrian!*" the coxswain called back. This was merely nautical custom and formality. In fact, several telescopes had carefully tracked the gig's progress since it left the British frigate across the harbor. The same telescopes had also noted, the day before, the broad pendant of a commodore which flew from her masthead.

With extended boathook the coxswain reached for the old ship's starboard mainchains, hooked on, and drew the gig close in to her hull. With decades of practice behind him, the officer gracefully climbed up the accommodation ladder and stepped through the elegantly carved entry port. He paused, tall and dignified, and gazed politely at the boatswain's mates as they piped him on board. He then formally touched his hat with his right forefinger.

At the ship's bow a loud bang and a jet of smoke introduced the first gun of the salute. Clearly, the Americans were very much ready to honor a distinguished guest this morning. The screech and twitter of the boatswain's calls ended, and the last echo of the fifteen-gun salute rolled slowly around the harbor—actually, echoes of thirty guns, for the *Cambrian* had returned the salute gun for gun. The officer walked forward between the two parallel lines of boatswain's mates, side boys, and marines, who stood rigidly at attention in their finest rigs as they paid him ceremonial respect.

At the end of this short path stood an American officer, also rigid at attention with a telescope under his arm, who had just lowered his hand from his own hat.

"Welcome aboard the United States Ship *Constitution*, sir. We are honored by your visit. I am Amasa Paine, first lieutenant."

The visitor's eyes flickered for a moment at the mention of the ship's name—much as they had the day before when the captain of the port had announced her arrival. "Good morning, young man. I am Commodore Henry Ducie Chads, and it's I who am honored by your kind greeting as well as this most welcome opportunity to visit your fine ship. Furthermore, I'm in haste to offer to you any and all assistance which I—or the facilities of Her Majesty's Navy or the British India Office—can provide."

"That's most gracious of you, Commodore. If you please, my captain's been ill and thus was unable to greet you on deck. But if you'll kindly follow me, it'd be my pleasure to escort you below to the great cabin. The captain's most anxious to meet you and offer some refreshment."

"That would be delightful, Mr. Paine. Pray lead the way."

With a courteous gesture Paine proceeded aft, past the towering mainmast and the enormous capstan, and then paused at the aftermost hatch. "Sir, if I may go ahead . . ." The lieutenant stepped briskly down the companionway ladder.

Chads lingered a moment, then looked back at the entry port. He glanced quizzically about the ship's weather deck—a flush deck from bow to stern with no raised quarterdeck or poop deck. There was a very large hatchway forward, but on either side of it were wide expanses of solid deck, definitely not the open waist and narrow gangways between quarterdeck and forecastle that one might expect on a ship this old. He also noticed that the weather deck, fitted as it was with all the usual and expected equipment and accouterments—which included a considerable number of large-caliber carronades—presented an appearance of more order and repair than the squalor of the ship's exterior had led him to expect. His gaze lingered on the ship's substantial double wheel just aft of the companionway. He then observed a large number of seamen on deck, for the most part pale and lethargic, who—now that the ceremony was over—sat and even lounged in various attitudes of despondency. What might have been amazement on Chads' part, upon seeing this further unseamanlike display, was preempted by his foreknowledge of so many ill among the crew.

Lieutenant Paine waited patiently at the foot of the ladder, one deck down. "This way, sir," he said as he motioned the commodore aft. He knocked on a white-painted door trimmed in natural wood, opened it, and stepped through. Chads had paused for another moment to look forward with narrowed eyes. He thoughtfully examined the two lengthy rows of large, long-barreled black cannon on this, the ship's main gundeck. Again he saw a goodly number of seamen who appeared less-than-robust, taking their ease, faces turned toward the sunlight and slight breeze which came in through the open gunports. Chads turned and followed Paine into the cabin.

"Commodore, if you please, may I name Captain John Percival, commanding the *Constitution*. Captain, this's Commodore Henry Chads, in command of Her Britannic Majesty's Ship *Cambrian* as well as Her Majesty's other ships and vessels on this station."

Captain Percival, known throughout the U.S. Navy as 'Mad Jack' from the days of his impulsive, headstrong youth, had been sitting at the large table that dominated the center of the cabin. He had been pulling at his stock in the humid, eighty-degree weather which was only slightly relieved by the open gunports and stern windows. Favoring his right arm, he had struggled to get to his feet when he heard Paine knock. He now carefully stood, supported by a crutch, and looked every bit his sixty-six years. Leaning slightly against the table, Percival assessed his visitor, who appeared to be in his late fifties. He carefully extended his left hand in greeting.

"Welcome aboard the *Constitution*, Commodore."

"Thank you, Captain Percival," said Chads, who briefly took 'Mad Jack's' hand with both of his. "I'm delighted to be here and to make your acquaintance. However, I'm distressed to see you and so many of your ship's company in not quite the best of health."

"You're very kind, sir, and on that note I beg your pardon for not being able to receive you on deck. This damned gout or rheumatism or whatever it is has laid me pretty low, I can tell you. Mr. Balestier—the American consul, as of course you know—has kindly invited me ashore. Perhaps a few days' rest and Mrs. Balestier's cooking might help me. No doubt it will. Very gracious of them." Percival's face lit up as a thought struck him. "By the way, did you know that Mrs. Balestier's father was Paul Revere, that famous Bostonian—or infamous in your eyes, probably—for his actions at the start of the American Revolution?"

"No, indeed, I did not," replied Chads.

"Well, nevertheless, my bigger problem, as you've no doubt observed, is my men. I have more than 150 of 'em down with dysentery. Frankly, Commodore, we're here to get well and refit. We must before we can proceed with our voyage. And please forgive the wretched appearance of the ship." 'Mad Jack' shook his head, clearly embarrassed. "She looks like the very devil, I know, but it's all we could do to sail her this last month, let alone maintain her."

"Captain Percival, there's nothing for which you need to apologize," replied Chads with a dismissive gesture. "I quite understand. In fact, the substantive reason I'm here is to offer you any assistance we can provide. Our medicos stand ready to come on board, and we could take a considerable number of your men to hospital if anything like that would be agreeable. Whatever we can do to help you and your men back to health—and your ship to a more ready condition—would be our profound pleasure. My facilities are yours to command."

"This is extremely kind of you, Commodore," said Percival. "Particularly kind," he went on, trying to choose his words carefully as he thoughtfully studied his visitor, "as this last year's seen unusual tension between our respective governments. Tension over the boundary dispute in the Oregon territory. Other things. Indeed, sir, I'm not sure relations between our two countries have been this poor these last thirty years. In fact, to be frank, I wasn't quite sure what the nature of our welcome here might be."

"Stuff and nonsense, Captain," replied Chads. "That business is between London and Washington—between Mr. Peel and Mr. Polk. To the best of my knowledge our countries are at peace today; what the future'll bring belongs to the future. You and your men are fellow seamen in need, and that's enough for me."

"You are very good, sir, most gracious. I appreciate your kindness more than I can say," said Percival.

"You're quite welcome. It's settled, then. We'll start to make arrangements this afternoon." Chads paused for a moment. "Captain . . ." he began. His voice trailed off.

Percival waited a moment for Chads to finish his thought. "The commodore was about to say?"

"Yes. Ah, Captain, by any chance, could this vessel be the same *Constitution* that was so successful during the Anglo-American War—the War of 1812—and became known in your service as *Old Ironsides*?"

"Why, yes, sir," replied Percival, beaming. "*Old Ironsides* she surely is. In fact, that very same Paul Revere we just spoke of made her original copper fittings when she was built in Boston, back in '97. Do you know her at all?"

Chads looked out an open gunport. His gaze settled upon the deep blue water of the harbor and his eyes reflected the intense sunlight. "Oh, yes. Yes, I do know her. It was thirty-two years ago, and I daresay something like nine thousand miles from here. I was *Mister* Chads, then, first lieutenant of His Majesty's Frigate *Java*. At the end of a long and terrible afternoon, unsteady from my injuries, I stood right about here—in this very cabin— talking to your predecessor, a Commodore Bainbridge. Interestingly enough, Captain Percival, I recollect that Mr. Bainbridge was like you—also on crutches—due to wounds he'd received that day."

Chads paused and briefly bowed toward Lieutenant Paine. "I also knew *your* predecessor as first lieutenant—a Mr. Parker, who at that same interview stood about where you are now." He again gazed out through the gunport. "On that day this fine ship—*Old Ironsides,* indeed—was masterfully maneuvered, and it made me truly regret that she weren't British. It was really 'Greek met Greek,' you know—for after all, we were and are of the same blood. In any event, that unfortunate day was the twenty-ninth of December, 1812. I remember it all pretty well." With a slight smile, Chads turned back around to face the amazed Percival and Paine.

CHAPTER 1

North Atlantic Ocean
710 nautical miles east of Boston
Vicinity 41°42' N 55°48' W
Wednesday, August 19th, 1812
6:45 p.m.
Winds from the north

The U.S. Frigate *Constitution* backed her main topsail and, as her way came off, slowed virtually to a stop. She now lay quietly across the stern of H.M. Frigate *Guerrière*. Twenty-five American gun captains looked down the barrels of their short weather-deck 32-pounder carronades or their long main-deck 24-pounder cannons. In quiet voices they directed their crews to make whatever slight adjustments were needed to point each piece at the center of the *Guerrière*'s already much-battered stern. The *Guerrière* was for all purposes a complete and sinking wreck. All three masts had fallen and trailed in the water, dragging along a confused mass of sails and rigging. Large sections of her sides had been smashed in by the *Constitution*'s heavy shot, and around thirty of those shot had pierced the *Guerrière* well below the waterline, which allowed tons of water to pour into her hold at a rate far beyond the crew's ability to pump it out—even if that crew were not already exhausted. And of those Guerrières, more than 100 had been killed, or wounded, or were missing.

From the *Constitution*'s quarterdeck came a hail across the water, magnified and metalicized by a brass speaking trumpet: "Have you struck?" There was no reply, but a few moments later the White Ensign fluttered down from the stump of the *Guerrière*'s mizzenmast and a cannon was fired to leeward. On the *Constitution*'s quarterdeck a small boarding party was told-off, clambered down the ship's side, and threw itself into the No. 2 cutter which had just been pulled alongside. It and two of the *Consti-*

tution's other boats had been lowered, as the ship cleared for action, and had been towed astern during the battle where they were instantly ready for use—and reasonably safe from shot.

Only a few strokes of the oars brought the cutter off the *Guerrière*'s starboard quarter. The leader of the boarding party, Lieutenant George Read, cupped his hands and called up to the officers he could see on deck. "The ship, ahoy! Sir, Captain Hull's compliments, and wishes to confirm if you have indeed struck your flag."

There was a pause, in fact a lengthy pause, which caused the Americans some alarm. A shout of "What's afoot?" was heard from a seaman as he peered out of a gunport on the *Constitution,* followed by another: "Let's sink 'em!" However—finally—a dry, educated English voice floated down to the American boat. "Well, I really don't know. Our mizzenmast is gone, our mainmast is gone, and upon the whole, you may say we have struck our flag."

A few minutes later Lieutenant Read and several of his boat's crew came up the *Guerrière*'s side and onto her deck, carefully timing their climb against the wild rolling of the essentially dismasted ship. Read quickly spotted the captain on the quarterdeck and made his way toward him. All the while the lieutenant guarded his balance against the steep roll; with all three of her masts now nothing more than wreckage afloat in the water, their stabilizing pressure on the hull was gone and the *Guerrière* rolled like a log in the trough of the sea. Read skillfully watched his step as he looked around. The deck had the appearance of a slaughterhouse. A number of the crew were employed in unceremoniously throwing some of the many dead overboard. In addition to the considerable amount of blood, the deck was also extremely slippery with switchel—a rustic molasses and rum drink prepared before the battle by the *Guerrière*'s crew, who had been confident that they would serve it to the Americans when they captured the *Constitution.* For some reason they had hoisted the puncheon aloft on the *Guerrière*'s mainstay, from where the switchel had rained down everywhere when the cask was shattered by a shot during the fight.

Some of the gun tackles were not fast, and thus several of the cannons were loose and surged dangerously from one side to the other. Some of the seamen and petty officers had apparently broken into the spirit rooms and were already intoxicated. Along with the groans and screams of the wounded, the noise and confusion of the survivors made the whole scene one from hell itself. Midshipman Henry Gilliam, who walked close behind Lieutenant Read, tore his gaze from the appalling sight and looked out to sea.

"Good God," he said, mostly to himself, as he tried to assimilate it. "Pieces of skulls, brains, legs, arms, and blood lie in every direction. I've never seen *anything* like this. Damn it! The screams of the wounded are enough to make me curse the war."

On board the *Constitution*, Captain Isaac Hull stood by the bulwark next to Carronade No. 16, his telescope trained on the cutter hooked to the *Guerrière*'s side. His eyes strained to pierce the falling darkness. Lieutenant John Shubrick stood on the other side of the massive and brutal-looking gun—still quite hot from the battle—peering through his own glass. "Captain, during the action, did you per chance hear some of the men cheer and claim the ship is made of iron?"

"No, John, I didn't," replied Hull as he turned toward him with a surprised look. "What's it all about?"

"Well, sir, early on a few of the enemy's shot apparently struck the side, failed to penetrate, and fell into the sea, whereupon some of the men who perceived this cried out, 'Huzzay! See where the shot fell out? Her sides must be made of iron!'"

"Ha!" exclaimed Hull. "Ha! Iron, is it? I like it; I do indeed. You know, of course, our sister the *United States* has the rather unfortunate nickname of 'Old Wagon,' due to her being a poor sailer. Commodore Decatur has the devil of a time trying to stop his men from so calling the ship, and from calling themselves 'Wagoners.' I think 'Old Ironsides' has a much better ring to it— perhaps that's how our dear *Constitution* might now be known." Hull tugged at the seat of his too-tight trousers, which he had split during the excitement of the battle. "I see some irony to it. There're those who think it's that same *United States*—and not *us*—which has the hardest and stoutest sides of our 44-gun frigates."

On board the *Guerrière,* Read came up to the British captain and touched his hat. "Sir, I am Lieutenant George Read, United States Navy, third lieutenant of the U.S. Frigate *Constitution*. My captain, Isaac Hull, Esquire, desires me to request your presence on board the *Constitution* at your earliest convenience. In addition, may I offer to you the services of our surgeon? It appears that you have many killed and wounded, and I perceive you are injured yourself."

"That's most kind of you, Mr. Read," replied the *Guerrière*'s captain, "but I can't possibly deprive your wounded of care in order to help mine."

"Oh, sir, just never you mind about that. We only had a handful of wounded and they've all been attended to. Our surgeon's quite at leisure." Read broke off as he realized how this remark added to the captain's already palpable embarrassment concerning this terribly one-sided battle.

Fifteen minutes later, visibly hampered by his wound—a graze across his back from a musket ball—the British captain awkwardly climbed up the *Constitution*'s accommodation ladder. Captain Hull met him at the entry port and helped him onto the quarterdeck. "Sir," the Englishman began as he rigidly stood, obviously in pain and somewhat dazed. "I am Captain James Richard Dacres. I regret that it's my painful duty to surrender to you His Britannic Majesty's Frigate *Guerrière*."

"Captain Dacres, I am Captain Isaac Hull. Welcome aboard the United States Frigate *Constitution*." Dacres nodded and proffered his sword. He tried to place the hilt in the American captain's hand, but Hull pushed it away. "No, no, I won't take the sword from a man who knows so well how to use it. Please come below to my cabin and we'll attend to your injury."

Dacres started to walk aft with Hull but then suddenly stopped and faced him. "Captain Hull, what've you got for men? I've lost a hundred of mine. And I—I am finished, I'm entirely ruined."

"Oh," replied Hull with a smile. He was sorry for Dacres' misery but for a moment unable to contain himself. "As to that, Captain Dacres, I've met you with only a parcel of green Yankee bushwhackers."

"Bushwhackers? They're more like tigers than men—I never saw men fight so. They fairly drove us from our quarters. My decks are running with blood."

"I deeply regret the loss of life this day's seen," said Hull, his smile gone. "Sure, I don't mind battle—the excitement carries one through. But the afterward's truly fearful. It's dreadful to see so many fine lads killed and so many others wounded and suffering."

"Captain Dacres," Hull continued, taking him by the arm, "we'll try to save your ship if we can but even now I perceive she's sustained too much damage. Most of my boats'll swim and I daresay one or two of yours will also. Thus we'll work through the night to bring your men across. Is there anything left on board that you'd particularly want saved?"

"Oh, yes, yes," Dacres replied after a moment. "My mother's Bible."

CHAPTER 2
NORTH ATLANTIC OCEAN

North Atlantic Ocean
830 nautical miles southeast of
St. John's, Newfoundland
Vicinity 41°04' N 35°24' W
Thursday, August 13th, 1812
9:30 a.m.
Winds westerly

The U.S. Frigate *Essex*, 32 guns, had left New York on the fourth of July. Today was the fortieth day of her first war cruise, and she began it by standing to the southward, sailing under single-reefed topsails. She wore British colors—any ship could fly false colors, up to the point when she opened fire, as this was a common and completely legal *ruse de guerre*. This morning she sighted to windward—purely by chance—H.M. Ship-Sloop *Alert*, 20 guns. At first the Americans misidentified the *Alert* as a merchant ship because she presented the appearance of an armed British West Indiaman. The *Essex*'s captain, David Porter, was really on a hunt for a British frigate of a match to his own. Nevertheless, he was certainly interested in this smaller vessel.

As a coincidence, three days earlier, Porter had kept all hands busy with alterations to the *Essex*, so instead of looking like the trim, beautiful, and dangerous warship she was, she now looked like an old and indifferently kept merchant ship. Her gun stripe— the broad ochre band which ran down the length of her gunports, typical of warships—was painted out to match the rest of her black hull. Her half-port gunports had been tightly closed, tapped in, and painted over, and now were invisible to the eye even with a telescope. Her topgallant masts were housed, her clean and open cross-tree platforms were built up to appear as bulky crow's nests, and her yards and sails were trimmed in a careless manner. Neither officers nor marines wore their uniform coats, and all hands on the weather deck comported themselves in a leisurely, decid-edly un-naval, manner. Now her crew stealthily deployed two "drags" at the stern. These drags were previously rigged bundles of canvas and line that, when opened under water, would create a significant counter pull to the forward motion of the ship. Thus, when the crew set more sail, the *Essex* would appear to be ear-nestly on the fly—but would really be easy to overtake.

Once the drags were out and began to open, Porter quickly sent men aloft to shake out the reefs and spread more canvas. He then altered course to move away from the *Alert*. Porter also had other men simulate alarm by moving about on deck in a confused manner—all in an effort to help the British believe that the *Essex* was a defenseless commercial vessel desperately trying to get away from an unknown threat.

Taking all this in, the British officers on board the *Alert* not surprisingly concluded that this "chase" must indeed be a mer-chantman, probably an American, and thus the *Alert* bore down on the *Essex* under a press of canvas. On her nearer approach, the *Alert* raised a British ensign and pendant, and so identified herself as a commissioned warship. Accordingly, the *Essex*'s crew took a strain to keep their motions out of sight. They went to quarters and cleared for action—but left the ship's gunports sealed. Her heavy battery of 32-pounder carronades hid behind those ports, fully loaded and ready. The *Alert* fired the traditional gun across the American ship's bow; the *Essex* submissively hove-to. The British ship passed under the American vessel's stern. At that point the *Essex* brought down her British ensign and ran up the Stars and Stripes. In response the *Alert* rounded on the *Essex*'s lee quarter and, while her crew gave three cheers, fired a broadside of grapeshot and canister—to little effect as the broadside delivered hardly more injury than did the cheers.

Porter roared out a series of orders. The *Essex* spun around, a second American flag appeared at the gaff, the crew slammed open her gunports, and with an incredible thunderous roar, fifteen car-ronades hurled 480 pounds of iron roundshot into the *Alert*, rak-ing her as she wore. With the ship suddenly, surprisingly, and vio-lently stricken, many of her astonished crew threw down their equipment, deserted their posts, and ran below decks. Now it was the *Alert*'s turn to try to flee, in all earnestness, not in any sham. But in an instant the *Essex* ranged alongside, hoisted a flag which bore the motto "Free Trade & Sailors' Rights," and fired several more shots into her hull.

With a number of men down, as well as a shocking amount of

seawater already seven feet deep in the hold and rapidly on the rise, the British captain wore his ship round onto the other tack. This was to bring the many below-waterline shot holes above the surface in an effort to prevent his ship from sinking. He then took stock of his situation, which only took him a moment. The *Alert* fired a musket to leeward and struck her colors—a complete surrender after an action that had lasted only eight minutes between the first shot and the last.

Porter took verbal reports from his officers, mostly to the effect that the *Essex* had received only a few musket balls and grapeshot in her hull and sails. He laughed out loud when the carpenter remarked, "Sir, the greatest injury we've sustained is in your cabin—your windows are broke by the concussion of our own guns."

Still smiling, Porter picked up his speaking trumpet and hailed the vanquished enemy, "What ship's that?"

"His Britannic Majesty's Sloop *Alert*, 20 guns, Thomas Laugharne, master and commander," was the response. "What ship is *that*?"

"The United States Frigate *Essex*, 32 guns, Captain David Porter. Good morning to you, sir, and you will kindly stand by for my boat."

CHAPTER 3

H.M. DOCKYARD, PORTSMOUTH

H.M. Dockyard, Portsmouth
Portsea Island
Hampshire, England
50°49' N 1°05' W
Thursday, September 10th, 1812
2:38 p.m.

"Hip... hip... hip..." The crew of the blue-painted gig pulled smoothly and steadily as the coxswain softly called the time. As the boat moved across Portsmouth Harbor the slight breeze gently rippled the water. A young officer sat in the sternsheets beside the coxswain. He was a lieutenant in his early twenties with a ruddy complexion, light brown hair, and hazel eyes. His feet were firmly braced against his brass-bound sea chest. His undress round hat was pulled low to provide some relief against the afternoon sun, which glared down from an unusually clear sky. The coxswain threaded his way among the congested mass of ships, lighters, piers, and wharves which crowded the greatest and busiest naval base in the world. As they passed between the Scavenger's Jetty to the north, and the Pitch House Jetty to the south, they entered the dockyard's Great Basin. Arrayed straight ahead were the four dry-docks which bordered the east side of this sheltered staging area. The lieutenant glanced to the right, looked beyond the empty South Dock, and admired the row of massive red-brick store-houses—the Present Use Storehouse the closest. He then looked to the left. His eyes narrowed as he focused upon the tall, particularly beautiful frigate which was moored against the basin's north side.

"Thar she be, zir, 'is Britannic Majesty's Ship *Java*," said the coxswain with a broad smile. With a gesture the officer ordered the coxswain to stop. "Ease all," he barked, "rest yer oars." As the men ceased to row and the way came off the gig, the lieutenant studied the frigate with full attention.

She was indeed a beautiful and graceful-looking ship, which spoke to her French origins. Not for nothing were Spanish and French naval architects widely considered the best in the world, who could consistently combine the most elegant form with the most effective function. She was, the lieutenant already knew, 152 feet in length along the gundeck, she had a beam of 40 feet, and her burthen was slightly more than 1,070 tons. HMS *Java* was actually the late 40-gun French frigate *Renommée*, captured in a brisk action off Madagascar in May 1811 after she sustained a shocking loss of 145 men killed and wounded. Among the dead that day had been her captain, and among the severely wounded her first lieutenant.

She had been built in Nantes just seven years ago. Though she had seen more active service than many French ships, she had been maintained reasonably well, and though her losses in men off Madagascar had been terrible, her material damage had not been severe. A valuable prize of war, she had been brought into the Royal Navy. After a slow and roundabout journey to England she recently had spent several weeks here in one of the drydocks. Thus significant dock work had already been finished. Now, for nigh on a month, she had lain in the basin, busy with the details of fitting out, taking on board stores and provisions, and working through the various routines required to get a ship ready for a long voyage.

She had been recently painted, a uniform black relieved by a minimum of gold and white trim at bow and stern, and a deep-yellow stripe which ran the length of the gundeck. This stripe, regularly broken up by the black squares of the gunports, gave the ship the standard "Nelson checker," so-called in tribute to Vice Admiral Lord Nelson whose favorite color scheme it was. At this point, seven years after Nelson's death at Trafalgar, this appearance had essentially become the navy standard. The ship was many tons light and thus she rode high, showing quite a bit of her new below the waterline copper sheathing. This was only to be expected because it was obvious that her great guns were not yet aboard, not to mention she had only begun to take aboard the many tons of water, provisions, and stores which would be needed. Much of her standing rigging appeared complete but virtually none of her running rigging was as yet in place.

The lieutenant could see a number of men at work on deck, some on the rigging and some apparently on the gun tackles. A couple of these men noticed the gig and called out to the sole blue-clad officer in sight. The lieutenant in the gig observed this and nodded, whereupon the coxswain set his men back in motion. A few pulls on the oars brought the gig to the ship's side. "Pin 'er, Bill," called out the coxswain, and the bowman reached out with his boathook and caught fast at the mainchains. "Thankee, men," said the lieutenant as he stood up. He clapped onto the handropes and climbed the shallow steps mounted on the ship's side, greatly assisted by the *Java*'s tumblehome—the graceful inward slope of the outer hull. He came through the entry port and as he stepped down onto the quarterdeck his eyes swept the busy scene. He looked keenly at the many activities making the ship ready for sea, and then faced aft and doffed his hat in respect to the quarterdeck and the colors. The blue-coated officer he had observed from the gig approached; they both touched their hats in compliment to each other. As he extended his hand the young officer spoke first. "Good afternoon—I'm Chads, first lieutenant."

"Oh yes, Mr. Chads, glad to have you aboard, sir," returned the older man with a smile and a handshake. "I'm delighted to make your acquaintance. I'm Robinson, sailing master. The captain's been expecting you these past two tides. I understand that you and he served together for several years in the old *Iphigenia*—to include the action at the Mauritius in the year ten. Indeed, sir, he speaks extraordinarily highly of you. He'll want to see you directly; will you allow me to see you below?"

Chads followed Robinson down the companionway and aft to the great cabin. The master tapped on the light wood of the door and called, "Captain Lambert, sir, it's Lieutenant Chads come aboard at last."

The door flew open. "By God, Henry, it *is* you!" cried Lambert as he shifted pencil and papers to one hand and with the other he clapped Chads on the shoulder. "Welcome aboard," he continued as he drew Chads into the cabin. "Thank you, Mr. Robinson, I know you must return to the deck, but if you're at leisure in an hour's time I'd be delighted if you'd join us for dinner." Robinson bowed, said he was infinitely honored, and retraced his steps.

"My dear friend," said Lambert as he waved Chads to a chair, "take off your coat, sit down, and loosen your stock. Pour yourself a glass of that claret—well, at least Clements, that wicked old Gosport wine-seller across the harbor, *says* it's claret. I dare say you've had a long several days travel."

"Long but tolerable, sir," said Chads, "not so bad on the whole. I was a little sorry to leave the *Semiramis* but I'm delighted to be back with you." Lambert smiled and also sat as he spread his papers down onto the table in front of him.

"Henry, let me give you a *précis* of how things are coming along. At this point, as I told you in my letter, I've only a general notion of Admiralty's plans for us—and that just verbally. I expect my written orders soon with all the horrid details. However, I can tell you that we're bound for India. We're to carry out despatches to India and several other stations along the way, and we're to carry out the newly appointed governor of Bombay—a Lieutenant General Thomas Hislop—and his suite. Lastly, we're to carry out a considerable supply of stores—particularly copper sheathing—for ships building at Bombay. Let me see," he continued as he poked at one of his papers. "Ah, yes, they're the ship of the line *Cornwallis* and two ten-gun sloops, the *Chameleon* and the *Icarus*."

"Really, sir," said Chads, one eyebrow raised. "Letters, passengers, stores. Couldn't all these things go out in an Indiaman or a packet? Why a frigate? On the face of it, I must say it appears to lack glory."

"Well," replied Lambert with a smile, "I daresay they could, and I daresay it does. Yes. However, after we deliver all our papers, passengers, and stores the *Java* is not to return home, but is to be attached to the East Indies squadron. We're to bolster the force of Sir Samuel Hood, so in light of that their lordships no doubt think it's all terribly efficient. In any event, the *Java* came out of drydock in early August and's been here in the basin since. I should think we'll haul out to moorings in the harbor around the first of October. I could wish it would be sooner. I came on board in the morning of August twentieth, hoisted the pendant, and took charge of the ship agreeable to my commission. The whole thing was done with precious little ceremony. No point, really, as you can well imagine there was hardly anyone else present aside from the standing officers and myself." Lambert drummed his fingers on the table.

"The weather's been pretty tolerable," he continued, "moderate breezes and fine for the most part. Actually it's been damned pleasant. It's only rained three times and that only briefly. Since mid-August we've had a party of dockyard mateys employed fitting out the ship for a few hours every day—usually in the forenoon. They even came on board last Sunday, for all love, though as you know that's not usually their custom. I really must say they've been pretty useful at a whole variety of work, so I suppose I should give 'em their due and refer to them as 'artificers.' As you know, they seem to like that expression rather more than 'mateys.'" At that both men smiled and shook their heads. In general terms the Royal Navy's dockyard workmen had a reputation for independence, arrogance and, at times, remarkable corruption. At the same time, however, they could be extraordinarily skilled and hard workers.

"In addition to the dockyard men, we've also been blessed with several gangs of harbor-duty men brought on board from several vessels. More than the others, one of these has been the harbor-service ship *Gladiator*—there, you can just see her a little beyond the entrance to the basin." Lambert waved a hand towards the graceful expanse of the cabin's stern windows. "On a typical day—again, to include the odd Sunday—we see from ten to thirty such men come aboard. Thus far Mr. Armstrong, he's the gunner, has been the primary beneficiary of their aid; as of today they've worked for him seven days. They've scraped and repainted the gun carriages and have fitted the gun tackles and breechings. I daresay you saw some of that sort of thing on deck just now as you arrived."

"Yes, sir; just so," replied Chads.

"We only have a handful of our own crew on board at present, and those essentially just the officers. So, until we get our full drafts of men, we're extraordinarily dependent upon the dockyard mateys and the harbor-duty men to get us fitted out, provisions stowed, and otherwise ready for sea—and for a very long voyage at that. Oh, we've received most of our marines—that was on August twenty-ninth—but by no means all of 'em. As to stores, well, they come on board slowly. To date," he paused to consult another list among his mass of papers, "we've taken aboard 92 pounds of cask beef from the schooner *Vesta* and 304 pounds from the sloop *Cherub*. From the Victualling Office itself the numbers are a little more substantial: 1,102 pounds of fresh beef, 1,568 pounds of bread, 366 pounds of cheese, 5 large bags of vegetables, and 3 casks—that's 194 gallons—of wine." He stopped and scratched his ear.

"As you've seen, we await our great guns. I hope to have 'em come aboard in the next fortnight or so. The French guns were, of course, taken out; as you know the differences in calibration, weights, and measures demanded it. Can't very well put an English eighteen-pound ball in a gun made to take one of nineteen pounds seven ounces—it just won't do."

Chads nodded. "What exactly will our armament be, Captain?"

"Oh, we'll officially fit her out as a thirty-eight," said Lambert, "so it'll be pretty much the usual, which is to say a few more than that. Twenty-eight 18-pounder long guns on the gundeck, fourteen

32-pounder carronades on the quarterdeck, and on the fo'c'sle two more carronades and two 9-pounder chase guns."

Lambert looked up at Chads and smiled. "Well, Henry, that's it. I expect the rest of this month'll repeat this pattern and, as I mentioned, I hope we'll haul out of this damned cramped basin no later than the first of October. I think, on the whole, things are coming along pretty well though I'm not quite easy in my mind in regard to our manning. As you of all people know, everything else can be of the top order, but if we don't have a crew—I mean a full crew with a good proportion of right seamen among 'em—then it'll all come to naught."

The rest of September did, in fact, proceed much in accord with Captain Lambert's expectations—and to his fears. Fortunately, the unpredictable English weather continued to smile upon him, mostly fine and pleasant with only a few cloudy days and only five days with some scattered, light rain. The artificers came on board for another thirteen days—and separate gangs of dockyard riggers reported for eight days—all of whom brought the *Java* ever closer to her full material readiness.

In addition, drafts of harbor-duty men came on board almost every day and fell-to on a myriad of vital tasks. These men, infinitely useful and generally cheerful seamen borrowed from other ships, were at this point priceless surrogates for the *Java*'s continuing lack of her regular crew. They spent another two days assisting the gunner with the tackles, breechings, and carriages in preparation for when the great guns should be brought on board. Then—again on an almost daily basis—they brought on board and stowed a seemingly never-ending stream of provisions and stores, all critical for a large ship getting ready for a long voyage and foreign service. Such items were obtained from several sources which included various provision lighters and hoys, the harbor-service hulks *Speedy* and *Cuba*, and of course the dockyard's vast storehouses. The duty men not only had to handle the stores but also had to crew the lighters, hoys, and hulks, which included alternately bringing the lighters and hoys alongside the *Java* and then returning them to their moorings. During these twenty days a considerable amount of additional provisions came on board and was carefully stowed. This included large amounts of fresh beef, cask salt beef, oatmeal, bread, vegetables (at this time of year mostly cabbages, onions, carrots, and turnips), cheese, butter, sugar, and wine.

Bringing on board the fresh water was an enormous task in itself. Somewhat unusually, during a three-day period mid-month, they received and stowed twenty-six 400-gallon iron tanks. While the iron water tank for shipboard use was not anything like a new invention, the introduction in the previous year of Lieutenant George Truscott's improved pump had greatly facilitated the Royal Navy's transition from the traditional wooden water cask. Not only could a large iron tank hold more than a cask; more important the tanks could be stowed with much more efficient use of space. Deep down in the hold tiers of these close-fitting cubes were superior to casks, for due to their odd shapes even closely packed casks left considerable gaps and open spots. The Truscott pumps could easily move water in-and-out of the tanks and, for that matter, using leather hoses they could just as easily move water to the galley. They could also fill small tanks on deck; such tanks potentially could eliminate the centuries-old traditional scuttlebutts for ready-use drinking water. Thus, after these new tanks were stowed, over a five-day period the duty men toiled to bring on board over ninety-five tons of water—with two-hundred eighty more tons needed before the *Java* should leave port.

Indeed, the *Java* was gorging herself full—as she must—for once at sea her hungry and thirsty crew would consume close to one-and three-quarters tons of food and drink per day.

In the afternoon of the twenty-second Lambert called Chads and Robinson to his cabin. "See here, gentlemen, the port-admiral's flag lieutenant just brought me the Admiralty's formal confirmation for victualing. I'm very glad to have it indeed, since we're hip-deep in getting it done anyway. Ha!" Chads took the proffered papers and read aloud for the benefit of the master.

To Hy Lambert Esq.
Capn Java
Portsmouth

To complete for foreign service.

Having ordered the Stores of the Ship you command to be completed at Portsmouth for foreign service, that Provision to six Months of all species including Wine or Spirits, on having so done repair to Spithead for orders holding Yourself in constant readiness for sailing.

Given on 21st Sept. 1812

Vice Adm. W. Dommett
Rear Adm. J. S. Yorke
Rear Adm. G. J. Hope

"Well, sir," said Chads as he looked up from the letters—for there was also enclosed a copy of the Admiralty's parallel orders to the Victualling Board—"thank God for that. Thus far, on the whole, the victuallers have seemed willing enough, but this should cause 'em to stretch out even a bit more."

Of course the steady stream of supplies did not include just water and victuals, but also boatswains' and carpenters' stores of all kinds, from the enormous—such as the four huge anchors and the eight cables of 17½-inch circumference—to the miniscule—such as the twenty-four 20-second sand glasses. The anchors, cables, and hawsers alone had caused the duty men four solid days of backbreaking effort to get them aboard and secure them. In the case of the cables and hawsers, this included carefully coiling and stowing their seemingly endless lengths in the tiers below decks.

Naturally, all of this work was done under the careful eyes of the standing officers as well as the particular expertise of the first lieutenant and the sailing master. Indeed, it was generally agreed that it *was* all going pretty well. But, it was the crew, or rather the lack thereof, which kept Lambert restlessly tossing in his cot at night. For, despite the assurances of the Admiralty *and* the port admiral that men—plenty of men—would shortly come forth, Lambert found no comfort. The prodigious amount of work that had been done since the *Java* came out of drydock had almost all been accomplished by dockyard workmen and harbor-duty men. A ship without a crew was really no ship at all, but by the end of September the only true ship's company that were aboard were Captain Lambert himself; Mr. Chads, first lieutenant; Mr. Herringham, second lieutenant; Mr. Buchanan, third lieutenant; Mr. Robinson, sailing master; Mr. Humble, boatswain; Mr. Armstrong, gunner; Mr. Scott, purser; Mr. Kennedy, carpenter; Mr. Jones, surgeon; Mr. Falls, assistant surgeon; Mr. Barton, captain's clerk; John Smith, cook; Lieutenants Stewart and Davis and fifty-four Royal Marines; the master-at-arms; two master's mates; seven midshipmen; two first-class volunteers; one second-class boy; nine third-class boys; five able seamen; two ordinary seamen; and three landmen.

The dawn of Thursday, October first, ushered in a cloudy morning with moderate and variable winds. Crew or no crew, the dockyard superintendent had deemed the *Java* fitted enough and ballasted sufficiently. Thus, at six bells in the morning watch, using four hawsers alternately attached to various dolphins—dolphins being the heavy posts found along the quays and on pilings driven into the mud—she was warped out of the shelter of the

Great Basin. Once in the crowded harbor, about pistol-shot distance—fifty yards—off the South Jetty, she was secured to fixed mooring buoys just alongside the *Cuba* hulk. Captain Lambert was pleased—this movement was certainly a milestone in the *Java's* preparations and was in accordance with the private timeline he had formed in his mind when first given this commission. Moreover, the dockyard and the Victualling Office both seemed determined to hurry-along the *Java* in accordance with their own schedules. As a matter of fact, that very afternoon—despite the heavy rain that had inundated most of Hampshire—an ordnance lighter appeared alongside with two of the *Java's* twenty-eight 18-pounder long guns on board. It also brought out marine First Lieutenant Robert Mercer; he was the replacement for Lieutenant Stewart who had been transferred to the marine headquarters ashore.

Indeed, all of the supply and fitting-out activities that the ship had seen for the past twenty days continued for the next twenty, and if it were possible it appeared that they continued at an even more rapid tempo. Moreover, while the flow of dockyard workers on board had essentially ceased with the departure from the basin, the stream of daily harbor-duty men had, if anything, increased. The captains of three other ships anchored in the bustling harbor were particularly generous in their support. HMS *Barham*, 74, sent on board sixty men for four days who focused upon fitting and setting rigging and on pointing lines; the *Dannemark*, 74, sent fifteen men for six days who concentrated on fitting rigging and drawing stores from the dockyard; and the *Barfleur*, 98, sent eleven men for eight days who worked on fitting rigging and making gaskets. Other gangs of harbor-duty men labored five more days getting in spars, fidding the topgallant masts, crossing the yards, pointing lines, and bending sails.

At work alow rather than aloft, several more gangs toiled for eight days as they cleared, scraped, and washed the decks, and additionally pointed, spliced, rounded, and bent the cables. It took four days to stow the fore and after holds as well as the fore and after spirit rooms, and another two days to pump more fresh water down into the tanks from a lighter lashed alongside. Three days' labor was needed as a stream of provision and spirit lighters were brought alongside; these supplies included additional fresh beef, salt pork, bread, flour, butter, raisins, wine, beer, and even ten chaldrons (360 bushels) of coal. Finally, other duty men worked for seven days to draw and stow various additional bosuns', carpenters', and sailing-masters' stores, as well as receive and clean the ship's five boats (a 32-foot barge, a 26-foot launch, two 25-foot cutters, and an 18-foot gig).

All of this supply effort was somewhat complicated as the *Java* was now moored in the harbor. Just as when she was in the Great Basin, on most days the duty men had to crew the lighters, hoys, and barges to bring them out to the ship and back—as well as make the effort to load and unload them. The worst two days of all, however, were October ninth and tenth, when a succession of lighters brought out the remaining forty-four great guns. Those days presented the back-breaking and hernia-risking labor involved to hoist the incredibly heavy iron monsters on board—followed by the subsequent careful strain demanded to coax the guns onto their carriages on the quarterdeck and forecastle, and even more difficult, down below on the gundeck.

Receiving the guns on board was, clearly, a critical step forward, so Lambert naturally felt considerable relief to have it accomplished. This did not, however, prevent him from immediately tackling another equipment concern which he, Chads, and Robinson had much in mind, and which so far neither the Admiralty nor the port admiral had addressed. Unwilling to wait any longer, on October thirteenth Lambert wrote Admiralty second secretary, Mr. John Barrow, that

> As I believe H.M. Ships in General proceeding to the East Indies are supplied with a Chronometer, I have to request that you will solicit My Lords Commissioners of the Admiralty, that His Majesty's Ship under my Command may be supplied with one, together with the usual Charts for that Station, and I have the honour to be
>
> Sir –
>
> > Your most Obedient Servant
> >
> > Henry Lambert

The next evening, over brandy and coffee, Lieutenant Chads brought up a third subject which also weighed heavy in Lambert's thoughts.

"Captain, in regard to our poor purser, is there any progress in regard to his situation?" Amid the incredible activity of fitting out, Mr. Scott had had the misfortune to rupture a blood vessel.

"No, Henry, I'm afraid not," replied Lambert. "In the opinion of our surgeon, as well as a prominent doctor in Gosport, he's got no chance to heal properly if he travels into the heat and humidity of the East Indies. So, I've appealed to first secretary Mr. Croker that Scott be exchanged with a Mr. Outon, purser of HMS *Endymion*, who I'm told wishes very much to go to India. Unfortunately, I just received word that Admiralty's disregarded my proposition, and's assigned poor Scott to an inactive ship in the harbor."

"Sir, that's unconscionable," Chads instantly protested. "He'll be ruined." In fact, Edward Scott faced grave financial loss. In charge of supplies such as food and drink, clothing, bedding, candles, and the like, pursers bought almost everything on credit and very much acted as private merchants, with the crew as their customers. "He's a good man of good character. He's invested a considerable amount of his own money into the *Java*'s supplies, and now's got no opportunity to recoup those funds."

"I know it well, Henry," sighed Lambert. He stared at Chads for a few minutes, then drew paper, pen, and ink from a drawer. He began another letter to secretary Croker; the pen furiously scratched the paper while Chads impassively looked on.

His Majesty's Ship <u>Java</u>
Portsmouth
14 October 1812
Sir,

   In consequence of my Lords Commissioners of the Admiralty offering to remove Mr. Edward Scott, Purser of His Majesty's Ship <u>Java</u> under my Command to the <u>Topaze</u>, an old six-and-thirty Laid up in Ordinary, I feel it necessary to Request you will represent to their Lordships that the Injury, which he had unfortunately received <u>on His Majesty's Service</u>, has alone induced the necessity of his leaving this Ship, and that had the <u>Java</u> been intended for any other Station, I should have been most Happy to have kept him as my Purser. I therefore, in justice to his deserving character, and in consideration of the heavy Loss that he has sustained in fitting out and now having to Resign the <u>Java</u>, you will be pleased to move their Lordships to give him a Ship <u>equally</u> Good which is soon to be Commissioned.

                    I have the honour to be
                         Sir
                    Your most Obed. Humble Servant
                    H. Lambert – Captain

Unlike the preceding twenty-some workdays since Lieutenant Chads reported on board—actually the whole time the ship was in the basin—the fall weather now ceased to favor the *Java*. Indeed the master, Mr. Robinson, was obliged to record in his logbook only one "fine" day, while showing three cloudy days, nine days with showers of rain and, maddeningly, six days of heavy rain. On Sunday, the eighteenth, the weather came on to blow in earnest with strong gales of wind and heavy rain from the west and west-northwest, which caused all routine work to be suspended. In fact, it required the topgallant yards to be sent down on deck and the topgallant masts to be struck and housed in the topmasts. The next day turned even worse as the wind increased to heavy gales with driving rain. At daylight, Lambert ordered even the lower yards to be sent down on deck, and two hours later he had the top-gallant masts sent all the way down as well.

Finally, at four bells in the forenoon watch, he struck the top-masts. Now the *Java*'s tophamper was at a bare minimum to best ride out the storm, which left the roaring wind with little to push against except the hull of the ship itself. Most of the other ships in the harbor did not take measures quite to these levels. On the other hand, unlike the *Java,* most of these other ships had full crews on board who could promptly handle any suddenly emer-gent problems of heavy-weather seamanship—such as spars carry-ing away, mooring lines parting, guns breaking loose from their tackles, and the like. Indeed, the relatively few and miserable harbor-duty men who, as fate willed it, were unlucky enough to have been caught on board the *Java* had a tough go of it. However, at five bells a party of riggers, dispatched by an uncharacteristi-cally sympathetic dockyard superintendent, braved the harbor's rough water and came on board to help secure everything. Warmly received with grateful halloos, smiling faces and slaps on the back, the riggers ran lifelines everywhere and rushed about to apply pre-venter braces, trusses, and clew garnets to any gear that might be likely to part.

Although the storm continued from the west and west-northwest, by midnight it had abated considerably—at this point only fresh breezes, showers of rain, and squally. Then, shortly after dawn, when sixty harbor-duty men came on board from the *Bar-ham*, Lambert came to a decision.

"You know, our provisions and stores are fairly complete," he said to Chads as they stood beside the mizzenmast, "and we've hoped to take the ship out to an anchorage at Spithead this week. When it came on to blow I was afraid that plan was dished, but if the weather continues to moderate as it has the last few hours I think we may go ahead. In fact, if we can get a number of things done today we may proceed—even as early as tomorrow." He took off his hat, rubbed his forehead, and smiled. "Thus, Mr. Chads, I'd be obliged if you'd have the men sway up the lower yards and topmasts, set up the lower and topmast rigging, and then—when the God-damned rain comes to a stop—have the topgallant masts pointed."

As it came to pass, all that Captain Lambert desired—and more— was quite finished by late afternoon. At three bells in the first dog watch, however, Lieutenant Chads briefly delayed the departure of the Barhams. Their last task had been to bring aboard an additional 450 pounds of fresh beef and another 648 gallons of beer, so it therefore occurred to Chads that the men might welcome an issue of some of that beer before they left.

Wednesday, October twenty-first, dawned cloudy with moderate breezes. This day marked the seventh anniversary of the Battle of Trafalgar and the death of Lord Nelson. However, the occasion passed essentially unremarked because early-on, when one-hundred men from the *Barham* came on board, Chads had them immediately sway up the topgallant masts and cross the topgallant yards. As that work approached completion Lambert had a gun fired to signal for a harbor pilot—whose boat shortly arrived alongside.

"Slack water now, Captain," Chads reported. "First of the ebb any minute."

"Thank you, Mr. Chads." Lambert looked about him. The deck was lumbered and there was more disorder than order apparent. Yet, it was only to be a short voyage—two and a quarter miles as a crow might fly, though a little further as a ship must sail in order to clear the sand banks. "Make sail when you're ready."

"Aye aye, sir," replied Chads. "Mr. Herringham there." The second lieutenant stepped forward from the taffrail.

"Sir?"

"Mr. Herringham, suppose you should have the deck, and should you be desired to take the ship out to Spithead, how would you do it, and where should you place us?"

"Well, uh...sir..." Herringham replied as he considered. "With this favorable wind I'd unmoor and—clearing the Hard, of course—steer essentially south-southeast out of the harbor. I'd then bear southwest, the Sturbridge Buoy straight ahead, wanting to keep in four to five fathoms and wanting to keep Ashdown Mark above the trees. I'd observe the wind and tide, and I'd hope to anchor at Spithead with Southsea Castle bearing, um, northeast-by-east, and the Kicker Point northwest-by-north, in something like six fathoms. I think this'd place us where the captain desires, which would fall within the limits of the best anchorage at Spithead. And it wouldn't be too far from where the East Indiamen and merchant ships generally anchor on the Mother Bank to the westward of the Sturbridge Buoy."

"Very well, Mr. Herringham," said Chads formally, "that sounds like a capital course of action; pray make it so. Take charge of the deck and get the ship underway, and when there take any berth that convenience may suggest."

"Aye aye, sir." Herringham looked about him, pondered the gentle breeze and the now-flowing ebb, and cleared his throat. "Ha-hmm. Stand by at the moorings... hands aloft to loose tops'ls...loose the heads'ls!" He gave his orders clearly and confidently; both Chads and Lambert relaxed a little. Although Herringham had been a lieutenant for only two years, he was far from inexperienced: he had been at sea for over seven years and was a hardened veteran of Trafalgar. Thus, the *Java* slipped her moorings and made sail out of Portsmouth Harbor—for the first time sailing as a British man-of-war. Even with the loaned crew from the *Barham*, the challenges of the harbor's entrance, and with sandbanks seemingly everywhere, Herringham handled it all pretty well. He needed only minimal assistance from the harbor pilot who stood next to him.

Forty minutes later the ship came to anchor at Spithead with the best bower; Herringham immediately had the Barhams secure moorings with a cable each way, best bower to the west and small bower to the east. Satisfied, the lieutenant crossed the deck and touched his hat to Chads, pretending that Lambert was not right next to him. "Sir, we're moored in six and a half fathoms. Marks at the mooring: Kicker Point nor'west-one-half-north, and Southsea Castle nor'east-by-east. We have moderate breezes and fine weather."

"Very good, Mr. Herringham, well done indeed," replied Chads.

The rest of the day saw considerable activity. The Barhams furled sails, bent sheets, sent down topgallant yards, worked at rounding the best bower's cable, and got the sheet anchor secured on the gunwale. Later in the afternoon the harbor pilot and the exhausted Barhams left the ship. The most significant event, however, occurred just as Mr. Herringham's moderate breezes and fine weather became fresh breezes and rain. The ancient 84-gun *Royal William*, the harbor guardship, sent on board a draft of forty-four men—finally, the first significant contingent of what would become the *Java's* real crew. In addition, the harbor-service ship *Gladiator* sent aboard one man—a seaman not destined as a Java but rather a supernumerary ordered for the crew of one of the ships building in Bombay.

At a late supper in his cabin Lambert brimmed with good spirits. "Here, a glass of wine with you, Henry," he said to Chads. "This has been a red-letter day, to be sure. We got out of Portsmouth—admittedly not very far!—which I nevertheless call a real step forward in our preparations for our voyage to the far side of the world. And, we at last start to see the beginnings of our own crew come aboard. Though, I must say I'd hoped for more seamen from the guardship's draft—well over half these men are landmen. Oh, thank you." Lambert took the last of the steak-and-kidney pie. "And I forgot to mention this." He got up and fetched a paper from his desk.

"What's that, sir?" queried Chads.

"More orders from my lords commissioners. The pilot brought it out this morning. Nothing we didn't really expect—see for yourself," said Lambert as Chads took the paper.

To Hy Lambert Esq.
Captain Java – Spithead.

To give Lt Genl Hislop & Aide de Camps
    a Passage to Bombay
You are hereby required and directed to receive on board
the Ship you Command Lt General Hislop and his two
Aides de Camp and give them a Passage to Bombay, when
you proceed thither, victualling them during their Continuance on board in the same manner as your Ship's
Company.

Given 17 Oct. 1812.

Rear Adm. J. S. Yorke
Rear Adm. G. J. Hope
Mr. J. Osborn

"Captain," said Chads, "I wonder, do you know this general? I've heard his name, but can't rightly say I know anything about him."

"I've heard of him as well," replied Lambert, "and I was told a few things before I left London. He's from a military family, his father and two elder brothers also soldiers. Indeed, both brothers were killed in India some time ago—in the early '80s I believe. He's seen a fair amount of service—at the siege of Gibraltar, in Ireland, at Toulon, in Corsica, and in Germany. He's been *aide-de-camp* to both General Dundas and Lord Amherst, and his German service was a special mission ordered by the Prince of Wales. He's spent a great deal of time in the West Indies—fifteen years it seems—up until last year. He commanded the 39th Foot at the capture of Demerara, Berbice, and Essiquibo, and he later became lieutenant-governor at Trinidad. Just two years ago he commanded the 1st Division at the capture of Guadeloupe. He's a permanent major-general, but's been given the local rank of lieutenant-general along with this current appointment as commander-in-chief at Bombay."

"Very impressive," said Chads. "Well, perhaps he'll tell us some stories of his service during our voyage. Do you have any idea as to when we might see him and his officers?"

"No, Henry, not really," replied Lambert, "but I'm given to understand it may be as late as the second week of November. No matter, we still have considerable preparations to make of our own."

Indeed, the *Java*'s next four days at Spithead saw much of the same activity as her previous days at Portsmouth Harbor moorings and in the Great Basin. Lighters brought alongside an additional ton of bread and a hundred pounds of oatmeal. The provision depot-ship *San Ildefonso* (formerly a Spanish ship, captured at Trafalgar) sent over three butts of fresh water. Some aspects of the provision efforts and supply routines were more challenging at this point as the ship was now some three miles from the dockyard—the distance much lamented by Mr. Buchanan, the third lieutenant, and the crew of the blue cutter after being sent in several times to draw boatswain's stores. One of these boat expeditions finally took ashore the miserable and unfortunate purser, Edward Scott, and returned with the Admiralty's choice for his replacement, James Pottinger.

The *Java*'s Spithead moorings were ideal if one cared to monitor the many arrivals and departures to and from Portsmouth. Indeed, the anchorage was incredibly busy—just as were the harbor and the dockyard itself. The sheltered water was alive with considerable activity; ships, lighters, and boats of all description moved about left, right, and center. These next four days saw several warships pass close aboard: arrivals included the harbor service ship *Ardent* as well as H.M. Ships *Aboukir*, 74, and *Boxer*, 12; coming out were the *Barfleur*, 98, and the *Magicienne*, 36. On her way out to the Mediterranean, the *Barfleur* came pretty near the *Java*. A number of men briefly stopped work to peer at her—even as did Lieutenant Chads with the assistance of his glass—in the hope of seeing on her quarterdeck her famous captain. Surely the hatless, blue-coated officer by the taffrail must be Sir Edward Berry, who had once been Lord Nelson's flag-captain as well as his confidant. Berry was also one of very few officers who wore three of the special Naval Gold Medals, having commanded ships of the line in the battles of the Nile, Trafalgar, and San Domingo.

The *Java*'s crew—now a few true Javas, no longer purely dock-yard mateys and harbor-duty men—were busily employed. They cleared hawsers, scraped and cleaned the lower deck and the quarterdeck, struck the topgallant masts and lower yards, and stowed the new provisions as well as the boatswain's stores. Perhaps not surprisingly, all this work had to be done in less-than-hospitable weather. The wind, which ranged from strong breezes to fresh gales, came generally from the south and west. In addition to their spirits being brought down by the predominant heavy clouds and haze, the men were thoroughly soaked and chilled by two long days of rain—heavy rain.

CHAPTER 4

U.S. NAVY YARD, CHARLESTOWN

U.S. Navy Yard, Charlestown,
across the Charles River from
Boston, Massachusetts
42°37' N 71°06' W
Thursday, September 10th, 1812
4:15 p.m.

The marine sentry outside the USS *Constitution*'s great cabin stamped and clattered as he came to attention. He rapped twice on the shuttered door and called out, "The master to see you, Captain."

Isaac Hull gazed out the stern windows, lost in thought. His eyes focused upon Boston's Old North Church, which was clearly visible in the pleasant afternoon sun. He gestured to his steward to open the door, which exposed a smiling blue-coated officer. His left arm was cradled in an off-white canvas sling which contrasted pleasantly with his uniform.

"Come in, come in, Mr. Aylwin. How is your shoulder today?" Hull's open Connecticut face reflected his concern, since he hoped for a good report but was fearful of the opposite.

"Oh, very well, I thank you, Captain. I seem to be healing better than expected—or at least better than the surgeon feared." Twenty-three days earlier one of HMS *Guerrière*'s marksmen had shot Aylwin in the shoulder. "In fact, per your orders, we have the working party told-off ready to retrieve our bower, so I'd like to take charge, with your permission."

"Well, certainly, if you're quite sure you're up to it." Hull frowned, unconvinced. "What says the surgeon?"

"Truly, sir, I'm fine, and Dr. Evans has no objections. I'll take the second cutter's crew, as well as thirty other men. Young Midshipman Belches will assist me. It'll be good experience for him. *Gunboat 58* is alongside. We'll go on board momentarily."

Today the *Constitution* was secure at her moorings in the navy yard. But eleven days ago she had been at anchor in the deep water of Nantasket Roads. She had been close to the lighthouse in Boston's outer harbor—in the process of returning to port after her victory over the *Guerrière*. They had just completed the enormous task of transferring the many wounded British prisoners to the hospital on Rainsford Island, and were otherwise mostly prepared to proceed on into Charlestown. At five bells, however, that morning's orderly plan fell into chaos when an unidentified squadron of five warships abruptly swept in from the northeast. Ships coming southwest toward Boston from Massachusetts Bay were likely British, so without a moment's hesitation Captain Hull had axmen cut the cable and then hurriedly made sail. Barely able to keep ahead of the unknown ships, Hull ran the *Constitution* in for the protection of Boston's outer-harbor forts. A short half-hour later the ships were positively identified to be American rather than British; nevertheless, under the circumstances, cut and run had been the sensible thing to do. There was no use fussing about it. But, now, it was time to retrieve that anchor and its cable.

"Very well, Mr. Aylwin, make it so. I hope it gives you little trouble."

"Thank you, sir," replied Aylwin, with a grin. "I'm quite sure that it'll behave much as all large, obstinate, obdurate, and cross-grained pieces of iron will, for they know well the advantage they hold over us." Aylwin's humor faded. "Captain, if I may, I've heard you may be leaving the ship?"

"Yes, John," said Hull, "I'm afraid I must. I suppose some'll say I hide my face, mortified at the news from Detroit about my uncle William who's surrendered the Army of the Northwest to the British. I *am* mortified, to be sure, though really no one should judge the poor old general 'til all the particulars are known." He pulled back his chair and sat down at the desk, rubbing his right eye. "It's something else, however, that actuates my departure. My brother in New York, also named William, has died—and he's left a widow and children. I feel I must come ashore for as long as it takes to settle his affairs and to make arrangements to provide for his family. I'd rather stay here, of course, but there's no one else to help them. I must go and do this; it's the least I can do for them."

"I'm heartily sorry to hear it, Captain," replied Aylwin, "but I quite understand."

"Thank you. Well, I mustn't keep you. Bring me back that anchor. I'm determined that I'll not give Commodore Bainbridge—for it's he who'll be your new captain—a poorly equipped ship."

For the past few days, despite his serious injury, Mr. Aylwin had been indispensable in the efforts to ready the ship for further operations. Because there had been relatively minor damage to her hull, the most serious problems for *Old Ironsides* (as the crew had indeed now started to call her) were aloft, which was Aylwin's special purview as sailing master. The ship could not begin another wartime cruise until all mast, rigging, and sail damage inflicted by the *Guerrière* was repaired. While some of the necessary work had already been done, which included some at sea in the immediate aftermath of the battle, the heavy and serious work had really begun just last Monday. The damaged sails and yards were sent down and taken ashore, and the crew had unrove the running rigging. On Wednesday the crosstrees were sent down from the topmasts, and by Thursday the rigging was removed from the lower masts. On Friday the crew and the dockyard craftsmen had been busy with a myriad of tasks. Among other things they cleared the last of the old rigging and prepared to unship the mainmast.

Also on Friday the surgeon, Amos Evans, went into Boston to the Exchange to dine and read the newspapers. He had little he could contribute to the refit of the ship, and the crew continued to be both reasonably healthy and remarkably accident-free throughout this period. As a result, Mr. Evans took every opportunity to see the sights of Boston and collect what information he could about world and national events. Today upon his return to the ship he was met by Lieutenant Beekman Hoffman—who, next to the sailing master, was his closest friend on board.

"Doctor, it's good to see you, it surely is. What have you learnt today?"

"Good day to you, Beekman. Well, it so happens that I've learned a cartel has arrived from Halifax and it brings, amongst other prisoners, Captain Crane and the other officers and crew of the *Nautilus*." The USS *Nautilus* had been a brig-of-war armed with twelve 18-pounder carronades; on July seventeenth she had gained the dubious distinction of being the war's first vessel lost on either side. She had been captured, off northern New Jersey, by a British squadron comprised of the ship of the line *Africa* and the frigates *Shannon* and *Aeolus*.

"They said that Admiral Sawyer at Halifax detained six of our seamen under pretense that they were English subjects," Evans continued, "and sent them to England for trial. When Commodore Rodgers heard of this he stopped the cartel—at that moment getting under way with the *Guerrière*'s crew—and took twelve seamen out of her to be dealt with as they treat ours."

"Ha!" snorted Hoffman. "Good for Commodore Rodgers, the old tartar."

"They also said that the British have treated our prisoners in Halifax badly and that the officers were stuffed into the cockpit every night and kept there 'til morning. Also that the *Constitution*'s midshipman, John Madison, had his sword taken from him by the *Statira*'s captain, who after he stamped on it threw it overboard with the remark 'There's one damned Yankee sword gone.'"

Hoffman said nothing, though he shook his head several times and displayed an angry expression. Evans went on.

"On a brighter note, the various newspapers lead me to believe that the people of the United States, at least outside of New England, say and do many handsome things in consequence of the *Constitution*'s victory over the *Guerrière*."

"I'm glad to hear that," said Hoffman. "How different from around here. The dear Lord knows the Federalist diehards in Boston appear to entertain the *Guerrière*'s officers more liberally than they do the *Constitution*'s."

"Oh, look here, Beekman," said Evans, who changed the subject and waved a slim book at him. "I purchased this, a celebrated work, just published in New York by the author of *Salmagundi*."

"*Salma* what?" replied Hoffman, completely lost, only able to imagine *solomungundy*—a stew of leftover meats found both ashore and afloat.

"*Salmagundi*. It was published about five years ago and was quite the thing. It's a satirical piece about the follies of the day which utilizes great wit and considerable good nature. I don't believe anything like it's ever before been produced in America. Anyway, this new piece—and the author is one James Paulding—is called the *Diverting History of John Bull and brother Jonathan, by One 'Hector Bull-us.'* It's a comedy about the settlement of the thirteen colonies and the subsequent revolution against England, and takes inspiration from the sentiments which led to the present war. I'm told it's making much noise among the political parties in the United States."

"Very well, Amos," said Hoffman. He smiled and slapped the

surgeon on the back. "I'll depend upon you to read it carefully, and then I'll be obliged to you for an entertaining and informative *précis*."

On Saturday the surgeon again went on shore. Rather than taking a walk all the way into the city, he confined himself to a visit with Mr. Morris, the *Constitution*'s first lieutenant. Morris was in quarters ashore as he convalesced from his wound received during the battle with the *Guerrière*. Even so, Evans did manage to pick up more news of interest to his shipmates, which he quickly shared with Lieutenant Hoffman and Captain Hull upon his return.

"I heard that the merchant brig *Adelaide*, the prize we took on August fifteenth, was retaken by the frigate *Statira* and sent into Liverpool," Evans said. "Not Liverpool in England, of course, but Liverpool in Nova Scotia. Our prize crew returned in the cartel yesterday. They said that the *Statira* fell in with the *Adelaide* at night on George's Bank."

"Did our men have any intelligence in regard to the *Statira*?" asked Hull.

"Yes, Captain. They reported that the *Statira* mounts 52 guns, appears to be badly manned, and is otherwise much inferior to our frigates of equal rate. I was also told that it appears that the *Statira* was very near Commodore Rodgers' squadron the other night without the latter knowing 'til it was too late. If only they'd taken her. In any event, all the Americans that returned in the cartel are still considered prisoners of war, but are recommended by Admiral Sawyer for an exchange with the soldiers taken by Captain Porter and then paroled. One British army lieutenant and two private soldiers'll be given in exchange for one of our navy lieutenants." Evans stepped closer to Hull and lowered his voice.

"Another report says that a fisherman saw Captain Porter engaged with two British frigates off Cape Ann yesterday, and that the fisherman saw them capture Mr. Porter. But Captain, I really think this last's just more anti-war, anti-Madison, Federalist and Yankee hoaxing and humbugging, which you know many New England citizens are prone to practice."

Sunday, the thirteenth, was cloudy with strong breezes from the northwest which followed a night of rain and wind. The crew continued to clean the ship and to work at other needed activities. In the early afternoon Lieutenant Hoffman and Surgeon Evans returned on board; they had spent the morning in Boston. They saw Captain Hull taking the air on the quarterdeck, and when he waved at them they walked over. They both raised their hats in salute.

"Sir," began Hoffman, "the report of the day is our frigate *Essex*'s arrived in the Delaware River after she took a British sloop-of-war, the *Alert*, which mounts 20 guns. Captain Porter sent her into Halifax as a cartel with 300 prisoners. This report comes pretty straight and is probably correct."

Hull slapped his thigh and grinned from ear to ear. "Huzzay!" he shouted. "Huzzay! Gentlemen, I hope it's correct. Captain Porter's a fire-eater; upon that you may depend. It'll be the first of many for him, I warrant. What else have you learned? Anything, Doctor?"

"Oh, Captain, nothing which signifies like the news about the *Essex*," the surgeon replied. Hoffman looked at Evans with a smile, his eyebrow raised. Evans hesitated a moment, then said, "Well, sir, much to my annoyance, we heard another parcel of *Yankees* as usual cursing 'Madison's ruinous war' and trying to abuse, ridicule, and humbug us naval officers." Hoffman interrupted with an even broader smile.

"Or, Captain," said the lieutenant, "as I would put it, they tried to pour cold water down our backs." Evans nodded and went on.

"I wish all His Majesty's loyal subjects would return to their own much-loved and dear old England and not hang like a cyst on the back of our government—thwarting all its views and trying to pull it under water. Damn it, in my opinion, one domestic traitor is worse than twenty foreign, avowed, and open enemies!"

"Easy, Mr. Evans, easy," replied Hull as he took his arm. "Remember that I'm also one of those *Yankees*, and you know *my* views. I assure you that we New Englanders are not *all* against the war. It's not just you gentlemen from Maryland and Virginia who desire to twist the tail of the British lion."

Evans colored slightly and said, "Of course, Captain, of course you're right. I humbly beg your pardon."

They were interrupted by the return of Midshipman Belches and a number of men from Nantasket Roads. As he came through the entry port, Belches observed Hull on the quarterdeck and approached him with his hand to his hat and a downcast expression.

"Captain, Mr. Aylwin's respects. He humbly requests if he may have a fresh gang of men. I'm sorry to report that in our attempts to recover the anchor we were right thoroughly swamped and the first gang like to all drowned." He observed Hull's horrified look.

"Oh, no, sir!" he went on hastily, "no one was killed, but all was pretty well soaked, froze, and bedraggled I do assure you."

"Very well, Mr. Belches," responded Hull, looking much relieved. "Mr. Hoffman, at the turn of the tide, please be so kind as to dispatch Mr. Eskridge and a fresh working party to aid the master. Mr. Belches, see to your men. Desire the cook, with my compliments, to find something warm for them. See they shift into dry clothes, and see you do yourself. Doctor, perhaps you could make sure there aren't any injuries."

That night saw rain, but the next day, Monday, was pleasant with light and variable winds. At six bells in the middle watch young Midshipman Eskridge returned on board. He brought a further request from the master for even another relief of men, since the wayward anchor continued to put up considerable resistance.

At four bells, in the morning watch, a gang of seamen was told-off and sent on shore to the dockyard to repair sections of old rigging and measure new. In the mid-morning Mr. Evans again went into town, but shortly returned in great haste to talk to the captain.

"Sir, I read the newspapers at the Exchange. The report of the day was that three British frigates have been spoken off Cape Cod. It's said they wait for Commodore Rodgers' squadron to come out of Boston. They've heard of the capture of the *Guerrière*."

"Have they indeed?" said Hull. "Well, I daresay they spoil for a fight now—if they wasn't before."

"There was more, Captain. I heard confirmation of that report about the *Essex* and the *Alert*. The *Essex*, it appears, had disguised herself as a merchantman before the *Alert* commenced a fire upon her. In return, the *Essex* opened her ports on her for the space of eight minutes only, which killed and wounded several of the enemy—but none of the *Essex*'s crew was touched."

"I am amazed," said Hull. "What a remarkable victory. Captain Porter's the complete master of our trade and I honor him for it. And I thank you for this most welcome intelligence."

At noon *Gunboat 58* finally came alongside with the master, his working party—and the recovered bower anchor—to considerable cheers from the crew.

The next day was a brisk and pleasant fall day. The Constitutions spent most of it in efforts to clean ship and polish brightwork, because at eight bells in the afternoon watch Commodore William Bainbridge's boat came alongside. Captain Hull was on the *Constitution*'s quarterdeck, resplendent in full-dress uniform, stationed on the starboard side. The ship's commissioned and warrant officers arranged themselves behind him, likewise attired in their best uniforms.

"Mr. Morris," Hull formally called out to the first lieutenant. "Would you be so good as to turn up the hands?"

"Aye aye, sir."

The boatswain's calls wailed and shrilled throughout the frigate. Aside from those already on deck, the rest of the crew streamed up through the hatchways and formed up in divisions. The marines, as might be expected, were perfection in their attire, and the petty officers, men, and boys were a sight all to themselves in their finest rigs.

For some time, the two marine musicians—drummer and fifer—had been playing various martial and maritime airs from the forecastle. During a pause, they heard the officer of the watch call out a challenge, and then a crunching sound as a boat touched the ship and hooked on. They nodded to each other and then burst into ruffles and flourishes (as best just the two of them could). The boatswain's calls and honor guard of sideboys and marines welcomed Commodore Bainbridge as he came up the side. He let go the new baize-covered side-ropes, looked about him, and then walked aft. He took a position on the quarterdeck's larboard side and came to attention. Morris came up to Hull with his hand at his hat brim, slowly, still in some pain from his gunshot wound. He was, in fact, lucky to be alive since wounds to the abdomen were so often fatal.

"Ship's company fallen in and correct, sir."

"Thank you, Mr. Morris."

Hull stepped up onto the slide of the carronade opposite the wheel. A flush-decked ship had many advantages, but one disadvantage was the absence of a raised quarterdeck with an elevated vantage point. He cleared his throat, unfolded a piece of paper, and began to speak loudly enough for all on the weather deck to hear.

"I shall now read to you a portion of a letter which I just received from the Honorable Mr. Hamilton, the secretary of the navy. It goes as follows:

> Dear Captain Hull, I have it in special charge from the President of the United States to express to you, and through you, to the Officers and Crew of the frigate *Consti-*

tution the very high sense entertained by him of your and their distinguished conduct in the late action with his Britannic Majesty's frigate, the *Guerrière*. In this action, we know not which most to applaud, your Gallantry or your Skill. You, your Officers, and your Crew are entitled to and will receive the applause and the gratitude of your grateful Country.

Hull refolded the letter and put it in his coat pocket.

"Men, I'm fully in agreement with Mr. Hamilton's remarks. You all, each and every one of you, have earned my highest respect and my deepest thanks. You answered the call of your country in its need. You've carried the war to the enemy where he deemed himself supreme. In July, during those four harrowing days when we were almost caught by a squadron of his finest ships, you showed him that American seamanship was equal to—dare I say *superior* to—the best in the world. And in August, when we met and destroyed the *Guerrière*, you taught him that the men and ships of the U.S. Navy are nothing to be trifled with." Hull paused and glanced about the sea of upturned faces. "More than all things, I'd like to continue my service with you and to sail again, with you, to challenge the foe. But that's not to be. I must go ashore, at least for awhile. I need a furlough to attend to some private concerns that simply can't wait. Thus, I must say farewell to you and to the ship, our dear *Constitution*—or *Old Ironsides*, as you have recently renamed her." There were scattered huzzays and laughter among the crew.

"As you know," Hull continued as he adjusted his hat, "in addition to the last two years as captain, I previously served on board almost five years as a lieutenant. If I hold any ship in our navy as a favorite it's surely this one." He stopped a moment as if to gather his thoughts. There was no way he nor anyone else could guess it today, but fate would will it that in a naval career that would last another twenty-nine years he would never again serve on board the *Constitution*. "Men, farewell. I commend you to your new captain, Commodore Bainbridge. And, I commend you to the enemy, whom you will continue to chastise. Until we meet again, may you all find fair winds and flowing water!"

Hull stepped down from the carronade and walked stiffly over to where Commodore Bainbridge stood. He unfolded a second piece of paper, and Lieutenant Morris shouted, "Off hats!"

"Orders from the Honorable Paul Hamilton, Secretary of the

Navy of the United States of America," Hull said. He read the orders as strongly and clearly as he could— somewhat mechanically, trying hard to not allow any emotion to affect his voice. The orders were short and to the point. When he finished he again glanced at the first lieutenant.

"Mr. Morris, please have the goodness to haul down my pennant."

"Aye aye, sir."

The long, narrow commissioning pennant came slowly down from the main peak, a lengthy, formal descent. Bainbridge then stepped up onto the carronade next to him, and in turn produced a paper which he carefully unfolded and read in a loud and equally mechanical voice:

> By the Honorable Paul Hamilton, Secretary of the Navy of the United States of America. Whereas Captain Isaac Hull of the United States Ship *Constitution* is removed to the Command of the Charlestown Navy Yard, You are hereby required and directed, upon this order being delivered to you, to repair immediately on board of the United States Ship *Constitution*, now lying in the Charlestown Navy Yard, and to take upon you the Charge and Command of the aforesaid Frigate *Constitution*, willing and requiring all the Officers and Company belonging to the said Frigate to behave themselves in their several Employments with all due Respect and Obedience to you their Commander; and you likewise to observe as well the Printed Instructions and all Orders and Directions you may from time to time receive from your Superior Officers in the United States Naval Service. Hereof you nor any of you may fail as you will answer to the contrary at your Peril. And for so doing this shall be your Order. Given at the City of Washington, to William Bainbridge, Esquire, hereby appointed Commander of the U.S. Frigate *Constitution*.

"Hoist my pennant, Mr. Morris, if you please."

"Aye aye, sir."

The broad, short commodore's pennant rose slowly up to the main peak. When it broke out, the gun salute began from the forecastle, the sharp reports echoed around the buildings and docks of the yard.

Hull and Bainbridge ceremoniously faced each other.

"Commodore," said Hull, "I've indeed been fortunate in defeating the enemy, but not more so than my brother officers will be if they, in turn, fall in with that enemy. Where there is anything like equal force you'll find that they're not at all invincible. And that enemy will find they are not now fighting Frenchmen and Spaniards." Bainbridge nodded but made no response. Hull paused a moment.

"Well, then," he said, "that's it." He raised his hat with his right hand. "Sir, may I have your permission to leave the ship?"

Bainbridge raised his hat in turn. "Permission granted, sir."

Hull settled his hat squarely back onto his head, turned, and quickly walked toward the entry port. The boatswain stepped forward from where the group of warrant officers stood, and in a voice that could reach the maintop in a hurricane he shouted, "Three cheers for the captain! Hip! Hip! Hip!"

"Huzzay!" heartily boomed out over four hundred voices.

"Hip! Hip! Hip!"

"Huzzay!"

"Hip! Hip! Hip!"

"Huzzay!"

The boatswain's calls shrilled, the drum rattled out ruffles, the marines presented arms, and the sideboys touched their foreheads with their gleaming white gloves. Hull paused at the port, took off his hat, and gazed about the deck. He then turned abruptly and went down the accommodation ladder.

As he stood at attention with the other warrant officers, the surgeon thought the scene altogether moving. He had known that the crew held Captain Hull in great affection and respect, but even so the heartiness of the cheers and the quantity of tears surprised him. But that surprise was nothing like what came next.

He heard several voices call out from the crew, to Hull, who was now in a boat pulling briskly away from the *Constitution*.

"Sir, don't go!"

"Captain, don't leave us! Stay with us an' we'll go out an' take the damned *Africa*!"

"Captain, take us with you!"

"Please, transfer us—to *any* other vessel!"

From where he stood, Evans could just now see Hull. He sat in the boat, staring back at the ship. If he heard the voices that called to him he gave no reaction.

Commodore Bainbridge, on the other hand, had clearly heard the voices. He shook with rage. Extremely red in the face, he stepped up onto the same carronade from which Hull had spoken.

"What d'ye mean by these outbursts?" he shouted. "What the devil do'ye think you're about? Who here's ever sailed with me before and refuses to go again?"

"I have!" rang out from several men.

"I sailed with you in the *Philadelphia*," called out one, "an' I was badly used. It might well be different now, but I'd prefer a-goin' with Captain Hull—or *any* of the *other* commanders." Additional voices, more muted, were also heard to the effect that they had sailed with him before and did not wish to sail again.

The armorer, a petty officer named Hayes, was less muted in the expression of his dissatisfaction, and to those he added a few more blatantly insolent and mutinous expressions. "Kiss my arse, ye whoreson bastard. I'll not sail with you."

"Shut your goddam mouth!" roared Bainbridge. "I'll see you brought to court-martial. Master-at-Arms! Master-at-Arms, there, d'ye hear me? Place that man under arrest and confine him below—no, belay that. Place him in irons and send him on board the gunboat." He gestured alongside, where *Gunboat 58* had remained after she had delivered the wayward anchor.

Bainbridge made a visible effort to master himself. In a calmer voice he said, "Lads, this is coming it pretty high. This state of affairs cannot be allowed. You must recollect your duty. I shall go ashore and return tomorrow morning, when we shall finish this."

He stepped down from the carronade slide, turned to the first lieutenant, and spoke in a fiercely quiet voice. "Mr. Morris, call over the marine officer. Tell him that I desire sentries posted about the ship. I charge you and him—and all the lieutenants—*at your peril*, there shall be *no* desertions from this ship tonight! Do you take my meaning, sir? Good! Dismiss the hands. I shall be back on board the ship in the morning."

Ignoring Morris' salute, Bainbridge spun on his heel and walked rapidly toward the entry port, following in Hull's footsteps. He hardly paused for the marines' honors and boatswain's calls before he disappeared over the side and into his boat.

The officers looked hard at each other for a moment, then dismissed the crew by divisions. It was a somber crew of Constitutions who then went about the ship, completing the work that had been scheduled for the day.

Despite the unhappiness with which Tuesday closed, Wednesday began with at least pleasant weather. At four bells another gang of seamen was told-off and sent to the dockyard to continue work on the rigging. As they left *Old Ironsides*, they studiously avoided looking at two men who sat on the deck by the binnacle with their iron-bound hands in their laps. During the night these men, amazingly eluded the notice of the eighteen sentries who were posted all around the ship, crept over the side and into the second cutter. For several hours they waited in the darkness under the shadow of the ship. Finally they deemed it safe, and as they realized that rowing would create considerable noise, they cast off and floated down to and alongside one of the gunboats anchored close-by. They had hoped to push unobserved to the shore. However, an alert sentry on the gunboat discovered them, reached out his musket, hooked on to the cutter, and drew them close under the gunboat's quarter—at which point both men were captured. Now they sat in irons, fearfully awaiting the commodore.

At two bells in the forenoon watch the commodore came back on board and was received with all due pomp and pageantry.

"Mr. Morris," he called out once he gained the quarterdeck.

"Sir?"

"Call all hands, if you please." Once again the boatswain's calls shrieked throughout the ship, and once again the crew streamed up through the hatchways to form in divisions. Bainbridge stepped up on a carronade.

"My men, what do you know about me?" There was a half-minute of silence, then a voice called out.

"In the year three, at Tripoli, sir, some of us were with you at the capture of the *Philadelphia*." If Bainbridge felt any irritation at the reminder he had then surrendered one of the finest ships in the navy, he did well to conceal it.

"Well, men, come on a cruise with me now, come cheerfully, and I'll do by you all that the service allows." Another long half-minute of silence. Bainbridge shifted his feet, cleared his throat, and played his last card.

"Ha-hmm. Men, you see here at my feet two of your shipmates. As you know, they were caught in the middle of the night—caught with the *red hand*, mind you—as they deserted the ship. I need not remind you that the penalties for desertion are severe—a court-martial will likely hang them, or at the least award five hundred lashes apiece." He paused to let his words sink in.

"Now," he began again, "if you'll consent to come on a cruise with me, willingly, with no more outbursts and no more lurking discontent, and do your duty as right seamen in the United States Navy, then I shall release your shipmates, and I shall not punish them as they deserve. What say ye?"

This time there was no silent pause. Bainbridge could hear neither specific words nor individual voices. But he could hear what sounded like a murmur of assent as the crew discussed his appeal among themselves. That, and the number of nodding heads he could see, encouraged him to push for closure.

"Very well, then. Master-at-Arms, release the prisoners." The master-at-arms and one of the ship's corporals stepped to the binnacle and removed the shackles from the two men, who stood up and looked around, grinning in disbelief.

"Mr. Morris."

"Sir?"

"Dismiss the hands. There's still plenty of work and more to get ready for sea. We can afford to waste no more time."

"Aye aye, sir."

CHAPTER 5

U.S. NAVY YARD, CHARLESTOWN

U.S. Navy Yard,
Charlestown, Massachusetts
42°37' N 71°06' W
Wednesday, September 16th, 1812
10:00 a.m.

Commodore Bainbridge, it seemed, had been successful. His arguments to persuade the *Constitution*'s crew to "recollect their duty," and to willingly and cheerfully consent to the cruise, appeared to have struck home. The ship thus settled back into the routines of resupply and preparation—as well as the not-so-routine activities of significant refit and repair.

Much of Wednesday saw pleasant weather with many of the men engaged in taking an inventory of—and then packaging—an enormous amount of sailing master's stores. Some of the more interesting of these included seven old hand lead-lines, one snatch-block for deep-sea lead lines, two log reels and lines, fifteen half-hour sand glasses, twenty-four 20-second glasses, twenty-four 14-second glasses, seven pieces of bunting (white, blue, and yellow), four copper hand-pumps, six fishing lines, two speaking trumpets, fourteen compasses (azimuth, brass, and wooden), twenty flags of other nations, three sets of telegraphic signals, eleven signal lanterns, fourteen British signal flags, and thirty-nine charts.

After the wardroom's mid-day dinner, Mr. Aylwin reminded Mr. Evans that they were engaged to his brother, Mr. W. C. Aylwin, for an afternoon in town. As it turned out the master's duties required his presence on board—but he insisted that Evans keep the appointment. This he did and then returned much later in the evening. He filled two mugs with coffee and sought out Aylwin, in the fore-hold, to share his day.

"Good evening, John, I hope I see you well?"

"Yes, Amos, thank you," replied Aylwin as he accepted one of the mugs. "How was your excursion?"

"I had a very pleasant day with your good brother," said Evans. "He first took me to the Athenaeum, which is in a large house at the eastern point of the Common. What a wonderful place! What a magnificent library— modeled, I was told, after the Athenaeum and Lyceum in Liverpool. They aim to collect the great works of learning and science in all languages for the use of their members and of scholars. It appeared to me they have several thousand valuable books on all subjects. Fortunately your brother is a member, so the institution was free to me once he introduced me. In the lower room they file the newspapers of the day. In the third story they keep the books of John Adams, which includes many German, Italian, and French works. No books can be taken out of the house but persons are at liberty to sit there and read. Oh, John, I beg your pardon—" Evans noticed Aylwin's broad smile. "Of course, you know all this perfectly well."

"That's all right, Amos. I'm pleased you enjoyed it. What else did you do?"

"Well," said Evans, "your brother had a difficult time tearing me away from the Athenaeum, but in the early evening we hired a one-horse gig which cost us $1.25 each—an *amazing* price—and thus we rode out to Cambridge to see the 'Fresh-pond.' We amused ourselves by strolling about. Of course, we didn't walk all the way around it; I understand the lake covers almost 160 acres. Your brother told me that in winter ice is cut out of it, packed in sawdust, and shipped to many places to the south. You New Englanders are an enterprising set of fellows, to be sure!"

"Indeed, we truly are," replied Aylwin, again with a smile. "Ice and timber figure significantly in Charlestown's list of exports. Perhaps you should talk to Mr. Tudor at his wharf just adjacent to the river; it's he who's the main shipper of ice—all the way to Havana and even to Rio Janiero."

"Rio Janiero—incredible!" exclaimed Evans. He drank some coffee. "Anyway, your brother and I then found a light supper of fried chicken and coffee—for which we paid 62½ cents—and then we returned to Boston. As I said, it was a very pleasant day, and I'm profoundly sorry you couldn't come with us."

"Oh, well, there'll be another time, Amos, I'm sure," replied Aylwin. "The afternoon here went pretty well. In fact, while you were gone, some *ladies* came on board to visit the ship."

"Really?" said Evans, always interested in opportunities to socialize and thus a little disappointed.

"Don't look so glum," said Aylwin, "for you'll see these same ladies tomorrow. The commodore invited 'em to dine on board, and has also invited you, me, and some other officers to join them."

The next week saw considerable activity on board the *Constitution* with all hands—from the commodore on down—busily employed with the repairs of battle damage and with preparations for the upcoming cruise. The weather contributed its own challenges. The wind was consistent from the northeast. However, the individual days fluctuated from reasonably cool and comfortable on Thursday, Saturday, and the following Wednesday, to cold and unpleasant the rest of the time. Friday and Sunday even brought forth strong gales and rain. As the men settled into the heavy work routine there was little additional evidence of malcontent among them. The only incident of consequence was Ordinary Seaman Timothy Cogstall's removal to the gunboat when Bainbridge was apprised of certain mutinous expressions the seaman had foolishly uttered. Save for Thursday and Sunday, at dawn every morning a gang of expert riggers—with a few sailmakers included—was told-off and sent on shore to the Yard as harbor-duty men. All hands were formally and meticulously mustered on Thursday, Sunday, and then again on Tuesday. Although all the Constitutions were volunteers, from the discontent expressed after the change-of-command ceremony Bainbridge was still worried about desertion. And, for those of the crew who could swim and might be contemplating jumping ship, Charlestown was extremely close to where the *Constitution* was moored. The ship's work was also interrupted for several hours on Saturday with a general exercise of the great guns—which was not live-fire, of course, while the ship was in the navy yard.

As he had been told to expect, Mr. Evans did indeed receive an invitation to dine in the great cabin. So, on Thursday at four bells in the afternoon watch—shaved almost raw, dressed in his best uniform, and accompanied by Mr. Aylwin, Lieutenant Hoffman, and Lieutenant John Contee of the marines—he rather stiffly entered the cabin. The commodore, equally stiffly, introduced them to Mrs. Bainbridge, Miss Bainbridge, Miss and Mrs. Heyliger, Miss Nicholson, a Dr. Trevett, and a Lieutenant Broom. Evans was unclear as to who exactly the latter two gentlemen were; but he was pleased to learn that the ladies were the commodore's wife, elder daughter, sister-in-law, mother-in-law, and sister-in-law's friend.

He was even more pleased when Mrs. Bainbridge—who apparently had heard that he was a devotee of the theater—wanted to know if he had seen anything recently.

"Why yes, ma'am, I have, too."

"Oh, Dr. Evans, pray tell us about it," said Mrs. Heyliger.

"Well, ma'am, the other evening I went to the theater for the opening of the season. I found the theater neat and convenient, although a trifle small. I do have to confess that the scenery didn't at all meet my expectations. The house was a mite thin though the orchestra was tolerably filled. There weren't many ladies in attendance—indeed it seemed that naval officers formed the major part of the audience."

"What was the play, Mr. Evans?" inquired the commodore in his quarterdeck rasp.

"Sir," replied Evans, "they performed the *Exile of Liberia*, along with *Catherine and Petruchio* for the afterpiece. This last's actually Shakespeare's *Taming of the Shrew* as altered by Mr. Garrick."

"And?" said Bainbridge.

"Well, Commodore," Evans began hesitantly, a little unsure of his ground where Bainbridge and reviews of the theater were concerned. "I thought both pieces were fairly murdered with all the parts completely overacted. A Mr. Young, a mouthing, hectoring, bully-like fellow, acted the parts of 'Daran' and 'Petruchio.' Mrs. Young, an extremely beautiful woman, acted the part of 'Alexina.' A Mr. Entwistle—a tolerable buffoon and blackguard song-singer—received much applause from the gallery and pit when he performed the part of 'Sirvitz.' Oh," he interrupted himself, breaking into a laugh, "the pit observed the whipping part of the *Taming of the Shrew* with great applause! But—along with the indifferent scenery—the actors were for the most part dressed all out of character. For example, Russian sailors were dressed like English sailors, the 'Governor of Liberia' was dressed in an American colonel's uniform with but little alteration, and so-on. Overall I found it more tedious than otherwise, particularly the performance of that Mr. Young. I'd recommend he study Hamlet's advice to the players at first opportunity."

"Really, sir, and what might that be?" curtly inquired Mrs. Heyliger, not at all understanding the illusion.

"Why, ma'am, it's about forty lines from—if I'm not mistaken—act three. Part of it's something like

50

Speak the speech, I pray you ... trippingly on the tongue. But if you mouth it, as many of our players do, I had as lief the town crier spoke my lines. Nor do not saw the air too much with your hand ... you must acquire and beget a temperance that may give ... smoothness. O, it offends me to the soul to hear a robustious periwig-pated fellow tear a passion to tatters, to very rags ... I would have such a fellow whipped for o'erdoing Termagant. It outherods Herod. Pray you avoid it."

"Mr. Evans," began Miss Nicholson, who did not seem impressed by this recitation and so changed the subject. "Pray forgive a personal question but I'm a little perplexed. I comprehend that you're the *Constitution*'s surgeon and thus the medical officer. But even in the short time I've been on board today I've heard you addressed as both 'mister' and 'doctor.' Are you a doctor, sir?"

"Alas, dear lady, no," replied Evans with a smile. "While I have considerable training and a number of years experience in the practice of medicine and surgery, I am not a university-educated physician. That's actually the case with most naval surgeons. Thus, those who address us as 'doctor' do so merely out of courtesy—though I daresay it's also a mark of respect due to our demonstrated skill and knowledge. However, it's my hope to attend university and become a physician some day. Should I be fortunate to remain attached to ships which call Charlestown home, perhaps after the war I might be able to attend the medical school at Harvard College."

"Amos studied for several years, ma'am, under Dr. Rush," interjected Aylwin.

"Really, sir?" said Mrs. Heyliger with great interest. "With Dr. Benjamin Rush, from Philadelphia?"

"Yes ma'am," said Evans, "I had that privilege indeed. He's a great man as a physician, humanitarian, and patriot, and very much an inspiration to me."

Thursday had also seen considerable disassembly of the mainmast in preparation for the lower section being taken out and repaired. In fact, the lower main and foremasts had each been pierced through by eighteen-pounder roundshot from the *Guerrière*. Though both sections had thus far been stout enough to bear their injuries, neither Bainbridge, Aylwin, nor the navy yard superintendent believed that *Old Ironsides* should begin another war-cruise without repair or replacement. However, in 1812 the U.S. Navy had no drydock—the first would appear some twenty years later. And, at Charlestown, the navy had no sheer-hulk nor even a substantial wharf to lash a ship alongside for major repair. As a result, a set of sheers—two long and sturdy spars—were floated out from the yard and with great effort got on board the ship itself. Thus, with the exception of Sunday, the next four days continued with heavy labor: they dismantled the fore as well as main masts; they sent the topmasts, spars, and rigging ashore; they rigged the sheers; they stepped the mast blocks; and, finally, they hoisted-up the sheers. On Monday, in addition to the mast and rigging work, ship's carpenters—augmented by others from the Yard—began some considerable woodwork. This was to repair the starboard quarter gallery, as well as cut bridle ports in both the starboard and larboard bows. The quarter gallery had been damaged and briefly set on fire during the *Guerrière* action. The new bridle ports, cut midway between the forward gunports and the stem, were envisioned to ease the ship's mooring and unmooring. They would also enable the rigging of a towing bridle, and would serve as gunports to allow the bow chasers to fire directly forward.

Monday afternoon Mr. Evans accepted an invitation from his colleague, Dr. Robert Thorn. The occasion was dinner on board the *Constitution*'s sister-ship *President*, which was moored just a few hundred yards away. In addition, Lieutenant Charles Morgan and Midshipman William Taylor departed for brief leaves of absence, while Midshipman Allen Griffin transferred to the frigate *Chesapeake*, which was also in the Yard.

Tuesday's dawn saw the now-daily routine of the rigging gang being sent ashore to work in the Yard. It also saw the third day of significant carpentry at the quarter gallery and the bridle ports. The major event, however, was saved for late afternoon. It was then that the crew rove the purchase blocks, trimmed the sheers, knocked out the wedges, manned the tackles, and hove the lower mainmast out—much like drawing out a bad tooth. They carefully lowered it to the water and used the launch to tow it to the Mast Yard. Wednesday brought forth nothing so dramatic: riggers went ashore; carpenters carried-on at bow and stern; topmen took off the fore- and mizzen trestle-trees and sent them to the Mast Yard; shipyard plumbers came on board to replace the heads forward as well as the water-closet in the quarter gallery; the gunner's mates made a huge number of new wads; and the rest of the men worked on the mainstay, the collars of the spring stay, the middle bobstay, the spritsail yard, and made new gaskets. Lieutenant Shubrick returned on board from the City of Washington, where he had been dispatched by Captain Hull in late August with the news of the victory against the *Guerrière*. He brought with him a new chronometer which he promptly entrusted to the commodore. Evans dined ashore at the Boston Coffee House where, he reported to his friend Aylwin, he obtained a very good dinner served by a very pretty girl.

The next week was essentially a copy of the last. Cold, rainy, and disagreeable weather was the mode—with the exception of Sunday and the following Tuesday, which were fairly pleasant. There was some fluctuation in wind direction; however it generally came from the northwest and west. The gangs of riggers and sail-makers were sent to the Yard as duty men every day, but were now also joined by gunner's mates, carpenter's mates, and painters. By Friday the carpenters and plumbers had finished their work on the quarter gallery and the bridle ports. Material continued to flow from the Yard to the ship: new mizzen trestle-trees, the old mizzen stay (to be taken apart and the fibers worked-up into new nippers and gaskets), the fore rigging (to be set up when the foremast was replaced), some of the refurbished mizzen shrouds, and a new kedge anchor. Beyond all of the things supplied by the Yard, the ship's company was constantly busy with the fabrication or repair of various items on board such as nippers, ropebands, gaskets, and deadeyes.

On Thursday, at two bells in the first dog watch, the ship beat to quarters and the crew was mustered; on Saturday—at eight bells in the afternoon watch—the same events were repeated with the crew additionally exercised at the guns. Thursday also saw a U.S. Army recruiting officer come on board to turn over a shamefaced seaman named George Mitchell. Mitchell had deserted from the *Constitution* weeks before and then had enlisted in the army to receive the recruitment bounty of eight dollars. It was all for naught; Mitchell was clearly a sailor and the army officers and sergeants quickly smoked out the truth. Thus, on Friday, Mitchell was given a dozen lashes at the gangway and then confined on board the gunboat to reflect upon his conduct. The punishment for desertion could have been far more severe. But, Bainbridge was still at work with his strategy of leniency; still trying to solidify the Constitutions behind him. After Mitchell's flogging, which if anything many of the ship's company found amusing, all hands were employed washing clothes, bags, and hammocks.

Mr. Evans was able to go ashore three times during this week.

On Friday he went to the Navy Agent's office on ship's business. He then walked to the Exchange and the Coffee House to look through their newspapers. On Sunday he walked around Boston with Lieutenant Contee, and they saw—as he later told Aylwin—"many pretty girls coming from and going to church." It was Saturday, however, when he once again spent the entire day with Mr. W. C. Aylwin. Unfortunately, John Aylwin was once again buried in ship's work and unable to join his brother and friend in town. But, as always, Aylwin was later blessed with Evans' detailed report.

"Dammit, John, I wish you could've joined us! We walked all over the town. We looked to see what was playing at the theater, we saw Franklin's monument, and then we went over to the State House. I was particularly impressed by the State House—it much reminded me of the capitol in Annapolis. From its top we had an elegant view of the town and the surrounding country." Evans waved his arm in a circle to indicate the panoramic vista.

"We saw the senate and representative chambers," he continued. "In the former are a musket, a horseman's sword, and a cap and drum taken from some Hessians at the Battle of Bennington in 1777—together with a framed complimentary to General John Stark for that occasion. In the other chamber there's a large codfish hung up to represent the staple commodity of the state. Over the speaker's chair is a noble head of General Washington. The seats are well arranged, but due to the number of the members it's very crowded. This leaves no room to write—having no tables—so they go into the adjoining rooms when they wish to do anything of that kind. The council chamber is a neat, well-finished, but plain room. In one of the other rooms are four inscription stones from a monument that formerly stood on Beacon Hill—but have been removed in consequence of the ground on which it stood proven to be private property. The stones describe the principal events and most prominent and fortunate features of the Revolution and those that led to it. They also have an exhortation to posterity not to forget the expense, toil, and trouble with which the surrounding blessings were achieved."

"Very interesting, Amos," said Aylwin. "I'm glad you got to see these things. I've been there myself, but it's been quite a long time ago. Did you see anything else?"

"Oh, yes. We went by the Coffee House before we came back to the ship. There were several notes of interest posted amongst the newspapers. There was one that particularly appeared to be bad news for us, John. It said that Admiral Sir John Borlase Warren has taken command of British forces at Halifax—and has brought with him four ships of the line and twelve more frigates."

"Oh," said Aylwin, "oh, my. No, Amos, that is definitely *not* good news."

"No. And another note reported—in fact corroborated—some earlier good news for the *British*: in July the French Marshal Marmont was defeated by General Lord Wellington with considerable loss in Spain—at Salamanca—and Marmont was severely wounded. I'm afraid such information will reanimate the enemy's efforts not only against the French—but also against us."

"Yes," said Aylwin, "I quite agree." He considered for a moment as he toyed with the fringe of the new epaulet on the left shoulder of his coat. He was no longer the sailing master, but now a lieutenant, having received a commission two days before in recognition of his outstanding work since the commencement of the war. "Dare I ask if there was anything more?"

"Well, only this," replied Evans. "Captain Hull's uncle, General Hull, has arrived home near Boston. This, of course, has caused much fresh speculation on his conduct and his surrender at Detroit. The British—of course—but also the damned Yankees and Federalists overly much take his part, which I find a suspicious circumstance."

"Very interesting," said Aylwin again, thoughtfully. "Well, regardless of what happened, I feel for the old man, for Captain Hull, and for their whole family."

The ship's work, in which Lieutenant Aylwin was buried, was now even more intensely focused upon the masts and rigging. Much of Saturday was devoted to the rigging of the mizzenmast and the fixing of the fore rigging. Greatly daring, considering that the ship was moored in middle of an extremely religious community, Bainbridge determined to work through Sunday. They started at six bells in the middle of the night when the master took a party of men into the Mast Yard to retrieve the repaired mainmast. This was the new sailing master, Mr. John Nichols, who had come aboard earlier in the month when John Aylwin had been promoted from master to fifth lieutenant.

Six hours later saw the crew tow the mainmast alongside, whereupon garlands were lashed onto it and with enormous effort it was got up on deck. Then, since the sheers had groaned and "complained" so audibly when the mast had been removed, Bainbridge sent to the Mast Yard for two additional spars to reinforce them. As the new spars came alongside so did two new midshipmen; reporting on board were a young Mr. McCarty and an even younger Mr. Nixon, both of whom just had time to shift into work clothes and join the working party which got the spars up and along the sheers. Almost all of Monday, and Tuesday morning, was devoted to rigging the sheers and making them secure for stepping the lower mast. Then, at two bells in the afternoon watch all was ready, and with considerable effort on the part of three-fourths of the crew, the mast was hove-up to the vertical and then carefully stepped into place. Next, gangs of men anxiously coaxed it down through deck after deck until its butt finally rested in its place firmly seated on the keelson. At that point it was tightly wedged in. A swarm of topmen now spent the rest of the day and most of Wednesday working the mast. The got the main rigging over the masthead, got the mizzen top over, and set up the mizzen rigging. At the same time another body of men undertook the immense job of unsecuring the sheers. Once that was done, they transported them forward preparatory to taking out the foremast, and then lashed them tight.

CHAPTER 6

U.S. NAVY YARD, CHARLESTOWN

U.S. Navy Yard,
Charlestown, Massachusetts
42°37' N 71°06' W
Thursday, October 1st, 1812
Strong gales from the south and east, rain

Thursday, the first of October, not only began a new month but it also opened the fifth month of the war. It found *Old Ironsides* and her crew still deeply immersed in repair and resupply with considerable hard work still left to do. The New England fall continued to make things even harder, for during the first week every day save two presented cold temperatures, strong gales of wind, and rain. Weather notwithstanding, Commodore Bainbridge increased the pace of the work, worried that the ship would not be ready to sail by October's end. He now kept all his skilled crewmen on board most days. He allowed the gunner's mates, sailmakers, painters, riggers, and carpenters to go to the Yard—as harbor-duty men—two out of seven days. He also required the men to work a second Sunday in a row and, in so doing, took some severe criticism from various Bostonian clergy.

Thus, this first week of the month saw a myriad of activities. The Constitutions bent the lee cable to the sheet anchor; lashed the purchase blocks for heaving out the foremast; made plats and gaskets; set up, fixed, and fleeted the main and mizzen rigging; got the top over the mainmast head; turned-in the deadeyes of the main rigging; got the main cap on; got the main topmast and topgallant mast on end; fidded and rigged the main topmast and main topgallant mast; made fast the catharpins in the main rigging; rattled down the main, mizzen, and mizzen topmast rigging; crossed the main and mizzen topsail yard; got on board a new trysail mast, spanker gaff, and crossjack yard; and sent a spare topsail to the frigate *United States*. They also laid in the ground tier of fresh water and started on the next tier of casks (that enormous job took three full days), and then took onboard a large amount of firewood. Finally, they received from the Navy Agent eighty-one barrels of salt beef, fifty-one barrels of salt pork, and a puncheon of spirits.

On Thursday, at four bells in the forenoon watch, the men successfully hove out the lower foremast, lowered it to the water, and towed it in to the Mast Yard. On Monday the repaired mast was towed back out from the Yard and lashed alongside, and then on Tuesday the crew hove it up and in. With great relief the men observed that the most difficult part of this particularly complex job—the refurbishment of the lower main- and foremasts—was complete. They now began to disassemble the sheers and get them down on deck. The next day saw them lower the sheers to the water and tow them ashore.

Almost everything else that happened that week was anticlimactic to the masts' removal and reinstallation. Yet it was significant that four new master's mates and a new lieutenant reported on board. The latter was Mr. George Parker, who replaced Mr. Charles Morris as first lieutenant. Morris, now much recovered from his wound, had been promoted to master commandant. This was not only a personal recognition, but also as a compliment to the ship relative to the victory against the *Guerrière*. On Saturday, at two bells in the first dog watch, the ship beat to quarters and all hands were mustered at their stations. On Sunday the crew was mustered again and formally rated. In a crew that was all volunteers, and who for the most part were veteran seamen and had been on board working in teams for over five months, it was no real surprise that there was an abundance of able seamen, a lesser number of ordinary seamen, and very few landmen and boys.

As the date of the hoped-for departure approached, Mr. Evans got caught up in more of the preparations and spent a little less time on shore. Even so, on Friday, he had gone to the theater once more to see a play called *The Foundling of the Forest*, "performed," as he related, "or rather butchered" with an afterpiece called *The Guerrière and the Constitution*. In fact, he had walked out early, since the afterpiece had been "a foolish and ridiculous thing." On Monday he went on shore and found a large bookstore where he purchased a number of medical and other books. He then looked through the newspapers at the Coffee House and came away even more (if that were possible) "disgusted with the Yankees" for the considerable anti-war, anti-Madison, and anti-navy commentary he found. On Tuesday he went on shore to take a requisition to the Navy Agent, and from there to an apothecary shop to bargain for needed medicines. The Navy Agent, Mr. Amos Binney, seemed to be at leisure and also appeared pleased to speak with the *Constitution*'s surgeon.

"Ah, Dr. Evans, I hope I see you well," he said in greeting with a broad smile.

"Tolerably, Mr. Binney, I thank you," replied Evans, "I hope that your affairs progress? You seem much-less harassed than the last time I saw you."

"Indeed yes; yes sir," said Binney. "Of course as you know, I had a, well, shall we say *very* hard time of it for some weeks. I was but newly appointed, poorly staffed, and poorly equipped to support so many warships here at Charlestown in time of war." He went on, warming to the subject. He passed Evans his snuff box.

"It's really an ill-developed navy yard, you know. The establishment affords no real advantage or facility for naval purposes. We've about twenty-five acres with temporary wooden buildings situated on grassy tidal flats. Except for the commandant's house—which is actually quite grand—and the marine barracks, there's not much more to it. There's just a parade ground, carpenter's shop, blacksmith shop, timber shed, a small hospital, the saltwater mast pond or yard, a rudimentary rope-walk, and piles of cannon, shot, and ballast. Unenclosed, it's even exposed to the inroads of cattle from the highway! It's really more a supply depot than a shipyard. There's only a modest wooden wharf—indeed, sir, private wharfs have to be rented for even basic repairs. We vitally need a stone wharf and a building slip."

"On the subject of supplies, every ship seems to require complete supplies of provisions and every kind of stores. And on my arrival I was but newly hired, I had no experience, I had no precedents, nor forms, nor instructions. I was obliged to create a whole system from the chaos that surrounded me, and I was always short—or wholly destitute—of funds. I had to resort to the banks and even to my friends for money on loans and on interest. I was overwhelmed with requisitions from the public ships in every department—pursers, boatswains, carpenters, gunners, armorers. Frequently I had half a dozen midshipmen, with as many boats' crews, simultaneously calling for stores."

"Mr. Binney," exclaimed Evans, "I knew you were quite hard pressed, but didn't realize how bad your situation really was."

"Indeed, sir," replied Binney, "I was at my wits' ends. Then, thankfully, Mr. Hamilton—the secretary of the navy, as you know—came handsomely to my aid. On the eighth of September he authorized a cash warrant for $33,000 to be paid to me! I then could repay the loans I'd gotten. And I had money for repairs, pay, provisions, contingencies—and even, my dear sir, medicine! It actually exceeded the amount I'd asked for, but Mr. Hamilton gave me more. This's how he stated it, 'so that no inconvenience may arise to the public service. We are extremely anxious to get all our public vessels to sea with the least possible delay—and we confidently hope that every assistance on your part will be promptly rendered to effect this desirable object.'"

"Well, sir," said Evans, "I congratulate you. With the efficient system you've established, and now that you're well-funded, this yard'll soon stand second to none, I'm sure."

On Wednesday, Evans went in to Boston for additional medicine and medical supplies. On the way back he stopped by the Common to watch a military review.

"It was very interesting, John," he told Aylwin upon his return, "there were two regiments of infantry, some cavalry, and some artillery. They looked and marched well, but the first infantry regiment fired badly. On the other hand, the Boston Hussars are an elegant corps and they dress superior to anything of the kind I've ever seen—even in Maryland or Virginia. They're uniformed after the Polish Hussars, which is to say elegant. The other regiment, Sargent's Light Infantry, is a fine formation; they march, fire, and perform the difficult evolutions with great precision and exactness."

"Well, Amos," replied Aylwin with a straight face, "could it be that—perhaps—there's yet hope for some of these Yankees?"

On Monday, Commodore Bainbridge posted a letter to Philadelphia—to a new friend, merchant ship-owner and master mariner William Jones. In the letter he apprised him of progress and asked him for advice and suggestions for any fruitful ways to annoy the enemy.

U. S. Frigate *Constitution*
Boston 5 Octr 1812

Mr. William Jones, Esqr, Philada

My dear Sir, Entertaining the highest opinion of your judgement due to your vast experience, I beg you will give me your opinion & advice <u>freely</u> & <u>fully</u> in regard to a plan of Cruizing.

My command consists of the Frigates <u>Constitution</u> & <u>Essex</u> & Sloop of war <u>Hornet</u>. We can carry between 4 & 5 months Provisions and 100 days water. The <u>Constitution</u> will be ready to leave Boston with the <u>Hornet</u> in 20 days. The <u>Essex</u> I shall order from the Delaware River to meet me at a place to be fixed. In your opinion, which would be the best Place, off <u>Maderia,</u> or the <u>Cape de Verd</u> Islands? In your observations be pleased to mention the best places for receiving Supplies of Water & Provisions. I intend to keep my Cruizing Ground as secret as possible in order that the Enemy may not disturb me. I trust I shall always be freely disposed to meet them Ship-for-Ship & Man-for-Man in which event, I pledge you my word, you shall have no cause to blush for my conduct.

Commodore Rodgers' Squadron consists of the <u>President</u>, (one of the finest Ships in the World—in fact, I offered Rodgers $5,000 to change Ships, which he declined), <u>Congress</u> & <u>Wasp</u>. Comdr Decatur's Squadron is the <u>U. States</u>, <u>Chesapeake</u>, & <u>Argus</u>. Rodgers & Decatur will leave here shortly on a Cruize but wither bound I know not. Having had to give the <u>Constitution</u> <u>all</u> new lower <u>Masts</u>, many other Spars, & an entire new Gang of Standing Rigging, besides patching her <u>Wooden</u> Hull, keeps me very busily employed—last Sunday I took in the Main Mast, & this Sunday I am taking in the Foremast. So, you'll perceive, I dare even break the Sabbath in this Religious Land.

I believe the Squadron of Sir J. B. Warren has only 2 Seventy fours & one <u>first</u> <u>rate</u>; I think it probable they would have to Cruize on our Coast, to <u>over-match</u> our large Frigates.

Mrs. B. joins in great regard & best wishes to Mrs. Jones & yourself. And believe me Dear Sir, to be with Sentiments of warm friendship, yours

Wm Bainbridge

The next week started out cold with fresh breezes and even gale-force winds which came into Charlestown from the northwest. However, as the wind backed to the southwest it latterly brought several pleasant days, which a little light rain did not entirely spoil. Work on the masts and rigging dominated the days' activities. The men turned in the foremast rigging and then began the seemingly endless heavy work to completely reestablish the foremast, repeating much of the activity that had previously been done to set the mainmast back up. They also got up the crossjack yard; rigged the spanker boom and gaff; got out the booms of the standing jib and the flying jib; set up the lower rigging; and stayed the masts.

In addition to the mast, spar, and rigging work, the crew was still busy taking in stores and provisions. Mr. Binney sent on board thirty-four more casks, breakers, and hogsheads of spir-its—containing 4,463 gallons—which completed the Spirit Room's requirements. He also sent on board 1,287 gallons of molasses, another thirty barrels of salt beef, thirty-six more barrels of salt pork, twenty-four kegs of butter, and a considerable quantity of firewood. A steady procession of ship's and Yard's boats brought more casks of water, which were stowed with great labor under the direction of the master. This week Bainbridge allowed the gunner's mates, sailmakers, and painters on shore only one day as duty men. But, at the same time, carpenters and joiners from the Yard spent only one day on board the ship as they finished various re-quired projects.

On Thursday, the eighth of October, all hands briefly paused in their work to watch two small squadrons depart Charlestown, heading for Boston's outer harbor and from there the open sea. Bainbridge laconically entered the event in his journal:

> Sailed on a Cruize the United States Frigates <u>President</u>, Commodore John Rodgers; <u>United States</u>, Commodore Stephen Decatur; <u>Congress</u>, Captain John Smith, and the Brig <u>Argus</u>, Master Commandant Arthur Sinclair.

On Sunday, at six bells in the forenoon watch, a messenger came on board with a response to Commodore Bainbridge's letter to Mr. Jones. Bainbridge was most anxious to read it but he was just in process of taking a formal muster of the Constitutions. As part of that muster (and in lieu of divine services) Bainbridge then read to them, in a tuneless bellow, the forty-two articles of war (*An Act for the Better Government of the Navy of the United States*). He felt his relationship with the ship's company had stabilized fairly well since the incidents of the change-of-command. But, he also thought it might be the right time to remind them that his ab-solute authority as captain was backed by the full weight of the law, and not just by the capricious agreement and good will of the ship's company. When he had finished with the articles he had Lieutenant Parker dismiss the men. Bainbridge himself hurried down to the great cabin and to Jones' letter.

Philada 8th Octo 1812

My Dear Commodore Bainbridge,

I proceed to comply with your request for Ideas of a Cruise for the Squadron under your Command, which your own Experience & Intelligence renders almost superfluous. The positions which I consider the best for intercepting the British trade I mention in the order of distance from our own Coast.

First off, Cape Carnaveral in the coast of Florida. You will intercept to a certainty everything from Jamaica through the Gulph & have the ports of Georgia & the Carolinas near you, which your prizes can reach in 3 or 4 days.

2d. The Crooked Island passage to intercept the trade from the East end of Jamaica. A great many fine Ships go through in small squadrons, these would be fine game for you.

3d. From 1 to 2 degrees North of Corvo and Flores in the Azores; this is an excellent position. The West Indies Fleets and small squadrons pass near these Islands and then steer a more Northerly course. (Commodore Rodgers was _too_ _far_ North when on the Maredian of the Azores— which is why he made no captures in his earlier Cruize).

4th. Range along the Coast of Portugal in the track of the convoys between Britain & the Straits of Gibraltar and thence pass to the Westward of Madeira, Teneriffe, and the Cape de Verds—or from the Azores direct to the Verds if it is thought the eastern route would be likely to expose your route to the Enemy. I would pass just to the Westward of the Verds and cross the Equator in about 22° West, where you may fall in with some of the Indiamen out-or-home or some of the trade to-or-from the Cape of Good Hope, Isle of France, &c. Here you may also replenish your water from the rains, as I presume you would <u>not</u> wish to touch at Teneriffe or the Cape De Verds Isles for that purpose. And, I do not think you have much to tempt you to stay long near Madeira, where our own Vessels will discover and expose your Route.

5th. The Coast of Brazil where the British drive a valuable trade, and the cargoes are frequently in a very convenient Commodity, Viz, Gold in Bars and Coin and other compact valuables.

6th. If you go further south than this I would advise you to touch at Tristan Da Cuna Island where you can get refreshments and water; you will find there a good bay and anchorage. Thence I would look off the Cape of Good Hope for the trade that may be passing. If you can learn of any Vessels lying in Table Bay you may, by running in under English Colours, perhaps have a chance of cutting them out.

7th. A Brilliant Cruize ought no doubt be made in the Indian Ocean. There are numerous places where you could replenish water, and the Ships you would probably take would furnish you with an abundance of provisions. You might also calculate upon getting a partial Supply of Cordage and other Naval Stores out of your prizes. Upon mature reflection, however, there appears to be <u>too much left to chance</u> to warrant such an enterprise with so important a part of our Gallant little Navy. The distance and absolute deprivation of a Single friendly Port to refit in case of Accidents—to which you would be much exposed—and which the Men with the dread of disease, seems to forbid so hazardous an enterprise.

Nevertheless, I have forwarded to you the best practical work of information that I have met with, viz, Elmore's <u>British Mariner's Directory and Guide to the Trade and Navigation of the Indian and China Seas</u>, and for the China Seas you ought to have Horsburgh's <u>Atlas of the East Indies and China Sea</u>, as well as his <u>Directions for Sailing to and from the East Indies, China, New Holland, Cape of Good Hope, and the Interjacent Ports</u>. The homeward bound British Indiamen pass the Cape of Good Hope from the Middle of Jany to the last of March and April—the China fleets about a month later—and pass the equator in about Longt 22° W about five weeks after they pass the Cape of Good Hope, touching at St Helena on their way down. The Outward Fleets leave the Channel from the latter end of Jany to the beginning of April, pass the Equator from 18° to 25° as the Winds admit, and pass within 5° or 6° of Brazil (some much nearer) and sometimes touch at Rio Janeiro. As much time would be lost in your route from the Coast of Brazil to the Cape, in which you would meet with <u>Nothing</u>; look into the Cape and return in the track of the Indiamen, passing near St Helena and touching at Ascension Island. You will determine whether it would not be better to limit your Cruize to the Coast of Brazil, touching at Rio for supplies, and if on that station your success should not equal your expectations you can soon return to the Northward, ranging along the West India Islands and select your cruizing ground according to circumstances.

In this course you will pass near the little Portuguese Island of Ferdinand Noronha off the NE point of Brazil. It has a good Harbour on the NW side and has a Governor & small Garrison. The colony is made up of male exiles and convicts. Here you will find firewood, water, and refreshments—particularly turtle. I have passed within a league of it on my return from China and as I approach'd the Island found a WNW Current which continued for three days at the rate of 40 Miles in 24 hours.

In whatever situation you may be placed I am well assured that a high sense of National and Personal honour, guided by vigilance, skill, and intrepidity will mark your conduct, and that the fruits of your labours may be a rich harvest of glory, wealth, and happiness is the Sincere wish of your respectful friend,

Wm. Jones

Monday saw most of the men employed for most of the day in refining the new rigging. This activity was, however, interrupted by Mr. Ludlow, the purser. He called forth the ship's company by divisions and "served out slops." Slops, in this case, amounted to an issue of material from which the men could make themselves hot-weather clothes. The routines of the ship were again slightly altered as Mrs. Bainbridge came on board, with some other ladies, around six bells in the afternoon watch. However, those routines were not significantly impacted by this visit. This is because the commodore chose to invite none of his officers to dine with the ladies, as he preferred to dine with them alone. However, at two bells in the first dog watch, the commodore, his guests, and the entire ship's company all came together when he beat to quarters and held a general non-firing exercise of the great-guns and small-arms. Mrs. Bainbridge and the other ladies seemed most impressed by the evolution. On his part, Commodore Bainbridge was visibly pleased by the exercise and by the ladies' evident interest.

CHAPTER 7

U.S. NAVY YARD, CHARLESTOWN

U.S. Navy Yard,
Charlestown, Massachusetts
42°37' N 71°06' W
Tuesday, October 13th, 1812
Strong gales from the N.E., rain

Tuesday morning began cold in New England with considerable white frost. It was *very* cold for the season. This weather included gales and rain from the northeast which, through the day, lightened only slightly. At daylight the ship's company was mustered by divisions. After breakfast the Constitutions undertook a further long, laborious day of sea preparations; they stowed the booms, spare spars, and spare topmasts, received on board four chaldrons of sea coal, and received a lighter of water. At four bells in the forenoon watch the *Constitution*'s second, third, and fourth cutters—along with the *Hornet*'s launch—rowed in to the yard's Rope Walk in order to bring down the sheet cable and two hawsers. All these boats, with the Yard's scow in addition, were necessary since the sheet cable (required, of course, for the sheet anchor) was 22 ½ inches in circumference and 127 fathoms from end-to-end, the one hawser was seven inches in circumference and 150 fathoms in length, and the second hawser was five inches around and 140 fathoms long. In the later afternoon some of the men bent the new sheet cable to the anchor. Most of those men then went up to the Mast Yard, floated the mainyard down and alongside the ship, got it aboard, and began to rig it. Other working parties bent the topsails and the fore topmast staysail.

After dinner the commodore sat with his clerk, John Hagerman, and composed orders for Captain Porter. David Porter was an old friend of Bainbridge, who now commanded the third ship of the squadron. Bainbridge could speak with Master Commandant James Lawrence of the *Hornet* almost daily in Charlestown, but as Porter was readying his ship in the Delaware River, south of Philadelphia, more formal communication was necessary.

U.S. Frigate <u>Constitution</u>
Boston
13th October 1812

Captain David Porter
Commr U.S.F. <u>Essex</u>

Sir,

As soon as the Frigate <u>Essex</u> under your command is prepared for sea, you are hereby directed to proceed with-out delay to join me at sea. Enclosed is a detail of my in-tended movements which you will be pleased to receive as your guide for finding me.

I shall sail from this Port by the 25th Instant, and shall shape my course in the most direct way for the Cape De Verd Islands, where I shall stop at the Island St Yago in Port Praya Bay to fill up my water. I presume I shall leave there at furthest by the 27th November, and hope I shall meet you there.

From Port Praya Bay, I shall proceed to the Island Fer-nando Noronha, at which place I shall get Refreshments, and expect to leave there by the 15th December, and thence cruize along the Brazil Coast, as far South as Cape Frio un-til the 15th January, at which time I intend to pass by Jan-erio, and cruize between that place and the Island St Sebas-tian until the 1st February. I shall stop at said Island (Se-bastian) to receive some Refreshments, and shall Leave it on the 3d February and proceed to the Island St Catherine, which place I shall Leave by the 15th February.

I shall then proceed off the Island St Helena and cruise to the southward of it. In this station I intend to remain, to intercept the returning Ships from India, until the 1st of April.

Should any unforeseen cause or accident prevent our meeting by the 1st April next, you must then act according to your best judgement for the good of the Service on which we are engaged. I herewith transmit you a copy of my instructions from the Navy Dept. in order that you may know the Latitude I am acting under, which I consider <u>completely discretionary</u>.

I shall be extremely anxious for us to meet, to communicate more fully, and for me to receive your able assistance in advice and cooperation. With best wishes for the health & Success of yourself, Officers & Crew, I am &c.

Wm Bainbridge

At midnight Mr. Evans collected one of his surgeon's mates, handed him a mug of coffee, and bade him sit with him in the dimly lit sick berth.

"John Armstrong, do you observe yonder sick man, Roberts? He was attacked suddenly with delirium and stupor with slight convulsive symptoms. He insists that he will die at two o'clock, and is much disturbed when he hears the bell struck, and counts every half hour. I've given him laudanum with wine every hour. He has, alas, complete possession of the superstitions of his messmates. I've requested the officer of the deck to not strike the bell at half after one and two. So, I intend we sit up 'til that hour to watch the effect of firm impression on a debilitated frame."

The next morning Lieutenant Hoffman caught the eye of Mr. Evans as he rushed across the forecastle with his list of tasks in hand. Evans leaned against the foremast, sleepy and glum.

"What cheer, Amos?" called Hoffman, "why so long in the face? I collect your patient indeed expired in the middle watch?"

"Hullo, Beekman," replied Evans, "no, he didn't die, I'm pleased to say. He remains alive, and in fact better than he was, though nevertheless I intend to send him to the hospital."

"Well, then, what's amiss?"

"The marine officers are cross with me for I also intend to send three of their men to the barracks as unfit for sea service. But that's of no moment. What really has me put out this morning is that a newspaper came aboard with distressing news of the elections in my home state. I swear, Beekman, if all the enemies of this country were in Hell itself, democracy would still have been triumphant in Maryland!"

"Why, what's happened?" asked Hoffman, not truly understanding or interested, but he expected some amusement from his friend's overly developed passion for politics.

"Oh! Well, as you know the damned Federalists, where I come from, generally support Mr. Madison's administration—and the war—more than those around here in New England. Nevertheless, there are a pack of extreme Federalists in Maryland who rival any up here. Last summer one of them, a newspaper editor, constantly attacked the president as a puppet of the French. He continually denounced the administration and questioned the propriety of the war in the most disrespectful terms. Well, a large mob—this was in Baltimore—did him and his colleagues some injuries and then ran them out of town. Yet now it comes to pass that this editor—Alexander Hanson is this reptile's name—has had the unmitigated gall to stand for election to the United States Congress. He states that this is because of the war's 'absurdity' and that it's absolutely necessary to elect a representative 'who'll vote for a speedy end to the war.' He styles himself a 'friend of peace and commerce,' forsooth. What a farce! Yet, yet—he in fact was elected! What miserable dunces the people are to be so easily gulled. I tell you, Beekman, some days I'm entirely sick of this rascally world."

The next week saw the preparations for sea continue. Each day was a little more frenetic as the commodore fretted about meeting the date he had set for sailing. The weather cooperated, by and large being calm and generally pleasant except for the fog, cold, rain, and gales of wind on Wednesday, Friday, and the following Friday.

These days found the men working more on the masts. They hove up the mainyard; set up the fore rigging and stayed the foremast; rove the running rigging; got up the Bentinck shrouds; bent sails (fore and main courses, topgallants, royals, staysails, topgallant and royal studding sails, flying jib); and set up the mizzen, mizzen topmast, main, and main topmast rigging. It was only on the first Wednesday that Commodore Bainbridge spared some men for harbor duty—the rest of the days he kept all on board for ship's work.

Sent by Mr. Binney, a considerable amount of provisions came on board during this time. This included a full lighter plus another 240 barrels of bread; thirty barrels of flour; eight barrels of rice; eight casks of peas; thirty barrels and seven hogsheads of beer; and 136 boxes of cheese. Other supplies flowed from both navy yard and navy agent. A lot of it was brought alongside by *Gunboat 58*: two 21-inch cables, four 5-inch hawsers, twelve sailmaker's palms, thirty sail needles, four 2-foot rules, fifty-four fishhooks, four sides of leather, eleven scrub brushes, one barrel of tallow, seventeen pounds of marline, eleven pounds of whipping twine, fifty-eight iron hanks (a small hoop used to hold sails to stays), sixteen wooden hanks, a quantity of new sails, sand for the deck, and various other stores for the boatswain, carpenter, gunner, cooper, and the other warrant officers. Much that came out with the gunboat was for the sailing master: two topgallant masts, three topsail yards, one main yard (in two pieces), and one topgallant studding sail boom. The rest was a prodigious collection of rigging blocks and deadeyes; there were over two hundred blocks—single, double, treble, and sister—which ranged between five and twenty-five inches in diameter, and there were thirty deadeyes which ranged between seven and fourteen inches across. A final load of provisions came on board on the twenty-third when the sloop *Eagle* came alongside. Both ships' companies spent the afternoon transferring sixty-eight barrels of sauerkraut, six barrels of cranberries, nine barrels of horseradish, and additional large quantities of cheese, salt beef, salt pork, firewood, rum, and tobacco.

On top of stowing all the provisions and stores, the crew kept busy with many other final preparations for sea. For three days they fitted the tackles of the great guns; for two days they painted (whitewashing the berth deck and cockpit, blacking the bends, and painting the sides); they stowed the booms; and they scrubbed hammocks and bags. The purser publicly obliged those men ragged or in want of bedding to take such slops as they needed—all species of wearing apparel, bedding, and the like. The daily activities were by no means confined to just seamanship, supply, and logistics; on the evening of the twentieth the ship beat to quarters and the crew mustered at their stations. This event was then repeated on the twenty-second—followed by a non-firing exercise of the great guns and small arms.

One of the major events of this week, in order to more readily collect some final provisions, was the movement of the ship from the navy yard in Charlestown to a position just off the commercial heart of Boston. On October sixteenth, during the afternoon watch, the commodore caused the men to unmoor ship, loose topsails, and slowly drop down to the city. After this had been done—Bainbridge leaving it to his officers—the midshipman of the watch, Mr. Baury, reported to the commodore in the great cabin.

"Sir, Mr. Shubrick's respects and we've come-to with fresh moorings in six-fathom water just opposite Long Wharf. If you please, we've ninety fathoms of the best bower one way and forty fathoms of the small bower the other."

Two days later, while the *Constitution* was still just off the city, Surgeon Evans found another opportunity for an adventure.

"I hired a chaise, John," he told Aylwin later that evening at supper, "and I went out on the Taunton and Newport Road to Paul Revere & Sons Rolling Mills. It's beyond Canton, seventeen miles from Boston. They have a furnace to smelt and refine pigs of copper, and cast bells, cannon, and the like, and a mill with which they roll the copper into plates—or should I say sheets. There's another mill for the purpose of boring the cannon. I was treated with much politeness by a Mr. Eyres, one of the firm. He then walked with me to the Cotton Factories, a short distance lower down the stream. At one of them they gin, card, and spin the cotton by machinery and also have some looms. At the other they card and spin wool, and make stuffing for ladies' pelisses out of cotton."

"Oh, my, Amos, ladies' pelisses," Aylwin laughed as he tried not to spill his wine, "my word!"

"Yes, John, ladies' cotton pelisses. You choose to jest but it's something new in this country and's consequently kept *very* secret by the owner. Anyway, the country between Boston and Canton is hilly and rocky, but in a much higher state of cultivation than I'd expected to find it. I stopped at a store in Canton and was accosted by an elderly man. He wanted to know whether I'd give him a seat in my chaise and carry him as far as his house, which lay about two miles on my road. I answered in the affirmative and he amused me on the passage as he told me what the neighbors would say to him the next day, and how many inquiries would be made of him to know with whom he'd had a ride. I took the hint, and I recollected what Dr. Franklin had said of the Yankees, so I gave him my name, abode, business, and the like. He gave me a cordial invitation to stop at his house and drink some brandy, but as I wanted to get back to the ship I declined."

Four days' work off Long Wharf found *Old Ironsides* complete in victuals and stores, so it was that at daylight on Wednesday, October twenty-first, Commodore Bainbridge had the hands clear hawse and unmoor. At six bells in the forenoon watch, the wind being surprisingly fair, the *Constitution* made sail and got under way, moving seaward through the outer harbor toward the deep-water anchorages. As she closely passed one of the harbor forts she was saluted by three loud cheers from the garrison, and the amused and delighted ship's company cheered back with great enthusiasm. Barely an hour after unmooring, at noon, she came-to in

President Roads with the larboard anchor. Although he was extremely anxious to get completely out to sea, Bainbridge realized that event was probably a few more days away. He decided to have the ship securely moored with two anchors, and so veered out fifty fathoms cable each way.

That afternoon, once again, Mrs. Bainbridge and several other ladies came on board to dine in the great cabin—and once again the commodore invited none of his officers to join them. Those officers instead dined together in the wardroom, one deck below, as was their routine.

"Gentlemen, I've heard some of the seamen refer to the commodore as 'Hard Luck Bill,'" remarked Evans as he passed the port. Because the great cabin was situated immediately above the wardroom, as they sat at the table the officers could occasionally hear traces of Bainbridge's voice—as well as those of his female guests. "Will you tell me what that may signify?" Lieutenant Parker looked sharply at Evans and seemed to be consider a response, but it was Lieutenant Shubrick who spoke.

"It's because, Mr. Evans, the commodore's had several unfortunate—ah—shall we say *incidents* in his past while in command of public ships of war."

"Oh?"

"Yes," said Lieutenant Hoffman in a quiet voice. "Three in particular come to mind."

"Gentlemen," broke in Parker, "be circumspect in your remarks."

"During the undeclared 'quasi-war' with France," continued Shubrick, with a glance at Parker, "Mr. Bainbridge was given the 18-gun schooner *Retaliation* as his first command. One day in November, 1798, as she sailed just off the Virgin Islands, the *Retaliation* approached two large warships which Mr. Bainbridge assumed were British. However, the first ship—*not* British at all—was actually the 36-gun frigate *L'Insurgente* which suddenly broke out French colors and fired a shot across the *Retaliation*'s bow. Simultaneously the second ship, the French 44-gun frigate *Voluntaire*, ran out her guns, ranged close aboard, and hailed the *Retaliation* with a demand to surrender. Well, without a moment's hesitation, Mr. Bainbridge hauled down the American flag."

"Which made him," interjected Lieutenant Morgan, "the first officer of the new United States Navy to strike his colors."

"Then," continued Shubrick, "in September of 1800 Mr. Bainbridge was in command of the small frigate *George Washington*.

He was sent to the Med to carry despatches to the U.S. consul in Algiers—as well as carry several tons of foodstuffs and naval stores to that same place."

"Food and stores carried in a man-of-war?" asked Evans, puzzled.

"Why yes, Doctor," replied Shubrick. "Surely you know that for several years we—as well as a number of European countries—paid regular tribute to the Barbary States: Morocco, Algiers, Tunis, and Tripoli. This was in order to ensure protection from their proclivity to seize and plunder Christian ships and enslave their crews."

"Well of course I know that, Mr. Shubrick," responded Evans irritably, "everyone knows that. But I thought the tribute was in money."

"Sure, Amos, for the most part it was," said Aylwin, "but often it was in goods and stores too."

"Well," continued Shubrick, "upon their arrival at Algiers, Mr. Bainbridge anchored his ship well inside the harbor. This certainly facilitated landing his cargo of tribute. But it also placed the ship very much within range of the city's many batteries of heavy guns. This was an unfortunate thing, for the despotic Dey of Algiers then decided that he'd commandeer the *George Washington* in order to transport his ambassador to Constantinople. And not just this ambassador but also a hundred other people and many gifts for the Sultan of Turkey. Gifts such as slaves, ostriches, horses, sheep, cattle, antelopes, parrots, lions, and tigers. What's more, the Dey decided that the ship must fly Algerian colors while on this task to Constantinople." He paused to drink some of his wine.

"Well, did he do it?" pressed Evans.

"Oh, yes indeed, Doctor, and many a tear fell at this instance of national humility," replied Morgan. "At two o'clock on the ninth of September the colors of the United States were struck and the Algerian flag was hoisted on the main topgallant masthead. Thus, the USS *George Washington* sailed all the way to Constantinople flying a foreign despot's colors."

"I see," said Evans. "Now that you mention it, I know this story, though I did not connect it to our commodore." He reflected a moment. "You mentioned a third situation?"

"Gentlemen, I again advise discretion," said Parker, clearly uncomfortable.

"Yes, sir, of course," said Morgan. He thought for a moment. "The last incident, Doctor, and probably the worst, occurred in October of the year three when we were actively engaged in warfare with the Barbary powers. Mr. Bainbridge then commanded the 36-gun frigate *Philadelphia*. Incidentally, Mr. Porter—who now commands the frigate *Essex* and is soon to join us—was his first lieutenant. Anyway, as it happened one morning, the *Philadelphia* was on station outside the harbor of Tripoli. A raider which belonged to the Bashaw of Tripoli was discovered as she tried to enter the harbor, so the *Philadelphia* naturally gave chase. However, when it became obvious that the enemy vessel couldn't be caught, Mr. Bainbridge gave up the pursuit, bore up, and headed back out to sea. Unfortunately, the *Philadelphia* then struck the unmarked Kaliusa Reef and stuck fast, just at the edge of the harbor. In desperation the commodore tried several things. He set more sail to try to push over the reef; he likewise reconfigured sail to try to back off the reef; in order to lighten ship he caused the great guns and the anchors to be thrown overboard and tons of fresh water to be pumped into the sea; and he even had the foremast cut down. It was all for naught. After five hours of fruitless labor, and with Tripolitan gunboats rapidly approaching, Mr. Bainbridge surrendered to the enemy. He handed his fine ship, himself, and 300 prime American seamen over to the Bashaw."

"So, Mr. Evans," said Shubrick, "in a five-year period our commodore hauled down the flag of the United States *three times* in the face of the enemy—*without any fighting*. It's really no wonder he's called 'Hard Luck Bill.' Ha! The *true* wonder is that he continues to be employed at all. In fact— "

"That'll *do*, gentlemen," Parker broke in, "that will indeed do. I believe we've sufficiently covered the subject. A glass of wine with you, Doctor. I'm sure I've heard that a little wine does wonders to rectify the humors and aid the digestion. Yes? Splendid! Then let us drink to...smooth sailing and...*good* luck."

At daylight on Saturday morning, before they were piped to breakfast, the crew hoisted in, stowed, and secured for sea all the boats save one.

"After the hands finish breakfast," Bainbridge said to Parker, "have them bring aboard the water from the gunboat." During the night, *Gunboat 58*—that all-purpose workhorse—had come alongside with many more casks of drinking water. These needed to be stowed on top of the ground tier of water casks which had been laid in during the first week of October. "When that's done, I'd be obliged if you'd hoist the topgallant yards and then loose the sails to dry. There's a cool wind from the northwest this morning which will answer very well for such work."

"Aye aye, sir," responded Parker. "I'm afraid we still have much to do to clear the ship for sea."

At six bells in the forenoon watch Bainbridge called the first lieutenant over once again. "Parker, before the hands go to dinner, beat to quarters, if you please. We needn't clear for action. I know very well, and I'm grateful, that we have a veteran crew—and also one that's been hardened in battle. Nevertheless, the minute we clear yonder Boston Light on Little Brewster Island we may be fighting for our lives. Thus, after almost two months in harbor, I believe the men—and the officers too—need to resume thinking about our warlike skills."

Later in the afternoon it crossed the chronically impatient Bainbridge's mind to stand to sea even if things were not totally in order. The tide favored it, but the impetuous thought had barely formed when the wind hauled round from the northeast and east and would not permit it. Partially to make himself feel better, at two bells in the first dog watch Bainbridge beat to quarters for the second time in the day. This time, however, he also had the men exercise the great guns, but again without firing.

It was well the ship had not abruptly sailed in the early afternoon, for that morning Mr. Evans had imposed upon the officer of the watch who resignedly put a boat at his disposal. He had then gone on shore and ventured into Boston for one last look around and to make some final farewells. On the way in he and the boat's crew observed that the USS *Hornet* had gotten underway from the navy yard and was proceeding into the outer harbor, presumably heading for the deep-water anchorage near the *Constitution*.

CHAPTER 8

ATLANTIC OCEAN

Atlantic Ocean,
620 nautical miles west of
La Palma, Spanish Canary Islands
Vicinity 29°00' N 29°30' W
Sunday, October 25th, 1812
9:00 a.m.
Wind from the south; heavy sea running

The 44-gun frigate USS *United States*, sister to the *Constitution* and the *President*, was sixteen days out of Boston. Commodore Stephen Decatur, U.S. Navy—*already* famous as a hero of the Tripolitan War—was intently seeking a single-ship encounter with a British frigate.

The 38-gun frigate HMS *Macedonian* was four days out of Madeira. Captain John Surman Carden, Royal Navy—*hoping* to become famous—was desperately seeking action with a French or American frigate; either would do.

They both got their wish.

In the long hour and a half of the hard-fought engagement the *Macedonian* suffered terribly. The Americans fired almost seventy broadsides and as a result not less than one-hundred roundshot had penetrated the *Macedonian*'s hull; many of those had gone all the way through-and-through and out the other side. The *Macedonian* had nothing left standing but her mainmast and her foreyard on the stump of the foremast. With the exception of one small gig all of her boats were destroyed, and out of her 300 officers and men 36 had been killed and 68 were wounded. In shocking contrast, only five British shot had struck the hull of the *United States*, and she had lost only five killed and six wounded.

Leaving the *Macedonian* to wallow helplessly, considerable flotsam and jetsam all around her, the *United States* ceased fire, moved about two miles off, and began to make minor repairs and fill new gunpowder cartridges. However, any improvements to the *United States'* ability to continue fighting accounted for only part of this surprising move. More important, in Decatur's mind, a break in the fighting might allow the British to catch their breaths, to take stock of their situation, and to realize they had lost this battle. Accordingly, after about an hour, the *United States* ran back down for the *Macedonian* and took up a raking position off her larboard quarter.

On the British ship's quarterdeck Captain Carden conferred with his officers. The Macedonians had worked hard—extremely hard—during this last hour as they tried to get their ship ready for further action. But it was all in vain. She remained helpless and unmanageable. The first lieutenant, David Hope, still ardently advocated fighting on; however Carden, supported by the other officers, concluded that he had no option but to surrender. A seaman named Watson reluctantly hauled down the torn ensign. He tried to bundle it into his arms, but overcome by emotion, as well as the flag's enormous bulk, he finally had to let it fall to the bloody deck.

Decatur immediately sent a boat to take possession of his prize—and to bring to him the British captain. The boat shortly returned and Lieutenant John Nicholson strode across the quarterdeck. He doffed his hat to Decatur and reported.

"Commodore, as we had perceived, the enemy's the *Macedonian*, 38 guns, Captain Carden. At present she's a perfect wreck—an unmanageable log. If we're to save her we must get to work at once. And, sir, her losses in men are shocking! Fragments of the dead are distributed in every direction. The decks are covered with blood and there's one, continued, agonized yell of the unhappy wounded. Sir, it's a scene of my fellow-creatures so horrible, I assure you, it's deprived me of the pleasure of our victory."

Decatur touched his own hat. "Thank you, Mr. Nicholson. Please assemble the carpenter, sailmaker, and surgeon, as well as their mates. Also muster at least half of the marines and report to Lieutenant Allen. As you say, we must get to work at once, for by the Lord God I intend to save that ship and bring her home as a prize. Directly I welcome our guest, I'll join you on board the *Macedonian*." Decatur stepped over to the British captain, who had followed Nicholson through the entry port and now stared about him, apparently amazed at the *United States'* lack of both visible damage and spilled blood.

"Carden. Carden! Carden, it's I, Decatur." The British captain turned to him, distracted and seemingly uncomprehending. The contrast between the two officers was striking. Carden had been dressed in his best uniform for the *Macedonian*'s formal church services held earlier that morning; although his uniform was certainly the worse for having gone through the battle, he still presented a dignified and even resplendent figure. Decatur, on the other hand, wore his usual at-sea undress of farmer's homespun and straw hat. Carden, struggling with shame and mortification, was grave and somber; Decatur, having won—decisively—his first blue-water battle, was all animation and cheer.

"Carden, I'm Stephen Decatur. This is the U.S. Frigate *United States*. You know me—from your stay in Norfolk last winter." Realization came to the British officer. He nodded, and held out his sword, which he had detached from its belt as he had stepped onboard the American ship. Decatur pushed the sword back. "I can't receive the sword of a man who's so bravely defended his ship," he said with a smile, "but I will receive your hand." Carden bowed, and shook Decatur's offered hand. He reattached his sword to its belt.

"Decatur," he said slowly. "I'm an undone man. I'm the first British naval officer that's struck his flag to an American."

"May I inform you, sir, you're mistaken," replied Decatur, with a grin. "The British frigate *Guerrière*'s already been taken, on August nineteenth." Carden stared at him, blankly. "My dear sir, the flag of a British frigate was struck before yours. The *Guerrière* was beaten, seized, burnt, and sunk by our sister ship, the *Constitution*."

Decatur grew even more cheerful as the immensity of his victory fully overtook him. He was also thinking about the real possibility that he could repair the *Macedonian* and, rather than sinking her like the *Guerrière*, triumphantly bring her back to the United States as a prize. He called out to several of his marines who were close by; he adopted a serious air and pretended to chastise them while he pointed at Carden.

"You call yourselves sharpshooters, but you've allowed this tall and erect officer, on an open quarterdeck, to escape your aim! How was it that you let such a figure of a man survive unscathed?" Instantly catching himself, Decatur realized this was in poor form and he also, finally, comprehended how Carden felt. He took the British officer's arm. "Your pardon, sir, my sad attempt at jocularity was unforgivable. Indeed, I'm told that the losses among your men are shocking. Despite my tasteless joke I'm heartily relieved that you were *not* injured."

"Thank you, Decatur. Lord above, your grape and canister came through our ports like leaden rain—everywhere carrying death in their trail. And, though you choose to jest, I daresay upwards of forty of my shipmates fell close around me on my quarterdeck." Carden turned to watch the first of several boats start their short journey to the *Macedonian.* Decatur moved a few steps away. William Allen, the *United States'* first lieutenant, joined him. They both studied the British captain, whose bowed figure now leaned against the bulwark as he stared at the wreck of his ship.

"It seems a strange coincidence, Commodore," said Allen. "Strange that this far out we've fought a ship and captain we knew from before the war."

"Yes, Mr. Allen, it surely does." replied Decatur. "It's been only nine—no, no, eight—months since the *Macedonian* was in Norfolk, awaiting their ambassador's despatches. My wife and I had Carden and his officers to our house twice—well, of course, you know that, for you were there—and he came on board the *United States* once. As you recall, we talked of many things—to include what would happen if our two ships met in action." Decatur smiled. "He was so confident of a different outcome than this one."

"You know," the commodore went on as he adjusted his straw hat, "for me fully one-half the satisfaction that arises from this victory's destroyed when I see poor Carden's distress. And I don't think that the news of the *Guerrière's* earlier defeat has made him feel better at all—if anything, it seems to have compounded his misery." He shrugged his shoulders. "Well, perhaps we can console him."

CHAPTER 9

SPITHEAD ANCHORAGE, England

Spithead Anchorage
The Solent
Hampshire, England
50°46' N 1°08' W
Monday, October 26th, 1812
6:00 a.m.

"Come in." Captain Lambert swallowed the last of his coffee and looked up from his desk. Lost in thought, he barely heard the hesitant knock outside HMS *Java*'s great cabin. In response to the summons Mr. Midshipman Keele peeked in and, as he caught his captain's eye, straightened to attention.

"If you please, sir, Mr. Chads' duty and fresh breezes west-by-north and cloudy weather. Also we have a lighter just along-side—from the *San Ildefonso*—with eight more butts of water."

"Very well, Mr. Keele," replied Lambert, "thank you. My compliments to Mr. Chads and I'll be on deck directly."

Lambert nodded in satisfaction as he came up the companion-way and looked about. The water was indeed already coming aboard and the sails were loosed to dry from the preceding two days of heavy rain. There was still a great deal left to do before the *Java* would be prepared to leave England, and her captain was a bit concerned that she would not be ready in time to suit the Ad-miralty—or for that matter, to suit the unknown general who was no doubt anxious to depart for his new post in India. Agreeably, considerable activity had been arranged for today and actually through the rest of the month. In addition to the water, this day would see the *Java* draw more stores from the dockyard—as well as a hoy come alongside with the *Java*'s requisition for around seven and a half tons of gunpowder. It should also see a draft of men come aboard from H.M. Ship-Sloop *Coquette*; men not designated as ship's company but rather as supernumeraries for the ships at Bombay. However, this was not entirely good news: when last he was at the dockyard Lieutenant Herringham had learned that the *Coquette*'s crew was apparently in some sort of disarray and disaffection, tantamount to mutiny. Upon hearing this news Lambert was disheartened. The inclusion of fifty prime seamen was a godsend, faced as he was with an incomplete crew and many of those untrained landmen, but fifty budding mutineers was a gift he could well do without.

At four bells in the forenoon watch the powder hoy came down from the dockyard. Its red flag noisily snapped in the breeze as the hoy replaced the *San Ildefonso*'s lighter alongside. All hands, save those who comprised two boats' crews sent to draw stores, fell-to and quickly got the 170 barrels of powder on board. Then, at four bells in the afternoon watch, several boats did indeed bring on board the fifty men from the *Coquette* along with their dunnage. Lambert watched keenly from the quarterdeck as his lieutenants took them in charge. Some of the men gazed about curiously, while some kept their eyes on the deck. In general, they conveyed an impression of sullen indifference, the sight of which galvanized Lambert into action.

"Mr. Chads, there!" he hailed, "be so good as to call away my gig. I shall go in to the dockyard."

"The admiral will see you now, sir," said the flag lieutenant. Lambert walked in to the mahogany-lined office and sat down in the upholstered chair at which Admiral Sir Richard Bickerton pointed. While the Commander-in-Chief, Portsmouth, finished signing a folder of documents, Lambert studied the somber portrait of Lord Nelson above the ornate desk. Upon a moment's reflection, Lambert was not at all surprised to see Nelson looking over Bickerton's shoulder; during 1804 and part of 1805 Bickerton had been second-in-command to Nelson in the Mediterranean and certainly had been one of his favorites.

Finally Bickerton threw down his pen and looked up. "Good day to you, Lambert, and I give you joy of your new command. I understand that the *Java*'s preparations for sea are going well?"

"Yes, sir, ah—pretty well, I thank you," replied Lambert. "The dockyard turned her out in fine form, the victuals and stores come aboard apace, and she's indeed getting into high order."

"Good! Capital," said Bickerton.

"However, um, sir, I'm much less sanguine about my manning.

I've just now received some drafts of men, and I must say that so far I'm rather concerned at the enormous number of landmen come aboard. Almost sixty are raw, untrained Irishmen who've never smelt salt water in their lives—except in crossing from their own shores to England."

"Come, Lambert," returned the admiral, "we all must put up with landmen now and then. Prime seamen don't grow on trees, you know, particularly this late in the war."

"Oh, yes sir, of course. I only hope my next draft'll consist of a little more right seamen. And, sir, my real cause of alarm is the draft of men I received even today." Lambert paused for a moment. "Sir, as of course I'm sure you know, these men—fifty altogether—aren't actually meant for the *Java*'s crew; they've been sent on board as supernumeraries for the ships building in Bombay. But, sir, they're from the *Coquette*. They're disaffected, they're troublemakers—God's my life, sir, I'm told they're practically mutineers—and I'm most dismayed with the prospect of admitting such men into my ship!"

"I quite appreciate what you say, Lambert," Bickerton said slowly. "To be sure, the *Coquette*'s an extremely unhappy ship, and—to be quite frank—we've decided that we'll break up her company and send them here-and-there to other ships. This is nothing new; you've no doubt seen such measures taken before. They're not all of 'em disagreeable by any means. Most are merely led astray and maligned by a few bad apples. You and your premier—Chads—are officers of vast experience, with remarkable fighting records, and are of the highest character. You will soon whip the *Java*—and these men—into first-rate order, I'm quite sure." Lambert opened his mouth to further remonstrate, but Bickerton had looked back down at his desk and picked up his pen.

"I'm sorry, Captain Lambert, but there's really no help for it. In the end we'll send you enough true, loyal seamen I assure you, but take these men you must. In any event, in regard to both your Coquettes and your Irishmen, a voyage to the East Indies'll give you plenty of opportunity to make 'em into a good crew."

"Aye aye, sir," responded Lambert, tight lipped.

"By the by," Bickerton continued, "it appears you may be able to do *me* a service. Presently anchored off the Mother Bank are two John Company ships readying for sea—let me see, yes, here it is, the *Atlantic* and the *Cape Packet*. They're bound for Calcutta and they should be ready to sail in a week or so. Their masters have expressed their intent to sail as soon as ever they can, escort or no, but I won't have it. Too many damned French privateers about—not to mention Americans. So, I desire you convoy them until your courses naturally diverge in the Indian Ocean. They can just wait a few days for you; I'm sure that's all it will be."

"Aye aye, sir," Lambert repeated.

"And," Bickerton went on, "for the first part of your voyage—perhaps for a fortnight—you'll also be accompanied by two more vessels, H.M. brigs *Port Mahon* and *Derwent*. They'll part company with you at some point to be determined, but at first you'll be quite the little squadron.

"Yes, sir. Aye aye, sir," replied Lambert once again as he got to his feet. He realized the interview was over.

Despite Admiral Bickerton's assurances, Lambert remained profoundly concerned, saved from dwelling upon it only by the heavy activity of the next six days—activity complicated by the ups-and-downs of the fall weather. The wind was really of no consequence; it ranged from light to moderate, generally from the west and southwest. Both the thirtieth and the thirty-first saw half-days of rain, but these were nothing compared to the heavy gales and equally heavy rain of the twenty-seventh. This forced Lambert to strike lower yards and topmasts and get the topgallant masts down on deck. The gales abruptly moderated on the twenty-eighth, which allowed the crew to then sway the lower yards and topmasts right back up, as well as facilitated the pointing of topgallant mast rigging.

Additional provisions continued to come aboard, which included a cask of peas, several large bags of vegetables, three quarters of fresh beef, four tons of beer, and six tons of water. On Thursday a lighter came alongside with several tons of iron bolts and copper sheathing destined for the new ships building at Bombay. The discharge and stowage of these materials took the efforts of all hands for the entire day. And, in an attempt to come to terms with the tremendous quantity of gunpowder which had come aboard on Monday, Mr. Armstrong and a working party spent the better of two days filling smaller kegs and ready-use cartridges.

Considerable boatswain's, carpenter's, sailing master's, and sundry stores were brought alongside in lighters or were fetched from the dockyard by the ship's boats. All of these things then, of course, required significant effort to clear the seemingly always-lumbered decks and properly stow the items below. On Wednesday the *Java* received a new six-oared gig as well as an impressive amount of baggage which belonged to Lieutenant General Hislop. That afternoon also saw a Royal Marine messenger come on board with a letter which bore the Admiralty's incongruous fouled-anchor seal. Lambert signed for it and took it directly to his day cabin. He called to his steward for tea while he tore it open.

To Henry Lambert Esq.
Capt. Java Spithead

Java: to proceed with Lt Genl Hislop and Despatches to Bombay (calling at the Cape), join Sir Saml Hood and follow his orders

You are hereby required and directed as soon as you shall have received on board the ship you command Lt General Hislop and his Aides de Camp, agreeably to our order of the 17th Inst., together with such Despatches as may be entrusted to your care, and put to sea the moment wind and weather will permit and proceed without loss of time to the Cape of Good Hope and having landed any Despatches which may be intended for that Settlement, you are to make the best of your way to the Isle of France and having landed the Despatches for that Island you are to proceed to Bombay, where you are to land Lt General Hislop, and his suite, with the Government, and those Despatches destined for that Presidency, and then to proceed and join Vice Admiral Sir Samuel Hood Bt. at Madras or wherever else he may happen to be, and putting yourself under his command follow his orders for your further proceedings.

Given 26 Oct. 1812—

W. Dommett
J. S. Yorke
J. Osborn

Lambert read the orders twice as he drummed his fingers on the table.

"Pass the word for the first lieutenant," he called, the cry immediately echoed by the marine sentry perpetually stationed outside the cabin. Chads quickly came in, perfectly aware that orders or something like had just come on board.

"Ah, Henry, here they are at last," said Lambert. "They say

nothing I didn't already know but, as always, it's good to have 'em written and in one's hand."

"Indeed, Captain," replied Chads as he read the proffered document. "Well, we just received an enormous amount of the general's baggage and private stores today, so I daresay he'll not be far behind. Lord, when you look at his many things on top of the considerable shipbuilding materials, the supernumerary hands and their dunnage, and every-which thing, the master and I are at wit's ends to try and stow it all. It will be desperately difficult to clear for action, I daresay."

"I'm well aware, Henry. As to the general's arrival we may still have a fortnight, but we must complete stores with utmost speed. It's still the crew about which I'm the most concerned. On Monday the admiral's flag lieutenant told me we're to receive a small number of men from the *Royal William*. Well, that was to have been yesterday—those infernal gales no doubt brought that plan by the lee—but it could come to pass today. He also said a larger draft should come aboard by Friday or Saturday. Lord, I surely hope so!" Lambert unconsciously touched his fingertip to the wooden table-top for luck.

In fact, just a half-glass later saw one of the *Royal William*'s boats alongside bearing six boys, as part of the complement, as well as thirteen men as supernumeraries for Bombay. Lambert, working at his desk close to the stern windows (pleasantly bathed in the light which came through the six curved, sloping sections which ran across the entire width of the cabin), received the news from the midshipman of the watch with nothing more than a nod.

The receipt of the last admiralty order, and the thought that General Hislop and his staff would soon come aboard, reminded Lambert that he needed to address the issue of the general's ac-commodation. On board a frigate the captain lived in relative splendor. Even though he had to share the space with four pon-derous 18-pounder cannon, nevertheless his quarters were larger (about nine-hundred square feet) than the cabins allocated to all the rest of the officers put together. Thus, it was obvious that Lambert was going to have to share this beautiful, commodious, airy space with his high-ranking passenger. The captain actually occupied three cabins here at the after-most part of the gundeck: the great cabin all the way aft, something on the order of twenty-eight feet wide and fourteen in depth, illuminated by that elegant array of windows; the smaller coach, essentially the captain's din-ing room, slightly forward and on the larboard side; and then the bed place or sleeping cabin which mirrored the coach on the starboard side. Lastly there were the two small quarter galleries, on either side of the great cabin, lit by their own windows to the stern and to the sides. Partitioned off from the great cabin, each quarter gallery contained a commode—and both were normally reserved for the captain alone.

The general's *aides-de-camp*—please God he bring only the two previously mentioned—would be accommodated somehow on the berth deck and mess in the wardroom with the *Java's* other officers. The ship's officers lived in small cabins—each one averaged a tiny forty-two square feet—arranged in two rows on either side of the wardroom, all at the after part of the berth deck. If the general should bring any servants they would sleep and mess with the crew more forward on that same deck. The general himself, however, would need to be in here. Lambert raised his voice to the marine sentry. "Pass the word for the carpenter!" As always, the cry was instantly taken up and moved forward, which resulted in a tap at the door a few minutes later followed in turn by the sawdust-covered form of Mr. Kennedy.

"Ah, there you are, Chips," said Lambert, "I beg pardon for interrupting your work. Pray take a chair. As you know, we are to carry an army general and his presumably small staff on our voyage to India."

"Yes, sir, so I've understood."

"If it were a mere commodore which came with us, particularly someone I knew, I'd just shove over in here, share-and-share alike. But this officer is far senior to me—something much like a vice admiral—and of another service entirely, and I don't know him at all. So, in this case mere shoving over won't do. We must do something more formal. At first I thought I'd give up the entire cabin and crowd into the wardroom, where I'd displace Mr. Chads and the whole establishment down there. Or, I could simply give over the great cabin and restrict myself to my coach and sleeping cabin. I've known either arrangements on other ships in like circumstances. But on reflection I believe it would be better to divide the great cabin fore-and-aft. This'll require more work, to include the fabrication of another bulkhead. But it'll allow each of us—the general and me—separate entrances to the half-deck, the exclusive use of one of the smaller cabins, half of the great cabin, and one of the quarter galleries. May I have your opinion?"

"Well, sir, I believe your second scheme's the superior one," replied Kennedy without hesitation. "H'as you said, it'll require some work, to be sure—and o'course it'll be h'another section of bulkhead we'll 'ave to strike below when we clears for h'action, but still I believe it'll h'answer for the better."

"Very well, Chips," said Lambert. "I won't burden you personally with the labor. You're busy enough at present. I'd already made a request for dockyard joiners to come aboard for this purpose—as well as to fit out a couple of small cabins below for the general's aides. When the joiners do come on board—I hope later this week—I desire you acquaint them with the particulars and keep your eye on them. You may directly draw the needed materials from the yard."

Kennedy stood up and touched his forehead. "Aye aye, sir. Very 'appy to be o'service."

Lieutenant Chads, and the other lieutenants, spent much of the next two days employing what crew they had with various tasks about the ship. These were things that certainly needed to be done, but they were things that from the doing were also good training for the mostly inexperienced men. Thus, they loosed sails to dry and then furled them (between the periods of rain); ranged the sheet cable; lashed the booms; scraped the outside of the ship; exercised the boats (heaving them up from the water and then down again) and they even turned deadeyes in afresh, rove new lanyards, and set up stays. The anchorage and the harbor mirrored the activity on board the *Java*; during this time H.M. frigate *La Loire* and brig-sloop *Peacock* sailed close-by on their ways into Portsmouth, while the frigate *Fylla,* sloops *Hope* and *Plover*, and a number of other vessels took advantage of a southwest wind and departed St. Helen's Road into the Channel.

On Friday this flurry of activity was interrupted. A procession of the *Royal William*'s boats came alongside bearing 137 men specifically for the *Java*'s true complement. The officers received these men with delight mixed with relief. As he gazed down at them from the quarterdeck, Captain Lambert received them with mixed emotions. He rejoiced in the number of men, but as he watched them come aboard and assemble in the waist he recognized that the vast majority had been gathered from the press gangs and the prison hulk, with few right seamen among them. The sight of those from the hulk brought Lambert's spirits even lower than they had been. Not unexpectedly they had little in the way of personal belongings—nor did many of the pressed men for that matter—but what really struck him was their sullen and churlish demeanor, their pale unshaven faces, and the evident marks on their wrists and ankles from their recently cast-off irons. It was quite true that any man could swab a deck, haul on a rope, or push a capstan bar round-and-round. For centuries the Navy had been making seamen from whatever grist came to its mill; yet, even so, there were limits.

"Lord," said Lambert to himself, "oh, Lord."

The next day, Saturday, October thirty-first, saw the new men fumble about as they tried to help to stow the most recently obtained stores, victuals, sailcloth, and cordage—which lay about everywhere cluttering the weather decks. It also saw them try to generally acclimate and orient themselves to the ship and her routines. Then, at two bells in the first dog watch, the officers and petty officers called all hands to formally size-up and rate the ship's company. After the initial rating process was over the officers began to compile their watch and quarter bills. It was indeed no surprise to see that the notation beside fully one-third of the names was "landman"—all-too-frequent to give any comfort. The proportion of "ordinary seamen" to "able seamen" was uncomfortably high as well, for strictly speaking an ordinary seaman was little more than "one who can make himself useful on board, but is not an expert nor skillful sailor."

Another worry took some of Lambert's attention at this point. As if he needed another distraction he found himself embarrassingly short of personal funds. After considerable hesitation he decided he put his pride aside and penned an appeal to Admiralty second secretary Barrow.

> H. M. Ship Java
> Spithead
> 2 Novbr. 1812

Sir,

I am extremely sorry that I am compelled to lay this Requisition before My Lords Commissioners of the Admiralty, but from private reasons feel it an imperious Duty I owe to Myself and Family to state on My Honor since collecting My Bills for the numerous necessary Articles of equipment I conceived requisite for a Voyage to the East Indies for the reception of Lieut. General Hislop and Staff: That, I am £150 out of pocket exclusive of the further unavoidable Expenses I shall be at in procuring further necessities at the different places I am to touch at between here and Bombay. I trust therefore that Government will allow

me some Remuneration in addition to the little I have received from the Honourable East India Company,

and I have the Honour to be

Sir

Your Most Obedient Servant

H. Lambert

Notwithstanding the overabundance of landmen, the *Java*'s
preparations for sea proceeded rapidly throughout the first week
of November. This was only slightly hampered by three rainy days
at the start. Fortunately, the end of the week saw a balance with
three days of particularly fine weather and light winds. In fact,
those winds—which had been predominantly from the northwest,
west-northwest, and north-northwest—obligingly suited Captain
Lambert's plans by a gradual shift around to the northeast, east-
northeast, and finally east.

The process of organizing the crew continued on Sunday.
When the watch and quarter bills had finally been completed, and
when the division officers ceremoniously reported their divisions
all present on deck and even sober, Lambert formally read to them
from the Act of Parliament and the Articles of War.

"For the regulating and better government of His Majesty's
navy, ships of war, and forces by sea," he began, his voice clear and
penetrating, his timing and cadence effective, his delivery honed
and polished by hundreds of previous readings.

"Whereon, under the good providence of God, the wealth,
safety, and strength of this Kingdom chiefly depend; be it enacted
by the King's most excellent Majesty, by and with the advice and
consent of the Lords spiritual and temporal, and Commons in the
Parliament assembled, and by the authority of the same, that from
and after the twenty-fifth day of December, 1749, and subsequently amended, the articles and orders hereinafter following, in
time of peace as in time of war, shall be duly observed and put in
execution, in manner hereinafter mentioned."

Lambert leaned against the quarterdeck railing and spoke rapidly but not hurriedly. He laid them out in succession, thirty-five
articles in all. He began with the requirement for public worship
according to the liturgy of the Church of England. After that appeal to diligent reverence, the rest of the articles instantly got
down to business, coldly underscoring a considerable length of
punishable offenses: swearing, cursing, drunkenness, and un-

cleanness; giving information to the enemy; giving aid to the enemy; withholding information from superiors; activity in the nature of spies; failure to preserve captured documents; embezzlement of property from ships seized for prize; pillage or evil-treatment of prisoners; failure to prepare for fighting; cowardly crying for quarter; cowardly yielding to the enemy; failure to duly observe orders in time of action; withdrawing or keeping back in time of action; failure to pursue the enemy; failure to assist a known friend; delay or discouragement of action on any pretence; desertion; failure to protect merchant ships; misuse of mariners of merchant ships; making or endeavoring to make a mutiny; uttering any words of sedition or mutiny; concealing a traitorous or mutinous design; attempting to stir up a disturbance; contemptuous behavior to a superior officer; striking, or offering to strike, a superior; disobeying a lawful command of a superior; quarreling or fighting with other persons in the fleet; wasting or embezzling stores or ammunition; setting fire to anything not appertaining to the enemy; negligently steering and thus hazarding a ship; sleeping on watch; negligently performing duty; committing murder, sodomy with man or beast, or robbery; making a false muster; failure to apprehend and hold a criminal; and behaving in a manner scandalous, infamous, cruel, oppressive, or fraudulent. The long list of specifics ended with the final article, a general one often referred to as the "captain's cloak," which enabled every captain to employ a catch-all when necessary:

"All other crimes not capital, committed by any person or persons in the fleet, which are not mentioned in this act, or for which no punishment is hereby directed to be inflicted, shall be punished by the laws and customs in such cases used at sea."

When it was finally done, and Lambert had closed his book, he hoped that the messages had gone home. This was certainly due to the remarkably wide-range of topics, but it was also due to the grim and unrelenting recital of the punishments allowed. Embedded in the words he had just read were seven utterances of "punished with death," three of "upon pain of death," and fourteen of "shall suffer death." As he gazed out upon the sea of faces—an utterly silent sea—he saw nothing but grave, solemn, and serious expressions. This was true not only among the seamen who had heard the articles many times before, but also the many landmen who had just heard it for the first time, and now reflected upon just what it entailed to be persons subject to naval discipline.

Time for reflection was limited, however, for this Sunday also saw the crew employed aloft with various activities which then continued throughout the week. They rattled the shrouds afresh, enlarged and resewed the mizzen royal sail, stropped blocks, made points and nippers, and resettled various sections of rigging. Their seemingly endless toil was by no means reserved for work solely aloft. Sundry stores and supplies continued to flow into the ship, some delivered by dockyard lighters and some fetched by the *Java*'s boats. Six more cases of copper and an equal amount of iron bolts came aboard, which took almost a full day to properly stow away. The decks constantly needed to be cleared of all these materials, and those decks were washed as the clutter and clearing allowed—not every day as would be the routine once at sea, but certainly enough to maintain reasonable appearances. There were even opportunities on two of these busy days to wash clothes and scrub hammocks.

Again, fortunately, much of the work necessary to ready the ship also doubled as equally necessary, and indeed critical, training for the raw crew. Sail drill and general proficiency aloft were of particular concern to the captain, first lieutenant, and master. Thus, even though the rain necessitated several occasions for loosening the sails to dry, the crew was obliged to loosen and then furl the entire suit every day save Friday—whether they really needed it or not. Similarly, when the sails were furled each day at sunset, Mr. Chads also had the boats hoisted up and stowed again, not that such evolutions really required being done for operational reasons. In a like vein the men were exercised aloft in even more sophisticated activities; every day save one, at two bells in the forenoon watch, the crew was required to rush up each mast to cross the topgallant and royal yards. Then at sunset, which was at this time of year around three bells in the second dog watch, they were obliged to send them back down and strike them on deck.

The incessant parade of shipping in-and-out of Portsmouth continued to flow by the *Java* close aboard, which always added to the crew's very-real sense of frenetic naval activity. On Wednesday, during the now-routine sail drill at sunset, the surgeon joined the master at the taffrail to watch a particularly busy spectacle of ship movement.

"Good evening, Mr. Robinson," he said, "quite a display I find."

"Well, there you are, Mr. Jones, and good evening to you," responded Robinson. "It is indeed. I've long been convinced that no where can give one the fullest sense of the maritime superiority of our country than right here in the Solent. The quantity of merchant and naval shipping coming, going, and at anchor is simply staggering. Look—this very moment—amongst naval vessels leaving harbor you see the *Warspite*, 74; *Minerva*, 32; *Magicienne*, 24; and *Niemen*, 40. *Magicienne's* captain is the Honorable William Gordon, a friend of our captain, and *Niemen's* captain is Samuel Pym, decidedly *not* a friend. Then over there are the brigs *Minerva*, 18; *Columbine*, 18; and *Zephyr*, 16. And at the same time do you see the ships coming in to harbor? There's the famous *Indefatigable*, 44—her captain's John Fyffe—the *Diomede*, 50—Captain Fabian—and the brig *Rolla*, 10." All this while Robinson had pointed every which way with his telescope. He now tucked it under his arm and opened the ledger-like volume he held in his left hand. Warming to his subject, he went on.

"As I just have my logbook here I'll tell you even more. The last few days have also seen the departures of the ships *Barham*, 74; *Doris*, 36; *Nemesis*, 28; and *Crocodile*, 22; the brigs *Derwent*, 16; and *Saracen*, 18—she's just been built—the sloops *Alonzo*, 16; *Racoon*, 18; and *Atalante*, 18; the schooner *Pickle*, 16; and the storeship *Weymouth*. Vessels arriving have been the *Stag*, 36—she was just built, too—the *very* famous *San Josef*, 114; and the brig *Fervent*, 12. There, Doctor, aren't you amazed? My short list here contains more ships than the entire navies of most countries."

"Amazed I am, most certainly, Mr. Robinson," replied Jones. "At times I confess I despair of victory against Monsieur Bonaparte and his allies—and now the Americans too, it would seem—but I do take heart. With a navy—and a carrying trade—such as ours, and if we are true to ourselves, how can we not prevail?"

"Well, sir," said Robinson. "I believe our navy is capable of performing anything—and everything."

In the great cabin, immediately below them, Captain Lambert and Lieutenant Chads were in the midst of a far less pleasant conversation.

"There's no question, sir," said Chads. "Of course none of the hands will bear witness, but that don't signify. Armstrong and one of his mates, King, overheard Gordon plainly. He was among a group of Coquettes, pitching it hot as to what's all wrong with this here ship, how the Coquettes are picked on continuous, that it don't have to be borne, and that there were *remedies*, if they comprehended his meaning."

"God's my life," said Lambert.

"Sir." agreed Chads, shaking his head. "So Armstrong immediately called for Neale and they straight away had him clapped in irons."

"Very well," said Lambert. "So that's for Gordon. What about Johnson?"

"Well, Captain, at almost the same time though in a different part of the ship—and I am certain the incidents are coincident—Johnson was among several in the party sending up the mizzen royal yard under Mr. Robinson's direction. I was standing nearby, merely observing, and they were moving pretty slowly so I remarked something very like, 'hoist away chearly, lads.' In response Johnson spoke something under his breath. I said, 'you there, what's that you say?' whereupon he looked straight at me and again spoke under his breath, but this time I distinctly heard the words 'whoreson bugger.' Robinson was walking toward me and apparently he heard it too, for he instantly called over two marines and had 'em clap Johnson into bilboes on the half-deck."

"God help us," said Lambert. "Henry, this is damned serious business. I wish I were as certain as you the two things are not related. Regardless, we must take decisive action. They must be flogged, and soon." Chads nodded, again in full concurrence.

"In fact," Lambert went on, "I've been expecting something like this what with all these disaffected Coquettes, the gaolbirds, and some of the other pressed men. Thus, not only must these villains be flogged, we must positively make an example of 'em. Dammit, Henry, *you* know more than any man that I heartily dislike the cat, that I'm no hard captain, no Tartar. But there's no arguing that it must be used on occasion—and this occasion must stand as a sharp demonstration to the rest of the crew."

"What's more, this came from the port admiral today." Lambert waved a paper in the air. "It's a copy of a letter he received from the first secretary of the Admiralty. Apparently Sir Richard wrote the Admiralty after my visit when I expressed my concerns about our manning. I'm afraid it did no good—here, see for yourself." He passed the document to Chads.

Admiralty Office
October 31, 1812

Sir,

Having laid before my Lords Commissioners of the Admiralty your Letter of the 26th instant, acquainting me with your interview with Captain Lambert and his laudable anxiety of mind in regard to the manning of the Ship he commands; I am commanded by the First Lord to acquaint you that whilst Captain Lambert has a right to be concerned about being short of Complement with respect to experienced Sailors, his Lordship is very much satisfied that H.M. ship in question is far from ill-manned, and that he has every confidence that Captain Lambert and his Officers will be able to instill a firm and right sense of Naval discipline into the Crew, and with constant exercise at Sail drill and at the great Guns and small Arms &c, make them fit for any Service in short order.

I am, Sir,
Your humble servant,

J. W. Croker
First Sec'y, Admiralty

Adm. Sir R. Bickerton,
Commander-in-Chief, Portsmouth

"Well, sir, that seems clear enough," said Chads with a scowl. "Indeed, very clear. If my lord Viscount Melville in Whitehall's satisfied, then I daresay we must be satisfied here. So, we've a long voyage ahead of us and an indifferent crew. And train them we must but, as his lordship says, we also must firmly establish discipline—and that sooner rather than later. That in mind, I suppose that today's incidents in some ways present an opportunity. Sir, do you think two dozen lashes, or even three?" There was a pause as Lambert considered.

"Three dozen, I believe," he said at last. "The message must be clear, not even so much to Gordon and Johnson but rather to all the rest. It'll make no difference to Gordon. He appears to be a poor seaman and a brute. It'll do him no good, and yet it'll likely make him no worse. I'm a bit more concerned with Johnson; he may have only forgot himself. If so, it's his hard luck. It cannot be helped."

Thus, as four bells rang out the next morning, Captain Lambert came up the companionway ladder and onto the quarterdeck. Chads walked over to him and touched his hat.

"Hands to punishment, sir?"

Lambert nodded. The boatswain, Mr. Humble, had overheard their words and already anticipated the order. He instantly roared out, "All 'ands to witness punishment!" The calls of the boatswain's mates began their screech and twitter. The men came forth from all parts of the ship, assumed their places within their divisions, and toed their newly assigned lines on the proper deck seams. Similarly, the officers took position on the quarterdeck, resplendent in best coats and gold lace, and the marines formed a line abaft the mizzenmast which also came forward along both starboard and larboard sides, splendid in scarlet jackets, white cross-belts, twinkling brass, and gleaming muskets—with bayonets fixed. Humble and his mates had already turned-up and made fast a grating at the fore end of the quarterdeck; he nodded to Lambert to indicate its readiness. The ship's company fell silent, all eyes upon their captain, who had moved slightly forward of the mizzen.

"Thomas Gordon," said Lambert, his face set unusually hard and his voice cold and quiet yet quite audible to all. He continued as the seaman stepped forward in the company of Neale, the master-at-arms.

"You are charged with making mutinous expressions. Mutinous expressions! On some ships you'd be charged as a full mutineer, and hanged. Is it possible you spoke in ignorance? No, I think not. It passes all belief. Whatever the case, it will not do. This is an extremely serious matter, Gordon, and though this time I shall not cause you to hang, there are dire consequences nevertheless." Lambert raised his voice slightly and called out, "Have this man's officers anything to say for him?" Gordon's division officer and the first lieutenant were silent. There really was nothing that could be said in the enormity of the offense—as well as in the face of the captain's visible anger. "Very well. Do you have anything to say for yourself, Gordon?"

"No, your honor."

"So be it," replied Lambert, and then raised his voice again, "John Johnson." Johnson—a supernumerary able seaman—essentially mimicked Gordon's motions from a moment before as he stepped forward in the custody of Blagdon, the ship's corporal.

"And you. You are charged with offering contempt to the first lieutenant. Contempt and disrespect. What were you about? There's hardly a ha'penny's difference between contempt and mutiny, Johnson. As I said—and you should very well know—mutiny means the rope. Have this man's officers anything to say for him?" It was really only Chads who could have spoken, and of course he did not. "Do you have anything to say for yourself, Johnson?"

"No, sir, thankee kindly, your honor."

"Very well. Strip." Both men slowly took off their shirts and laid them on the deck.

"Seize them up, in turn," said Lambert.

"Seized up, sir," said Humble a minute later as Gordon stood bound to the grating, his arms outstretched.

"Mr. Barton," said Lambert to his clerk, "read the nineteenth article of war, if you please."

Chads called out, "Off hats!" and then Barton began in a high, clear tone.

"Nineteen: If any person in or belonging to the fleet shall make or endeavor to make any mutinous assembly upon any pretence whatsoever, every person offending herein, and being convicted thereof by the sentence of a court martial, shall suffer death; and if any person in or belonging to the fleet shall utter any words of sedition or mutiny, he shall suffer death, or such other punishment as a court martial shall deem him to deserve; and if any officer, mariner, or soldier in or belonging to the fleet, shall behave himself with contempt to his superior officer, being in the execution of his office, he shall be punished according to the nature of his offence by the judgement of a court martial."

"Three dozen apiece," called out Lambert. "Bosun's mates, do your duty."

Ceremoniously, Humble pulled the cat-o'-nine-tails out of its red baize bag and passed it to Darby, the largest of his mates. Darby twirled the handle which forced the nine lengths of whip to separate and fly loose. Then—as the marine drummer began a roll—the boatswain's mate lashed forward with the first stroke. Gordon, staggered by the impact, screamed hoarsely. As the blows continued Gordon continued to howl, at times barely able to draw his next breath, his feet doing a bizarre dance on the now blood-splattered deck as he squirmed against the unyielding bindings. Mercifully, long before the end of the three dozen lashes he passed out and hung silent and still. The only sounds which remained were Humble's formal count, the hiss of the tails, and the wet impact. Finally it came to an end. Humble and Darby cut the seizings and carefully passed the unconscious man to two of his mess-mates, who carried him below to the sick berth. Then, the whole business was repeated. Johnson was led forward, white with terror. Humble passed a new cat to Harrogan, who replaced Darby.

Most of the crew and the officers appeared able to watch the floggings dispassionately, though there certainly were pale faces, tightly closed eyes, and sympathetic tears to be seen. This was particularly true among the young midshipmen and ship's boys. Both Lambert and Chads repeatedly glanced about the deck. They studied the men carefully and were satisfied that there were no signs of outrage or protest. Three-dozen lashes was a severe sentence, to be sure, but the charges were themselves extremely grave. Since there had been many witnesses to both incidents the entire ship's company knew that the offenders were guilty—guilty beyond redemption. Chads met Lambert's eyes. Both were happy the bloody business was over, yet they were also both guardedly confident that the hard display had made a solid impression on the men, particularly the former Coquettes.

"Hands to breakfast, Captain?" asked Chads.

"Yes, Mr. Chads, if anyone's still got any appetite. After breakfast, loose sails and cross topgallants and royals, if you please, and then have all hands turn-to and ready the ship for today's ceremony."

"Aye aye, sir."

Thus, a few short hours later, a hesitant tap at the door heralded Mr. Midshipman Salmond, who brought Mr. Chads' respects and the news that all was ready on deck. Lambert threw down his pen and motioned Barton to follow. They walked out of the cabin and up the companionway to the quarterdeck, where Lambert clapped his number-one scraper on his head. As he came up on deck he suppressed the grin which had spread across his face, for the scene was magnificence itself. What had opened as a breezy and cloudy day had become very fair and fine. Fully dressed out, the ship was ablaze with color. The gentle wind played with every flag, streamer, pennant, and jack that the *Java* owned—displayed from, it seemed, every part of her masts, yards, and rigging. The rest of the ship was a splendid sight as well: decks, guns, falls, and hammock-cloths immaculate; officers resplendent in their best gold-laced uniforms; and all hands gorgeous in their Sunday-best embroidered shirts, brass-buttoned jackets, and ribboned hats.

The noon observation had just been completed, and thus the officer of the watch reported that he believed that, if the captain pleased, it was twelve.

"Make it so, Mr. Buchanan," said Lambert. As eight bells rang out Buchanan touched his hat, turned away, filled his lungs, and bellowed, "Away, aloft!" The majority of the crew ran for the shrouds, both larboard and starboard. They raced up as quickly as might be expected due to the numbers of landmen—and due to the considerable care being taken to avoid getting tar on best clothing. The men laid out onto each yardarm. When the teeming mass finally came to a stop, everyone in position, Lambert took off his hat and in the fullest voice he could muster cried out, "Three cheers for the King!"

"Huzzay...Huzzay...Huzzay!" roared out some four-hundred voices. The seamen hung onto their perches aloft and the officers on deck pulled off their hats and held them across their breasts. As the last cheer faded away Mr. Armstrong touched a slow-match to the starboard bow-chaser and so began the gun salute. As he came from forward aft he ignored the watch in his hand. Mirrored by the senior gunner's mate who walked down the larboard side with his own slow-match, Armstrong paced from gun-to-gun with the traditional timing ritual.

"If I weren't a gunner I wouldn't be here,"—boom!—"I've left my wife, my home, and everything that's dear,"—boom! As he fired the seventeenth gun the gunner stopped and faced aft, and upon meeting his captain's eye he removed his hat and bowed. The last of the *Java*'s salute—as well as those of the many other ships in Spithead—still echoed around the anchorage, and enormous clouds of white gun smoke slowly rose and dissipated into the sky.

Immediately the boatswain's calls summoned the hands to dinner, which brought forth the usual running feet, the clang of mess-kids, and the roar of conversation.

"I still don't see wot's this 'ere fuss about," said George Herue. One of the ship's smallest boys, he spoke to his equally small mate Benjamin Pauling as they ran to join their mess.

"Which h'it's about wot they call the Gunpowder Treason Plot, which 'appened almos' two-'unnert years ago," replied Benjamin. "This wicked old cove, Guy Fawkes was 'is name, an' some other fine fellows tried to blow up King James the First—God bless 'im—and Parlyment altogether."

"'E wot? Wot fer?"

"'E did it on account 'e was a papist, and 'e din't much like the laws wot was then against papists. But h'it din't work, see, and 'e got caught, an' they served 'im out proper as you might just h'imagine, George. So now h'it h'is that every year since, an' on the very same day I thank you, we cheer the king and we cheer old Mr. Fawkes too, as you might call 'im, wot fer? 'Cause he buggered h'it all up, the old bastard, an' the king's alive, that's wot fer!"

Saturday morning saw Captain Lambert and Lieutenant Chads standing by the taffrail, deep in conversation about final preparations for sailing. The noise and bustle of the hands employed variously about the ship provided a comfortable background. But, shortly after four bells rang out, they were interrupted by Herringham, the officer of the watch, who approached with fingers to his hat brim.

"Beg pardon Captain, Mr. Chads, but if you please there's a boat from the dockyard fast approaching. I daresay it's the paymaster as we were told to expect this morning."

"Very well, Mr. Herringham," replied Lambert, "kindly muster the hands, and have a chair and table brought up for the clerks' convenience."

The boatswain's calls echoed throughout the ship, superfluously it seemed. The Javas clearly anticipated the order and instantly abandoned their work. They came both rapidly and cheerfully to mass along the larboard side of the quarterdeck and gangway. There they stood, fidgeting, smiling, and joking among themselves as the pay clerks and several marines came on board, laden with a number of heavy sailcloth bags. The visitors quickly established a position next to the capstan.

"Silence there, silence fore and aft," called out Chads. He took reports from the division officers and then turned to Lambert. "If you please, Captain, all hands present, relatively clean, and sober."

"Thank you, Mr. Chads," replied Lambert, who then raised his voice. "Men, as you very well have noticed, the paymaster's clerks are here to pay you wages to date as well as two months' pay in advance. Now do not expect any additional pay during our intended voyage—at least until we reach India." This intelligence was received with wide grins, scattered cheers, and a general buzz of approval. Smiling, Lambert turned to the clerks. "Well, you may certainly carry on, gentlemen."

"Addison," called out the senior clerk, and instantly there Addison was. He pushed his way through his shipmates, pulled off his hat, and respectfully approached the table.

"David Addison, sir, if you please, able, starboard watch, fo'c'sle."

He saw his name checked off and the tarnished coins slapped down onto the capstan head—roughly three months' pay—which he scooped into his hat. As he moved over to the starboard gangway he stirred the coins with his fingers. So passed the next two hours, a long muster indeed, but which all bore with remarkable patience. Finally, Valgard Workey, ordinary, collected his pay and crossed the deck, which caused the happy ship's company to be dismissed by divisions.

The next two days saw all hands busily employed as they made various final preparations for sea—and prepared to receive the general who was now expected on Tuesday. However, an unexpected arrival came Sunday as two boats slid alongside with three naval officers and their sea chests. Came on board Master and Commander John Marshall, along with Lieutenants Christopher Aplin and James Sanders, as well as Assistant Surgeon Matthew Capponi. All of these officers carried orders which required the *Java* to convey them to India where they would be attached to various ships on that station. They were shown below where Captain Lambert welcomed them with sherry and some pleasantries. The pleasantries, on Lambert's part, masked his irritation at this new surprise. They also masked his concern about where to find accommodation for three more commissioned officers and another warrant officer on his already overcrowded berth deck. He dismissed the lieutenants and the surgeon into Mr. Chads' care, and then offered Marshall another glass.

"Well, Commander Marshall," said Lambert, "I see from your orders that you were promoted from lieutenant the twenty-fourth of last month, and that you shall take command of the sloop *Procris* when we reach the East Indies. I heartily give you joy of both events, and as is proper under the circumstances we'll address you in future with the courtesy title of 'captain.' Have you served in the east before?"

"Yes, sir," replied Marshall, "indeed I have. Shall I tell you a bit of my background?"

"Certainly; please do."

"Well, sir," said Marshall, "in 1800 I came on board the *Aurora*, Captain Caulfield, as a first-class volunteer and soon after was rated as midshipman. I served on the Lisbon and Mediterranean stations, and then changed to the *Latona*, Captain Sotheron, in the Baltic and Channel. In 1803 I removed to the *Grampus*—again with Captain Caulfield—at first on the Guernsey station and then as we sailed to the East Indies. In 1805, as a master's mate, I followed Captain Caulfield into the *Russell*. A year later I was made acting-lieutenant by Rear Admiral Pellew. I served with him in the *Culloden*, to include the action at Batavia Roads. I passed for lieutenant in 1806 and then the next year I returned to the

Russell. In 1809 I moved to the *Aboukir*, Captain George Parker, and took part in the unfortunate Walcheren expedition. For the past three years I've been in the North Sea, the Baltic, and just recently in Russia, where I commanded a gunboat at the defense of Riga."

"Well, you've seen some pretty active service, so you have," said Lambert. "I'm heartily glad to have you on board. I'm sorry I can't offer you good accommodation, however, with the hellish overcrowding I face. I'll do the best I can for you—we'll make you and the lieutenants some small partitioned cabins on the berth deck next to the army officers. And let me say that I and my officers will be grateful for your assistance as we try to make something of all the infernal lubbers we have as crew."

"Oh, never mind about accommodation, sir," replied Marshall with a smile. "I can sling a hammock anywhere. But thank you sincerely for taking me—and the other stray officers too—on board at the last minute. I'm sure I can speak for them to say we'll be very happy to assist you in any way we can."

The wind came fairly steadily from the east, which Lambert hoped would last, please God. He wanted to reposition the *Java* and the convoy a little farther to the west as soon as the general was embarked. Monday turned out to be rainy most of the day, but at eight bells in the afternoon watch—in the hope that Tuesday would see clear weather—Lambert hoisted the signal for the convoy to unmoor. He also hoisted a jack at the foretopmast as a signal that the general could come on board if convenient.

Tuesday was cloudy at first, but as the day wore on the weather indeed turned fine with light breezes. Very early—two bells in the morning watch—the *Java* sent boats to the *Ildefonso* with a number of empty casks. They shortly returned with four tons of water, which caused the crew considerable labor to secure it in the hold. Lambert studied the other ships in the convoy through his glass, and was not at all happy with the lack of activity displayed by his two Indiamen. He hoisted a second signal to unmoor—and this time punctuated it by firing a cannon. At four bells in the afternoon watch the *Java* herself unmoored and at the same time signaled the convoy, again firing a gun, to weigh anchor. By six bells the *Java* had hove short on her own cable and was directly above her anchor. Lambert, now frustrated by the Indiamen's seeming inability or unwillingness to follow orders, cocked his eye at Chads.

"Henry, this passes all belief. If this's how it's to be once we're at sea it's going to make for a damned unpleasant voyage. Repeat the goddam signal, if you please. I'm going below. Let me know the moment we see anything of our distinguished passenger."

As it turned out, happily, it was only a few minutes which Lambert had to wait.

"Mr. Robinson's duty, sir," reported Frederick Morton, midshipman of the watch, "and the port admiral's barge approaches. He believes it's the general and his staff at last."

"Oh, very well, Mr. Morton," replied Lambert, "my compliments to the master and I'll be on deck directly." A few minutes later Lambert gained the deck and studied the barge, now positioned to come alongside at the *Java*'s starboard mainchains. It was indeed Sir Richard's barge, extremely fine with a finely attired crew, but in the stern sat not the admiral nor any naval officer at all, but rather three army officers resplendent in scarlet coats and gold lace. As the seaman in the barge's bow caught his boathook into the mainchains, Lambert glanced about the deck. Despite the busy preparations for getting under way the Javas had worked hard to maintain the ship's pristine appearance since last Thursday's 'gunpowder treason' commemoration. The decks and accouterments were perfect and the accommodation ladder elegantly rigged with new-covered manropes. As they held their polished silver calls at the ready, the boatswain and his mates were fine in their best rigs and the sideboys were equally impressive in their new white gloves. The marines, of course, were fit to be seen by royalty—crossbelts pipe-clayed, buttons polished, hair powdered, and all fully prepared to stamp-and-clash and present their gleaming bayonet-fixed muskets at the right moment.

As the general's hat came in sight, and then even with the deck, the ceremony came alive. The sideboys knuckled their foreheads, the boatswains' calls shrilled, the marines mechanically and precisely executed their drill, and the bowchaser boomed out with the first of the eleven-gun salute. The general, a tall and dignified officer, stepped down onto the deck, hand to hat, and slowly walked aft followed by his officers. Lambert in turn stepped forward. He dropped his own salute and shook the general's outstretched hand.

"Welcome aboard, General Hislop. I am Captain Lambert. His Majesty's Frigate *Java* is honored to have you and your staff on board and to take you to your new post at Bombay. Speaking of which, may I give you joy of your command and your recent promotion?"

"Thank you kindly, Captain," replied Hislop with a friendly smile. "We're much honored to be on your fine ship. May I present my *aides-de-camp*? Major Walker and Captain Wood."

"Delighted, gentlemen," said Lambert as he shook their hands. "Sir, please allow me to name my officers: my senior lieutenant, Chads; Lieutenants Herringham and Buchanan; Mr. Robinson, master; Mr. Humble, bosun; Mr. Armstrong, gunner; Mr. Pottinger, purser; Mr. Kennedy, carpenter; Mr. Jones, surgeon; and last but certainly not least, Lieutenant Mercer of the Royal Marines."

"Gentlemen," said Hislop, shaking their hands in turn with obvious good humor, "it's indeed my pleasure. I'm sure that we'll all get to know each other very well before we reach India, and I greatly look forward to it."

Lambert stepped back and gestured toward the deck at large. The deck already showed no sign of the recent ceremony and was now alive with seamen who moved to various ship-handling stations.

"Sir, we'd just hove short and, now that you and the last of your dunnage are aboard, we and the convoy'll weigh and shift to an anchorage more-or-less six leagues to the west. For days the wind's been foul, but today it's obligingly come round to just what we need and I mean to take advantage of it. Thus, if you'll step back with me to the taffrail you shall have a splendid vantage point from which to observe the maneuver. I'm afraid that much of my crew are untrained landmen, but still I hope that we shall carry it off in a creditable fashion."

So it was that the *Java* weighed anchor and made sail in company with her tiny convoy. Much to her officers' embarrassment, the gun-brigs and even the Indiamen executed both tasks more quickly and efficiently than did the *Java*. Her landman-heavy crew was both a little slow and a little clumsy—just as the officers had expected and feared. The maneuver was finally done, but after almost two hours had passed the light wind had moved them only half-way to where Lambert had wanted to be. As darkness fell upon his unhandy crew and with no Solent pilot on board, Lambert decided it would be prudent to wait for daylight to proceed. As she hoisted the signal for the convoy to anchor, the *Java* herself came-to with her best bower in eleven and one-fourth fathoms. They were just off shore from the Isle of Wight at the mouth of the Newport River, with Cowes Point bearing west-southwest.

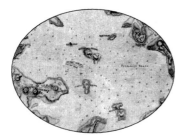

CHAPTER 10
PRESIDENT ROADS, BOSTON

President Roads
Outer harbor, Boston, Massachusetts
42° 20' N 70° 56' W
Tuesday, October 27th, 1812
10:00 A.M.
Fresh breezes; winds from the west

Commodore William Bainbridge, U.S. Navy, paced the weather side of the *Constitution*'s quarterdeck. His head was down and his hands were tightly clasped behind him. Up and down, up and down, his quick steps and stiff turns telegraphed both agitation and excitement.

Four bells rang out. Bainbridge stopped abruptly as though he had waited for the sound.

"Mr. Parker!" he boomed out, though the first lieutenant stood only six feet away.

"Sir?" replied a startled Parker.

"It's time. Weigh the starboard anchor, if you please, and heave short on the larboard. Loosen sails."

"Aye aye, sir."

The last two days had dragged on interminably for Bainbridge as he impatiently saw the completion of the final preparations for sea. The wind had not helped as it came in gale force from the south and southeast—and brought squally weather and then heavy rain. The day before yesterday a final collection of fresh-water casks and breakers had been sent on shore, filled, and returned. The crew had stowed the boats, secured the spare spars, cleared the hawse, set up the mainstay and the main staysail stay, and in general got last-minute things ready. Twice each day—at noon and at two bells in the first dog watch—the commodore beat to quarters and all hands were formally mustered.

Early today, however, the wind had both decreased and veered to the westward—and the tide was favorable. Parker reported to Bainbridge that all was in readiness on board and that the *Hornet* had signaled the same. The new sailing master, Mr. Nichols, expressed his concurrence. He added that he was content with the ship's draft of water astern at 23 feet 3 inches and ahead at 21 feet 11 inches. At six bells in the afternoon watch, the wind now fair from the west, the *Constitution* weighed her larboard anchor, made sail, and stood to sea. The *Hornet*, in company, mimicked her every motion. As the ships got under way they passed a cartel brig packed with exchanged American prisoners-of-war from Halifax. The men on the cartel saluted the warships with three cheers which were duly answered with considerable enthusiasm, particularly as the Constitutions recognized their own Midshipman John Madison, who waved and capered at the brig's railing.

At one bell in the first watch Lieutenant Hoffman approached the commodore and touched his hat.   "Sir, if you please, Boston Light bears west-½-north, three and one-half leagues distant."

"Very well, Mr. Hoffman," replied Bainbridge. "Carry on."

Now the crew catted the larboard anchor (hoisted it straight up to the cat-head in the bow), then fished it (hoisted its flukes upwards), and finally stowed it on the anchor bed. Just after five bells in the first watch they set the main course to capture more wind—now just light airs which came from the north. Yet, not long after midnight, it came on to blow with dirty weather that gave no indication that it might move on. In fact, by four bells in the middle watch Bainbridge was compelled to agree with the officer of the watch—now Lieutenant Morgan—that the fore and main courses needed to be hauled up. No sooner had that been done when the winds headed them off east-by-south and then abruptly shifted east. The commodore waited a moment while the leadsman in the mainchains took another sounding. He reported thirty-eight fathoms now, but another check just three hours later would show no bottom at all.

"We'll need to about-ship, gentlemen," said Bainbridge.

"Aye aye, sir," replied Morgan.

The master stepped to Morgan's side. "Stations for stays!" he roared in a full, carrying pitch. The calls of the bosun and his mates shrieked and twittered, which hurried along almost seventy seamen to their stations. The crew quickly got ready for this routine, yet reasonably complex, evolution. The sail trimmers fell-in by divisions, although some of them went directly aloft to clear rigging and shift backstays. The mizzen boom was hauled over by the mizzentopmen while others shifted the topping lift. An experienced helmsman took the wheel. The captains of the forecastle, quarterdeck, waist, and afterguard supervised the braces and bowlines as they were thrown off their belaying pins and flaked down on the deck—ready and clear for running.

"Ease down the helm!" The jib sheet was eased and the weather mizzen sheet was hauled to windward.

"Helm's a-lee!" The waisters let go the foresheet and the afterguard checked the lee forebrace. The forecastlemen checked the foretop bowline.

"Rise tacks and sheets!" The forecastlemen let go the fore tack, the waisters let go the main tack, and the foretopmen manned the weather fore clewgarnet. Simultaneously, the maintopmen manned the main clewgarnet and the quarterdeckmen hauled up the lee clew of the mainsail.

"Mains'l haul!" The waisters let go the main preventer brace and top bowline and the quarterdeckmen let go the main topsail brace. The afterguard let go the mizzen braces and bowlines. Then the waisters let go the main bowline. The forecastlemen handled the main preventer brace and shifted over the headsails. The maintopmen manned the main topsail brace, got down the main tack, and handled the main sheet. Concurrently, the mizzen topmen manned the mizzentopsail brace and hauled the crossjack brace, and then the afterguard let go and overhauled the main clewgarnets.

"Of all, haul!" The afterguard let go the forebrace and the lee foretopsail brace, and then let go and belayed the lee foretopgallant brace. The forecastlemen let go the head bowlines, the topgallant bowlines, and the foretop bowlines—and then got down and overhauled the fore tacks. Finally, the maintopmen and the quarterdeckmen hauled aft the fore sheet and the quarterdeckmen hauled the fore brace. The ship thus passed from the one tack to the other. Yet, hardly twenty minutes went by before the wind obliged Bainbridge to wear ship (not quite as complex a maneuver as tacking) and stand towards the *Hornet* to the southwest—and then wear again a half-hour later, to now head northeast-by-east.

This intensive sail-handling in fact set the pattern for the next dozen days. Over the course of those days the commodore congratulated himself countless times for having such a high number of experienced sailors on board. The wind and weather seemed determined to test thoroughly the material condition of the ships and the seamanship of the men. Every one of those days seemed to present variable winds, changing sea-states, and fluctuating weather. The common conditions were mists, haze, rain, squalls, gales, high seas, and heavy swells. The winds came from the south, southeast, southwest, west, west-northwest, northwest, and north-northwest—and they shifted, veered, and backed with maddening frequency. Thus, every day, and every night, saw the on-deck watch—if not all hands—continuously called up and sent aloft. They set, adjusted, or shortened sail; they wore ship and tacked ship; they sent up and then struck topgallant and royal yards; they took in and shook out single, double, and even triple reefs; they set and took in stormsails; they set and took in studding sails (not to mention shifted studding sails from starboard to larboard and then larboard to starboard as the wind veered and backed); and they sent down worn or torn canvas and bent new in place. While a few of the voyage's first days required only seven or eight altera-tions of sail configuration, several days involved twenty or thirty. Consequently, the crew was continuously cold, wet, exhausted, and frustrated, for despite all this effort the *Constitution* and *Hornet* averaged only six and one-half knots as the hours and days went by. And, it was a challenge to stay on the courses—southeast, southeast-by-east, and east-southeast—that would take them to the Cape Verde Islands.

Indeed, the men, and the officers as well, underwent consider-able hardship as they incessantly pitched and rolled on the stormy seas. The surgeons of both ships became extremely concerned about the continuously wet berth decks; concerns which were as well-founded as they were inevitable. Wooden ships always leak a little no matter how new or how well-built. This is particularly true in bad weather as the seams both above and below the waterline continuously flex with the motion of the ship. Thus, each day re-quired a number of men to work at the pumps for several hours to reduce the amount of water in the bilges. In addition to the water that worked itself into the ships, the men *brought* plenty below as well. The crews' hammocks, bedding, and clothing stayed damp—if not actually wet—for the men inevitably got soaked from the fre-quent rains when they were topside or aloft, and they really had no place in which to dry themselves or their clothes. Moreover, the crowded berth decks presented hard living even without the wet conditions. It was slightly more tolerable in *Old Ironsides*, where a seaman had a space around thirty inches wide to sling his hammock and the berth deck had a clearance of almost six feet. But on board the smaller *Hornet* a man might only have hammock space twenty-four inches wide, and the deck was only five feet, five inches high.

This is not to say that there were no brief periods of relatively calm and clear weather, for of course there were. The crews took every advantage of such times to dry their clothes and hammocks and even to attempt drying some of the constantly soaked sails.

Then, on top of everything else, the commodore found himself not quite happy with the *Constitution*'s anchor stowage relative to blue-water sailing. As a result, the weary men found themselves further heavily employed as they got the stream anchor on board and unstocked it. They also found themselves tasked to shift the waist anchor farther forward. The men who drew the next job which struck the commodore's mind were more fortunate; though somewhat messy, the labor involved to draw six pounds of soap from the purser and then apply it to the wheel ropes was nothing in comparison to shifting anchors.

Indeed, one could never have said that the intensive sail-handling—punctuated by attempts to eat, sleep, and dry things—were all that the busy men had to do. The commodore also kept his mind focused upon his tiny squadron's warlike nature. Thus, with hardly any exception, each of these days witnessed the ships beat to quarters and formally muster the crews—and on two of those days the ships completely cleared for action, the marines practiced sharpshooting, and the gun crews exercised the great guns. Additionally, considerable flag signals were passed between the *Constitution* and the *Hornet*, some for operational communications, but some just for practice.

It was no surprise that this close to the American coast other ships were to be seen. Although Bainbridge was keenly interested in engaging with British warships, privateers, and merchant ships—and, certainly, retaking American merchant ships that had been captured by the British—he let the first three sightings go by uninvestigated. However, for some reason the fourth sighting, on the twenty-ninth, intrigued the commodore; he shortened sail on board *Old Ironsides* and signaled the *Hornet* to pursue. After a half-hour of excitement the chase turned out to be nothing more than an American merchant brig. No one was particularly surprised nor disappointed, and the exercise with the two warships working together as a team was worth the effort for that reason alone. Then at noon, four days later, the masthead lookouts discovered another sail on the lee bow; both ships hoisted British colors and packed on sail to chase. Within an hour a boat from the *Hornet* boarded the strange sail—a brig wearing Spanish colors. She was shortly released upon proving her papers to be in order. Tuesday, the fifth of November, presented a copy of this incident. At seven bells in the afternoon watch the warships sighted a strange sail to the southeast. Both ships cleared for action and made sail in chase. They came up to the stranger after an hour and a quarter. All three ships backed their main topsails and hove-to, whereupon a boat from the *Hornet* boarded the vessel. At this point the routine was altered in that the boat did not return to the *Hornet* but came across to the *Constitution*. A few minutes later, to the greeting of the sideboys' salutes and the bosun's calls, Master Commandant Lawrence came onto the quarterdeck accompanied by a tall, thin man dressed in civilian clothes. The commodore received them in the great cabin with small glasses of port.

"Commodore Bainbridge," said Lawrence, "please allow me to name Captain Skinner of the American merchantman *Star*, twenty-five days from Cadiz via Lisbon, bound for New York."

"A pleasure, sir," said Bainbridge somewhat impassively. If he were at all pleased at the introduction he hid it tolerably well. "I dare to say Captain Lawrence likes your papers and your story, so to what do I owe the favor of your visit?"

"Commodore," interjected Lawrence, "he has some news from Europe I thought you might like to hear." Bainbridge looked expectantly at Skinner.

"Yes, sir. Well, it's from Russia, and I guessed that you wouldn't have heard. The French've taken Moscow! The Emperor Napoleon himself entered the city on the fourteenth of September. That is, if the reports and newspapers are correct, and I believe them to be. The French defeated the Russians at a place called Borodino in the first week of September, which allowed for the French movement toward Moscow. It's reported that the casualties at Borodino was terrible; around 70,000 killed and wounded."

"Indeed?" replied Bainbridge as he refilled Skinner's glass. "Well, Mr. Emperor Napoleon Bonaparte has some experience entering the capitals of countries with whom he goes to war. It's a pity that London's yet to appear on that list. Did the Russians at all try to prevent this unseemly event?"

"Well, sir," said Skinner, "as I said, after the Russians were defeated at Borodino the French were able to move forward unopposed. I'm not sure that I can add anything more, other than by this time—my news is obviously several weeks old—Monsieur

Bonaparte's expected to be in St. Petersburg, chasing the czar. I presume he thought the czar would've given up once his capital was taken. Kings and such generally do, it seems."

"I daresay," said Bainbridge. "Well, Captain ... Skinner, I won't detain you further. New York beckons you, I'm sure. Thank you for the most fascinating news."

It was on Sunday, November eighth, that the tiny squadron had its most interesting encounter. The morning had seen squally weather but by noon it had cleared up with fresh breezes from the west-northwest. The foremast lookout discovered a sail two points on the lee bow, whereupon the *Constitution* and the *Hornet* made all sail in chase. After an hour and a half they caught the chase, and per usual all three ships shortened sail, backed their main topsails, and came to a stop—which, per usual, enabled the *Hornet*'s boat to board the strange brig.

"So, then what happened?" asked Surgeon Evans later, over coffee in the wardroom. He had been below most of the day with three cases of venereal disease that would not respond to any treatments he could think of.

"So then," replied Lieutenant Aylwin, who had been officer of the watch during all the excitement, "she proved to be an American merchantman named the *South Carolina* of Philadelphia. She was bound for that city, coming from Lisbon. As she came-to she broke out American colors. We and the *Hornet* broke out English colors—ain't we sly Amos? We pretended to be an English squadron and we said we was going to seize her and send her into Halifax as a prize. Well, when he heard that bit of news, the American captain, a cheeky fellow named Richard Gaul, said he was in ballast. Then he produced a British license and was thus happy to prove to us Englishmen that he had a protection to trade. Well, Amos, don't you just wish you'd been there to see that old codger's face when they told him we was really Americans—and that we'd caught him red-handed in trade with the enemy? Ha! Pretty damned chagrined, I wager. Then the old rascal had the gall to say we'd worked to wind'ard of him *this* time, but he'd be damned if we ever did it to him again. So, then, along with a few hands, the acting-master of the *Hornet*, I think you've met him—Bill Cox— was put on board as prize master. Her victuals looked a little thin, so we sent over the stern cutter with a barrel of beef. Just think, Amos, of all the prize money we'll get when the government sells her."

"I hope so, John," said Evans, "and I hope it's the first of much more to come. You made a pun, by the way—*Captain Gaul had a lot of gall*."

Aylwin winked and smiled. "Well, I suspect that you and the commodore are of one mind in the notion of prize money. Anyway, at one bell in the second dog watch we waved goodbye to Mr. Cox and filled away ourselves, to the southeast-by-south. This was just as more rain, squally weather, and a heavy swell reappeared." Aylwin drank some of his coffee. "You know, sometimes I do like a good blow, but I've gotten heartily sick of this weather of late. And for all this work—the hands turned up to trim sail time and again, watch after watch—I think we've not come more than 1,500 miles to show for it. I suspect the commodore hoped by now we'd have come more like 2,500."

"I know what you mean, John, I do indeed," replied Evans. "I'm grow concerned for the crew's health. Aside from their general weariness, and that we're on short rations, the berth deck's been continually wet since we left port—and that's nigh on to thirteen days."

"Injuries? Rheumatism? Arthritis? Chills?" asked Aylwin.

"Yes, sure, all you mention—although far fewer injuries than I'd have expected. Yet far more other things we've carried with us from harbor: gonorrhea, chancres, buboes, even a tapeworm, forsooth. One man sees me daily because he has 'bouts of giddiness' when he turns to work. On the other hand, another man *insists* on going to duty just to receive his grog—although *he* is truly *not* well." Evans stared into his mug for a minute.

"John, I'm not quite clear on what the squadron's orders are. Are you, at all? That is, of course, if you're at liberty to discuss?"

"Well," replied Aylwin, "the commodore certainly hasn't been forthcoming, that's for certain—how different he is from Captain Hull. As I comprehend it, we're to generally sail about, annoy the enemy's commerce, and afford protection to *our* commerce. His honor has thus decided to sail almost three-thousand miles, clear across the Atlantic. We proceed with all haste to the Cape Verdes where the British usually have considerable shipping. We'll stop at Port Praya for water and to rendezvous with Captain Porter and the *Essex*. From there we'll all cruise southwesterly in the common sea lanes, and then turn more southerly back across the ocean to the waters off Brazil, where the British have much commerce. We may cruise off the Brazils for a month or even two. Of course it all depends upon our good or bad luck in meeting the enemy. If we haven't met many, or *any*, by that point we may then range as far as St. Helena Island. The vicinity of St. Helena's often frequented by the big ships of the Honorable East India Company as they return to England—*very* heavily laden indeed—from India and China. So, here's to it, Amos!" Aylwin clunked his mug against Evans'. "Happy hunting."

CHAPTER II

THE SOLENT, HAMPSHIRE, ENGLAND

The Solent
Just offshore from the Isle of Wight
Hampshire, England
50° 47' N 1° 17' W
Tuesday, November 10th, 1812
6:30 P.M.

Despite the unusually busy day, certain fundamentals of H.M. Frigate *Java*'s shipboard routines remained constant. For example, the ship's cook and the captain's steward remained indifferent to the embarkation of special passengers, and the shifting of the anchorage, and threw together a light supper for the senior officers. They had made good use of the fresh provisions and even delicacies readily available in Portsmouth and Gosport. The officers crowded around the table in Captain Lambert's half of the reconfigured great cabin. General Hislop, Commander Marshall, Major Walker, Captain Wood, and Lieutenants Sanders and Aplin were entertained by Captain Lambert, Lieutenant Chads, and the senior marine officer, Lieutenant Mercer. After the cloth was drawn, and as the officers nibbled at Essex cheese and passed the decanter of burgundy, Hislop caught Lambert's eye.

"Captain, our impending departure's brought forth to my mind something I learned as a schoolboy, which may be appropriate. In trying to recall my Virgil, it seems to me that when Aeneas and the surviving Trojans were about to sail to Italy, his father Anchises offered a cup of wine to the heavens and cried, 'Great gods, whom Earth and Sea and Storms obey, Breathe fair, and waft us smoothly o'er the main.'"

"Bravo, sir, well said!" replied Lambert. "I daresay we've a little farther to travel than did the pious Aeneas, so the sentiments are perhaps of even more relevance."

"Captain," interjected Chads, "before supper our new military friends pressed me to relate how the once-French frigate *Renommée* became our dear *Java*. I daresay I could do a passable, workmanlike job of it, but you're the grand master of the tale, so I implore you, would you please undertake the task?"

"Indeed?" said Lambert, "If that's the case I'd be most happy." He swept his glance around the table and saw expressions of genuine interest and anticipation. He nodded, took a sip of wine, and cleared his throat. "Ha-hmm. Well, gentlemen, so it was that on the second of February 1811, not quite two years ago, three French 40-gun frigates—Mr. Chads' dear *Renommée* (commanded by a Commodore Roquebert), the *Clorinde* (Captain St. Cricq), and the *Néréide* (Captain Lemaresquier)—sailed from Brest. They had on board 200 troops each and a goodly supply of munitions. They were bound to the Indian Ocean, to the Île de France—or as we call it, the Mauritius. Our capture of that island in early December of the year ten was, of course, not yet known in Europe. Bad weather nearly separated the frigates the first night, and a continuance of contrary winds occasioned the squadron to be eighteen days just going the first 200 leagues of the voyage. On the twenty-fourth of February, when he read some Lisbon newspapers found on board a Portuguese ship, the French commodore gained intelligence that a British attack was intended—and had perhaps already been made—upon the Mauritius. On the thirteenth of March the frigates crossed the line. On the eighteenth of April, in latitude thirty-eight degrees, they doubled the Cape of Good Hope, and on the sixth of May, being the ninety-third day since their departure from Brest, they arrived within five miles of Île de la Passe—which is the tiny island situated at the entrance of Grand-Port on the southeast side of Mauritius. Soon after midnight a boat from each frigate was despatched to the shore to gain intelligence."

Lambert again cleared his throat and leaned forward. He clearly knew this story extremely well and enjoyed the telling.

"The night was calm, and yet not a musket shot nor any other disturbance could be heard. This encouraged the hope that the island was still in French possession. Daylight on May seventh arrived, and the colors hoisted at the fort upon Île de la Passe were indeed French, but they were unaccompanied by any French private signals." Lambert paused, with a knowing look. "Indeed, it was actually our people attempting a *ruse de guerre*."

"This lack of private signals gave Commodore Roquebert his

first serious alarm. And then, at sunrise, five sail hove in sight to loo'ard. Two of these five were unarmed vessels, probably coasters—but the remaining three were the British 18-pounder 36-gun frigates *Phoebe* and *Galatea*, Captains Hillyar and Losack, and the 18-gun brig *Racehorse*, Captain de Ripe, all part of a squadron which'd been ordered to cruise off Mauritius to endeavor to intercept this same French squadron. They were also to look for two others—the new 40-gun frigates *Nymphe* and *Méduse*, from Nantes, of whose expected arrival information had also been received. The British ships began to approach the French. Simultaneously, the *Galatea*'s gig was despatched—with intelligence of the French squadron—to Captain Schomberg of the 18-pounder 36-gun *Astrea*, which lay in Port Louis on the northwest side of Mauritius. Captain Hillyar, as you may know, was a favorite of Lord Nelson, and Nelson had more than once commended Captain Schomberg for his unusual zeal." Lambert sipped some of his wine.

"In the course of the forenoon the *Renommée*'s boat was able to return with the information of the colony's capture. The three French frigates now tacked and stood to the east'ard, followed by the three British ships. At sunset the French squadron bore southeast of the British, distant about three leagues."

"At eight a.m., on the eighth of May, the French frigates bore up and, with a light air of wind, stood towards the *Phoebe* and *Galatea*. These, with the *Racehorse*, wore shortly afterwards and steered to the west'ard in the direction of Île Ronde—a small island to the northeast of Mauritius—then distant about five leagues. With the odds against him, wishing to have a commanding breeze with which to maneuver, and expecting at every moment to be joined by the *Astrea* from Port Louis, Captain Hillyar now *avoided* rather than *sought* an engagement." Lambert paused and again looked around the table, where several of his audience had raised their eyebrows.

"Towards evening, when the two squadrons were scarcely five miles apart, Commodore Roquebert decided to discontinue the chase and hauled up to the east'ard. On May ninth, about noon, the *Phoebe* and *Galatea* bore up to join the *Astrea*. The French ships were now lost to view. The three British frigates then steered for Port Louis, and on the twelfth came to anchor off the harbor."

"Having slipped the British squadron, Commodore Roquebert then resolved to try a surprise upon some place on the windward side of Île Bourbon—or Île Réunion—about thirty leagues southwest of Mauritius. The boats of the French squadron, which had on board a division of troops, attempted to disembark at a post that was known to be weekly manned, but were prevented by the heavy surf. Thus disappointed, the French commodore stood across to the coast of Madagascar to endeavor to obtain provisions. On the evening of the nineteenth the ships surprised the small settlement of Tamatave, in Madagascar. The garrison of Tamatave consisted of about 100 men of our 22nd Regiment which—except for a small proportion—were sick with the endemial fever found in that country. This settlement had been taken from the French, on the twelfth of February, by that same detachment of British troops sent there by Mr. Farquhar in the 18-gun brig-sloop *Eclipse*."

"Sir," Walker broke in, "who's Mr. Farquhar"

"Oh, your pardon, Major," replied Lambert. "Mr. Robert Farquhar's an old John Company man, installed as governor of Mauritius in 1810 after the place was taken by Admiral Bertie." Walker bowed his thanks from his chair.

"On May twentieth," Lambert continued, "Captain Schomberg, with his three frigates and brig-sloop, approached Commodore Roquebert. Schomberg had sailed from Port Louis on the fourteenth, directly for this spot. The British ships now chased with a light breeze from the west-by-north; however, the French continued lying-to awaiting the return of their boats from Tamatave. The *Renommée*'s boat at length came off, and then the French commodore formed his three frigates in line of battle. He placed the *Renommée* in the center, the *Clorinde* ahead, and the *Néréide* astern. In the meanwhile the British closed in as fast as the light and variable winds would permit, with the *Astrea*, *Phoebe*, and *Galatea* in line ahead and the *Racehorse* nearly abreast of the *Phoebe* to loo'ard. At four o'clock p.m. the French frigates, being on the larboard tack, wore together. The British ships now approached on the starboard tack and, as soon as the *Astrea* had arrived abreast of the *Renommée*, the latter opened fire at long range. Then the *Astrea* returned fire as did the *Phoebe* and *Galatea* as they advanced in succession. Thus—"

Lambert leaned forward and rapidly arranged the salt cellar, the butter dish, his wine glass, and four biscuits on the tablecloth as he tried to convey the exact situation to his audience.

"Having passed out of gun-shot astern of the *Néréide*," he resumed, "the *Astrea* prepared to tack and renew the action. But, as one might expect so near to land—Madagascar in this case—the cannonade produced a calm to loo'ard. As a result, the *Astrea* missed stays and was barely able to wear, and scarcely accomplished that before there was an entire cessation of the breeze. Of course, from their weatherly position the French ships felt its influence the longest. The breeze didn't quite leave them until the *Clorinde* and *Renommée* had bore up and stationed themselves—in a most destructive position—across the starboard quarters and sterns of the *Phoebe* and *Galatea*." Lambert waved his hand to indicate that his guests should not forget to keep the bottle of port from circulating round the table.

"Now, gentlemen, this was a good time for the *Racehorse*, with her particular facility for using sweeps, to take a position close athwart the hawse of the *Néréide*. At this time a distant and partial cannonade was going on between the *Néréide* and the *Astrea*. Well, the *Racehorse* indeed began to sweep but stopped to open fire *long* before her shot could reach the French frigate. In consequence, the *Astrea* made the signal to 'engage more closely.' Regardless, owing to the loo'ard position of the *Galatea*, and the efforts of the *Phoebe* to support her consort by backing her sails, the two ships lay nearly abreast of each other, in this manner—" Lambert again busied himself rearranging his table-top squadrons, and then suddenly looked up.

"Forgive me, gentlemen, I warm to my story, and I daresay go on-and-on. The tale hasn't grown too tedious, I trust?"

"Oh, no, sir," exclaimed General Hislop, "no, indeed. Pray continue; we are intrigued."

"You're too kind, sir," replied Lambert. "Well, then, on the starboard quarter of the *Phoebe* lay the *Renommée*, and on *her* starboard bow the *Néréide*. The *Néréide* had just cleared herself from the *Astrea* and *Racehorse*, then about a mile and a half ahead, and like them was handicapped for the want of wind. But then, around half-past six, a light air from the southeast enabled the *Phoebe* to close the *Néréide* in a raking position. She had hitherto been able to bring only her bow guns to bear on the *Néréide*, and her quarter ones on the *Renommée*, as the swell alternately hove her off and brought her to. So, at the end of twenty-five minutes the *Phoebe* completely silenced the *Néréide*. But then the *Phoebe* was obliged to break off because the *Renommée* and *Clorinde* fast approached to support their nearly overpowered consort. These two frigates, which in the meantime had kept their broadsides to bear by the aid of their boats, had battered the *Galatea* terribly. Her cutter had been cut adrift by a shot while being towed astern, and then her jollyboat was sunk just as a tow rope was being handed on board, and scarcely were the tackles got up to hoist out a third boat, when another shot carried away the foreyard tackle. Some seamen then got sweeps out of the head, so finally the *Galatea* was able to get her bow round and open her broadside upon her two antagonists—particularly upon the *Renommée.*"

"Now, the *Renommée* and *Clorinde* made sail to support the *Néréide*. The *Galatea*—with her masts much wounded and her hull greatly shattered—hauled towards the *Astrea* and *Racehorse*, and at around eight o'clock p.m. ceased her fire. Then, as the *Galatea* passed to loo'ard of the *Astrea*, the *Galatea's* foretopmast fell over the larboard bow and her mizzen topmast fell upon the main yard. Having at this time almost four feet of water in the hold, her masts badly wounded, and her rigging cut to pieces, the *Galatea* was clearly in too disabled a state to continue fighting. She hailed the *Racehorse* for assistance, and so Captain De Rippe sent on board eleven men." Lambert paused for a moment to accept a cigar from his steward, and then light it.

"The *Astrea* then wore round onto the larboard tack. After he took stock of the situation, Captain Shomberg signaled the *Racehorse* to follow him as he intended to renew the action. And so at about half-past eight the *Astrea*, *Phoebe*, and *Racehorse* bore up towards the enemy whose lights were now visible in the west-nor'west. It appears that after the *Renommée* and *Clorinde* had obliged the *Phoebe* to break off from the *Néréide*, the latter—on account of her disabled state—was ordered by the commodore to make for the land. But, the *Renommée*, followed by the *Clorinde*, hauled up in line of battle to renew the engagement. Then the *Clorinde* lost a man overboard, and in bringing-to in order to pick him up necessarily dropped astern of the *Renommée*. However, Commodore Roquebert gallantly stood on his course alone, and at ten o'clock came to close action with the *Astrea*. With a heavy fire of round, grape, and musketry, the *Renommée* attempted to lay athwart *Astrea's* hawse—but, aware of the numerical superiority of her opponent's crew and embarked soldiers, the *Astrea* avoided coming in actual contact."

"After an animated cannonade of about twenty-five minutes, during which the *Phoebe* fired raking shot at the *Renommée* and the *Racehorse* gave broadside fire, the French ship made the signal of surrender. Captain Hillyar ordered the *Racehorse* to take possession of the *Renommée*, but that brig, just at this moment lost her foretopmast from an earlier shot and was unable to comply. Captain Schomberg then sent on board the prize—in a sinking boat!—only seven men: a lieutenant, a lieutenant of marines, and five seamen. Then the *Astrea* and *Phoebe* made sail after the *Clorinde* which had shamefully kept aloof during her commodore's gallant action. Now the *Clorinde* was under a press of canvas on the larboard tack, endeavoring to escape. The chase of the *Clorinde* was continued until two o'clock a.m. on the twenty-first. On account of the perfect state of her rigging and sails, the *Clorinde* gained considerably on the *Astrea* and *Phoebe*. The two latter now wore to cover the captured *Renommée* and to form a junction with the *Galatea*. Then, at that very moment, the foretopmast of the *Phoebe*, from the many earlier wounds it had received, fell over the side."

"The *Phoebe*, besides the loss of her foretopmast, was badly wounded in all her masts, her sails and rigging much cut, and her hull struck in many places, with seven men killed and twenty-four wounded. The principal damage to the *Astrea* was in her sails and rigging and was not really significant. Out of her complement two were killed and sixteen wounded. I've already told you of the disabled state of the *Galatea*'s masts and rigging. In addition, she had fifty-five shot holes in her hull and her stern was also much shattered. Her loss was sixteen men killed and forty-six wounded. The *Racehorse*, notwithstanding that some chance shot had knocked away her foretopmast, appeared to have escaped without any loss."

"Pray, Captain," interrupted Hislop. "What was the state of the French at this point?"

"Well, sir," replied Lambert, "The *Renommée* sustained a loss of 93 men killed and wounded. Among the former was her gallant captain, Commodore Roquebert, and among the severely wounded was her premier, Lieutenant Defredot-Duplanty—who only went briefly below to have his wound dressed, and then came back up and fought the ship in the bravest manner. The *Néréide* had her captain and 24 others killed, and 32 wounded. The *Clorinde* reportedly only had only one man killed and six wounded, probably occasioned by the fire of the *Galatea*."

"With respect to the *Renommée*, *Néréide*, and *Clorinde*, they weren't quite as formidable as some of the French frigates which we've encountered in recent years. However, the broadside force of both the *Astrea* and the *Galatea* was 467 pounds, and that of any one of the three French frigates was 463 pounds. The complement of the latter, even without the embarked troops, far outnumbered that of the three British frigates. In point of size the French frigates also had the advantage: the *Renommée* measured 1,073 tons, the *Clorinde* 1,083, and the *Néréide* 1,114. Therefore, the difference in guns, men, and size between a British 18-pounder 36-gun frigate and a French 40-gun frigate rendered the parties in this action about equally matched—that is, if you make due allowance for the side which possessed the fewer in number of men."

"The *Renommée* had been roughly handled by the *Galatea*. But had the *Clorinde*, when the *Renommée* was attacked by the *Astrea* and *Phoebe*, given to the former the support that was in her power, the *Renommée* in all probability would've effected an escape—and that without the slightest disparagement to the *Astrea*."

"The resolute conduct of the *Néréide*, as she didn't surrender to the *Phoebe* after she'd sustained so heavy a loss in killed and wounded, in some degree redeems the shyness—shown on two previous occasions—of Captain Lemaresquier. Well, that is unless we're to consider that, as he fell in the action, the credit of *not* striking his colors is due to the next officer in command, Lieutenant Ponée. With respect to the *Clorinde*, the behavior of *her* captain on this occasion perfectly agrees with his embarrassing behavior on a former occasion. Indeed, in an action six years ago, Captain St. Cricq abandoned his commodore. Now he does the same in May 1811. In the first instance flight did not save him; in this instance it does save him. Upon the whole, if some glory was lost to the French navy by the misconduct of the *Clorinde*, more was gained to it by the good conduct of the *Renommée* and the *Néréide*. In any event, at daylight on the twenty-first, the *Astrea*, *Phoebe*, and *Racehorse* discovered the *Renommée* and *Galatea* to windward."

"As he did not know, of course, that the *Renommée* had been captured, and as he got no answer to his signals from the *Astrea* and *Phoebe* because of their great distance off, Captain Losack in the *Galatea* thought it could very well be the French squadron which was in sight. So, while the captured *Renommée* bore up to join the *Astrea* and *Phoebe*, the *Galatea* made the best of her way to Port Louis. Once the *Renommée* had closed with the British ships, the French prisoners were taken out and a proper, larger prize crew was put on board."

"Now, Captain Schomberg turned his attention to Tamatave. As the damaged state of the *Phoebe* didn't allow her to quickly beat up against the wind and current, Captain Schomberg despatched the *Racehorse* in advance to summon the French garrison at Tamatave to surrender. On the evening of the twenty-fourth the *Racehorse* rejoined the *Astrea* with the intelligence that the *Néréide* was at Tamatave. Since this was the nearest port in which he could get his ship repaired, the *Néréide*'s surviving senior officer,

Lieutenant Ponée, had proceeded straight there. He immediately moored the *Néréide* in the most advantageous manner to resist the British attack which he hourly expected to be made. "So, the *Astrea, Phoebe,* and *Racehorse* immediately made sail for Tamatave. But, because of a strong gale, they were prevented from getting in sight of the French frigate until the afternoon of the twenty-fifth. No one in the British squadron possessed any local knowledge of the spot, and it was considered impracticable to sound the passage between the reefs without being exposed to the fire of the frigate and a battery of ten or twelve guns. So, Captain Schomberg sent in, to the French, Captain De Rippe with a flag of truce and a summons of surrender. In that summons the French were informed that the '*Renommée* and *Clorinde* had struck after a brave defense.' The inference that Schomberg intended here's pretty clear, and such a *ruse* can be allowed in such cases, but I might comment that an officer should always be cautious how he signs his name to a document. If such a document bears, on the face of it, what may afterwards be considered a lie, it could well translate into a touchy point of honor. As you know, the *Clorinde* had run away and was out of the action—but she had not surrendered."

"Regardless, Lieutenant Ponée, like a brave man, refused to unconditionally surrender. Rather, he proposed to deliver the *Néréide* to the British, and the fort as well, on the condition that he, his officers, his ship's company, and the troops in garrison on shore should be sent to France without being considered prisoners of war. These terms were acceptable. So, on the twenty-sixth, Captain Schomberg took possession of the fort of Tamatave and its dependencies, as well as the *Néréide* and a vessel or two in the port." Lambert sat back in his chair and looked around the table.

"Gentlemen, permit me to comment on an interesting thing about our *Renommée*. It'll be remembered that only two officers and five men were sent to take possession of the *Renommée*, which had then a crew of nearly four-hundred officers and men. In this state of things it's a surprise that the French didn't try to retake their ship. Indeed, it appears that many of the crew wished to do so. However, there was an army colonel named Barrois on board—who, in accordance with the etiquette of the French service, was now the senior officer after the death of Commodore Roquebert. This colonel acted upon a principle of honor which some French naval captains would do well to imitate, and refused to give his sanction. The colonel felt that as the ship had been clearly and formally surrendered, he was duty-bound to honor that formal act. Hence, the British lieutenant and his few hands remained in quiet possession of the prize throughout the night, until the *Renommée* joined the *Astrea* and *Phoebe* in the morning of the twenty-first."

Chads rubbed his chin in thought, and with a slight frown said, "Captain, pray tell us the fate of the *Clorinde* and the infamous Captain St. Cricq."

"Certainly, Mr. Chads, since you ask. As we've disposed of two of Commodore Roquebert's frigates, we may well consider the missing third. By daylight on the twenty-first, the *Clorinde* flew as fast as ever she could and ran completely out of sight of both friend and foe. Then, after he ruminated awhile on his situation, your friend St. Cricq bent his course towards the Seychelle Islands where he came to anchor. Then, on the seventh of June, he set sail for a return to France. He stopped briefly at the Island of Diego Garcia for cocas, wood, and water, and eventually on the first of August, rounded the Cape of Good Hope. The rest of their voyage was filled with a number of adventures which included—with the French coast in sight—nearly being taken by Sir John Gore in HMS *Tonnant*. But, on the twenty-fourth of September, the *Clorinde* at last came to anchor in the road of Brest. However, it wasn't for long that the good captain of the *Clorinde* was allowed to enjoy the ease and comfort of a home port. For five uncomfortable days last March, Captain St. Cricq was tried by a court-martial for not doing all in his power in the action in which the *Renommée* had been captured; for separating from his commodore in the heat of the battle; and for omitting to execute the remainder of his orders—which did *not* direct him to return to France. Upon these charges he was found guilty, and thus he was sentenced to be dismissed the service, to be degraded from the Legion of Honor, and to be imprisoned for three years."

Major Walker slapped his hand on the table. "Capital! I do love a story where the villain gets his just desserts." Lambert smiled at him.

"Well, it's late, gentlemen, and I've kept you chained to the table far too long. So, let me conclude my story. The *Néréide* and the *Renommée*, being both new and particularly fine frigates, were brought in to the Royal Navy and added to the class of British 38s—the *Néréide* under the new name of *Madagascar*, and of course as you know, the *Renommée* under the new name of *Java*."

General Hislop pushed back his chair and stood up, followed by all the others. He raised his wine glass, and looked down the table at Lambert. "And here we are, Captain, in the *Renom-mée*'s—that is to say the *Java's*—great cabin, now knowing her much better. I drink to you, sir, and your fine ship. Thank you for the delightful tale."

CHAPTER 12

THE SOLENT, HAMPSHIRE, ENGLAND

The Solent
Hampshire, England
50° 47' N 1° 17' W
Wednesday, November 11th, 1812
5:00 A.M.
Clear weather; light winds from the S. and S.S.W.

At daylight, H.M. Frigate *Java* made the signal for her convoy to weigh. More or less in unison the ships made sail to the west-southwest. After about three hours of extremely slow progress they came into South Yarmouth Roads, shortened sail, and anchored. The master then approached Lambert and touched his hat.

"Sir, we've come-to with the best bower in nine and one-half fathoms water. The lead's brought up gray sand with small stone and broken shell. Hurst Castle bears west-½-north, and Sconce Point west-southwest."

"Very well, Mr. Robinson, carry on," replied Lambert. The master again touched his hat and turned away.

"Mr. Chads," said Major Walker, who stood beside the first lieutenant at the rail, "I'm loath to admit it, but I'm not quite sure I'm familiar with Hurst Castle."

"You astonish me, Major," replied Chads. "Surely you're acquainted with the 'Device Forts,' the thirty-odd fortifications for artillery constructed long ago by good King Henry the Eighth—places like Portland Castle, Southsea Castle, and Pendennis Castle? Well, this's but one of those, built at the end of that long shingle spit just there. The idea was to guard the western approaches to Portsmouth. As you can see, Hurst Castle commands the western end of the Solent, and situated as it is in this narrow part, its artillery can discomfort any would-be invader. And, that invader will already be confounded by the strong currents here which result from the significant tidal ebb and flow."

As the morning wore on, the weather deteriorated with fresh breezes and rain which then settled in for the rest of the day. At noon Lambert felt compelled to veer out a half cable in order for the *Java* to ride more comfortably, and at one bell in the first dog watch he ordered down the royal and topgallant yards and struck the topgallant masts. In fact, the next four days were filled with nothing but frustration. The convoy, as well as the *Java*, was ready to proceed. Lambert thus had every intention to sail but the English weather had no intention to cooperate.

Thursday saw their first attempt. At three bells in the morning watch—despite the light and variable winds, continuous rain, and generally thick, hazy weather—the *Java* sent up topgallant masts, crossed topgallant yards, loosed topsails, hove in a half-cable, and made the signal for the convoy to weigh anchor. At seven bells Lambert sent for a pilot as the *Java* and the convoy got under way. The ships moved slowly west-by-south with the wind from the east-southeast. At five bells in the forenoon watch the *Java* briefly hove-to to take on board the pilot. By two bells in the afternoon watch the ships carefully stood for the Needles Rocks—a row of three distinctive stacks of chalk which rose from the water off the west end of the Isle of Wight. By three bells they could see the rocks despite the deteriorating weather. But it was all for nothing; by seven bells the wind had shifted dead foul and the rain and fog had thickened to the point that no land nor landmarks were visible. Lambert, Robinson, Chads, and the Solent pilot agreed that they must discontinue the attempt and anchor. The convoy came-to with best bowers in Yarmouth Roads in fifteen fathoms water—not any great distance from where they had all started eight hours before and in fact no farther west at all.

Friday morning saw the convoy riding at anchor in a dead calm, the weather still hazy, rainy, and thick. At two bells in the forenoon watch the *Java* hoisted out the barge and sent her on shore for some water, with which she returned three hours later. As far as sailing, the officers saw today little chance of any better success than yesterday. In fact, by two bells in the afternoon watch the weather had turned squally with even more rain. This necessitated veering to a whole cable, and by six bells Lambert decided to send down topgallant yards and strike topgallant masts. By eight bells in the second dog-watch, however, the weather had moderated to light breezes with clouds and—thank God—the rain finally stopped.

"Good evening, General, gentlemen," said Lieutenant Chads, who joined the army officers and Commander Marshall at the leeward quarterdeck rail. "I hope I find you well."

"Oh, prime, prime, Mr. Chads, thank you," replied General Hislop, "and you as well, I trust. It's nice to be on deck with no rain! In fact, with the change in the weather we just speculated about our chances of putting to sea tomorrow but were loath to ask—lest we wantonly violate custom and break Captain Lambert's concentration." He smiled and nodded toward Lambert, who walked up and down the weather side of the quarterdeck, head down and hands clasped behind him, lost in thought.

"That's kind of you, sir," said Chads as he returned the smile, "and while as a distinguished and high-ranking passenger you certainly aren't bound to such custom, in the navy we do typically respect the captain's privacy at such times—unless of course the working of the ship demands interruption." They all watched Lambert for a moment, who for his part was totally oblivious of their interest.

"If I may be so forward, Mr. Chads," said Hislop, "it appears to me that your relationship with Captain Lambert is more than the usual one of inferior to superior?"

"Why, yes, sir," replied Chads after a moment of consideration. "I believe that's quite true. While presently he's my superior and companion-in-arms, I've served with him in the past, and I consider myself his particular friend as well as his lieutenant."

"So we've understood," said Marshall. "I wonder, if it wouldn't be presumptuous or indiscreet, could you tell us just a little about him?"

"Certainly, sir," responded Chads. "Henry Lambert is one of the finest officers in the King's service. Moreover, in my opinion, he's a fighting captain without equal. If you're truly at leisure for a moment, may I illustrate the point?"

"Oh, yes—yes, absolutely," exclaimed Hislop, while the others nodded assent.

"Well, sir, gentlemen, he's the son of a naval officer—Captain Robert Lambert—and thus entered the navy in 1795 on board the *Cumberland*, 74 guns, and saw action that same year at Toulon. He then removed to the frigate *Virginie* and further to the ship of the line *Suffolk* on the East India station. In 1801 he received his commission as lieutenant on board the *Suffolk*, and then later moved to the seventy-four *Victorious*, and then the *Centurion*, 50. Then, in the year three, Mr. Lambert was made master and commander of the 32-gun frigate *Wilhelmina*, which was actually a troop ship armed *en flûte*. As such she carried only her light guns—eighteen 9-pounders, two 6-pounders, and one 12-pounder carronade—and was manned with a weak complement."

"In April 1804, while she escorted a valuable country-ship towards Trincomalee, the *Wilhelmina* fell in with—sorry, this was just to the east of Ceylon—a powerful French privateer, the *Psyché*, 32 guns, commanded by a Captain Trogoff, a brave, skilful, and enterprising officer."

"Pardon me, sir," interrupted Captain Wood, "but what does the expression '*en flûte*' signify?"

"It essentially means without guns," replied Chads. "If you might picture the gundeck with the great guns removed, with the gun ports then with nothing behind them, then it would be like a flute; holes pierced down the side, with nothing behind them. It's indeed fairly uncommon for warships to sail about without their main armament, but it occasionally does happen for diverse reasons. In any event, fortunately for our story, the *Wilhelmina* at least still possessed her weather deck guns as I just described, so she wasn't totally defenseless."

"So, during the night the *Psyché* rapidly closed the British vessel. Commander Lambert directed the ship he escorted to beat a retreat, and then he lay-to to await the enemy. The *Wilhelmina*, being jury-rigged, had the look of a merchantman which may explain the readiness of the privateer to attack. At daylight—two full days later!—the two ships were within pistol-shot, the *Wilhelmina* to windward of the *Psyché*. This considerable delay was due to a squall which prevented the ships from closing, as well as a deliberate tactic on the part of Commander Lambert to draw the *Psyché* away from the richly laden British merchant ship. In due course, however, the two warships exchanged first broadsides as they passed on opposite tacks, and the *Psyché* hailed Lambert, fruitlessly bidding him to surrender. The *Psyché* tacked, the *Wilhelmina* wore, and, as the two ships' heads pointed the same way, a running fight began. The French fired alternate guns at the British vessel's rigging and hull. The damage which they inflicted brought the *Wilhelmina*, disabled, upon the starboard tack with her sails aback, and enabled the Frenchman to pass under her stern and deliver a raking fire. Commander Lambert, however, was able to again get his ship before the wind and engaged the *Psyché* with his larboard broadside. The *Psyché* closed to board. But she found the

Wilhelmina's people ready to continue the action yard-arm to yard-arm with the great guns and to give boarders a very warm reception. She sheered off a little—as she fired round, grape, and canister. Then she crossed the *Wilhelmina's* bows and raked the British ship, but when she tacked in another attempt to board she found herself raked in return. Both vessels now once more steered the same course. They closed for the last time, yard-arm to yard-arm, and fought 'til the *Psyché* had had enough—this was at seven a.m., two hours and ten minutes after the beginning of the action. Badly damaged, the *Psyché* crowded on all sail and—as she was faster and less damaged in her sails, masts, and rigging than was the *Wilhelmina*—succeeded in effecting her escape. Commander Lambert was in no state to pursue: the *Wilhelmina* had lost her main topmast; her bowsprit, main, and mizzen masts were badly wounded; her boats were shot to bits; and her hull was pierced in multiple places." At this point the officers all found themselves looking at Lambert, who still paced the quarterdeck's weather side.

"The *Wilhelmina's* previous captain had attached the greatest importance to gunnery," Chads continued, "and had drilled the crew constantly. The effects of his care were certainly seen in this action. Though the *Wilhelmina* was much cut up, she succeeded with her weak battery—remember, she was armed *en flûte*—in reducing the *Psyché* to an almost sinking condition. It was later found out that at the close of the action the privateer had forty-four men *hors de combat*, and some feet of water in her hold, whereas the *Wilhelmina* suffered a loss of only ten men. And, the *Psyché* was in many respects as good a ship as, or better than, most frigates in the French navy. She had an excellent—in fact, a famous—skipper and a well-trained crew, while her preponderance in force, whether of guns or men, was immense."

"So you can see, gentlemen, that in the circumstances Commander Lambert deserves particular praise for his splendid resistance to such odds. Indeed, the *Wilhelmina's* broadside weight of metal was only 100 pounds, versus the Frenchman's 240. So, even though his opponent was only a *privateer*, and not a true commissioned warship, the admiral thought nothing of that since he seized upon the first opportunity he had to promote Commander Lambert to "post"—that is to say, permanent—captain's rank. I make this point to stress that usually such promotion comes from the defeat of an enemy *national* vessel, not a privateer."

"Well," said Hislop, "a most enlightening story and it certainly illuminates Mr. Lambert's reputation as a fighting captain."

"Oh, but sir, the story improves!" said Chads with a grin. "Pray allow me to continue? Ah, thank you. Well, it came to pass that after his promotion to post captain, in December 1804 Mr. Lambert was given command of the 36-gun 18-pounder frigate *San Fiorenzo*. Still stationed in the East Indies, in February of 1805 he cruised along the coast about 500 miles northeast of Madras. On the thirteenth the *San Fiorenzo* stood on the starboard tack, with a light wind at west-sou'west, in search of the French 32-gun frigate *Psyché*, Captain Jacques Bergeret, who was reported to be off the town of Vizagapatam."

"The *Psyché*?" interrupted Walker. "Hold hard; didn't we just dispose of the *Psyché* in April 1804?"

"Indeed, Major, we—or rather Captain Lambert—did. But, in one of those strange twists of fate one sometimes sees, Captain Lambert was now destined to meet the *Psyché* once again. Now the *Psyché* was no longer a privateer but a French naval frigate. She'd been repaired and purchased for the national navy by General Decaen—the governor of the Île de France."

"Extraordinary!" exclaimed Hislop.

"Indeed, sir," laughed Chads, "but as Lord Nelson once said, 'In sea affairs, *nothing* is impossible and *nothing* is improbable.' So, the *San Fiorenzo* happened to discover three sail at anchor under the land to the south'ard. These were the *Psyché* and two British East Indiamen which had been recently captured by the *Psyché*. All three of these vessels immediately slipped their anchors and made sail, pursued by the *San Fiorenzo*. Light and baffling winds continued during the day, and towards midnight it became quite calm. Later, however, a light breeze sprang up, and the *San Fiorenzo* braced round on the larboard tack and made all sail—they also began to trim and wet the sails to quicken her progress."

"I understand what you mean to trim the sails, Mr. Chads, but what does 'wet' them signify?" asked Walker.

"Well, sir," replied Chads, "wet canvas'll hold more wind than dry, so if there's little wind but speed's essential, it may be worth the effort—and it's *considerable* effort—to wet the sails. The lower sails we can spray fairly effectively with the wash-deck pump or the fire engine. However, for the higher canvas it's necessary to reeve whips through the blocks on the yards, and then hoist buckets of sea water up and pour them over the sails. It's extremely hard work, and requires a good number of men to get enough water splashed about to do the job."

"So, in this way the chase continued throughout the night. The *San Fiorenzo* gradually gained until the early evening of the fourteenth, when all *four* ships raised English colors. At about eight o'clock p.m., the *San Fiorenzo* overhauled and took possession of the stern-most vessel of the three. This was the *Thetis*, late English merchant ship, and as I said a moment ago, recently a prize of the *Psyché*. From the crew of the *Thetis* it was learned that the other prize had been the merchant ship *Pigeon,* but was now the *Equivoque* privateer, of ten guns and forty men, commanded by one of Bergeret's lieutenants." The officers suddenly had to move a few feet to windward to accommodate a working party of seamen.

"They continued the chase under all sail," Chads went on, "and an hour later the *San Fiorenzo* got within gun-shot of the *Psyché* and fired a bow-chaser at her. The Frogs promptly returned that fire with two guns from their stern. Then the two frigates commenced a furious action, at the distance of about 100 yards, and continued hotly engaged until a few minutes before nine p.m. The *Equivoque* occasionally took part in it. At about ten o'clock the *San Fiorenzo* shot away the *Psyché*'s main yard, but the firing still continued with unabated fury. At eleven-thirty the *San Fiorenzo* hauled off to reeve new braces and to generally repair her rigging. Then at midnight, being again ready, she bore up to renew the action. But, just as she was about to reopen her broadside fire, a boat from the *Psyché* came toward her with a white flag. The boat bore a message from Captain Bergeret. He stated that although he believed he might bear the contest a little longer—at this point the chase and action had lasted upwards of forty hours—he'd decided to strike his flag out of humanity to the surviving members of his crew."

"And no wonder, sir. The *Psyché* had had three officers and fifty-four seamen and marines killed, and seventy officers, seamen, and marines wounded. They had gone into action with about 240."

"Good Lord!" exclaimed Hislop, "Well, I'm almost afraid to ask: what were the casualties onboard the *San Fiorenzo*?"

"Well, sir, it *was* pretty severe," replied Chads, "but not nearly so much as the French. She had a total of twelve killed and thirty-six wounded out of the 253 men and boys on board. The truth is that the two frigates, although *nominally* equal, were really far from being a match; the *San Fiorenzo*'s broadside weight was about 470 pounds to the *Psyché*'s 250, and her tonnage was around 1,000 to the *Psyché*'s 850—so it's a marvel to consider what a resistance the *Psyché* put up. And you really can't count the

Equivoque, for she only had about ten guns, and because the aid she afforded the *Psyché* was only occasional and inconsistent."

"Henry, do you know what happened to the *Psyché*, and to the captain, Bergeret?" inquired Marshall.

"Well, sir, as to the *Psyché*, she was added to our navy as a 12-pounder 32-gun frigate, but due to her age and damage done by battle and grounding she did not continue more than a few years in the service. Captain Bergeret's ultimate fate I'm afraid I don't know, other than to say he was taken prisoner to India, and that he was later sent to the Mauritius in an exchange with English prisoners of war."

"But, I do know that every Frenchman—and every Englishman, for that matter—who wishes well to the navy of his own country should forevermore hold in honorable recollection the heroic defense of the *Psyché*."

"Indeed, Henry, indeed," said Marshall, "but will you now tell us of Mr. Lambert's later activities at the Mauritius? You served with him there, I believe."

"Yes, sir, I did," replied Chads. He reflected a moment as he gazed out upon the sea. "In June of the year six, Captain Lambert returned to England to have some time ashore. But, in May 1808, he was appointed to command the frigate *Iphigenia*, 36 guns, and took her to Quebec and then back out to the East Indies. It was at that time that I first met him, because I was appointed as his second lieutenant. Over the next couple of years I grew to admire him as a right seaman and compassionate officer. It was in summer 1810, however, when I learned first-hand what an extremely intelligent, cool, and determined fighting captain he is. At that time we took part in the operations which eventually led to the capture of Mauritius, the complexities of which you gentlemen certainly know and thus I won't go into a great amount of detail."

"On August thirteenth, our squadron's boat attack upon the *Isle de la Passe*—in which I played a small part—went pretty well. However, the subsequent attack against the French squadron in Grand Port did not, alas. Perhaps disastrous is not too strong a word? As I said, though the operation was very complex I daresay it's reasonably well-known, so I'll briefly try to acquaint you with Captain Lambert's specific role. In the afternoon of the twenty-first the French commodore, Duperré, removed his ships to a position close off the town. He moored them with springs on their cables in the form of a crescent, such that the ends of his line were protected by reefs. As you know, a spring is a rope run from a ship to a jetty or an anchor such that when pulled upon will turn the ship in place. Commodore Duperré stationed his own ship, the 52-gun *Minerve*, just behind a patch of coral. Next to her was the *Ceylon*, 32, then the *Bellone*, 40, and lastly the *Victor*, 18. Our squadron consisted of the *Magicienne* (Captain Curtis), the *Néréide* (Captain Willoughby), our *Iphigenia* (Captain Lambert), and the *Sirius* (Captain Pym)—all 36-gun frigates. Captain Pym was in command."

"Mr. Chads," said Hislop, "forgive our tendency for rude interruptions, I beg you. But, didn't we hear of a vessel named *Néréide* earlier? Wasn't she the French ship captured in 1811 along with our *Renommée*—and renamed *Madagascar*?"

"The same name, General, to be sure," replied Chads. "It's merely a coincidence. They weren't the same ships. The one that became the *Madagascar* was built in France and named the *Néréide*. The one I've just mentioned was also built in France and named *Néréide*, and when we captured her in 1797 we kept that name in our service. But, since she was lost to the French service, they simply reused the name when they built another ship. Ships of the same name often swim simultaneously in different navies. After all, present at Trafalgar were three *Neptunes*, two *Achilles*, two *Swiftsures*, and two *Argonauts*."

"So it was planned that this *Néréide* should anchor between the *Victor* and the *Bellone*; the *Sirius* abreast of the *Bellone*; the *Magicienne* between the *Ceylon* and the *Minerve*; and the *Iphigenia* abreast of the *Minerve*. Thus, on the twenty-third, our squadron entered the tortuous channel and the reef-filled lagoon, and while under fire we stood along the edge of the first reef and made our way toward the French anchorage. The *Sirius*, going too far to starboard, took the ground. With the *Sirius* now a beacon for the rest of us, the *Magicienne* and the *Iphigenia* successively cleared the channel, but at five o'clock the *Magicienne* also grounded on a bank in such position that only six of her foremost guns could bear upon the enemy. Seeing what had befallen the *Magicienne*, we in the *Iphigenia* dropped our stream anchor and came-to by the stern in six fathoms. Then Captain Lambert skillfully let go our best bower and thereby brought our starboard broadside to bear upon the *Minerve* into which, at pistol-shot distance, we poured a heavy and destructive fire. By this time the *Néréide* was also in hot action; her captain steered for, and anchored upon, the beam of the *Bellone* at a distance just short of 200 yards. A furious cannonade began between these two ill-matched ships—and the *Victor*, from her slanting position on the *Néréide*'s quarter, also began to take an occasional part. At six o'clock, after having received fire from the *Magicienne* and the *Iphigenia*, the *Ceylon* hauled down her colors and Captain Lambert immediately hailed the *Magicienne*—in *quite* a thunderous voice I might add—and ordered her to send a boat to take possession. But at that very instant the *Ceylon* dishonorably set her topsails and tried to run on shore. At six-thirty the *Minerve*—which had her cable shot away by the *Iphigenia*'s continuous fire—made sail after the *Ceylon*. Both these ships grounded near the *Bellone*, but the *Ceylon* first ran afoul of the *Bellone*, which forced her to cut her cable and also run aground. The *Bellone*, however, lay with her broadside still bearing on the *Néréide*, and she was now reinforced by fresh men from the shore which dramatically increased her hitherto weakened rate of fire. This, in retrospect, was the turning point of the battle. As he sensed this, Captain Lambert decided to cut our cable and run down in pursuit of the *Minerve*, but he also saw that a shoal was directly between us and the French squadron."

"At a few minutes before seven o'clock the *Néréide*'s spring was shot away and the ship swung stern-on to the *Bellone*'s broadside. A most severe raking fire followed. To end this, and to bring her starboard broadside to bear, the *Néréide* cut her small bower cable, and then let go her best bower. Thus, she succeeded in turning. However, after an action that had already lasted five hours, the *Néréide* was essentially disabled, aground astern, and the greater part of her crew was killed or wounded. Captain Willoughby therefore ordered the now feeble fire of the *Néréide* to cease, and the few survivors of the crew to shelter themselves."

"At about ten o'clock the *Sirius* sent a boat to the *Néréide* with a request from Captain Pym that Captain Willoughby abandon his ship and come on board the *Sirius*. Willoughby damned the notion—he refused to desert his surviving men—and sent back word that he had struck his flag. Not knowing any of this, Mr. Lambert also sent a boat on board the *Néréide* to inquire why she had ceased firing, and received the same terse reply. At about one o'clock in the morning, after having been repeatedly hailed by the *Néréide*, the *Bellone* finally discontinued her fire. The *Iphigenia* and the *Magicienne*, whose cannonade had dismounted the guns at the close-by shore battery, also ceased their fire, and all was silent for a time. We later found out that the *Néréide*'s casualties were almost 230 out of 280 men. Injuries from splinters were uncommon numerous. We learned later that Captain Willoughby lost his eye and received a dreadful face wound which was from a splinter, and his first lieutenant was severely wounded by splinters in the throat, breast, legs, and arms."

"A few minutes past four o'clock Captain Lambert—who had previously sent a boat to the *Sirius* for orders—was directed by Captain Pym to warp the *Iphigenia* out of gun-shot."

"I'm sorry to be so ignorant, sir, and to again interrupt," said Wood, "but *warp?*"

"Not at all, Captain," replied Chads. "We'll make a right seaman out of you before we reach India, I assure you! To *warp*, in this case, was to move the ship by pulling her by cables attached to anchors carried out ahead in the boats, and then dropped. The ship was wound up to the anchor using the capstan, the cable passed to another boat with another anchor, the first anchor raised, and the ship wound up to the second anchor—on-and-on, hour-after-hour, the men soon exhausted as they wrestled the sodden nine-inch cables and the heavy, obstinate anchors. You do this sort of thing when the wind is unfavorable, the tide is in opposition, or within the narrow limits of a channel: we were faced with all three conditions. In such a channel you can only move about fifty yards each time, and often the ground is foul, the anchor doesn't hold, the anchor breaks, or it is lost altogether."

"Well, to resume, at that time Captain Pym still had considerable hope of getting the *Sirius* afloat, and thought he needed our help to heave her off. So, with tremendous effort, we began to warp by the stern with the stream and kedge anchors, and as we came close we sent the end of our best bower cable on board the *Magicienne* for her to use to try and heave off. This left us with only one bower anchor and cable. At daylight, when the *Bellone* recommenced firing, the *Magicienne* also renewed her fire back at the French. We, while warping, couldn't bring a single gun to bear—and in any event we'd previously fought so furiously that we were forced to send to the *Sirius* to get more 18-pound shot."

"By seven o'clock a.m. we'd warped the *Iphigenia* to the east of the long shoal. At this point Captain Lambert was convinced the battle was lost unless we took extraordinary and bold action. We thus prepared to run down and board the *Bellone* and the other grounded French ships, hoping to take them and even perhaps save the *Néréide*. Lambert sent me to the *Sirius* with this proposal, but Captain Pym gave me a negative answer, only to repeat that the *Iphigenia* must continue warping out to come to his assistance. As the French shot steadily hulled us, Lambert—in a right passion—sent again to Pym saying that we were obliged to renew the action in our own defense. Shortly after that a lieutenant came from the *Sirius* with a note which ordered Captain Lambert to continue firing if we must, but in any case we must warp out directly. We accordingly resumed our labors. As soon as we'd hauled a little further off, the French shifted their fire from us and concentrated upon the *Magicienne*. By ten o'clock we'd warped close to the *Sirius*, and then both ships opened a hot fire upon the French who were trying to remount the guns at the battery on shore."

"Some while later, it being found impossible to refloat the *Magicienne*, her crew jumped into her boats and were ordered to remove into the *Iphigenia* preparatory to her being set purposefully ablaze. The poor *Magicienne* had nine feet of water in her hold, was exposed to a heavy fire from the enemy, and had no means of effectively returning that fire. We, meanwhile, had been unable to get beyond the stern of the *Sirius* due to the strength of the breeze, so we came-to with our small bower. We had earlier lost our stream and kedge anchors—but we hauled on board the stream and bower anchors of the *Sirius*. Sometime earlier we saw that the French finally sent boats to the surrendered *Néréide* and thus took possession of her. Then, around seven o'clock, the *Magicienne* was set on fire by her captain and at eleven, rather spectacularly, she blew up with her colors flying."

"At four a.m. on the twenty-fifth we again began to warp, whereupon the French ships and a newly-erected shore battery recommenced firing at us and the *Sirius*. By seven-thirty a light air enabled us to run completely out of gun-shot. However, Captain Pym had decided that he must destroy the *Sirius* as every effort to get her afloat had proved utterly in vain. So, a great quantity of stores, to include some powder and shot, was moved from the *Sirius* to the *Iphigenia*. Then, at nine a.m., the *Sirius* was set on fire as her crew also came over to us. With the destruction of his ship, Captain Pym relinquished the command to Captain Lambert. I suppose that was somewhat ironic, as now the *Iphigenia* was the only British ship left from the original squadron of four."

"So, during that afternoon the *Iphigenia* continued her exertions to warp to the anchorage under the *Isle de la Passe*—which as you know we had taken and garrisoned a fortnight earlier—but owing to the foulness of the ground and the consequent loss of one of our bower anchors we made little progress. At daybreak, on the twenty-sixth, we found that we had driven considerably during the night and that our bow anchor's stock was badly broken. Regardless, we recommenced warping, but since we fouled our stream anchor we soon were obliged to get out an 18-pounder gun to heave out ahead in lieu of an anchor. And then, at noon, we were disappointed to observe that the *Bellone* had hove herself afloat."

"Well, the next morning found us still trying to warp out but still we made very slow progress—this despite our crew's great exertions and Mr. Lambert's remarkable seamanship. We then sighted three additional French ships working up to the *Isle de la Passe* from outside the reef, and by noon we were able to determine that all the original French ships in Grand Port were once again afloat. Thus, with the enemy seemingly in every direction, Captain Lambert rallied the exhausted crew and we prepared to fight both sides of the ship at once. Yet, a worse problem than the fatigue of the crew confronted us: after four days of fighting there was not ammunition enough on board to maintain an action of even short duration—even on one side only."

"I'm afraid, Mr. Chads," said Hislop, "you're going to tell us that this second squadron of French frigates put an end to any hope for the *Iphigenia*'s escape."

"Alas, sir," replied Chads, "I am. These additional ships were under the command of a Commodore Hamelin, the senior French naval officer on the station. They had come from Port Louis with the express intention of taking the *Iphigenia* and the *Isle de la Passe*, and to thus complete the victory for the French. So, at five p.m., Mr. Hamelin sent to Mr. Lambert a demand that he surrender the *Iphigenia* and the *Isle*. Naturally, Captain Lambert refused, and by sunset we had managed to work in close to the island, but unfortunately we couldn't obtain a good berth. Our situation worsened at daylight on the twenty-eighth, when we saw that, because of our insufficient tackle and the poor holding ground, we'd drifted into the middle of the passage. Then, at around seven o'clock, Commodore Hamelin sent in another flag of truce—again he demanded surrender—and at nine o'clock we received an additional summons to surrender from General Decaen, the governor at Grand Port."

"Captain Lambert then sent a reply to Hamelin—with a copy to Decaen—wherein he offered to surrender but set certain stringent conditions. Accordingly, General Decaen sent back a letter in which he pledged the faith of the French government that within one month he would send the crew of the *Iphigenia*, and the island's small garrison, to either the Cape of Good Hope or to England. He appended the usual terms that we wouldn't serve again until properly exchanged. The letter also contained a barely masked threat that if Captain Lambert didn't agree to these terms, the entire French force would attack and—when they would certainly carry the ship and the island—they'd accept no quarter but would put us all to the sword."

"Really!" exclaimed Major Walker.

"In this extremity," Chads continued, "with scarcely enough ammunition to support an action of half an hour, with very little fresh water to support upwards of 800 men—50 of whom were wounded—and surrounded by a force of five-fold superiority, Captain Lambert saw no alternative but to haul down our colors. Thus ended this terrible action in which the British navy lost four frigates." Chads again looked out to sea, his mind filled with the images of those dreadful six days.

"Sir, I'm afraid I haven't done justice to my topic," he said after awhile, "which was to show Mr. Lambert as a peerless fighting captain. I wish you could've seen him as he skillfully directed the warps as we traversed the tortuous, winding channel; coolly ignored the enemy's steady fire; constantly remained on deck seemingly everywhere at once; never showed fatigue even as the long, bloody action went on day after day; continuously devised new plans to disadvantage the enemy; at every moment encouraged and cheered-on the busy, exhausted men; held his temper reasonably well when confronting Captain Pym—convinced as he was that we could've turned the tide if Pym hadn't forbidden us from attacking the grounded French ships; and finally played out a losing hand with considerable grace and *élan*."

"Not at all, Mr. Chads," said Hislop. "We've all been in action and can well comprehend your meaning. You've described the battle prodigiously well and I picture the events as if I'd been there myself." He considered for a moment. "I can't recall the later specifics, I'm afraid. Did the Frogs honor the terms of the surrender?"

"No, sir," replied Chads as he turned back to look at him. "They did not. Captain Willoughby remained at Grand Port and was treated passably well—his severe wounds not admitting his removal. But not so his brother officers. Captains Pym, Curtis, and Lambert, with their respective officers and men—myself included, of course—were removed only as far as Port Louis and were treated in the harshest manner. We couldn't complain, however, for several ladies—taken out of some captured Indiamen—were thrown into the same prison and suffered the same privations. Where was General Decaen? You might well ask. Where was that gallantry of which Frenchmen are so apt to boast? Females made prisoners of war; nay, treated like criminals, and that by Frenchmen—Frenchmen who won't scruple to tell an Englishman that their country is half a century more forward in civilization than his. Ha!"

"Moreover," Chads continued, clearly angry with the recollection of the events, "we can't part with Commodore Hamelin without stating that the officers and men under his orders plundered us of almost everything—in so doing they added personal insult to Captain Lambert, who'd demanded and received an honorably negotiated surrender. Thus, in spite of the solemn pledge given by General Decaen—that the prisoners who capitulated to him would be paroled or exchanged within a month—we were played false. Indeed, the much larger British force that finally captured the Mauritius that succeeding December found us there still imprisoned."

"Soon after our welcome release, we captives experienced a most fortunate occurrence. On board HMS *Illustrious* in Port Louis, Captains Pym, Willoughby, Curtis, and Lambert—and their officers—were tried by courts-martial for the loss of their ships and were most honorably acquitted. The *Iphigenia* was recaptured in December as well. Captain Lambert was returned to command, and I was appointed first lieutenant at his specific request."

"Well," said General Hislop as he shook Chads' hand, "a happy note within a grim tale. Thank you for the story, Mr. Chads. I now prize Mr. Lambert's acquaintance even more than I did—as indeed I do yours."

Saturday morning, November fourteenth, opened cloudy with moderate breezes and then actually turned fine during the rest of the day. The wind, however, blew from the west and northwest, which precluded any real thoughts of departure. In the early morning some of the men were employed obtaining more water. Then, at two bells in the forenoon watch, the grating was rigged and all hands witnessed supernumerary landmen John Robinson and James White receive twenty-four lashes each for quarreling—an indication, perhaps, that the dreary wet days and forestalled departure were affecting morale. The afternoon saw the ship's company employed in various ways, mostly just to keep busy, which included fitting a new fore topsail.

Sunday started out with the promise of another good day, with light and variable winds from the east-southeast and southeast. So, at four bells in the morning watch, Lambert ordered the topgallant masts sent up, the royal and topgallant yards crossed, and the sails loosed to dry. He also took advantage of a literally passing opportunity; around eight bells he persuaded a dockyard lighter to come alongside—diverted from a delivery elsewhere—and took from her a final two tons of fresh beef and vegetables. By noon more thick, foggy weather began to roll in. Undeterred, Lambert felt the favorable winds should not be wasted. Making the signal for the convoy to weigh anchor, the *Java* herself hove-up her best bower and, around six bells in the afternoon watch, made sail. The captains of the gun-brigs—apparently extremely anxious to get to sea, got under way with remarkable speed and soon stood through the Needles and out into the English Channel. One of the Indiamen, however, had fouled her anchor; it was either tangled up in its own cable or caught on some underwater obstruction. Either way she was having the devil's own time with it, so at two bells in the first dog watch Lambert, fuming but unwilling to enter the Channel without both Indiamen—and with the fog increasing—once again signaled for the convoy to anchor. The *Java* furled sails and came-to, her best bower striking the seabed in seventeen fathoms, once again no great distance from Hurst Castle, which now bore west-½-north.

"This is madness," said Walker later as the wardroom took supper. He spoke to the table in general but then looked specifically at Robinson. "Raise the anchor—sail a few feet—drop the anchor—raise the anchor—sail a few feet more—be driven back twice the distance you just sailed—drop the anchor! If this's the much-acclaimed life at sea, I can just as well leave it to you sailors."

"Now, Major," replied Robinson, "one of the first things you must learn at sea is that everything we do—I cannot emphasize enough—*everything* is governed by nature: the wind, the weather, and the tide, and of these the wind is the dominant. Unlike you gentlemen of the army, who can march any direction you choose whenever you fancy, we simply cannot. Therefore—always keeping in mind this first thing—the second thing you must learn at sea is patience. It does no good to rant and roar, these things are and nothing can be done about it. Shall it console you that the great Captain Cook faced just such trials? For example, on his first voyage of exploration he had several false starts—just as we. The line from his journal reads something like 'I intended to sail, but due to the weather was obliged to let go another anchor,' and then he was obliged to wait six more days before he saw the wind and weather turn favorable. And, even that ill-fated Lieutenant Bligh—now Rear Admiral Bligh, if you please—had an extremely difficult time as he tried to get the infamous *Bounty* to sea. He made several unsuccessful attempts to get down Channel from Spithead due to contrary winds and bad weather—indeed at times he was forced back farther than he had got to earlier. It took him almost a *month* before a fair wind favored him."

"Oh, well yes, but Bligh—" began Captain Wood.

"No, sir," interrupted Robinson, "I know what you're going to say, and I won't have it. Say what you will about Mr. Bligh in other respects, but in truth there never was such a seaman nor a navigator, and if he had to bow to the wind and weather then who are we to do better? We may get to sea tomorrow and, if not, the day after, or a month after. India will wait for you, gentlemen, I do promise you."

Indeed the next morning presented another bleak appearance; cloudy, fresh gales, and rain. However, the wind—from the east-southeast—was fair. Lambert threw out the signal to weigh, and at six bells took aboard the pilot, hove-up the anchor, and set topsails. Both merchant ships rapidly and efficiently followed suit, no doubt their masters trying to make amends for yesterday's fiasco. An hour later they stood through the Needles. Due to the increasing wind Lambert decided to reduce the *Java*'s tophamper, so he sent down her topgallant yards and struck topgallant masts. By two bells in the forenoon watch the three ships were making almost four knots, the wind was from the east-southeast, the course was south-southwest, and Needles Point bore northeast at seven miles. Robinson stepped over to the captain and touched his hat.

"Captain, I much dislike to interrupt our progress, but I really should like to heave-to and stretch the swifters a little; I shouldn't think it would take more than ten minutes."

"Very well, Mr. Robinson," replied Lambert, "make it so." The *Java*'s sails were trimmed so that she fell off the wind and essentially stopped. Some of the experienced hands fell to tautening the swifters—the aftermost shrouds on the fore and main masts. It was not that the swifters had been set up poorly; it was merely the case that the motion of the open sea and the initial strain of a press of sail usually demanded adjustments in rigging. For that matter the stowage of the hold usually demanded adjustments as well. In fact, the master's mates were even now far below decks, ensuring that everything had been packed as tightly as possible, so that in bluewater sailing the ship's roll, pitch, and yaw would develop only minor shifting if any at all. Anything major would damage the cargo, damage the ship and, in the worst scenario, could roll the ship over if her stores cascaded from one side to the other. Every

British captain recalled that this very thing had even happened to no-less of a figure than Captain Sir Edward Berry (who had sailed past the anchored *Java* at Spithead just a few days past). Fourteen years ago, when he was the young captain of Nelson's flagship *Vanguard*, shifting cargo in a moderate Mediterranean gale had rolled the masts right out of the ship.

By noon the wind had increased to strong gales with rain. This made for exhilarating sailing after more than three months in the dockyard and the anchorage, the ships finally out at sea after the frantic weeks of fitting out. Exhilarating to some, perhaps. As the ships were now out of the lee of the Isle of Wight they felt the unrestrained waves of the English Channel, heaving and rolling, made even worse by the adverse weather. The veteran sailors and officers were neither particularly surprised nor affected, but to the many landmen and non-naval passengers it was truly an unwelcome change to feel the heave of decks underfoot. It was equally unpleasant to realize they had not yet appreciated the meaning of the expression 'sea legs,' nor, for that matter, the misery of being sea sick.

Lambert shortly made a signal to steer west, and an hour later the convoy caught up to the gun-brigs which had impatiently maintained position waiting for them. By six bells in the afternoon watch all ships were obliged to reduce sail to accommodate the wind and rain. But, by the time of the officers' supper—the hands had eaten earlier—the wind had moderated enough to reset fore and mizzen topsails and to comfortably steer south-southeast. So it remained for the rest of the day, which Lambert finished with a grateful glass of wine. He sat under a lamp, in his remaining half of the great cabin, as he wrote in his journal.

Monday, November 16, 1812. At last we got under Sail about 7 o'clock this morning, the Weather not very pleasant but the Wind serving. We put to Sea and left England, having on board 397 Persons including crew, marines, officers, supernumeraries, passengers and their servants, near 6 months' provisions and Stores, 28 18-pounder long guns, 16 32-pounder carronades, 2 9-pounder chasers, and considerable Stores destined for Bombay. The Convoy was in company, consisting of 2 Brigs and 2 Ships.

CHAPTER 13
MID-ATLANTIC OCEAN

Mid-Atlantic Ocean
1,520 nautical miles E.S.E. of Boston
Vicinity 33° 10' N 40° 59' W
Monday, November 9th, 1812
7:30 a.m.
Fresh gales, rain; winds from the west

For the men of the USS *Constitution* and the USS *Hornet*, this day at sea felt much like any of the previous week. The afternoon, however—and indeed every day for the next two weeks—would see the previous heavy squalls, strong gales, and rain moderated by occasional clear skies, light winds, and pleasant weather. The winds fluctuated half the time fair from the west but then again half the time contrary from the east, southeast, and east-by-south. The topmen and sail trimmers saw the daily activity slightly lessen, but only slightly. The efforts to set, take in, reset, and adjust sails were now more to gain every advantage of such winds as there were, rather than merely cope with foul weather and heavy seas. The light winds, and downright unfavorable winds, did their parts to slow the ships; during this time the average speed dropped slightly below six knots, much to the captains' frustration.

"After all, Mr. Parker," groused Bainbridge one morning, unusually talkative, "we've a Goddam rendezvous to meet. I set our first rendezvous with the *Essex* in the Cape de Verds at Port Praya Bay. I wrote Captain Porter to meet us there no later than November twenty-seventh. I hope we'll not miss him." Parker started to reply, then thought better of it. It seemed to him that even with the squadron's relatively slow progress they were roughly half-way to that destination and that they could reach the Cape Verdes in another nine days or so, well ahead of the scheduled rendezvous. But Parker refrained from rebuttal or even comment. In the short time that he had been on board he had discovered the commodore to be particularly moody and irascible and, on occasion, caustic and foul-mouthed. He was cold and aloof in regard to the seamen; he never allowed any of them to address him directly and commonly referred to them as "damned rascals." He was certainly more open to the officers, but even with them a withering rebuke was almost as likely as a pleasant word. As first lieutenant—the ship's second-in-command—Parker had thus far been treated politely if formally; he was certain the commodore would continue to spare him his acid tongue, and yet the lieutenant also felt disinclined to put that theory to any rigorous test.

Each day, except Wednesday, November eleventh, continued to see all hands sent to quarters, while the thirteenth found them also exercising the great guns by divisions. These warlike activities usually occurred around one or two bells in the first dog watch, although on Sunday the fifteenth the commodore had all hands sent to quarters a second time, whereupon he again read to them the articles of war in his loudest quarterdeck rasp. The somewhat calmer weather also allowed for other ship's work: the men overhauled the sail room where they restowed the sails to the best advantage; they restowed the starboard bower anchor on the gunwale; they restowed the spare spars; they cleared out the boats, washed them, and restowed them; they bent a new foretopsail; they re-set the lower fore rigging and the main rigging; they and fit new backstays. Occasionally the ships put their topsails to the mast and hove-to in order for Captain Lawrence to come and go; this was of no great surprise because, until Captain Porter arrived with the *Essex*, Lawrence was second-in-command of the tiny squadron and needed to know Bainbridge's mind in case of accident or illness. Moreover, if Bainbridge could be said to have any service friends Lawrence was certainly one of them; he had been a protégé of Bainbridge for years.

In fact, Master Commandant Lawrence and Commodore Bainbridge in particular, as well as *Old Ironsides* and the *Hornet* in general, maintained close contact as they thrashed their ways toward the African coast. During the next fortnight there were only a couple of days where flag signals were not exchanged, the ships did not close each other sufficiently for the officers to converse through speaking-trumpets, or the ships did not back their topsails and slow such that Lawrence could jump into his gig and visit Bainbridge in person.

During this time the two ships indeed plowed slowly along the commodore's course of southeast-by-east-½-east, or close to it, for while the winds were not anywhere like dead foul, they were often not anywhere like fair. Day-after-day the winds came steadily from the east, east-by-north, and southeast—though they also were variable and at times briefly hauled up to the west. The weather continued to be less than ideal as well. Except for that occasional clear and pleasant moment, and even a few hours of dead calm, the logbook displayed a litany of complaints: haze, squalls, rain, heavy rain, heavy swells, and of course incessant gales of all types (gentle, fresh, brisk, and strong). In the considered opinions of all hands, from Bill Bainbridge (commodore) through Bill Williams (powder passer), there were far too few hours of fair breezes, moderate breezes, and fresh trade winds.

On one of these days the actual appearance of the long-obscured sun impressed the surgeon, so much so that he had to rush a comment to his diary: *the sun shines out today for the first time in many*. And, in addition to the occasional, grateful reappearances of the sun, a couple of other anomalous events gained the attention of all hands: on the eighteenth the ships spent a relatively tense hour as they passed through a sea filled with prodigious tide-rips which trended northeast to southwest; this was followed two days later by an exhilarating eight-hour stretch when the ships logged a full ten knots, hour after hour. Yet despite that delightful but too-brief run, the squadron's overall speed continued to be slow. The ships did all that veteran and skilled officers and crews could think of in order to please the commodore and drive the squadron faster. Both ships sent their men aloft continuously to make and reduce sail, some days as often as thirty-five times in a twenty-four hour period, trying any and all sail configurations that might possibly gain another knot or even a fraction of a knot from the unfavorable wind and weather conditions.

Despite constant activity with the sails (set, take in, and otherwise trim), the officers continued to have no trouble finding other work for the men to address. On board the *Constitution*, the men got up new topgallant and topmast backstays, cleaned out the boats, and, upon two occasions, spread awnings and sails to catch rainwater—of which they were able to fill a number of casks. Moreover, with the commodore's determination to hone the fighting skills of the crew, every day found both ships beating to quarters in the early evening, while a few days further saw the great guns exercised by divisions. On the eighteenth, the seventy seamen designated as marksmen, as well as the sixty marines, were exercised by shooting at targets. This was followed a few days later by the men designated as boarders being likewise practiced at small arms. Neither did the commodore—the God-fearing commodore—neglect his crew's spiritual well-being. Every Sunday during this time found the men formally mustered before being sent to dinner, at which point a number of prayers were read out to them in a roar which certainly made up in volume what it lacked in thoughtful or nuanced inflection.

On the evening of Thursday, November nineteenth, Lieutenant Aylwin spotted Mr. Evans as he leaned over the taffrail. As the lieutenant approached he saw the surgeon throw something into the sea.

"What cheer, Amos?" he said as he clapped his friend on the back. "What in the world are you doing? Did you just pitch something overboard?"

"Hello, John," replied Evans, "yes I did, too. I threw a bottle overboard with the intention of ascertaining the current. The bottle contains a piece of paper on which I wrote the latitude, longitude, date, and my name, with a request that the finder would make it public upon it being found. The paper was oiled, and the bottle was corked, sealed, and a piece of tarred muslin tied over it. I do hope someone does find it."

"What a fellow you are, Amos, I'm sure," said Aylwin. "Not content to merely be a skillful surgeon, you're a zealous tourist, a tireless diarist, an enthusiastic admirer of feminine beauty, an irrepressible political observer, a devoted lover of the theater, and now, I find, a curious hydrographer. I am truly amazed!"

Twenty feet away from Aylwin and Evans, on the leeward side of the quarterdeck, the fourth lieutenant was having a less-pleasant exchange while he walked with the first lieutenant.

"Mr. Parker," said Mr. Morgan, "I'm a mite confused. I—indeed I thought all of us—understood that we've been headed for the Cape Verde Islands."

"Yes?" replied Parker.

"Yes, and that we intended to anchor in Port Praya Bay to take on board water as well as rendezvous with the *Essex*."

"Yes?"

"Yes, sir. But sir, on Tuesday the commodore altered course to the south-sou'west, and on Wednesday he altered it further to the south and then south-by-west. By my reckoning, and that of Mr. Nichols, we thus passed *between* the Verdes to the west and Gorée to the east on the African coast. If we was then intending to make

Port Praya on the south end of Saint Jago Island, then we should've further—on Wednesday—steered west-sou'west."

"Yes?" an impassive Parker said once again.

"Yes! Yes, Mr. Parker! But we did not. No, we maintained a course of almost due south, and today we continue due south. We have passed-by all the Verdes Islands—certainly to include Saint Jago and Port Praya. Are we not to stop? Are we not to water? Are we not to keep the rendezvous with Captain Porter and the *Essex*?

"It appears not, Mr. Morgan."

"But sir—!"

"Mr. Morgan," said Parker with a sigh, "the commodore has apparently changed his mind, and while Captain Lawrence may know his thoughts, the commodore hasn't seen fit to enlighten me. I daresay he shall, if it suits him."

"But, Mr. Parker," replied Morgan, "this defies all understanding. What *can* be in his mind? Sir, for heaven's sake, can't you ask him?"

"No, I can *not*," snapped Parker, impassive no longer. He now showed considerable irritation and frustration. "But, my dear sir, you certainly have my leave to approach him yourself if you feel *you* have the fortitude!"

"Mr. Parker, in my opinion it's your duty—"

"Mr. Parker!" roared Bainbridge's voice from, seemingly, the deck. Both lieutenants looked about in surprise, and then looked down. The skylight to the commodore's forward cabin was a few feet away. As they stared at it they noticed that it was slightly open.

"Yes, Commodore?" replied Parker after a second's hesitation.

"Kindly inform the officer with you that, fortunately, neither the commander of this squadron—nor the first lieutenant of the flagship—have yet to devolve into states of confusion such that they require opinions of no value, nor are they required to take advice from inferiors as to how to perform their duty."

"Aye aye, sir!" said Parker as he stared at an extremely red-faced Morgan.

"Furthermore you—and *that officer*—will be so kind as to get the hell away from my skylight."

During the next week the squadron's course indeed remained a mystery to all except Commodore Bainbridge and, perhaps, Captain Lawrence. The next two days saw the commodore again change headings—south-southeast and south-by-east—seemingly with the intention to take the ships into the South Atlantic toward St. Helena Island or perhaps the Cape of Good Hope itself, and of course even farther away from the untouched and unsighted Port Praya. But then, on Sunday the twenty second, he turned the ships south and then south-½-west; and, during the subsequent three days, he ordered courses of south-by-west, south-southwest, southwest, and finally even west-southwest. Thus, they now headed back across the Atlantic toward South America.

Regardless of which course was laid on any of these days, the wind continued to be problematic. In fact, to the profound discouragement of all hands, the entire week of November twenty-third saw the ships average only three and one-half knots. The weather also continued to play *Old Harry* with them; indeed, on Sunday the twenty-ninth the squadron had to push through extremely dark and heavy weather with blinding, torrential rain.

Still, a small proportion of the time saw fair weather, if not fair winds. This was the case on the afternoon of the twenty-sixth when Captain Lawrence and Lieutenant Stewart came on board the *Constitution*, the gunner fired a cannon, and they joined the commodore and several of the *Constitution*'s officers as they brought marine Private John Pershaw to a formal court-martial (Pershaw was accused of threatening the life of Midshipman James Delaney, found guilty, and sentenced to receive four dozen lashes at the grating). Moreover, on the twenty-seventh the light wind and calm sea permitted working parties to fumigate the ship with muriatic acid gas—killing a variety of fleas, lice, rats, and other vermin—an activity which was followed on the next day by white-washing both the berth and gun decks. While that white-washing proceeded on board *Old Ironsides*, the *Hornet*'s crew entertained themselves by practicing various maneuvers. They tacked, wore, headed first northeast, then headed southwest, stood in for the *Constitution*, stood out, and finally headed southwest-½-south.

Later, that same evening, Mr. Evans took the air on the leeward side of the quarterdeck. Two days of muriatic gas and whitewash fumes made the sea air taste absolutely delightful. After about an hour he was ready to go below when he was loudly addressed by Commodore Bainbridge, who had been leisurely strolling about the windward side.

"Halloo, good evening there, Mr. Evans."

"Why, good evening, Commodore," Evans replied, as he turned in surprise.

"Please walk over and join me," said Bainbridge with a smile. "I've been thinking about the lightning rod."

"Yes, sir, indeed, the lightning rod," said Evans, baffled.

"Oh, yes, Doctor, the lightning rod, a most efficacious device, to be sure. We have three, you know."

"Three, Commodore?" said Evans. "You astonish me, sir. Would they be on top of the masts, I wonder?"

"Aye, they are that, for sure," replied Bainbridge. "I wouldn't command a ship not so equipped. Some say they're of no use and object to the expense and effort, but I know better."

"Indeed, Commodore?"

"Oh, yes. Back in the year five, during the Tripolitan War, three American frigates lay at anchor amidst a British squadron at Gibraltar. A severe thunder storm arose with much lightning. The British ships had no lightning rods; each American ship did. As a result there was several strikes and considerable injury done to most of the British vessels—but the American ships suffered no injury except the destruction of one of their rods."

"Sir, that's...remarkable," said Evans. "I had never heard this."

"Oh yes, Doctor," said Bainbridge, "and what's more, I know that the Dutch church in New York had been struck four times over the years before a rod was hoisted to the steeple, since which time it's never again been injured. It was the only church in the city that had no rod. All the rest of the churches escaped injury in every instance. The Dutch objected to having one from religious principles, but were afterwards convinced of their error."

"I believe I've read that Dr. Franklin stated that the sphere of attraction of a lightning rod is about thirty feet—or a little less," ventured Evans.

"Nonsense, Doctor," said Bainbridge, "I've known it to be more than fifty feet in several cases, and I'm certain it might be much farther."

"But Commodore," replied Evans, "I should think that as the inventor of the device, Dr. Franklin—"

"Well, good night, Mr. Evans," said Bainbridge, yawning, "it's been most pleasant to talk with you. We must do it again some evening."

The next day, Sunday, opened pleasantly enough with light

breezes and clear weather. The crew was mustered, church was rigged, and the commodore gave a solemn homily in addition to reading the standard prayers. Dinner then saw the routine Sunday duff washed down with two-water grog. Prior to the hands being piped to that dinner, and before a fast-approaching cloud could block his view of the sun, the master took his meridian observations and declared that the squadron could be said to be at 0 degrees 24 minutes north and, that is to say, it could be considered to lay across the equator itself.

Accordingly, right after dinner the ships backed their foretopsails and slowed to a stop—they were barely making three knots anyway—which allowed *Neptunus Rex* to come aboard in full regalia, accompanied by his train. While all hands were summoned, the customary and expected salutations, quips, and jests were exchanged between Neptune and Commodore Bainbridge; of course, a mile away Captain Lawrence similarly faced his own King Neptune on the *Hornet's* quarterdeck. Once the greetings were completed and a convivial glass of wine drunk, Neptune then called out and required any and all who had *Never before Crossed the Very Line Itself* to step forward, redeem themselves, or be shaved. On board *Old Ironsides*, Mr. Evans and four of the new midshipmen presented bottles of brandy from their personal stores and thus quite legally purchased exemption. Neptune's "constables" then brought the remainder of the initiates one-by-one to the "tub," which was merely one of the boats filled with water. Then, with a huge brush the men were thoroughly lathered with a vile-smelling concoction, roughly shaved with razors made of great iron hoops taken from an old cask, and then pushed in backwards and thoroughly ducked. It was all over fairly quickly, for in the two ships full of veteran seamen, there were relatively few who had not previously undergone this ordeal. It went by quickly for other reasons as well: much of the lewd hilarity usually found in the ceremony was curtailed on a Sunday, the men were gravely aware that most of them were still in their best clothes from having attended church, and the master's previously observed cloud cover had developed into warm, but heavy, rain.

"Well," said Lieutenant Aylwin later that evening as he, Hoffman, and Evans leaned on the taffrail and admired the clearing sky, "if we hold to these latest courses, we head right towards Brazil and perhaps the Island of Fernando de Noronha itself." Hoffman looked carefully around before he replied.

"Noronha's the second rendezvous established with the *Essex?*"

"It is indeed, Beekman," replied Aylwin with a grin, "and—just perhaps—we may even actually stop there!"

In fact, the rain departed as rapidly as it had come up, and so the last day of November and the first day of December brought pleasant weather and moderate breezes from the east while the *Constitution* and the *Hornet* went about their routine activities. The two ships practiced maneuvers with each other, daily sent the men to quarters and, again, exercised the great guns. On board the *Constitution* the men took down a number of the principal sails— jibs, fore topgallant, foretopsail, fore course, maintopsail, and main topgallant—and bent new ones in their place. On Monday, Captain Lawrence came on board and spent the entire day in consultation with Commodore Bainbridge.

It further appeared that Lieutenant Aylwin's jest about a stop at Noronha Island might in reality come true. After Lawrence left the ship, Bainbridge directed that the stream anchor be got into the chains and that the anchor cables be cleared for bending.

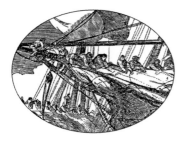

CHAPTER 14
THE ENGLISH CHANNEL

English Channel
30 nautical miles S.E.-½-E. of Lizard Point
Vicinity 49 57' N 5 12' W
Tuesday, November 17th, 1812
7:15 a.m.
Moderate breezes and rain

"A good first day, I should think, Captain," said General Hislop as he passed the plate of bacon. He had invited Lambert and Chads to breakfast. So they sat in Hislop's part of the *Java's* great cabin bathed in the gray light which came through the stern windows. "Although," he went on, "I might've wished for slightly finer weather."

"I quite agree, sir," replied Lambert. "Despite the weather and the constraints of standing through the Needles, I believe we made about fifty miles' progress. And despite today's weather appearing not much better we presently make about six knots, so I hope for"—he touched the wood of the table—"perhaps even as much as one-hundred twenty miles today. I wish I could've shown you Lizard Point but, unfortunately, it was obscured by darkness and clouds. Of course it's Land's End in Cornwall which's the westernmost place in England, but it's the Lizard—very far west, too—which is the southern-most tip. It's about ten leagues off to the nor'west—we couldn't see it now even if it were clear. Yes, sir," he stopped for a bite of breakfast. "We're off to a fine start, with even greater need and greater opportunity to turn our motley, mismatched, and lubberly crew into real sailors. I'm grateful to be at sea at last, and not remaining wind-bound in the anchorage for days—or weeks."

"A terrible fate, indeed," replied Hislop as he drank some coffee. "Apparently the master has given Major Walker and Captain Wood quite the lesson on this subject, citing no less authorities than Cook and Bligh. You know, it makes one wonder how Bligh's adventures may've turned out differently had his month's delay not happened." Chads took Hislop's glance and raised eyebrow as an invitation to reply; unless on specific matters of duty, lieutenants did not customarily speak to flag officers unless spoken to first.

"So Admiral Bligh's always maintained, sir. He believes the delay in sailing, compounded by the time lost as he tried to round the Horn, entirely ruined his schedule. Had he been able to directly reach Tahiti, bring aboard the breadfruit plants, and promptly return—rather than arrive late in the growing season and have to wait many months in idleness for the breadfruit to be ready to transplant—his men wouldn't have become so attached to the place, thus the mutiny wouldn't have occurred." Lambert started to comment but was interrupted by the midshipman of the watch, who presented Mr. Herringham's duty, and could the captain come on deck?

As Lambert gained the quarterdeck Lieutenant Herringham touched his hat. "Sir, foretopmast lookout sees a brig hove-to just ahead two points off the larboard bow. She appears to be British. Mainmast and stays'l all in a shambles."

"Very well, Mr. Herringham," replied Lambert. "I'll speak her, if you please. Hoist the colors."

The *Java* rapidly bore down upon the brig. She indeed had every appearance of a British merchantman with nothing particularly suspicious about her. When they had come to the distance of a pistol-shot, Lambert raised his speaking trumpet and gave the customary hail.

"What brig's that?"

A figure by the brig's rail, clad in a blue coat and who clearly waited for the question, replied through his own trumpet.

"*Harmony*, sir, of Plymouth. Twenty-six days out o' Halifax."

"What's amiss?"

"Sprung the goddam boom, yesterday."

"Do you need assistance?"

"Oh, no sir, thankee kindly. We've made some repair and're just about to try the stays'l again. At any rate we're close to home."

"What's the news?"

"Nothin' you don't know already, sir, I daresay. Out Canada-way Yankee privateers and national ships pretty thick."

"So, then, why're you sailing without convoy?"

"Why, sir, none were available—and we're pretty quick, usually."

"Well, Captain, I hope you don't regret that decision—even this close to home. Farewell!"

As the *Java* moved past the *Harmony*, Lambert waved his arm at her captain who doffed his hat in return. Lambert turned back to Herringham.

"Well, now, William, let's take advantage of the wind this morning. I believe we can sway up the mizzen topgallant masts and shake out all the tops'l reefs."

In fact, the rest of that day, as well as the next two days, saw a little rain but generally fair weather and good sailing; from noon-to-noon the convoy logged daily 135, 125, and 132 miles respectively. The wind came from the northeast, east, and east-southeast and the ships steered west, west-by-south, and west-southwest. The *Java* proceeded under easy sail; she made and shortened sail as needed to allow the convoy to keep up. The only other excitement was the sighting of a small northeast-headed warship Tuesday afternoon, which after an exchange of signals turned out to be nothing more than the homeward-bound gun-brig *Orestes*.

Friday, however, was a less-pleasant day by far. Overnight the weather rapidly deteriorated and brought squalls, strong gales, and an extremely heavy sea. At seven bells in the middle watch a sudden shift in the wind took the *Java* all aback, pressing her sails flat against the masts. In an attempt to recover, she wore and then ran off before the wind and around to the other tack, but the still-clumsy crew was still less-than smart in such an evolution. She wore twice more that morning and avoided being taken aback again, but by one bell in the forenoon watch Lambert felt compelled to heave-to, as did the rest of the convoy, all of which remained intermittently in sight. In the face of the dirty weather and the heavy swell, now from the southeast, the five ships remained hove-to for almost eleven hours and rode it out. Although the weather moderated in the evening and they were finally able to get underway, the day's total progress was only about sixty miles.

Frustrated by the dirty weather of the twentieth, Captain Lambert dearly hoped that the next few days might see fair weather, fair winds, and some resultant fine blue-water sailing. Saturday morning opened with every appearance of cooperation. Although it was raining, the accompanying fresh breezes allowed for the topsails to be set and a few hours' run at seven knots. However, at five bells in the morning watch, the *Java*'s lookouts found that one of the brigs was missing, causing Lambert to angrily heave-to and wait. An hour later the brig was seen to the westward and two hours more saw her rejoin the convoy. Then, just before noon, the lookouts discovered an unknown sail southwest-by-west. The convoy's course—southwest to south-southeast—appeared likely to bring them together. By five bells in the afternoon watch they were fairly close aboard. The chase, apparently a merchant-brig, seemed oblivious to their presence. The *Java*'s bow chaser rang out and the vessel hove-to in confusion. Chads, officer of the watch, ordered the courses taken in and the ship likewise brought-to. Five minutes' hallooing determined the brig to be unsurprisingly English, bound for Lisbon.

All through this same afternoon the weather deteriorated, and by midnight the fresh breezes had become squalls—which, in turn, became gales. Nevertheless, the convoy had averaged slightly more than five knots all throughout the day. Not what Lambert had hoped, but satisfactory all things considered.

Yet if Saturday had been only satisfactory, Sunday exceeded all his expectations. It started poorly. Two hours in the early morning were spent hove-to, bows to the southeast-by-east, while the *Java* and the Indiamen again waited for the two gun-brigs to come into sight. They had last been seen at sunset the evening before. However, as the brigs had planned to depart company today—bound for the Azores—and as the morning wore on, Lambert drew the logical conclusion that during the night they had altered course, slightly prematurely. Around two bells in the forenoon watch he shrugged his shoulders and had the convoy bear up and get under way. The gales which had developed during the night lasted half the day, and moderated to strong breezes a little after noon. However, the associated winds came steadily from the east and east-northeast, which drove the convoy southwest-by-south at a prodigious rate.

So it was that both Lambert and Chads took great delight as they showed the army officers hour after hour of impressive readings: seven entries of eight knots, then a seven-hour run at nine knots, and finally two hours at ten knots—all of which brought the full day's run to something in the range of 180 miles—extremely respectable, particularly as the Indiamen had also, surprisingly, managed to keep pace.

The next day turned out even better, to the continuing gratification of the officers and the passengers and even the inexperienced crew, all of whom caught at least some of the excitement of high speed and profound ocean sailing. The wind held steady east-by-north and east-by-east, the breezes fresh and strong, which drove the ships southwest-by-south to south-by-west. The watchkeepers gleefully cast the hourly log and reported steady eights, nines, and even a six-hour run of ten knots before noon.

The weather began to turn squally as the men finished their dinners. Despite the diminished visibility, it was just a half-glass later when the maintop lookout picked out a strange sail to the northwest. The *Java* left the Indiamen to proceed on the established course, wore ship, and packed on sail to investigate. In less than an hour she ran down the chase, which submissively hove-to without waiting for the warning gun. However, eager anticipation of a prize quickly turned to dismay. The *Java*'s green cutter was sent across, but as her boarding party scrambled up the side of what now appeared to be an American merchant ship, the cutter—shoved against the ship's side by an unusual double-crested wave stirred up by the squally weather—swamped, filled, and sank. Lieutenant Chads instantly had the gig hoisted out and led a second party across. He returned an hour later with the cutter's embarrassed but unharmed crew—as well as the second disappointment of the day. Although the chase proved indeed to be a Yankee, she was sailing from Lisbon to Boston under a license and thus was not liable for capture. The gig was hoisted up and the *Java* made sail, then wore ship to return to the convoy. Captain Wood, who stood by the taffrail with the other army officers, turned to his companions with a frown.

"General, Major, I have to confess I'm a bit confused. Why've we released an American merchant vessel? Why don't we seize her, and relish the prospect of the considerable prize money which'd come forth as a result?" Walker met Hislop's eye with a smile, and deferred to the senior officer.

"Well, Captain," said the general, "as you know, our land and naval forces continue everywhere the long struggle against the French, which requires enormous amounts of supplies." Hislop gazed across the quarterdeck at Lambert and Chads, deep in conversation beside the mizzenmast. "We particularly had been drawing grain, flour, and naval stores from North America, and this trade's particularly vital to support British armies in Portugal and Spain. So, despite the new state of war with the Americans, our consulates have been authorized to issue licenses to American citizens willing to continue such trade. Such documents instruct our naval officers—and our privateers, for that matter—to release, assist, and even protect any such ships they might encounter." Wood stared at his superior and shook his head.

"I know, Captain," Hislop continued, "it's almost beyond comprehension. War, politics, and necessity are terrible and confusing things, to be sure."

The *Java*, meanwhile, set topgallants and even topmast studding sails, trying to rejoin the convoy as quickly as possible and make up the time lost with the American ship. If anything she now tore along even faster than she had in the morning, and by the end of the day recorded a seven-hour stretch of eleven knots, which brought her day's run to an extremely gratifying 209 miles.

At two bells in the second dog watch all of the army officers were still on deck, where they enjoyed the strong breeze, the considerable heel of the deck, the high-flying bow wave to leeward, and the wide streak of copper visible on the windward side.

"Gentlemen," called a grinning Lieutenant Buchanan, the officer of the watch, "I fancy we sail pretty fast, perhaps faster than any time today. We're about to cast the log. Would you care to observe the procedure more closely?" The redcoats crossed the quarterdeck as James West, the midshipman of the watch, came forth. He carefully balanced on the sloping deck while he equally carefully carried the log, reel, and twenty-eight-second sand glass. He passed the glass to a quartermaster and assumed a position by the rail.

"Glass clear, sir," said the quartermaster. West held the reel as high as he could with one hand while he threw the log far out overboard with the other.

"Turn!" he shouted as the end of the stray-line shot by. The knots flew past—one every forty-seven feet, three inches—while the reel spun madly. As the last of the sand dropped down in the glass the quartermaster cried "Nip!" West pinched the line with his fingers, started to pull the log in, and counted the knots. He counted them a second time before he turned to Buchanan with a delighted grin.

"Sir, twelve knots, sir—twelve knots and one fathom!" he cried as he handed the equipment to the quartermaster.

"Very well, Mr. West. Jump down to the cabin with my respects and so inform the captain." Buchanan then turned to the army officers who had intensely watched West's every move. The lieutenant bowed and swept off his hat.

"General, gentlemen, I give you twelve knots and one fathom, if you please. If anyone asks you, you might say that one can always trust the French to build a damn fast ship!"

Perhaps Buchanan had spoken hastily—or at least should have touched some wood as he spoke—for it seemed from that moment on the favorable conditions of wind and weather, particularly as seen during the last two glorious days, gradually deserted the little convoy. Tuesday started brisk enough, which enabled the initial cast to show an exciting eleven knots and which even required the taking-in of studding sails, courses, and topgallants. However, as the morning wore on the clouds disappeared and the winds—east-northeast and northeast-by-east—moderated considerably, such that by eight bells in the morning watch Captain Lambert reset topgallants and courses and shook out all reefs in the topsails. But by four bells in the forenoon watch, and despite the enormous spread of canvas, the *Java* only could make six knots. The course was a steady southwest-by-south, and the weather was as fine and clear as could be imagined.

"Henry," said Lambert to Chads while they stood by the quarterdeck rail and looked down into the waist. "I'd hoped for another two-hundred-mile day today, but I don't think it'll happen. Yet, it's a beautiful day and the sea's smooth, so I think we'll take advantage of it in another way."

"Ah. The guns, sir?" replied Chads.

"Indeed. While the crew has been, and does, get good sail drill every day, thus far we've had no exercise at the great guns nor small arms at all—unless you offer to count firing a couple of salutes and a few shots from the bow chaser, which I do not. Let's have an hour at the guns, before the hands go to dinner, and really introduce them to it. It'll be a shambles, I'm quite sure, but only use makes master, and we need to get 'em used to it."

"Aye aye, sir," said Chads.

"Mr. Herringham," Lambert called to the officer of the watch. "Mr. Herringham, beat to quarters, if you please. I wish to exercise the great guns and the small arms. No, don't clear for action—we're so lumbered with extra stores, people, and baggage it'd take half the watch to accomplish and another watch to put it all back. Beating to quarters shall suffice for today."

The marine drummer boy began the roll. He started on the quarterdeck and then, slowly, walked forward on the starboard gangway to the forecastle while his drum thundered at remarkable volume. The men raced up and everywhere, and the warrant officers and midshipmen helped the bosun and his mates to push, prod, and pull the landmen into a semblance of correct station. The relatively few veteran seamen bore a hand as well, so that after a long ten minutes everyone, supernumeraries included, was approximately where he should be. Herringham finally approached Lambert and touched his hat.

"If you please, sir, hands at quarters."

"Very well, Mr. Herringham," replied Lambert. "Let's begin. Lieutenant Mercer." The marine officer stepped forward.

"Sir?"

"Please be so good as to arrange your men—those not serving the guns—along the larboard quarterdeck rail and the taffrail, and likewise take charge of the supernumeraries previously designated as marksmen. Run through the drill, and when you're satisfied that all essentially comprehend it, you may let each man fire three shots apiece. The bosun'll have some bottles suspended from the foreyard for you."

"Aye aye, sir."

"Mr. Chads," Lambert went on as he turned to the first lieutenant, "let's go through the great-gun exercise a half-dozen times, if you please. However, I daresay we won't fire live today. Unless the exercise goes uncommon well, that likely'll wait until the men appear able to rattle the guns in-and-out reasonably proficient."

"Aye aye, sir," replied Chads. Both of them hoped that the allocation of the few experienced seamen among the gun crews, and the distribution of the midshipmen, master's mates, and quarter gunners to every eight guns, would work tolerably well. In the past few weeks, Lambert and Chads, with Commander Marshall's assistance, had gone through multiple drafts of the watch, quarter, and station bills, trying to balance the pervasive needs of the ship with the few experienced men.

"Silence! Silence, fore-and-aft! Gun crews, starboard side!" shouted Chads, his orders being echoed by the lieutenants who commanded the various divisions of guns on the weather deck and gundeck. Each gun crew was responsible for a pair of guns, starboard and larboard. The crews would work the gun on the side being fought; but, if both sides of the ship had to be fought simultaneously the crews would have to split in two.

"Cast loose your guns!" On the gundeck the men loosened the frappings and tackles which normally pinned the cannon to the ship's sides in their stowed positions. The decorated wooden tompions were wiggled out of the muzzles and the lead aprons were removed from the flintlock firing mechanisms. Similar activities prepared the differently-configured carronades on the weather deck.

"Level your guns!" The gunport lids were opened, the sponge men raised the guns' breeches with their handspikes, and the gun captains thrust the quoins under the breeches to maintain each gun's now-horizontal position.

"Run out your guns!" The men heaved on the side-tackles hand-over-hand and thrust the guns' barrels out of their ports. This motion ultimately slammed the front-pieces of the carriages against the sides of the ship.

"Prime!" Loading was not required; in wartime the guns were usually stowed-away loaded in a constant state of readiness. Thus, each gun's captain now pretended to stick his cartridge-pricker into the touchhole to pierce the gunpowder cartridge already within the gun, and then likewise pretended to push a quill firing tube filled with fine powder down into the cartridge. He followed this by setting the gunlock to the half-cock—or safe—position and simulated filling the flintlock's pan with more fine powder.

"Point your guns—as they lie!" Chads felt this first-time drill was enough of a challenge without the additional complexities of elevating or traversing the cannon, so today they essentially dispensed with aiming.

"Make ready!" The gun crews ensured they were clear of the guns, carriages, and trucks in anticipation of the violent recoil when they fired. Each gun's captain stood well-behind the weapon as he held the trigger lanyard. Two of each crew held on to the side tackles.

Now, rather than actually giving the next command, Chads simulated having the gun captains fire. He then, following this same exact formal drill, had the guns run in and out several times, which got the men used to the routine of each step but again stopped short of actual detonation. It all went surprisingly well. At the sixth time, Chads looked questioningly at Lambert, who, after stroking his chin for a few seconds, nodded his head.

"Gun captains!" shouted Chads. "This time we shall fire the guns. D'ye hear me there! We shall fire two rounds. Give me your strict attention! Listen for the word. Do *nothing* without the word!" The drill began for the seventh time but this time cartridges were actually pierced, quills were inserted, and pans were primed. Then, two seconds after he gave the command "Make ready," Chads shouted "Fire!" Twenty-two gun captains, gundeck and weather deck, tugged their lanyards which tripped their flint-lock firing mechanisms. The *Java*'s starboard side erupted in crimson flame and white smoke; pieces of wadding and bits of non-combusted black powder flew everywhere. The multiple ear-splitting bangs—a little less simultaneous than one could have hoped—were instantly followed by the squeal of the long-gun trucks, the shriek of the carronade slides, and the deep twangs of the breeching ropes. These last took the force of the recoil and halted each weapon as it violently flew backwards.

"Stop your vents!" called Chads, and each gun captain shoved his vent-piece down his touch-hole, which blocked the burning embers and corrosive gases which rushed up and out. For a couple of seconds all hands looked outboard as almost two-dozen plumes spectacularly flew up from the sea, more or less four-hundred yards out. Then, the drill continued.

"Sponge your guns!" The spongers dunked their sheep's-wool sponges into the leather firebuckets and then shoved them down the barrels, twirling them to ensure all burning embers from wads and powder residue were extinguished.

"Load with cartridge!" Each gun's loader inserted a flannel car-tridge into his gun and then rammed it home. Then each gun's captain felt for its seating with his cartridge-pricker.

"Shot your guns!" The loaders now rolled solid iron round-shot—either eighteen pound or thirty-two pound balls—into the muzzles and rammed them home. After the next command—"Wad your guns!"—they inserted and rammed home wads—thick plugs of rope-yarn compressed and bound with twine.

"Run out your guns!" of course came next, and so the drill con-tinued until another broadside was fired—perhaps the second a little less ragged than the first. Chads maintained the sequence of orders; step followed step but now—once the guns were reload-ed—the crews reinserted the tompions, replaced the aprons, se-cured the tackles and breechings, and closed the gunports.

"Send the hands to dinner, Mr. Chads, if you please," said Lambert, and as the men scrambled off and formed into their messes, in extremely high spirits and talking excitedly, he shook his head. A rueful smile came across his face as Hislop and Mar-shall approached him from across the quarterdeck.

"Oh, my, gentlemen," said Lambert with a nervous laugh, "I did expect a shambles, and this was indeed pretty bad. I didn't keep careful time but it strikes me there was almost four—even four and a half—minutes between shots. I was encouraged by the first part of the drill to try a couple rounds in earnest, but the men are extremely slow, and extraordinarily clumsy. Captain Marshall, how went the small-arms exercise? It appeared you watched 'em very attentively."

"It went pretty well, sir, I must say," replied Marshall. "The marines showed excellent form and the other men seemed tolerably good pupils and not wholly inept."

"As far as the great guns, sir," added Chads, "perhaps it wasn't too awful, considering. After all, no gun burst by being double-charged, no arm was blown off by improper sponging, and though some men have been taken to the surgeon for sundry injuries, as far as I saw no leg was broken nor foot crushed by recoiling trucks. As we repeat this evolution in future I've every hope we can make the crew into right gunners—just as we've been seeing pretty good progress into making them true sailors. As you have remarked, 'only use makes master.'"

"Gentlemen," Lambert laughed, "you ever play the optimist with me. Would God allow you to be right!"

On the whole it turned out to be an extremely productive day. The gun drill, which undeniably proved the ship's unreadiness to engage in a real fight against a proficient opponent, was nevertheless a good first step in the rectification of the problem. And, despite the lighter winds and the resultant reduction in speed during the past couple of days, the convoy still managed a not-inconsiderable 150 miles' progress from noon to noon.

The next day—November twenty-fifth—began with the same moderate breezes and fine weather with the convoy averaging about six knots. Around two bells the peaceful morning routines were interrupted by a screech from aloft.

"Land, ho! Deck there! Land on the starboard bow," came the cry from the maintop.

"Ah, there it is. I've expected to hear that this last glass and more," said Mr. Robinson as he walked the leeward side of the quarterdeck with Major Walker and Captain Wood. Opposite them on the weather side Captain Lambert paced the same twenty-one feet up-and-down, entirely lost in thought. "Bearing west-sou'west—that'll be the small island of Porto Sancto," continued Robinson, "and it, the larger Madeira, the scattered *Ilhas Desertas*, and to the south the *Ilhas Selvagens* (we of course call 'em the

Salvages or the Dry Salvages) as well as many smaller is-lands—some no more than large rocks—all constitute the Madeira archipelago. It's said that Columbus himself lived on Porto Sancto, prior to his first voyage to the New World, and that the island's first governor was his father-in-law. As of course you know, we garrisoned Madeira in the year seven—a friendly relationship with the Portuguese, sure, while we continue to fight with them against the French in the Peninsula. And, the fact that we thus have prime access to their wine—that most excellent full-bodied Madei-ra—pleases *this* old man no end, I can tell you."

"I take it that we shall not land at Madeira or any of its associ-ated islands?" queried Walker.

"No, Major, I'm afraid not," replied Robinson. "We're well pro-visioned and it's somewhat out of our way."

"Pity. Can you at least describe it to us?" asked Wood. "General Hislop's been to Madeira before, but neither Major Walker nor I have."

"Why, certainly, Captain Wood, it'd be my pleasure," said Rob-inson with a smile. "Well, the first distant appearance of Madeira exhibits a bare and broken rock of huge dimensions which is pecu-liarly dark and gloomy. It's not until you make your way closer that you see the green flora which is everywhere scattered over the dark red soil. The terraced slopes—covered with a luxuriant tropi-cal vegetation—change that distant barren aspect into one of ex-treme beauty and fertility."

"The shores of the island are mostly lofty cliffs, jagged ridges, and sharp pyramids of rock which occasionally face the water with a perpendicular front one or two thousand feet in height. The cliffs are interrupted by a few small bays where richly cultivated valleys approach the water between the abrupt precipices. These narrow bays are the sites of the villages of Madeira, each with its little church at the outlet of the gorge. Throughout Madeira diligently cultivated terraces are visible on every side. These spots, with their white cottages clustered at the sea-shore, form an interesting con-trast with the broken and wild background."

"The capital of Madeira is Funchal, which's situated in a kind of amphitheater formed by the mountains. The landing at this town's on a stony beach and's accomplished with some difficulty on account of the surf. The streets of Funchal are very narrow, ex-tremely steep, without sidewalks, and, to our view, like alleys. However, they're well-paved and surprisingly clean. In the town there're many elegant establishments and much luxury among the higher classes. The poorer houses are generally of one story of which the exterior's usually whitewashed. They usually have but one entrance, the floors are paved with round stones, and the walls are of rough stone."

"As you leave Funchal for the country you find one continual ascent between vine-covered stone walls. The roadsides are lined throughout with flowers—among them fuchsias, digitalis, rose geraniums, punica granata, rosa indica coccinea, hydrangea hortensis, box-trees, and myrtles. The valleys're covered with the belladonna lily and the mountain passes appear like rich flower gardens left to grow wild. Oh, aye, riding about Madeira's beautiful. In general the roads are well made and easily and safely traveled on a pony. Ponies are used rather more than horses or mules."

"Oh, and let me not forget to mention that in the lower portions groves of orange and lemon trees are mingled with the vineyards. Then, as one mounts higher, bananas, figs, and pomegranates are seen, and again, still higher, the fruits of the tropics are interspersed with those of the temperate zone: apples, currants, pears, and peaches, while the ground is covered with melons, tomatoes, and egg-plant. Some of the peasants raise a little wheat, barley, rye, potatoes, sugar—and coffee too. Indeed, all kinds of vegetables and fruits are in abundance and not only sufficient for their own wants but also to supply the shipping that touches there. The markets're usually well-supplied with meat, poultry, and fish. And those vineyards! Oh, gentlemen, the vineyards—they occupy every spot that's susceptible to cultivation. Many of the terraces on which the vines are grown are cut into the sides of the hills, and the visitor can't but admire the labor expended on the stone walls that support them."

"The people of Madeira—of the lower orders—are industrious, sober, and civil, and although ignorant, I should say generally happy. There's little, if any, mixed blood among them. They are of the old Arabian stock. Dark hair, eyes, and complexions are most common. The men are above middle height, strongly built, and capable of enduring great fatigue. I've always thought that the women aren't particularly pretty, which I impute in part to the hard labor required of them."

"The men of the lower order are dressed in a kind of loose trousers which descend as far as the knee, with a shirt or jacket of gaudy color. The women wear bodices, with short petticoats of a variety of colors, in stripes. The children're poorly clad, apparently have but one garment apiece, and that generally dirty."

"The deportment of the poor's a mixture of politeness and servility. They invariably notice you as you pass; they take off their caps and then kiss their hands or make some other respectful salutation. The ignorance of the common people seems great. Few can read and still fewer write. Of course the language spoken is the Portuguese, but with a rapid utterance and a clipped or abbreviated style of words and expressions. Despite what I said earlier about the happiness of the people, beggars are numerous and one is much touched as well as tormented with them from the moment of landing. It's a surprise to find so many so persistent in such a fine island."

"Outside of Funchal, the houses would be called huts in our country. They're composed of walls of stone about six feet high. A roof rises on all sides to a central pole, are thatched with straw, and contain only one room. In the northern part of the island some of the peasants make their habitation in caves or in excavations on the hillsides."

"You were at some point, Master, going to speak more of the wine industry—surely?" asked Walker with a grin. Robinson laughed.

"Aye, Major, so I shall—I was about to get to it. Well, the inhabitants of Madeira are rightly jealous of the reputation of their wines, which are generally the engrossing topic of conversation. I was once able to visit a small wine works. On our approach to the building we heard a sort of rhythmic song with a continued thumping sound. Upon our entrance we saw six men stamping violently in a vat of grapes of six feet square by two feet deep, their legs bare up to the thighs. As they stamped the juice flowed off and was received in tubs. The produce of such an individual press is on an average about 50 gallons daily. Each gallon requires about ten bushels of grapes, and the general average is from one to three pipes of wine per acre annually."

"The south side of Madeira produces the finest wines. The kinds of grapes're various and the wines manufactured just as numerous. The common Madeira's obtained from a mixture of Bual, Verdelho, and Negro Molle grapes, and the Malmsey and Sercial from grapes of the same name. After being expressed, the juice's put into casks, undergoes the process of fermentation, is clarified with gypsum or isinglass, and a small portion of brandy is added—two or three gallons to the pipe. Many of the peasantry are employed as carriers with sheepskins filled with wine on their shoulders. About 25 gallons, which weighs more than 200 pounds, is a common load. One of the most remarkable things to see is a stout mountain lass trudge up a steep path—with ease—under a load that would stagger one of our dockyard mateys even for a short distance!"

"Well, Master," said Walker, "I shall savor my Madeira more in future, now I understand the effort which goes into it."

"No doubt, sir, no doubt," replied Robinson. "I beg pardon, gentlemen, but I must close my travelogue here as my duties draw me away at this time. But I do hope I've been of some use to you this morning."

"Mr. Robinson, you've fairly tormented and tantalized me!" cried Walker. "After such a wonderful description I'm devastated not to visit this apparent paradise on earth."

"Then I'll hope that, when you return from your duties in India, your ship will land there—many do, you know, homeward bound."

Once past the excitement of seeing the land, which remained in sight the rest of the day and the next day as well, the *Java* resumed her established routines. The breeze, however, steadily decreased. The convoy saw several hours in the evening without a breath of wind. They became totally becalmed, unable to make any way at all. The breeze picked up again just before midnight, but the day's run of only eighty miles was a disappointment.

Thursday morning saw the wind increase to light and then moderate breezes, southwest and southwest-by-south. This allowed the ships to proceed southeast-by-east and southeast-by-south—and average a little more than five knots. Just before the hands were piped to breakfast they were first piped to witness punishment: supernumerary ordinary James Simpson and ordinary Bernard McGuire received twenty-four lashes apiece for theft and drunkenness, respectively; and supernumerary landman James Hurley, landman Martin Galvin, and ordinary Robert Taylor received twenty-four, eighteen, and twelve lashes for neglect of duty.

By noon the moderate breezes had turned fresh and then squally which, at two bells in the afternoon watch, the *Java* turned to her advantage. She packed on sail and chased down a strange vessel to the east-northeast. Upon being boarded, the chase turned out to be only an Irish merchant brig bound from Cork to the West Indies, which the day before had somehow parted from a convoy shepherded by H.M. frigate *Circe*.

At four bells the strong wind split the *Java's* foretopsail, but the topmen immediately took it in and then bent a new one. By seven bells Lambert decided to send down topgallant yards and strike topgallant masts. The rest of the evening saw the squalls increase, later accompanied by rain and lightning. Still, regardless of the weather's challenge, the day's run reflected about 115 miles' progress.

The last four days of November were more discouraging in regard to wind strength and direction.

"After all, gentlemen," Chads explained to the army officers, shrugging his shoulders, "we may not *quite* be in the Doldrums—that region of low pressure and precious little wind to be found around the equator—but we *are* somewhat near the region called the Variables or the Horse Latitudes, where we might expect variable or shifting winds, with your occasional calm, squall, or rain."

"'Doldrums,' Mr. Chads?" asked Major Walker. "I've heard that term, sure, but never quite understood it."

"The nor'east and sou'east trade winds," replied Chads, "meet somewhat north of the equator, and this meeting creates an area or region called the Doldrums. There's often terrible thunder, lightning, water-spouts, frequent rains, and a continual succession of calms. Ships can sometimes be detained for days—or weeks—as they wait for a wind to carry 'em back into the trades."

"Is this a certainty? Will it happen to us?"

"It may or may not," said Chads, again shrugging his shoulders. "It's certain that it often happens, but just as often a ship's fortunate and avoids the situation. Ships occasionally cross far to the west, which sometimes helps. We'll do just that, and we may be fortunate."

Friday saw some of Mr. Chads' variable and light winds, then more squalls and heavy rain, such that the ships averaged only around two knots' speed for the entire twenty-four hour period. Saturday was essentially a repetition; the only reportable events that day were the flogging of landman John Kelly—eighteen lashes for uncleanliness—and the sighting of four strange sails. Lambert declined to chase any of them, not for lack of interest but for lack of wind. On Sunday the variable and light winds continued, and later in the day rain appeared which then turned into squalls, all of which contributed to cap the day's run at eighty miles. At five bells in the forenoon watch, the day still shining fair, Captain Lambert formally mustered the crew per divisions and inspected the men. And—as he carried no chaplain—he personally conducted an abbreviated church service which largely consisted of hymn singing. Monday, the last day of November, brought forth slightly better weather but enabled no greater speeds. At five bells in the morning watch the *Selvagens*—the Dry Salvages islets—were sighted at five leagues' distance and remained in sight until three bells in the first dog watch. They excited no real interest among the veteran seamen: the farthest points south of the Madeira archipelago, they were little more than barren and uninhabited rocks, were surrounded by dangerous reefs, had limited landing places, and had no sources of fresh water.

ILLUSTRATIONS

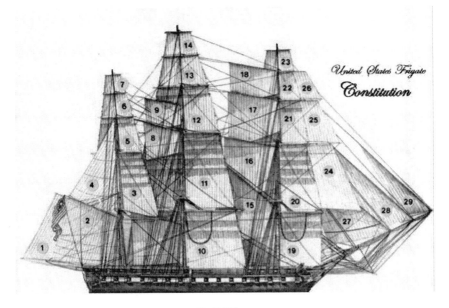

Sail Plan
United States Frigate *Constitution*

1 Spanker or Driver	11 Main topsail	21 Fore topgallant sail
2 Mizen sail	12 Main topgallant sail	22 Fore royal sail
3 Mizen topsail	13 Main royal sail	23 Fore skysail
4 Gaff topsail	14 Main skysail	24 Fore topsail studdingsail
5 Mizen topgallant sail	15 Main topmast staysail	25 Fore topgallant studdingsail
6 Mizen royal sail	16 Middle staysail	26 Fore royal studdingsail
7 Mizen skysail	17 Main topgallant staysail	27 Jib
8 Mizen topgallant staysail	18 Main royal staysail	28 Outer jib
9 Mizen royal staysail	19 Foresail or Course	29 Flying jib
10 Mainsail or Course	20 Fore topsail	

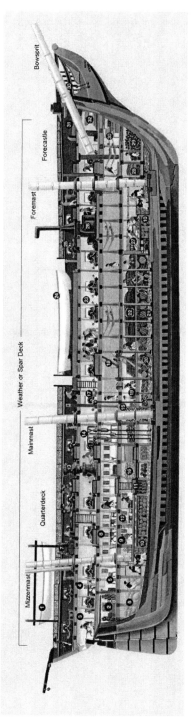

USS Constitution Cutaway

1. Cutter
2. Tiller room / Officers' stores
3. Captain's "great" cabin
4. Captain's dining cabin
5. Officers' cabins
6. Bread room
7. Steering wheel
8. Wardroom
9. Cockpit
10. Powder magazine
11. Spirit room
12. Warrant officers' cabins
13. Capstan
14. Chain (bilge) pumps
15. Shot lockers
16. Purser's / Clothing stores
17. Gun deck
18. Berth / Mess deck (crew)
19. Orlop deck
20. Hold
21. Ballast
22. Cable tier (anchor cables)
23. 24-pounder long guns
24. Launch
25. 32-pounder carronades
26. Galley stove / Galley
27. Sail room / Bosun's stores
28. Gunner's stores
29. Rigging blocks room
30. Sick bay
31. Manger
32. Manger
33. Heads (crew)

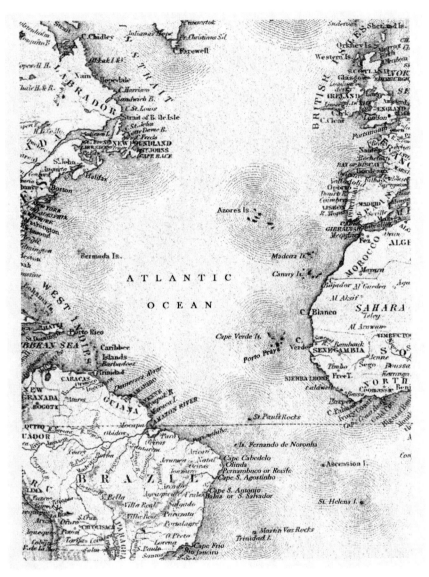

Chart of the Atlantic Ocean

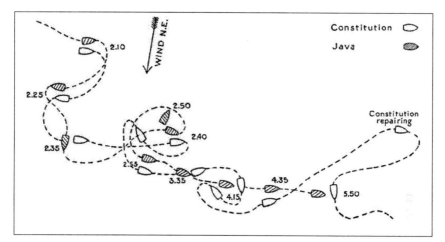

Track of Action between the USS *Constitution* and HMS *Java*
Original published in the *Naval Chronicle*, London, Vol.29, 1813

Commodore William Bainbridge
Commanding - USS Constitution
(1774 – 1833)

Lieutenant Henry Ducie Chads
First Lieutenant - HMS Java
(1788 – 1868)

Captain James Lawrence
Captain of the USS Hornet
(1781 – 1813)

Lieutenant General
Thomas Hislop
(1764 - 1843)

The USS Constitution today

CHAPTER 15

EASTERN ATLANTIC OCEAN

Eastern Atlantic Ocean
41 nautical miles north of the Canary Islands
29° 15' N 17° 43' W
Tuesday, December 1st, 1812
5:00 a.m.
Fine weather; moderate breezes

Tuesday, the first of December, began as a beautiful day. Steady and fair winds predominantly came from the south and south-southeast. These pleasantly drove HMS *Java* and her convoy along at almost seven knots, with the courses for the most part west-southwest and west-by-north. At eight bells in the forenoon watch, just as the hands were being piped to breakfast, the fore-topgallant lookout sighted the Peak of Tenerife to the south, as well as the northeast end of La Palma Island west-by-south-½-south.

"Gentlemen," smiled Hislop as he joined the master and the first lieutenant at the rail. "I perceive the famous Canary Islands are visible. I wonder if you'd be so kind as to tell me something about them."

"Certainly, General," replied Chads as both naval officers touched their hats in salute. "They're a considerable collection of small islands and rocks. There are, however, some significant ones, and they are seven. They lie from east to west, thus we'll find Lanzarote, Fuerteventura, Gran Canaria, Tenerife—of course you know Tenerife, sir, the largest of the islands, where Lord Nelson lost his arm in 1797—Gomera, La Palma, and Hierro. As he set out for the New World, in 1492, Columbus put into the port of Las Palmas on Gran Canaria, and as another story goes it was from Las Palmas that Sir Francis Drake had a Spanish cannonball fly through his ship's gallery—and right between his legs—in 1585."

"What?" exclaimed Hislop.

"Well, sir, true or not, it does make for a good story," said Robinson with a grin. "And to amuse you even more, you must bear in mind that the charming residents have named one of the islands 'La Palma,' while at the same time they call the capital of Gran Canaria Island 'Las Palmas.' They also require you to distinguish 'Santa Cruz,' the capital of La Palma, from 'Santa Cruz,' the capital of Tenerife."

"For the most part, sir," Chads interjected, "the islands are somewhat barren and even semi-desert. Fuerteventura is, after all, only about twenty-four leagues from northern Africa. The air temperature varies from eighty-six degrees to sixty-eight, and at times the peak of Tenerife—*El Pico de Teide*—has snow on it. The height of El Teide is considerable. Its perpendicular height, from actual measurement, is said to be 13,000 feet, though I really believe it to be somewhat less. Regardless, the nor'west trade winds are dominant in the islands between April and October, then shift further south."

"What do you know of their commerce, pray?" asked Hislop.

"Sir," replied Chads, "despite the general scarcity of water, they manage to produce some vegetables and fruit—grapes, dates, avocados, bananas—and they do have some goats, sheep, and cattle. The sea between the islands and the coast of Africa is rich in fish— particularly tuna, cod, bream, and mullet. The islands have a remarkable number of birds—I've heard as many as two-hundred different kinds—to include, of course, the canary."

"Of course, as the islands get their name from the bird."

"Well, um, no sir," replied Robinson. "In point of fact, just the opposite. It's said that an ancient expedition from Mauritania, some years prior to the birth of our Lord, found large dogs roaming the island. Someone therefore decided to call the islands *Insulae Canium*—the Islands of the Dogs—and so that name comes down to us presently as *Las Islas Canarias*. So, clearly, it's the birds that're named for the islands."

"Mr. Robinson, you astonish me!" laughed Hislop.

"Yes, sir, indeed," said Chads, smiling. "The master's knowledge is truly encyclopedic."

"Well, I could wish to land and look about your *Insulae Canium*," said Hislop, "but Captain Lambert tells me he intends no such thing."

"No, sir," replied Chads. "We're only a fortnight from home and our stores and water remain plentiful. We'll merely thread our way through these islands—and pass by La Palma and between Gomera and Hierro—as we continue south. However, in another fortnight or thereabouts we very well may come-to at the Cape Verde Islands or, as the Portuguese say, the *Ilhas do Cabo Verde*."

At noon Mr. Robinson took advantage of the particularly fine day. He gathered the master's mates and midshipmen and, all equipped with sextants or quadrants, they tried their hands at shooting the sun—attempting to find the ship's latitude by measuring the altitude to the sun. This was part of the master's continual efforts to improve their seamanship and navigational skills, but after ten minutes he abruptly dismissed them below to their dinners. As he walked over to Chads he shook his head with irritation.

"Well, sir, the observations of this day're pretty good—the air's extremely clear—but we might've made more, and better, if proper assistance could've been had from the young gentlemen. They seem to constantly seek nothing but pleasure for themselves, and as they've chosen to make this exercise a fatigue instead of a pleasure, well then, their observations cannot be depended upon!" Robinson touched his hat and strode off, muttering to himself. Chads hid a smile by looking out to sea.

By two bells the fine weather began to give way to clouds, fresh breezes, and squalls—which required three reefs in the topsails by seven bells, and limited the afternoon and evening runs to an average of just less than four knots.

The weather moderated after midnight and into the morning, and by eight bells the day shown fine with light winds from the southwest and west-southwest. Prior to being sent to breakfast the ship's company was mustered by divisions and once again witnessed a flogging: ordinary seaman John Callahan, eighteen lashes for disobedience of orders. Later in the day, frustrated by the light winds (the ships then only able to make two knots), Lambert again decided to turn the calm sea and fine weather to advantage and held another all-hands exercise of the great guns and small arms. On the whole it went much as it had eight days earlier. The gun crews were still extremely slow and clumsy, yet it would be unfair to say that there was no discernable improvement. Both the half-dozen simulated firings, and the two live firings after, were done with slightly faster times. And the men definitely showed more familiarity and even some confidence in handling the cannon and the other equipment. They also showed some sense of teamwork in the exercise, not anywhere equal to their growing proficiency in sail handling, but it pleased the officers all the same. It pleased the crew, too, as those not immediately reporting on watch queued for their late issue of grog and equally late supper; they talked and joked in extremely high spirits.

The early morning on Thursday brought cloudy weather and light breezes, which moved the ships forward at a little more than three knots. Sunrise, in turn, brought the sight of the Island of Ferro to the lookouts.

"Land ho! Land, three points off the larboard bow! Deck there, land, six or seven leagues distant!"

Lieutenant Aplin, the officer of the watch, inwardly congratulated himself for not having to decide whether to wake the captain with this news. The captain was already present on deck talking to General Hislop. Awakened earlier by the setting of the morning watch, neither officer had been able to get back to sleep.

"Sir, as we expected that'll be Ferro Island—the smallest and furthest southwest of the Canary Archipelago. It's a small island, yet it strangely possesses a goodly number of names."

"How so, Captain?" queried Hislop.

"Well, the earliest inhabitants—I believe called Guanches—called it 'Hero' in their language. I've no idea what, in this context, 'hero' would signify in English. However, when the Spaniards later came to dominate in the islands, they altered the name to the similar 'Hierro,' which as you know in Spanish means 'iron.' And, to make this more complex, among sailors the Latin word 'ferrum'—which also means 'iron'—subsequently gained widespread usage instead of Hierro, and thus we say 'Ferro' in present usage."

"If I'm not mistaken," said Hislop, "I believe I've also heard it called 'Meridian Island?'"

"Yes, sir, quite so," replied Lambert, "or, in Spanish, *La Isla del Meridiano*. This's because for several centuries Ferro's western tip, Orchilla Point, was understood to be the far western edge of the known world. The point also appeared to have no detectable magnetic variation, so sometime in the early 1600s the Spanish chose it as their prime meridian for navigation."

"What's the island like?" asked Hislop.

"I've never landed there myself, sir," said Lambert, "but the Master tells me it's quite beautiful, unspoiled, and tranquil. The coastline's rocky. The central plateau's very high, heavily wooded, and home to some cattle, horses, and goats. The town's called Valverde, and's said to be virtually unchanged since Columbus visited there just prior to his second voyage to the New World."

The rest of the day passed uneventfully, with El Ferro continuously in sight until darkness fell. Friday opened with extremely fine weather and variable light winds, but the breezes died out completely by four bells in the forenoon watch, which caused the three ships to slow to a complete stop and even to "box the compass:" their bows pointed this way and that; their sails hung limply from the yards. The calm lasted for almost eleven hours, until about two bells in the first watch, when some light airs finally came in from the north.

Friday's total run unsurprisingly measured only thirty-four miles, and by four bells in the forenoon watch Saturday gave every indication of offering only slightly better progress. In view of the light breeze and flat sea, Lambert once again ordered a gunnery and small-arms exercise. As it turned out, he, Chads, and Marshall all agreed there was little change from the drill three days before; but, if there were no visible improvement, at least there was no visible regression. What did catch everyone's eye was the subsequent small-arms exercise engaged upon by the master's mates and midshipmen. The army officers were particularly amused. Major Walker quietly remarked, "They appear much like the London Trainband of my grandfather's day, what with their muskets sometimes on one shoulder and then sometimes on the other. Ha!"

Fortunately, as before, there were only minor injuries reported. However, it was also reported that the sponger of one of the gundeck eighteen pounders, a landman named Thomas Hall, had not appeared for duty and, in fact, had been missing since "up hammocks" had been piped at seven bells. As soon as the guns were secured, Lambert ordered the crew to muster by divisions and then called for a painstaking search of the ship—particularly those spaces below the berth deck. This type of search assumed everything and nothing in its thoroughness—the missing man might have taken ill while below, or may have fallen down a hatchway, or for some reason might be hiding, or even may have been murdered and his body hidden by others. Thus, carrying lanterns, the officers and crew examined every square foot of the ship—the hold, the cable tiers, the storerooms, the bilges—but to no avail. Hall was missing, and at this point could only be assumed to have fallen overboard during the night, sadly unseen and unheard.

The first part of Sunday provided moderate if somewhat variable breezes, which allowed the ships to proceed at four to five knots. The remainder of the day saw the breezes fall off completely, which ultimately caused a seven-hour stretch that measured only one knot at each cast of the log. At four bells in the forenoon watch the Javas formally mustered by divisions, and Captain Lambert somberly read to them the Articles of War. When he had finished he closed the book and, as he looked around, picked up a second.

"Men, as all of us well know, we seem to have lost a shipmate. Although new to the sea, Tom Hall was a good lad and a good messmate. As such it's only fit and proper that we observe his untimely passing in a formal way. I haven't the words myself, but I've found some I think'll do." He opened the second book and began to read in a clear, carrying voice, although one somewhat softer than he had used for the Articles.

> When the Church buries a man, that action concerns me. All mankind is of one author and is one volume; when one man dies, one chapter is not torn out of the book, but translated into a better language; and every chapter must be so translated. God employs several translators; some pieces are translated by age, some by sickness, some by war, some by justice; but God's hand is in every translation, and His hand shall bind up all our scattered leaves again for that library where every book shall lie open to one another...

Lambert paused for a moment while he skipped a few lines in the text.

> No man is an island, entire of itself; every man is a piece of the continent, a part of the main. If a clod be washed away by the sea, Europe is the less, as well as if a promontory were...Any man's death diminishes me because I am involved in mankind...therefore never send to know for whom the bell tolls; it tolls for thee...

> No man hath affliction enough that is not matured... and...the bell that tells me of his affliction digs out and applies to me, if by this consideration of another's danger I take mine own into contemplation, and so secure myself by making my recourse to God, who is our only security.

The first three hours of Monday, the seventh of December, delivered another dead calm and a flat sea, with the ships stopped with their bows to the southeast. However, the wind sprang up around eight bells in the middle watch. It filled the slack sails, and suddenly the *Java* began to glide forward at four and then even five knots. But it was just an hour later that an angry Lambert was forced to heave-to and wait, for the sunrise brought no sight of one of the convoy, the *Cape Packet*. Visibility was even further reduced by the haze that had unusually come forth with the sun. However, around four bells in the forenoon watch the missing Indiaman finally came into view to windward, whereupon the *Java* and the *Atlantic* filled and made sail. At six bells the silver calls of the bosun and his mates piped "defaulters," and thus the ship's company mustered to witness punishment: landman William Long received ten lashes for neglect of duty and ordinary John Conway was given six for disobedience of orders. These were serious charges, but both men benefitted from reduced sentences which stemmed from their division officers eloquently speaking up for them.

The remainder of the day passed slowly with many of the crew employed in mending reefs and reeving new tiller ropes. The ships proceeded equally slowly. The hazy air and light winds barely provided steerageway and at times the winds ceasing altogether. The next day was much the same, seeing practically the same wind and weather as the last. Yet, around midnight the wind finally picked up, which enabled the last hour of the day to record a speed of six knots. Regardless, the overall progress of these two days was disappointing; even added together they only reflected about one-hundred miles.

Before he turned-in Lambert took a glass of Malmsey to his desk and added to the serial letter he was writing to his wife. It was a long letter, seventeen pages at this point, which awaited some future posting via some homeward-bound ship.

H.M. Frigate <u>Java</u>
8<u>th</u> December, 1812

Dear Caroline,

Today we served Wine to the ship's Company, the Beer being all expended to two Casks, which I intend to keep some time longer as the whole has proved good to the very last Cask.

I continue to be anxious over my overall weak and lubberly Crew, and indeed I often lie awake with worry. Their Gunnery is still quite poor, though I admit they do improve with each exercise of the Guns and Small Arms. And, it would be unfair and untrue if I told you the Crew's Skills as Seamen are not improving as well. However, their general level of Training falls far short of where it needs to be. For example, in the last four Days we were taken Aback no less than five times!

Now, I shall admit to you, dear Caroline, that the Winds have been unusually Variable and chancy, and not always the Regular and Prevailing winds we should expect from the Northeast Trades in these latitudes; such frequent Shifting does certainly increase the odds of being taken aback, but the Officers and Crew really ought to be better able to watch for the Changes and take appropriate Measures. Thankfully, we have not yet encountered a hard Gale nor a true Storm. Well, the Skills of sea-faring Men are of a laborious and dexterous Nature which can only be acquired by industrious application. God grant us enough Time to complete that process of Acquisition!

At Noon two days ago I found the Ship, by observation, ten miles ahead of the Log, which I suppose may be owing to a current setting in the same direction as the Trade Wind. Yet today we experienced a current setting Northeast-by-East, of about one-fourth of a Mile an hour. This somewhat surprised me, for I had formed the idea that the set of the Current should have been in the direction of our Course; but many careful observations with the Current-log, and the difference between our Astronomical observations, the Chronometers, and our Dead Reckoning gave the same results.

Tonight we saw the Sea exhibit remarkable Phosphorescence. My dear, seldom have I ever seen such a Display! Its brilliance was so great that it might truly be said to have the Appearance of being on Fire. The Army officers were completely amazed. My dear Caroline, I so wish you could have seen it, too!

The next three days were reasonably uneventful and in fact almost pressed copies of each other. The days' first parts saw moderate breezes and fine weather, and the remainders saw fresh breezes and haze. The winds were fairly constant, from the east and northeast; the courses were southwest-by-south, south-southwest-½-west, and southwest-by-west. While she occasionally reached the admirable speed of nine knots, the *Java* averaged around seven—still quite respectable—as she had to make and shorten sail as necessary for the Indiamen to keep up. Little disturbed the warship's set routines. Wednesday, at two bells in the forenoon watch, saw the crew formally mustered per divisions, while Thursday morning had the hands stow the booms afresh as well as lower and then sway back up the mainyard in order to refit its rigging.

Friday, however, had the small excitement of two landfalls. At six bells in the forenoon watch the lookouts discovered the small *Ilha do Sal*, the most northwesterly of the *Ilhas do Cabo Verde*—the Cape Verde Islands. This sighting prompted Lambert to haul to the wind on the starboard tack and have the cables bent to the anchors, for he had decided to stop briefly at Porto Praya, on the *Ilha de Santiago*—the Island of Saint Jago—which he now expected to raise early the next day. Thus it was no real surprise, late Friday afternoon, when the lookouts further noticed the north point of the *Ilha da Boavista* (the most easterly of the Cape Verdes) bearing southeast-½-south. The ships ranged down the west side of the island at a distance of about three miles. Chads had the deep-sea lead broken out, but they found no ground even with its forty fathoms of line. Hislop, carefully studied the island with his glass and then commented that there was little he could see but hills, sand, and palm trees.

"All too true, General," replied Robinson, "Boavista—or as we more commonly say, Bonavista—has been likened to a small piece of the Sahara Desert adrift in the Atlantic Ocean."

Saturday morning opened a day of fresh breezes and haze. At six bells in the middle watch the *Java* hauled to the wind on the starboard tack, and then, at two bells in the morning watch, she wore. Daylight helped the lookouts see the Island of Saint Jago, bearing southwest-by-south, distant four miles, pretty much where it was expected to be. This occasioned some discussion amongst the ship's company. Such talk even came into the wardroom as, between bites of breakfast, Major Walker sought some insights from the master.

"Mr. Robinson, I understand we raised Porto Praya early this morning. Could I further impose upon you for whatever information on the place you feel appropriate for us to know?"

"Certainly. I'm always at your service," replied Robinson as he put down his fork and wiped his mouth. "Porto Praya's a small, open bay situated on the south side of Saint Jago. Saint Jago's the most inhabited of the Cape de Verd Islands. It's long been a place where outward-bound warships, Guineamen, and Indiamen (English, French, and Dutch) have been accustomed to touch for water and refreshments. The town has a fort on top of a hill 200 feet above the sea. It commands the harbor, and were it properly mounted and garrisoned, it'd be a place of great strength. However it's almost in ruins. Of the other buildings, the gaol's the best, and next to that, the church. The governor resides in a small wooden barracks, at the far end of the plain, which commands a view of the bay and shipping." He drank a little of his coffee.

"Saint Jago presents a different appearance from Madeira—particularly the southeastern portion. There're many high peaks and mountains in its center which afford a fine background for the barren coastal scenery. The town of Porto Praya's situated on an elevated piece of tableland and looks well from the anchorage. The bay's not much exposed to the prevailing winds, but there's generally a swell that sets in which often makes landing unpleasant and difficult. The only decent landing-place is a small rock some distance from the town. It's under a high bank on which there's the fort I mentioned. Between this bluff and the town is an extensive valley in which are many date-palms, cocoanuts, and a species of aloe. Oh, thank you," he said as Captain Wood passed him some bacon.

"Upon landing, a stranger's immediately surrounded by a large number of the inhabitants with fruit, vegetables, chickens, turkeys, and monkeys—all who press him with bargains, and who're all willing to take anything for the purpose of obliging the customer. The walk from the landing to the town's quite tiring, and the road's deep with sand. The houses are mostly whitewashed stone, one storey high, partly thatched or tiled, and in general appearance resemble those inhabited by the lower orders in Madeira—but they're often not as nice. The streets are wide, and in the center's a large public square. The houses and streets're filthy in the extreme, and everywhere pigs, fowls, and monkeys appear to claim equal rights with the occupants and owners." He pushed his plate away and toyed with his napkin.

"The population's made up of an intermixture of descendants from the Portuguese, island natives, and negroes from the adjacent coast. Porto Praya contains around 2,000 people, I daresay. The language spoken appears to be a jargon formed by a mixture of the Portuguese and negro dialects, while most of the blacks speak their native tongues."

"Do I correctly understand that the captain intends to visit the port, and that we might possibly go ashore?" asked Woods, hopefully.

"That's the captain's intention," interjected Chads, who knew Praya fairly well but nonetheless sat at the table, sipped his coffee, and enjoyed Robinson's travelogue.

"Capital, Mr. Chads, capital!" said Walker. "Well then, Master, pray tell what sights must we see if given any opportunity at all."

"The first and greatest sight must be the town's common fountain," replied Robinson. "It's half a mile distant in a valley to the west of the town. It barely can supply the wants of the inhabitants and visiting shipping. Therefore, the drinking water's tolerable, but scarce, and it's hard to get it off shore on account of the great surf on the beach. This watering place's surrounded by a variety of tropical trees, such as dates, cocoanuts, bananas, papayas, sugarcane, tamarinds, grapes, oranges, and limes. When compared with the surrounding lands it may be termed an enchanting spot. What adds to the effect on a stranger is the novelty of the things that're brought together. On one side you find blind beggars, dirty soldiers, and naked children. On the other there are lepers, boys with monkeys, half-dressed women, assess not bigger than sheep, and hogs of a mammoth breed."

"How strange," remarked Walker.

"Yes, sir, so it is," replied Robinson. "Here, you find sailors watering and washing, chatting, and laughing. There, you see a group of *far niente* natives of all sizes, shapes, and colors—half clothed—with turbaned heads and handkerchiefs of many colors. In fact, the costumes here are so various that it scarcely can be said that any one of them's peculiar to the island. The men generally wear a white shirt and trousers with a dark vest. Others go quite naked except for a straw hat. Others again are in loose shirts. The children, for the most part, go naked. Regardless, all of the people are eager to derive some benefit from meeting you, particularly the beggars, who are equally obstinate with those found elsewhere and are certainly great objects of commiseration."

"When any vessels are in port, a market's held daily in the morning. The square in which it's held is quite large with a cross in the center. The market isn't of much extent, but a great variety of tropical fruits of the kinds I mentioned before are for sale in small quantities—as well as vegetables. These consist of cabbage, beans, pumpkins, squash, corn, potatoes, yams, and mandioca. Meat's not usually for sale—or I should say the only articles of this description are chickens four or five days old and some eggs. In order to obtain beef it's necessary to buy the cattle at the cattle-yard, where, on previous notice being given, you may choose those that suit you for slaughter. They are, in general, of small size and dark colored, and weigh between 250 and 300 pounds. Those I've seen were from the interior of the island where they're said to thrive well. Bullocks must be purchased with cash money, and the price at the time I was last here was twelve Spanish dollars a head."

"I've observed no trades except one small carpenter's establishment. A few shops're supplied with cotton, hardware, and the like. There are likewise a number of little wine shops where they also sell fruit—which they usually have in great plenty. The basic exports from the island are salt, wine, hides, goats' skins, and orchilla—the latter is a government monopoly."

"The climate of the Cape de Verds is said to be generally healthy—though exceedingly warm. It's subject to fevers which generally take place during the rainy months of July and August. There's an indistinctness in the atmosphere, that I've not experienced elsewhere, which causes everything to be ill-defined even though the day might be fair. The same appearance comes after a shower of rain as before. The temperature of the air's often 75 to 80 degrees Fahrenheit, and of the water around 80 degrees. The —"

At this moment the master was interrupted by Midshipman Martin Burke who crashed through the wardroom door. He steadied himself, blanched from the frowns and hard faces he observed, and hastily drew himself to rigid attention as he addressed the first lieutenant.

"I - I beg pardon, sir," he stuttered, "but the captain desires you—with his compliments—to come on deck when convenient. We've sighted a strange sail to the east'ard. She hoisted American colors upside down—and then let fly her sheets. We answered with our colors. It's very strange, sir."

"Is she a ship of war, Mr. Burke?" inquired Chads.

"Oh, sorry sir, no—she appears to be a merchantman, and she's makes no effort to escape us."

"Very well," said Chads, "please give the captain my respects and I'll be there directly."

Moments later—in fact essentially on Midshipman Burke's heels—Chads gained the quarterdeck and strode over to the captain.

"Ah, Henry, look at what we've stumbled upon," said Lambert as he proffered his glass. "American—in distress, apparently."

The *Java* ran down towards the American while she simultaneously took in sail, then hove-to close aboard.

"What ship's that?" called the officer of the watch— Lieutenant Buchanan—through his speaking trumpet.

"*William*, of New York," came the flat reply, "one day out from Bonavista. What're you?"

"Frigate *Java*. You'll kindly stand by for our boat."

Lambert gazed about his quarterdeck and found his eye linger upon Lieutenant Sanders.

"Mr. Sanders, a word."

Sanders sprinted over and touched his hat. "Sir?"

"Gather four topmen, a half-dozen marines, and jump into the blue cutter. Go take possession of that ship and see just what it is that distresses 'em."

"Aye aye, sir."

Lambert turned back to Chads. "Henry, let's also down the launch. Pick an older mid and eight reliable hands to man the prize. Let 'em gather some belongings and give 'em our latitude and longitude—in case we get separated. Their orders'll be to merely sail in company."

Fifteen minutes later Sanders stepped onto the deck of the Yankee. The master of that vessel, an older, shorter man, rose to meet him from where he sat on a crate.

"So, you're an Englishman, I guess?"

"I guess I am, too," replied Sanders, who tried not to smile while he also tried to imitate the American's nasal twang.

"Well, I thought we shouldn't be long in these waters afore we met some o' ye old-country sarpents. No offense."

"Oh, no," said Sanders, "not in the least, dear sir, and it'll make no difference in the long run. I guess I need to tell you that your vessel's a prize to His Britannic Majesty's ship the *Java*."

The American sighed heavily, and after a moment's pause said, "I know it. I'm a ruined man. I needed help from some vessel. I just prayed it'd not be English."

"I'm sorry for you, sir," replied Sanders, and he meant it. "From where do you come, and to where are you bound?"

"Come from the salt pans of Bonavista just to the north, an' bound home for New York. And that's what be our cargo—highest-quality Povoação Velha salt."

"What might your outward cargo have been?" asked Sanders, curious.

"Salted fish, flour, an' tobacco," was the answer.

"You've signaled distress, and you mentioned needing succor," said Sanders.

"Aye, Mister Lieutenant. We'd scarce completed loading when a gusty tradewind joined up with the already powerful current, causin' us to drag anchors. The next thing we knew the cables—too old, an' rotten maybe—parted under the strain, the one right after the other. Fortunately we found ourselves drivin' out to sea rather than drivin' towards the island. So here am I, with no anchors at all an' no length of serviceable cable even if I did."

"Well, sir, I'll say it again—I'm heartily sorry for your misfortunes—which now include the capture of your ship. In fact, I must now desire you and your men to collect your clothes and private ventures. My captain will presently send over a prize crew, and you'll need to remove to the *Java*."

"No need to be sorry, young man. You're just doin' your duty."

Sanders left the marines and hurried his cutter back to the *Java* to explain the situation. He passed the launch, with Midshipman J. R. Brigstocke and the prize crew, as they crossed in opposite directions.

"As you'd heard, Captain," said Sanders a few minutes later, "she's the *William*, as full of Bonavista salt as is possible. They'd just completed taking it all aboard when a gust of wind and a stiff current helped 'em part with both their anchors."

"Very well, Mr. Sanders," replied Lambert, "Thank you. As you saw, I've just sent Mr. Brigstocke and some hands to take her in charge and sail in company. Kindly go across once more, take out the *William*'s people, and retrieve your marines." Sanders saluted and walked off.

"Bonavista salt, says he!" exclaimed Chads as he rubbed his hands together. "Captain, I give you joy of your prize. She'll turn a pretty penny. About 300 tons, I should think, and about fifteen for a crew."

By four bells in the forenoon watch the *Java* had acquired a dozen downcast Americans along with their sea-chests. At least they nominally were Americans, for one man, Richard Robinson, was British and promptly volunteered for the *Java*'s crew, and four of the others were Italians. Regardless, everything was soon settled and organized sufficiently to permit the ships to get underway. Two hours later saw all four ships of the convoy approach the southern tip of Saint Jago and enter the harbor of Porto Praya. They came to anchor at the end of the bay, and as the bustle of the operation died down the master walked over to Lambert to give the formal report.

"Sir," he said as he touched his hat, "we've come-to in eight fathoms water with coarse ground. Marks at the anchorage are Fort São Filipe west-by-south-½-south, five miles distant, and the church in Praya-town close-by, north-northwest-½-west. And, we've got fresh breezes and hazy weather."

As quickly as possible the *Java* hoisted out several boats and sent them off to assist the *William*, carrying over to her a stream anchor and a cable. For the next hour and a half the boats' crews and the prize crew, led by the bosun, Mr. Humble, bent the anchor to the cable and secured the cable to the *William*'s windlass. That done, the anchor was cast and an appropriate length of cable veered away. The was hardly accomplished, however, before the anchor came home. It dislodged itself from the ground due to wind and current, and so the whole process had to be repeated. Shockingly, it promptly happened again; the men quickly recovered and then let the anchor go one more time. At this point a dozen telescopes on board the *Java* were focused upon the *William*'s bows, and for a half-hour all seemed to be finally secure. But at precisely seven bells in the afternoon watch the *William* was again, clearly, dragging the anchor. The ship and the *Java*'s boats noticeably dropped to leeward within Praya's bay.

"God damn and *blast* it!" shouted Lambert as he slammed his fist on the railing and tossed his telescope—an expensive achromatic Dolland telescope—into the scuppers. "What the bloody hell's the matter with that pack of God-damned lubbers? The next thing you know the sun'll set and in the darkness she'll be aground and lost!"

Chads started to say something about the coarse bottom perhaps completely foul and rocky under the *William*, but bit his tongue as Lambert spun on him.

"To hell with it, Henry! It's just been one damned thing after another this whole bloody commission! To hell with it! Call all hands this instant, weigh anchor, and make sail. Do you comprehend my meaning? No—we won't discuss it, Mr. Chads. Do what I say. Throw out a signal to the bloody Indiamen to do the same, and give 'em a gun to ensure they understand!"

The ship flew into a whirlwind of activity in obedience to the orders. Every officer and man was extremely concerned that the captain's blazing eye not fall upon him. Within an hour all four ships had weighed their anchors (a time consuming process even under the best of circumstances) and were under way. The *Java* briefly hove-to and recovered her boats, and as they came aboard their tired but talkative crews were shushed by their shipmates, who rolled their eyes significantly toward the quarterdeck. As the second dog watch was set, the convoy wore together and steadied upon a course of south-by-west, and all who cared to look now observed the southwest end of Saint Jago bearing northwest-½-west at three leagues distance.

On the forecastle Lieutenant Herringham came up to Lieutenant Chads, touched his hat, and spoke in a confidential voice.

"I beg pardon, Mr. Chads, but you'd mentioned the captain intended to stop at Porto Praya for water and vittles and, in fact, we'd come to anchor. Aren't we now to do that? Don't we need to replenish?"

"That *was* the captain's plan, Mr. Herringham," replied Chads, "but as you can see he's changed his mind. Our need for water and vittles isn't pressing. After all, we're not quite a month out of Spithead. It would've been good to pick up some fresh vegetables, fruit, and maybe a bullock or two—and of course it would've been equally well to take on board additional water—but certainly not issues of great need. And with any luck at all," he rapped the railing with his knuckle, "not more than another fortnight will see us close to the Brazilian coast—before we alter course for our run towards the Cape of Good Hope—so it'll be easy to put in at Recife or San Salvador to satisfy our wants. Dread naught, Mr. H. The captain knows what he's doing."

"Oh, yes, of course, sir," said Herringham, startled by this last. "Yes indeed, sir, thank you."

It was shortly after dawn on Sunday that Captain Lambert came on deck. The quarterdeck had just been washed, holystoned, and flogged dry. The officers present all moved to leeward, yielding the weather side for the captain's customary solitude. Despite the moderate easterly breeze and the perfect weather, the convoy had continuously made and shortened sail to accommodate the *William*—which had proved to be a shockingly slow sailer. At six bells in the morning watch, having studied the log-boards and noted the report of the log's last cast, Lambert crossed over to the officer of the watch. It was, this morning, Master and Commander

Marshall, who had early on volunteered to share in the watch-keeping rotation.

"Good morning to you, Captain Marshall."

"Good morning, sir," replied Marshall, touching his hat.

"I see we've averaged only five knots since we left Praya," said Lambert. "I've no intention of wallowing along at this rate until we reach Brazil. As soon as 'up hammocks' is piped and the officers and idlers are called, kindly veer out a cable and take the prize in tow. The *Java*'s a remarkably stout and fast ship. I believe she'll take the strain tolerably well."

"Aye aye, sir," replied Marshall, who then turned away to make the necessary preparations. While there was considerable labor involved to rouse out and haul aft an appropriate cable, it was not a particularly complex task. Indeed, by two bells in the forenoon watch, the *Java* drew the *William* forward at a full seven knots, which, as more and more sail was packed on, became eight knots and then even nine. The army officers, grouped at their oft-frequented post at the taffrail's leeward side, were amazed.

"Sir," remarked Major Walker to General Hislop, "I'd never have thought that such a sluggish craft on her own would be so graceful under tow, nor that as fine a ship as she is the *Java* could tow another vessel at such a prodigious speed." General Hislop merely smiled and shook his head in reply. After a moment he said, "It's well this's come to pass. I'm sure clipping along at this fine rate'll restore Captain Lambert to his usual pleasant self."

"Sir, since you mention it," said Captain Wood, "I was pro-foundly taken aback by the captain's outburst yesterday. Surely it was quite out of character?"

"Captain Wood," replied Hislop as he fixed him with a cold eye, "I've do not intend to judge nor justify to you an officer vastly your superior." He paused for a moment. "However, I'll say this: you shall find, in God's good time, that the burden of command can weigh heavily on an officer's shoulders. Moreover, this phe-nomenon can often be worse on naval officers than on we military officers."

"Sir?"

"Come, Wood, think. How often does a company of foot oper-ate independently from its parent battalion? How often does that battalion operate away from its regiment? An infantry captain's rarely far from his lieutenant colonel; the lieutenant colonel from his colonel; the colonel from his brigadier. It's similar with ships which sail together as a squadron or a fleet—in such case the commander of a ship's never out of sight or signal distance from his admiral. However, when a vessel's detached on independent duty, her commander bears the full weight of command, for his superior may be thousands of miles away—such as with us, right now. Since we passed by the Needles as we left Britain, Captain Lambert's been fully on his own. *Everything* is his problem and his responsibility. Even though I'm greatly his superior in rank, I'm merely a passenger on board his ship and I bear no responsibility nor authority whatsoever. And while he's got some good sea officers as his subordinates, he can delegate only a portion of his *authority* to them. He cannot share even one drop of his *responsibility*. I can tell you, from personal experience, a commander's nerves can become a little shredded over time. As you know, Mr. Lambert became a ship's captain quite young, and he's previously commanded three vessels in extremely intense actions against the enemy. Moreover, anxiety works like an acid, and a series of exasperations can have a corrosive effect on one's demeanor and outlook." He paused again to study the *William* at the other end of the tow rope.

"I really can't speak to Captain Lambert's burdens with any specificity, nor would I betray his confidences even if he'd shared them with me. However, I do know that the major concern he's got is the unusually large number of untrained men in the crew, on top of which's been the lack of time to weld all the men—trained and untrained alike—into an efficient team. The problems and even dangers of such a situation appear in the resulting general lack of fighting proficiency, as we've observed in the gunnery practice. They also appear in almost daily examples of clumsiness in regard to seamanship. While it's true that with every day which goes by the Javas do improve, and it's a certainty that with enough time the *Java* will evolve into a truly formidable fighting machine, she's not yet reached that enviable status. Thus, should we tomorrow come upon a competent enemy man-of-war, or should an unusual challenge from the sea or weather come upon us—a hurricane, for example—we aren't as ready as might be necessary. Thus, in this situation, I daresay our distinguished captain may display some occasional edginess. I'm quite sure I would, were I in his shoes."

CHAPTER 16

SOUTH ATLANTIC OCEAN

South Atlantic Ocean
Ilha de Fernando de Noronha
220 miles northeast of the Brazilian coast
3° 51' S 32° 25' W
Wednesday, December 2nd, 1812
11:00 a.m.
Pleasant weather; fresh trade winds

The U.S. ships *Constitution* and *Hornet* steered in for the body of the island. The *Ilha* had been discovered at four bells in the morning watch, bearing west-½-north, distant ten to twelve leagues. At dawn both ships had hoisted British colors in an attempt to confound any local Portuguese authorities. Then, at six bells in the forenoon watch, they slowly entered the Baía Santo Antonio on the island's northeast end. Commodore Bainbridge swept his glass around the bay, glanced up at his broad pendant to judge the wind's direction, and then motioned the first lieutenant to his side.

"Call all hands, Parker, if you please. Bring the ship to anchor."

"Aye aye, sir," replied Parker, who then turned to the bosun and the master to give the necessary orders. "Call all hands, Mr. Adams, and prepare to anchor. Mr. Nichols, stand by to furl the main t'gallant, royal, royal stuns'l, and the fores'l."

A short hour later found both ships riding at single anchor, taking in the rest of their sails, and swinging round to the wind and tide. Parker stepped over to Bainbridge, touched his hat, and gave him a report which told the commodore nothing he did not already know. He had been on deck for the entire evolution, but the formal report was customary and required, none the less.

"Sir, we've come-to with the larboard anchor in eighteen fathoms water, and we've veered out 120 fathoms of cable."

"Very well, Mr. Parker," replied Bainbridge. "Kindly signal the *Hornet* to proceed."

The smaller ship accordingly acted out the plan that Bainbridge and Lawrence had devised the day before; she promptly sent a boat on shore, which returned at four bells in the afternoon watch. Lawrence in turn came on board *Old Ironsides* to starboard, while a native catamaran simultaneously came alongside to larboard. Lawrence brought the welcome news that the Portuguese authorities would supply the squadron with whatever the island could offer. As if to accentuate this point, the three natives in the catamaran offered to sell their day's catch of fish.

"How did your interview with the Portuguese go?" inquired Bainbridge of Lawrence as he offered him a glass of Madeira. They both gazed out the great cabin's stern windows which, for the moment, faced the harbor's citadel.

"Very well indeed, sir," replied Lawrence, "despite the difficult landing through the surf." The younger man—in defiance of the eighty degrees air temperature and the staggering humidity—looked as tranquil and as cool as he always seemed to in his white hot-weather clothes. "I told the governor that I was Scott of the *Morgiana* and that you were Kerr of the *Acasta*, that we proceed from England to India, that we touch here for water and fresh provisions, and that we hope to rendezvous here in the next few days with the *Southampton*." The Americans had carefully crafted this deception to avoid possible reluctance to assist on the part of the Portuguese. While Portugal was officially neutral in regard to the war between Britain and the United States, she was very much an active ally to Britain in the war against the French. As a result, there was some question as to how hospitable Portuguese outposts would be to American ships—and particularly warships. Moreover, it was by no means certain that remote Portuguese outposts were even yet aware of the conflict, and Bainbridge was not interested in being the first to educate them. Thus, this ruse: there really was a British frigate *Acasta*, 48 guns, commanded by Captain Alexander Kerr and assigned to the Royal Navy's North American station; a real *Morgiana*, 18, Commander David Scott, assigned to the Jamaican station, and a real *Southampton*, 32, commanded by Sir James Yeo. With any luck the Portuguese would be deceived and willing to trade; more important, having been deceived they would not be able to pass along accurate or complete intelligence about the American squadron to any British ships that might soon follow.

"You think they've any suspicions?" asked Bainbridge.

"No, sir, not really," replied Lawrence. "The governor has no reason to doubt the story, and in any case I don't believe he'd even care. I think he's happy to sell some provisions and I think he's happy to have new faces to look at. He told me—his English's pretty good, but heavily accented—that we're the first ships to stop at the island in several months."

The island lay off the most northeastern part of the Brazilian coast. It was the "Botany Bay," as it were, of the Kingdom of Portugal. Its population consisted of a few natives, of some miserable and ill-clothed Portuguese prisoners, and a force of Portuguese guards in similar condition. Once a year a ship came from the mainland of Brazil, whereupon the Portuguese officers (and some of the guards) were exchanged, and new prisoners were incarcerated. There were no women among the exiles, nor on the island at all. None were permitted in order to make the exile even more unpleasant and lonely. There was not even anything that resembled a real boat on the island, so any movement to the mainland, by anyone, was impossible.

From a supply standpoint the island abounded in hogs, goats, fowls, corn, melons, coconuts, and a selection of other vegetables and fruits, as well as a great abundance and variety of fish in the surrounding waters.

For the Americans, Thursday started early if not bright. In the pre-dawn darkness, at one bell in the morning watch, the *Constitution* hoisted out her first, second, and third cutters, filled them with empty casks of different sizes, and sent them on shore—later also sending in the fourth cutter. It was a good day for it. Although it soon became extremely hot and humid, there were pleasant breezes from the east-southeast as well as a little cloud cover. While the boat crews were taken up with the watering effort, the rest of the crew was employed with work on the topmasts' rigging, painting the quarterdeck and forecastle, and sundry necessary tasks about the ship.

Unfortunately, the mission to obtain water was a failure. The island's prescribed watering place was near the beach, at the foot of the rock on which the citadel was placed. It was only with tremendous danger and difficulty that boats could approach, and subsequently that filled casks could be got back out through the surf. Some days, it would appear, wind and tide could make it all but impossible. Thus, at one bell in the second dog watch, the boats returned to the ship even though they had obtained no water on account of extremely high and heavy surf. Moreover, in the attempt, the second cutter had been stove in by the surf and was in a sinking condition, the fourth was seriously damaged, several of the seamen were nearly drowned, forecastleman Joe Roberts was much hurt being cast upon the rocks, and gun captain Davie Newark had his scalp split open by the chine of a falling water cask.

"Newark doesn't overly concern me," said Surgeon Evans later, "despite the bloody appearance of any such head laceration." He and Aylwin took their now-customary evening coffee as they leaned on the taffrail. "But Roberts' hand's another case entirely. They tell me both men had their injuries dressed by the surgeon of the garrison. He did a workmanlike job on Newark, but I surprisingly found Roberts' wound full of sand—and the tendons actually exposed."

"Perhaps he was distracted, or called away," replied Aylwin, equally mystified. "Which reminds me, one of the men in my division...Carter?"

"Ah, yes, Carter. He has some symptoms of scurvy. I don't put him on the sick list so that he mayn't have opportunity of being idle. I consider exercise of the first importance in his case. Yet, having said that, I'm worried about the short water and short rations. I may well see more symptoms of scurvy in other men quite soon, and I've stated such concerns to the commodore."

As it turned out, the Americans discovered there was no good landing place of any kind except for using a native catamaran—like the one the fishermen had used to approach the *Constitution* on her arrival. Common on the whole coast of Brazil, such things were essentially rafts made of a few logs which were steered by an oar and propelled by a lateen sail. A lee-board passed through the center which enabled the craft to go on a wind. Unfortunately there was only one of these conveyances allowed on the island—in fact, the same one they had already seen. It was kept in one of the forts, and it could only bear three men. Thus, the Americans found that despite the abundance of foodstuffs, water, and other things on the island, it was impracticable to obtain any significant amount of supplies. With great effort the boats were only able to bring off a small quantity of pigs, eggs, melons, cocoanuts, cashew nuts, and bananas. Two of the boats did make a second attempt at filling water, and this time returned with eight casks. The hands stowed the water and the few new provisions and, in so doing, did some rearranging of the hold. They found a barrel of sauerkraut had spoiled;

it was hoisted on deck, with due formality condemned, and thrown overboard.

The seemingly always-irritated and impatient commodore decided to depart on Friday afternoon. He assessed that the squadron had obtained all it practicably could from the island. This revised plan also meant that Bainbridge decided *not* to wait for the *Essex* to reach the rendezvous. He did, however, send in to the governor a letter addressed to Captain Yeo of HMS *Southampton*, but which was really intended for Captain Porter. Along with the basic rendezvous, Bainbridge had previously arranged this plan of subterfuge and clandestine communication between himself and Porter.

> My dear Meditteranean friend,
>
> Probably you may stop here; do not attempt to Water, it is attended with too much Difficulty. I learned before I left England that you intended to apply for a Station on the Brazil coast and that you would probably cruise from St. Salvador to Rio Janeiro. I should be happy to meet and converse on old affairs of Captivity. Recollect our Secret in those times, <u>that tried</u> men's souls.
>
> Your friend of his Majesty's ship <u>Acasta</u>,
> KERR.

After the American frigate *Philadelphia* was captured during the war with the Barbary states, Bainbridge and Porter had been imprisoned together at Tripoli for much of 1803-1804. The secret to which Bainbridge referred was the use of "sympathetic" or invisible ink, which is to say the careful employment of lime juice and heat. Thus, there was more to the message:

> I am bound off St. Salvador, thence off Cape Frio, where I intend to Cruise until the first of January. Go off Cape Frio, to the northward of Rio Janeiro and keep a lookout for me.
>
> Your friend.

When the *Essex* later arrived at Noronha, Porter played his part at being Yeo, so the governor dutifully gave him the letter. He knew exactly what to do, and thus it was easy for him to read that second part.

But that would be eleven days in the future. Today, at seven bells in the forenoon watch, the *Constitution* fired a gun and made a signal for all boats to return to their respective ships. At one bell in the afternoon watch, the first cutter came alongside towing a crude raft with a number of filled water casks. By three bells the water was stowed and the boats hoisted in. Both ships then weighed anchor and got under way. They stood off-and-on generally for the Brazilian coast, and by two bells in the first watch the *Ilha de Fernando de Noronha* bore northeast-by-east, four miles distant. At three bells the officer of the watch sent one of his midshipmen to the great cabin.

"Mr. Shubrick's duty, sir. The wind freshens, the *Hornet*'s off the larboard quarter distant one and one-half miles, and he'd like to set courses and topgallants."

"Very well, Mr. Fields," replied Bainbridge, "my compliments to Mr. Shubrick. He may make it so."

Saturday, the fifth of December, opened with clear, pleasant weather and brisk breezes. In fact the next ten days, except for brief rain showers on the sixth and the ninth, presented uniformly clear and pleasant weather with light to brisk breezes. This was so much so that after a few such days Mr. Evans was pleased to note in his diary that *the weather has been delightful ever since we have come on the coast of Brazil.*

As the squadron approached that coast, Bainbridge and Lawrence added some new evolutions to the ships' daily routines. Hands were stationed in the main chains with various lengths of lead lines to try for soundings. The frequency of the casts varied from once a day, once a watch, hourly, and even on the half-hours. The variance depended upon the perceived proximity of the shore, as well as the several captains' and watch officers' states of anxiety. Coupled with this precaution was a second one of significantly shortening sail (and at times heaving-to for several hours at a time) at night. None of the American officers had anything more than a general familiarity with the coast in this area. While Commodore Bainbridge desired to cruise for British shipping in sight of the land, particularly in the vicinities of Recife and San Salvador, he had no matching desire for his ships to run aground in the dark or on any uncharted reefs.

"In fact, Mr. Hoffman," said Bainbridge one morning. He

really more talked to himself than with the officer of the watch. "Take Pernambuco—or Recife as many call it. It's a principal seaport and the capital of its province, situated at the mouth of the Biberibe River. What actually forms the harbor is a large coral reef that runs in a line along the shore, and notwithstanding the reef itself, the harbor and approaches are shallow, often less than twenty feet."

"Why, sir, we draw at least twenty-three feet ourselves," observed the lieutenant, surprised.

"Really, Mr. Hoffman, you don't say."

Unsurprisingly, Lawrence and Bainbridge maintained a routine of daily musters, quarters, and gun exercises—now more than ever as the likelihood of action had considerably increased. These were generally held at the beginning of the second dog watch with the two ships a half to two-miles apart. The crews were also kept extremely busy as they made, set, and trimmed sail—as much as forty-five times in a twenty-four hour period. The ships coped with variable winds (some not at all favorable), while they tried to maintain formation with each other.

The two-day movement from Noronha Island to the mainland was fairly uneventful onboard the *Constitution* with the exception of several floggings. On Saturday, at six bells in the forenoon watch, all hands were called to witness marine private Anthony Reeves receive a dozen lashes, quartermaster James McCoy one dozen, and able seaman David Scott one-half dozen. Able William Mercer was placed in irons for attempted desertion at Noronha. After he heard their stories, as well as the positive remarks presented by their division officers, the commodore surprisingly excused and returned to duty quartergunner Charles Frank, able Timothy Cogstall, and William Burbank. Burbank was extremely lucky, as he was a private of marines accused of insolence to a superior officer, an offense which Bainbridge particularly hated.

It was just after dawn on the next day, Sunday the sixth, that the lookouts actually sighted the coast of mainland Brazil. The ships hove-to to take soundings, and thus found a depth of twenty-eight fathoms over a bottom of coral. Bainbridge, Nichols, and Aylwin observed on shore the ruins of a sixteenth-century fort, and concurred that they must be off Cape Cabedello, just at the mouth of the Parahiba River. This meant that they were about ninety miles north of Recife. The ships then stood off-and-on all day and through the night, moving slowly—no more than four knots—as they tacked and wore to the south and southwest. The crews saw a number of the native catamarans sailing about, mostly fishermen, some to windward and some to leeward. Early the next morning, at three bells, the lookouts sighted Cape Branco at ten leagues distance; by eight bells it was at six leagues and bore west-northwest.

"It presents the appearance of some of the high land in the Chesapeake Bay. Thankee, John," said Evans as he returned Aylwin's telescope. He had seen the well-wooded, cliffy point of white sand about one-hundred feet above the water. It was conspicuous when north or south of it, but it had blended into the land when they were directly offshore.

"It's said to be the point most farthest east in *all* of the Americas," replied Aylwin. "It's extremely hot with high humidity here, but as you've noticed this's relieved some by pleasant trade winds which come in from the ocean. This places us about eighty miles from Recife, and six-hundred from San Salvador."

The ships continued their slow progress as they stood off-and-on and beat to windward. They passed even more catamarans which were lying-to, fishing. The only unusual occurrence was the discovery that the foretopgallant yard was sprung; the topmen efficiently furled the sail, sent down the yard, got up a spare yard from the chains, rigged it, bent the sail, and sent it aloft. As if it took this as a cue, the next day saw the spindle of the trysail mast carry away, which required the topmen to briskly get the mast down, fit a new one, unbend the spanker, and bend another.

"I wonder what unusual tropical sights we shall see today?" Evans inquired of the wardroom while at breakfast.

"Well, Doctor," replied Nichols, "I expect the lookouts will discover the town of Olinda sometime this glass. It should bear west-by-south at about five or six leagues distance. It stands on the most elevated land in the vicinity of Pernambuco, and's remarkable for its white houses and churches interspersed with trees. Olinda Point's bordered by extensive reefs with breakers that stretch seaward nearly two miles—thus you've noticed we've slowed even more, and you hear the frequent cries of the leadsman? There's a lighthouse on Olinda Point, visible in clear weather to a distance of twelve miles. And then early this evening—if we maintain our present course and speed—I expect to come upon Recife."

"Ah yes," said Evans, "which's also known as Pernambuco."

"Just so, Doctor. It's the principal seaport of this region. Its commerce is significant; the exports consist chiefly of cotton, sugar, rum, hides, and dyewoods. Its imports are cotton and linen clothes, hardware, cutlery, silks, wine, flour, and salt fish. All kinds of supplies are to be obtained here and the prices are moderate. The fresh water's of good quality and can be gotten on board easily, and the only price for it is the cost of delivery. Many vessels—to include many British—put in there, particularly for water."

"I take it we shall not?" asked the junior marine lieutenant, William Freeman.

"No," replied Lieutenant Parker. "While the reef forms a fine harbor, it's not very deep. Mr. Hoffman, you know the commodore's mind on this. Pray enlighten us." Several of the officers, aware of Hoffman's earlier quarterdeck discussion with Bainbridge, laughed around bites of breakfast.

"Well, sir," said Hoffman reddening, "I—ah—the commodore feels the harbor too shallow for the *Constitution*."

"But surely we need victuals and water?" said Evans.

"Surely, Doctor," replied Parker, "but instead I daresay the commodore chooses to go into San Salvador—otherwise known as Bahia—which amazingly has an enormous, deep bay."

The ships continued beating to the southward in sight of the land, though they briefly hove-to mid-morning for Captain Lawrence to come on board *Old Ironsides*. The next day, the ninth, was a repeat of the last. However, at three bells in the forenoon watch, marine Private Pershaw was triced up to a grating and given four-dozen lashes—the sentence he had been awarded at his court-martial on November twenty-sixth.

"Merciful heavens," exclaimed Evans as all hands were dismissed from witnessing punishment, "was that not quite severe?"

"Yes indeed, Amos," replied Aylwin, "four dozen's quite severe. Yet, you'll reflect that his offense was pretty severe, too. I'll give him this, however; although quite young, he bore it much better than many hardy veterans would've done."

Around two bells in the afternoon watch a strange sail was discovered to the south. It stood toward the east, which stimulated both American ships to turn the second reefs out of their topsails, set their royals and courses, and begin a chase.

"So a *barque-rigged vessel* is in sight just ahead," grumbled Evans to himself as he lay brown paper soaked in vinegar on Pershaw's flayed back. "At least so say some of the wiseacres on board—with what justness we'll soon see."

"Arrumph?" mumbled Pershaw, his face muffled in the bedding of his sick-berth cot.

"Never mind," replied Evans, "I just find some of the men playing on my ignorance of sea affairs tiresome at times."

By seven bells the *Hornet* was alongside the chase, which hauled up her foresail and hove-to. *Old Ironsides* hove-to as well, four miles to the northwest, to await the result. Boats from the *Hornet* boarded the chase and then shortly returned, at which point the *Hornet* made sail to close the *Constitution*. Just before two bells in the first dog watch the *Hornet* ranged alongside. Both ships took in their royals, hauled up their courses, and laid their mizzen topsails to the mast. Dressed in his usual white, Lawrence leaned out over the railing and hailed Bainbridge through his speaking trumpet.

"She's a Portuguese brig from Pernambuco, loaded with salt. She departed Monday and's bound to Rio Janeiro. Her captain told me that the Portuguese here have just learned of the war between Britain and ourselves."

"Any news of shipping in Pernambuco?" called Bainbridge.

"Yes, sir. An American brig had just arrived loaded with flour, a ship from India had put in there in distress, two British ships were loading, and two others had recently sailed for London."

Just before darkness fell Evans and Aylwin were at the taffrail. They carefully juggled their coffee cups as well as Aylwin's telescope.

"See, right there, Amos," said Aylwin, who barely caught his cup from going over the rail while he helped Evans with the spyglass. "We're just abreast Cabo de Santo Agostinho, that promontory right *there*. You'll note the red cliffs with a church, and several cocoanut trees on the summit. The lighthouse can be seen up to a distance of twenty-four miles in clear weather. I'm told that at the point of the cape there's a brook of warm fresh water, called the Rill of the Ladies." Evans handed the glass back to Aylwin, who took it with some relief.

"Now then, this Cape Agostinho shouldn't be confused with Cabo de Santo Antonio, which we'll see in three or four days. Cape San Antonio's at the sou'west extreme of the land on the eastern side of the entrance to the great port of San Salvador. It's of moderate height, covered with trees, and can be seen from a distance of thirty miles in clear weather. Fort St. Antonio, with a lighthouse, stands on the tip of the cape, about 130 feet above high water."

On Thursday, the tenth, the commodore watched the sunrise and then ordered Lieutenant Hoffman to make all sail, course south-by-west, and to signal the *Hornet* accordingly. Thus, between six and seven bells in the morning watch, the Constitutions—imitated by the Hornets—packed on topsails, royals, staysails, flying jib, spanker, and topgallant studding sails. As a result, the squadron's day went by quickly as the ships tore along at eight knots cast after cast. The sail trimmers needed to make only minor adjustments during the day, which was fortunate, as the greater part of the gun crews found themselves spread out everywhere as they scraped the gun carriages and then painted them with black lead. Friday saw the men finish the carriages, only to then be tasked to scrape and paint the topmasts, topgallant masts, and booms, as well as reeve new wheel ropes. The ships had continued their rapid speed throughout the night as Bainbridge reckoned they were far enough out to sea—forty to fifty miles—that the risk of grounding was low; he did, however, keep the lead going every half-hour. At dawn he altered course to the west-southwest, and he found that the wind's force and direction allowed a second day of steady eight-knot measurements. The ships varied from this keen blue-water sailing only briefly, as they momentarily slowed for Captain Lawrence to come on board for dinner and then return.

At six bells in the afternoon watch the lookouts sighted a sail to the west. Both ships packed on even more sail in chase while they simultaneously made a considerable number of signals to each other. By eight bells the chase could be seen from the deck, and, finally, at two bells in the first dog watch the Americans came up with her. All three vessels hove-to, whereupon they made first a south-southwest and then a northwest drift. The *Hornet* sent her boat. After all the excitement, it turned out the chase was once again nothing more than a Portuguese merchantman going about her lawful, neutral, business. An hour later another sail was seen to the west; with little enthusiasm the squadron made chase but by eight bells in the first watch she could no longer be seen in the darkness. Not entirely sure of his position at this point, Bainbridge decided to heave-to for the night.

Saturday morning saw a piece of land appear which was judged to be that immediately to the east of San Salvador. The sea was filled with many small craft, which further indicated the large port was close by. At eight bells in the morning watch the *Hornet* again signaled she had seen a strange sail, so both ships began to chase, but gave it up an hour later. At four bells in the forenoon watch Bainbridge took the third cutter to the *Hornet*, and then returned right at noon as the Constitutions were piped to dinner. However, rather than collecting their mess-kids and going below, almost two hundred men assembled on the forecastle and along both sides of the main hatchway, all eyes on the commodore who stood beside the binnacle. As he noticed what was happening he moved forward, stopped beside the mainmast, drew himself up to his full height, and clasped his hands behind his back.

"Well, men, what's all this?" he called out in a steady voice.

"A word, your honor, if you please," replied one of the men in a slightly belligerent tone, backed by a chorus of mutters from the rest of the men.

"Yes?" said Bainbridge, alarmed and angry, but in careful control of himself.

"It's the vittles, sir," said another seaman.

"Yes?"

"And, sir, the water," said a third, noticeably supported by a rumble of agreement from the bulk of the men.

"Yes?"

"Commodore," said the first man, "we bin' on a allowance of one-half gallon of water per man per day ever since we left Boston. That may've been alright in the north, but it's damn well not enough in the God-damned tropics!"

"I see."

"And the vittles, sir," said the second man, "We bin' on three-parts of a daily ration since Boston. We're hungry all the time. Many of us are de... ah... debileetated. And if we gets sick, we don't get well but real slow-like." Bainbridge cast a frown at Evans as he guessed from whom an illiterate seaman came on to such a fancy word.

"Sir," said a different man, "you said we was going to put in at the Cape Verds, and get water and provisions, but then you just sailed right by. And then we didn't get much of nothin' at that damned little Portagee island. And now, you just up and sailed right by Recife, which everybody knows is a large port with vittles galore and plenty o'sweet water."

"Anyone else?" asked Bainbridge after a pause. There was some continued murmuring, but no other voice spoke up. "No? All right, lads, I've heard you. I comprehend your complaints. Now you listen close: I don't need to justify myself to *you* on *any* damned notion on *any* particular day. But, I will tell you this. My orders have taken us six-thousand miles already, they may take us another thousand into the South Atlantic, and they may even take us to the Indies or to goddam China itself on the far side of the world. Along the way I know *not* where and when we shall find water or victuals—and neither do *you*! And I know *not* if and when we may become becalmed for weeks far from land—and neither do *you*, my lads—so I conserve our provisions and water."

"You may not countenance it, and I don't give a damn if you do or don't—but the officers and I have also been on short rations. As to Recife, you sea-lawyers might know that despite prime vittles and sweet water the harbor ain't deep enough for the *Constitution*. As to that, we are right now just off San Salvador; some of you may know it as Bahia. It's a large port—much greater than Recife—and I make this promise: in the next few days we shall fill to bursting with victuals and water, and we'll not leave this coast until we do. Now get below to your dinners, and be thankful you have even that. Get below, and let's hear no more about this."

Below they went, if not entirely happy then at least somewhat appeased by the commodore's promise. At two bells in the afternoon watch Bainbridge ordered both ships to steer northwest and stand in for the land. Forty-five minutes later a ship was sighted, but the commodore elected not to pursue. During the night the ships stood off-and-on while they barely made steerage-way. Dawn presented the land, bearing north-northwest, distance six leagues. At two bells in the forenoon watch, Bainbridge signaled for Captain Lawrence to come on board the *Constitution*.

"My dear Lawrence," he began as he passed the decanter of port. They sat in *Old Ironsides'* great cabin. "If the wind serves I want you to proceed into San Salvador this evening—or more likely tomorrow. You'll seek out the U.S. consul for the port, Mr. Henry Hill—though I suspect he'll hastily come aboard *you* once he sees your colors. You must obtain as much in the way of provisions and water as the *Hornet* will hold—enough for both ships—for I don't intend to bring the *Constitution* in at this time. For the present I choose that the Portuguese not learn of our total force. When you come out of port, in a few days, we'll transfer the stores you'll have obtained for me. Moreover, before you go in, I want you to transfer some victuals and water to the *Constitution*. This is because you shall begin replenishment tomorrow, but we shall have to wait several more days for you to return."

"Yes sir, of course," replied Lawrence.

"Splendid. That matter out of the way, I need you to do something else just as important, or perhaps even more so. I hope to avail myself of all possible intelligence which might be in your power to gather from Mr. Hill—or anyone else at the consulate. Complete information's extraordinarily important for our squadron's successful operations while in these waters." He drank some of his wine.

"Therefore, you'll oblige me greatly if the following things might be within your means to ascertain. Oh, you needn't take notes. I've written a letter with the particulars for you to deliver to Mr. Hill. But here's a *précis* for your knowledge in advance:

"Is the Prince Regent, as well as the government of Brazil, well disposed to the United States?

"Which are the best ports to procure water and provisions on the coast of Brazil?

"Can I readily receive supplies at San Salvador?

"Would a vessel of war, which belonged to the United States, be safe and respected in such ports?

"What number of British cruisers are in these waters, and which are their ports of rendezvous? Do their ships of the line cruise off any particular ports?

"How are the British warships generally manned? Are their crews in general healthy?

"What number of English merchant ships are at San Salvador? Of what do their cargoes consist? Can Mr. Hill designate probable times when they might sail?

"What English vessels are expected at San Salvador?

"What's the best station off San Salvador to intercept English vessels bound in and out?

"Would an American cruiser be blockaded by British warships if she were to enter the port of Rio Janeiro?

"Do any of the English East Indiamen touch at Rio Janeiro—and if so at which times of the year?

"Do British whalemen stop at Janeiro on their homeward-bound passages?

"Have the British any trade to the suth'ard of Janeiro along the coast of Brazil, and from thence to the Rio de la Plate?

"How long would it take for information to go from San Salvador to Janeiro—and then for British cruisers to appear off Salvador after receipt of such information?

"That's quite a list, sir," said Lawrence, with a grin, after Bainbridge had come to a stop.

"Yes, well, regardless, do your best to find me some answers. And Lawrence, before you present Mr. Hill with my letter and these questions, make sure you do the civil thing. Tell him that although I haven't the pleasure of a personal acquaintance, yet his character's so well known to me that I salute him cordially with my best wishes and assurances of a desire to cultivate an acquaintance. Tell him I hold for him sentiments of real esteem. Tell him that, well, dammit, you know what to say; all that sort of thing."

"Aye aye, sir."

"In addition, you must positively assure him of my sincere determination that we won't cause him any embarrassment, in that the squadron shall not in the least violate strict neutrality. Nor shall we, by any act, interrupt the friendly understanding and amicable disposition which happily subsist between the prince regent of Portugal and the government of the United States."

"Yes, Commodore," replied Lawrence, "I believe I know just what to say. You can rely upon me fully."

"I know I can, Lawrence," said Bainbridge as he flashed a rare smile. "You have my full confidence."

As soon as Lawrence returned to the *Hornet*, he brought her close by on the *Constitution*'s weather beam. Then, from six bells in the forenoon watch until two bells in the second dog watch, the Hornets broke out, brought up, and carefully sent over fifty forty-gallon fresh water casks to *Old Ironsides*, while the Constitutions labored just as mightily to receive the many boat loads and stow them away. The *Constitution* also sent on board the *Hornet* three men to assist: quarter gunner James McCoy and seamen John Heart and Thomas Yates. For both crews this was hard labor indeed as they worked in the motion of the open sea, with the air and water temperatures each around 80° Fahrenheit and the humidity extremely heavy. Thus, the men welcomed the antics of the dozen live pigs which were also sent over—provisions obtained at Noronha Island—which provided some end of day amusement that was sorely needed.

By one bell in the first watch it was done. Among much hallooing between the two crews the *Hornet* filled away and headed toward the port, while *Old Ironsides* disappeared in the darkness off the *Hornet*'s starboard quarter. At four bells the *Hornet* struck soundings in thirty-three fathoms (sand and gravel bottom), with Cape San Antonio's light bearing north-northwest, distant about fifteen miles. Feeling uncharacteristically prudent, Master-Commandant Lawrence shortened sail, hove-to, and prepared to anchor.

CHAPTER 17
COAST OF BRAZIL

Coast of Brazil
In the approaches to São Salvador da Baía
7 nautical miles east of São Antonio Light
Vicinity 12° 59' S 38° 29' W
Monday, December 14th, 1812
5:45 a.m.
Variable winds with rain

At dawn the *Hornet* raised anchor and got under way. She made sail on the starboard tack, having spent most of the night riding to her kedge in twenty fathoms. At three bells she sent in a boat with an officer to make contact with the American consul and to request a harbor pilot. At that same moment Lieutenant Stewart, the officer of the watch, suddenly realized the ground was rapidly shoaling. The last cry of the leadsman surprisingly—shockingly— reported just four fathoms under the keel. With a startled look and emphatic nod from Captain Lawrence, the lieutenant instantly wore the ship to the south. Much to everyone's relief, the next cast of the lead showed a more comfortable sixteen fathoms. Keeping a leadsman taking soundings, the ship then stood off-and-on until a Portuguese pilot came out at four bells in the forenoon watch, at which point the *Hornet* stood in for San Salvador now five miles distant. An hour later she picked up her boat, which was sailing back out to meet her. But, when she had barely gained the harbor's mouth, the pilot chose to proceed no farther—much to Lawrence's irritation—so at six bells the *Hornet* came-to, with the starboard bower in twenty fathoms, to await the light of the next day.

The next morning came pleasant with light breezes and also—fortunately—found the pilot more content, so at seven bells the ship again got underway. With the captain, two lieutenants, and the master attentively at work with the pilot, the rest of the *Hornet*'s officers lined the rail as the ship entered the harbor.

"Lord above, Mr. Stewart," exclaimed Assistant Surgeon Hawkes, "this's an *enormous* bay. The entrance must be four or five miles wide."

"It is indeed, Micah," replied Lieutenant Stewart. "This's the grand Bay of All Saints, or in the Portuguese *São Salvador da Baía de Todos os Santos*. That's why we sometimes call it—and the city—San Salvador, but then sometimes call it Bahia. The bay extends to the north'ard for almost twenty-five miles, and its greatest breadth is about twenty miles. It has several islands at its head and several rivers run into it. It's a healthy place with an easy ingress and egress—though it's true the captain did choose to engage a pilot today. That's because only two of us have ever been here before—and neither of those in many years. It's quite convenient for vessels to call which need repair or supplies of any kind. However—with the exception of fresh meat, poultry, fish, vegetables, fruit, and firewood—the costs of everything here are *very* high, particularly for naval stores. Fresh water can be obtained in several places, to include between the city and Fort Gamboa under the public garden. The market's midway between the custom house and the consulates, near the water."

After an hour and a half's extremely careful progress the *Hornet* came-to, in fourteen fathoms, at a place immediately opposite the city's public gardens. As the anchor buried itself in the muddy bottom, the *Hornet* fired a formal salute of eighteen guns which was immediately returned by the circular fort of San Marcello do Mar. The echoes of the salute had hardly faded when Captain Lawrence came up the companionway and onto the quarterdeck. He already perspired in the heavy blue coat, white vest, and gold-laced cocked hat of his full-dress uniform. He tugged once more at the uncomfortable high collar and then jumped down into his gig, losing not a moment to call upon the U.S. consul, Mr. Hill.

As Lawrence's gig left the side of the *Hornet* it was immediately replaced by the first of several lighters which brought water and provisions. This first one contained 4,200 gallons of water. In fact, over the course of the day, and the next two days as well, clear and pleasant weather facilitated the acquisition of an immense amount of supplies: another 5,100 gallons of water, 810 gallons of wine, 58 barrels of bread, 18 barrels of flour, 100 bundles of sugar cane, 12 barrels of oranges, one bag of carrots, a cord of firewood, two boxes of candles, six new lanterns, ten live bullocks (with their associated 14 bundles of hay), and various quantities of yams, pumpkins, jerked beef, bananas, cocoanuts, mangoes, watermelons, hogs, and chickens (these last with their associated three bags of corn). Throughout the whole process the Americans were extremely pleased that the Portuguese officials treated them with considerable politeness and cooperation, and that several American merchants similarly yielded them a great deal of assistance.

By Thursday evening the *Hornet* was gorged full with supplies, and Mr. Hill had sent on board a letter—six closely written pages—with answers to Commodore Bainbridge's lengthy inquiries. Thus, at three bells in the second dog-watch, Captain Lawrence ran up his boats, weighed anchor, and stood out to sea. At midnight, uncomfortable with proceeding further in the pitch black of the night, he took in the royals and topgallants and came-to with the kedge anchor in eleven fathoms. San Antonio light bore northeast-½-east, distant two leagues.

The dawn brought light airs with rain. One bell in the morning watch saw the lookouts changed, the men of the starboard watch roused from their hammocks to come sleepily on deck, and the men of the larboard watch go below to turn-in. The ever-impatient captain immediately had the sleepy starbowlines weigh the kedge and set plain sail. By noon the rain had given way to pleasant weather with fresh breezes, Cape San Antonio bore northwest-½-north at about five leagues, and a strange sail was discovered which, upon approach, proved to be the *Constitution*. Just after four bells the ships joined company, hove-to, and Captain Lawrence came on board the flagship. At the same time both crews began the considerable labor of transferring water and provisions from the *Hornet*, only slightly inconvenienced by the clouds and rain which suddenly rolled in.

"Welcome aboard, Lawrence," said Bainbridge as he led him into his dining cabin, all smiles, with hopes for a positive report. "I'm just about to attack my dinner; you'll join me I'm sure. How did it all go?"

"Prime, sir, I thank you," replied Lawrence as he took the proffered seat and glass of wine. "The Portuguese were uncommon civil and gave us every assistance. Before we discuss those particulars, however, I do have one thing to report with which you'll not be pleased."

"Oh?" said Bainbridge, his smile entirely gone.

"No, sir. One of the men you sent on board me—McCoy—deserted while in the city, along with one of my men."

"Damn him!" shouted Bainbridge as he struck the table with

his fist. "Damn *them*! God damn them!" He sat rigidly, his face flushed and his lip trembling.

"Yes, sir. I'm very sorry," replied Lawrence. He flinched from the commodore's red-faced outrage. After a few moments of silence Bainbridge nodded his head.

"I tell you what it is, Lawrence. My crew, due to the constant drill and exercise we give them, are active and clever at the guns. Oh yes, they are, indeed. But I tell you in all other respects the damned villains are *inferior* to any crew I've ever had. Ever."

"Yes, sir," repeated Lawrence. He cleared his throat. "Ah, sir, Mr. Hill immediately contacted the captain of the port. They're optimistic that the deserters'll be run to ground without much trouble."

"Very well. Yes, very well," said Bainbridge as he tried to calm down. He picked up his spoon and rotated it in his fingers for a few moments. "How did you find Mr. Hill?"

"Commodore," Lawrence answered, glad for the change of subject, "I'm extremely grateful for Mr. Hill's aid. I cannot give him too much praise for his exertions. And, for his part, he wanted me to assure you that no event in memory has given him more real pleasure than the arrival of our squadron off this coast. He believes that he's freely communicated on every subject which he thinks possibly useful to further your mission in these seas, and he sincerely hopes that we'll rely upon him for any and every assistance that might be in his power to furnish for the promotion of our interests or those of the public service. He's sent you this lengthy reply to the inquiries you had me take in to him." Lawrence gestured to the sheaf of papers he had brought into the cabin.

"Splendid!" said Bainbridge. "I'll pour through it after dinner, but for now summarize, if you please. What does he tell us about San Salvador?" Lawrence paused a moment as the commodore's steward served them.

"Mr. Hill dearly loves this place and greatly warmed to the subject when asked," he said with a smile. "Let me see if I can recall it all. San Salvador's the capital of the province—and was in fact the first capital of Portuguese America, founded by the first governor-general—de Souza—in 1549. It has about 120,000 inhabitants. It stands on elevated land on the eastern side of the entrance to the bay, about two miles north of Cape San Antonio. It's built on a ridge which faces its anchorage to the west. It consists of an upper and lower town. The *Cidade Alta* contains several fine streets where the principal merchants reside. The *Cidade Baxa* consists mainly of one street of considerable length, which contains warehouses for inland produce and foreign goods—as well as a naval arsenal."

"The public buildings are the cathedral—built of marble—and said to be the handsomest building of the kind in Brazil, several other churches, the palaces of the archbishop and governor, a college, the town hall, the tribunal of appeal, the theater, several hospitals, a bank, and the exchange. Their export commerce chiefly consists of sugar, cotton, rum, tobacco, coffee, cocoa, and hides. The imports are mostly manufactured articles, flour, salt, iron, glass, and wine. We obtained most everything we desired in terms of victuals and supplies. The wine was a little dear, but coffee was just seven cents per pound, and the oranges—quite large ones, too—were $2.50 per barrel."

"During the day the prevailing winds will usually permit a vessel to reach the anchorage without tacking, as the most common are those from the east and sou'east. During the night the wind's weak, variable, and generally off the land. The water of the bay's generally deep—the fairway to the entrance has from thirteen to twenty fathoms, while much of the bay has depths which run from seventeen to twenty-five fathoms. The anchorage for warships is off the public garden in nine fathoms, muddy bottom, at about three-quarters of a mile from shore. The Portuguese vessels of war anchor nearer the arsenal." He paused to take a bite.

"During some of the year ships can refit and repair right at the anchorage. Lighters built for the purpose, with everything necessary to heave down vessels, are moored inshore of the loading ground, and I heard that even a large ship of 2,400 tons has been hove-down there. North'ard of the town, in Itapagipe Bay, there're merchant yards where ships can be repaired at all times of the year. The town and shipping are defended by several forts: the first's that on Cape San Antonio, a little to the north'ard are Santa Maria and San Diego, at the sou'west extremity of the town's Fort Gamboa and Fort San Pedro, and farther on's the circular fort of San Marcello do Mar which protects the navy yard. There're other smaller batteries along the beach and one on Mont Serrat point. On the land side the town is defended by various other fortifications." Bainbridge passed him the decanter of wine.

"Thank you, sir," said Lawrence. He refilled his glass and took a sip before he continued. "Thank you. Ample supplies are certainly available—and Mr. Hill says the same's true at Recife and Rio Janeiro. He also believes that while the Portuguese are indeed sympathetic to the British, he's sure that there's nothing to fear from the provincial governor nor any of the other authorities."

"Splendid!" said Bainbridge, at this point all smiles again. "Who's the governor?"

"Sir," replied Lawrence as he looked at his notes, "he's a count, the *Conde dos Arcos*. His name is Dom Marcos de Noronha e Brito."

"I see. Very well. What about the British presence?"

"Commodore, there's a sloop-of-war moored in Salvador Harbor. I also learned that there's a British seventy-four at Janeiro and a frigate at the river Plata. These last two, together with a brig-of-war, apparently constitute the entire British naval force on the Brazil coast. Another ship's said to cruise to the wind'ard of St. Helena Island. Several British merchantmen've just sailed from Salvador, but there are several more still in harbor. I'm told that forty to fifty of them come to Brazil each year and that the best place to meet with them's to the south, off Cape Frio. I was further told that ships bound to Salvador from England generally make the coast from six to twelve leagues to the north'ard of Cape San Antonio. A considerable quantity of specie's sent yearly, by British merchants at Janeiro to Recife, in order to purchase cotton. These vessels generally sail up the coast from four to ten leagues offshore."

"Specie—did you say specie?" mumbled Bainbridge from around a forkful of sea pie.

"Yes indeed, Commodore," grinned Lawrence, "and the British sloop-of-war I spoke of a moment ago—the one presently moored in Salvador—is reported to have as much as $1,600,000 in gold on board. She's the *Bonne Citoyenne*, and prepares to sail to England within ten or twelve days—they need to repair some leaks caused by grounding. I sent her captain, an officer named Pitt Burnaby Greene, a challenge to fight him ship-to-ship. And, sir, I took the liberty to pledge your and my honor that if he chooses to come out to meet the *Hornet*, in such a *rencontre*, the *Constitution* shall not interfere."

"Did you, by God!" exclaimed Bainbridge, once again laying down his utensils. "By God, Lawrence, you acted well, and it'd seem we've come to the right place. We'll cruise about for a number of days, both to the south'ard and north'ard of the bay's entrance. It'll be strange if between the two of us we can't catch something interesting as it comes in or out. And we'll need to pay attention—*very* close attention indeed—to your *Bonne Citoyenne*.

That's one we can't let slip through our fingers. Thus, you shall not go *too* far from the entrance." He stopped for a moment as he tried to mentally calculate his share of prize money should they be able to capture the British ship and her cargo of gold. Lawrence watched him for a moment with a smile on his face, as he had already done that same figuring the day before.

"No, sir. Indeed, sir," he replied. "Sir, what about you? Have you seen anything interesting these last few days?"

"Bah! No," said Bainbridge, "we merely cruised about, mostly south and east, five to six leagues off San Antonio. Early yesterday morning we did bring-to and board a ship, but she was Spanish, fifty-some days from the Canaries bound to Rio de la Plata. She had four-hundred passengers on board—male *and* female."

"Good God!" exclaimed Lawrence. "Mighty cozy, I'll warrant."

"Oh my, yes," agreed Bainbridge. "Mighty short on water too, as you can imagine, and thus their efforts to get water at Salvador. They come to the new world due to a famine produced by the locust last year. In any event, the ship hadn't spoke nor seen any other vessels during her passage."

The next day, December nineteenth, saw the *Hornet* on the *Constitution*'s larboard beam, as both crews continued to transfer provisions and stores from the one ship to the other. The day went by with moderate breezes and pleasant weather, with a midday sounding of twenty-six fathoms with a gravelly bottom. At five bells in the afternoon watch the ships parted company, the *Hornet* steered a little to the southwest and *Old Ironsides* steered farther to the northeast, in determined quests for British shipping.

"Farewell," said Bainbridge just before Lawrence jumped down into the *Hornet*'s gig. "I intend we separate for several days in order to cover as much expanse of sea as possible. Remember at all times, Lawrence, it's my positive order you carefully and strictly respect the neutral jurisdiction of this coast."

For the rest of that day, and indeed for the next four days, they cruised independently in their separate areas of responsibility. They occasionally tacked and wore—north, south, east, and west—and made and shortened sail as circumstances required. The weather was for the most part pleasant with light winds—the only exception was some squalls of rain on Tuesday evening, Wednesday morning, and Thursday morning. Both ships used Cape Antonio, and the Antonio light, as points of reference as they continuously ranged from six to twenty miles out and back. Both ships saw several strange sails each day, but concluded that most were small, local vessels, and thus rarely made chase.

Somewhat strangely, *Old Ironsides* saw more of interest to the north of San Salvador than did the *Hornet* to the south. On Monday her boats boarded a brig from Portugal—sixty-three days out from Oporto bound to Salvador. The brig's captain, accompanied by a Portuguese army officer, came on board the *Constitution* and talked with Bainbridge for a half-hour.

"Who was that soldier, John?" asked Evans of Aylwin as the Portuguese boat returned to the brig. Aylwin had been invited, along with Parker, to talk to the visitors.

"He's a colonel of cavalry, Amos," replied Aylwin, "and he's served in recent action in the Peninsula. He says if we've heard any rumors about a peace concluded between France and Russia, we should disregard. There's no truth to it."

"Well, I hadn't heard any such thing," said Evans. "Regardless, he's a distinguished-looking man and his uniform's quite neat and elegant."

The next day a boat from *Old Ironsides* boarded a Portuguese slaver, bound from the coast of Africa to San Salvador.

"It's always unpleasant to see the miserable slaves packed as they are into such ships," said the boarding officer when he reported to the commodore. "In this case it also appears that the poor wretches have the yaws. I saw the warts and nodules everywhere on their skins."

"I'm concerned to hear it, Mr. Shubrick," said Bainbridge. "Anything else?"

"Sir, only that the slaver had been spoken five days ago by a frigate which wore English colors. From their supposed position at that time, I surmise it may've been the ship we heard cruised off St. Helena."

On Wednesday both ships independently cleared for action, beat to quarters, and chased two ships—ever hopeful of a legitimate and lucrative prize. At one bell in the forenoon watch the *Hornet*'s boats boarded her candidate; alas, she merely proved to be another Portuguese merchant ship bound from Europe to Salvador. For her part, in the late afternoon, the *Constitution* sighted what appeared to be a large ship steering in the direction of Salvador. The Americans hurriedly packed on sail: topgallants, flying jib, spanker, staysails, lower and topmast studding sails, and main skysail—but to no avail in the light airs. Not only did *Old Ironsides* not close on the chase, by nightfall the chase had been able to increase the distance.

But, much to the Constitutions' relief, the next morning's rain-obscured sun displayed the chase lying-to at about seven miles distance. The *Constitution* was then forced to shorten sail and heave-to, in turn, as a squall of rain reached her. However, the weather did clear after a while, and around noon the *Constitution* made sail and made every effort to close but, just as before, was unable to appreciably gain. At two bells in the afternoon watch *Old Iron-sides* sighted the *Hornet* to windward; Lawrence apparently standing down with a view to cut off the same chase. The *Constitution* fired several shot, but they did not reach even half-way; however, as if in response, the chase suddenly stood-in for the land. At three bells the *Hornet* fired one shot, and then a second. The chase, which at this range clearly displayed British colors and had all appearances of being packet ship, now set staysails and jibs and ran in close for the shore. The *Hornet* immediately reacted; she took in her starboard studding sails, set her larboard studding sails, and hauled up. By five bells it was clear that the *Hornet* was having better luck than had the *Constitution,* as she rapidly gained on the packet. In fact, at six bells she was within musket shot; however, at this point they were within a half-mile of the shore, and were virtually in the entrance to the bay. Captain Lawrence pounded the quarterdeck rail in frustration, and gave it up. The *Hornet* took in her studding sails, hauled her wind, and stood toward the *Constitution.* For her part, the *Constitution* had earlier given up her chase of the packet after the *Hornet* had begun firing at it. In the meantime she had seized the opportunity to stop and board a brig coming out of San Salvador. Once again, to no one's surprise, it was a perfectly innocent Portuguese merchantman bound to Oporto.

At one bell, in the first dog watch, the *Hornet* sighted another large unknown sail to the east-northeast. Lawrence, determined to gain something tangible from this thus-far disappointing day, broke off his approach to the *Constitution* and tacked to the east. A half hour proved the sail to be only a medium-sized coaster, so the *Hornet* tacked back toward the west. Twice more that evening, at one bell in the second dog watch and two bells in the first watch, the *Hornet* again beat to quarters and began a chase, and twice more found nothing more than Portuguese merchantmen. Sometime after midnight, disgusted and tired, Lawrence wore to the northeast—where he hoped the *Constitution* now lay—and went to bed.

CHAPTER 18

EASTERN ATLANTIC OCEAN

Eastern Atlantic Ocean
300 nautical miles south of the Cape Verde Islands
Vicinity 9° 51' N 23° 35' W
Monday, December 14, 1812
Fresh breezes and cloudy, winds E.N.E.

Sunday had passed, uneventfully, into Monday. HMS *Java*'s tiny convoy flew along, watch after watch, at eight and even nine knots. The winds were steady from the east-northeast and northeast-by-north. Courses were correspondingly steady to the south-southwest and south-by-west. Monday's sole out of the ordinary event was another all-hands great-gun and small-arms exercise, which culminated in the now routine two rounds being fired from each cannon. There was, Lambert and Chads were grateful to note, more evidence of further improvement in regard to speed and smoothness during the drill. At the same time, however, there was an unusually sharp increase in the number of injuries associated with the exercise; in the sick-berth Mr. Jones and his assistant surgeons, Mr. Falls and Mr. Capponi, were inundated by a stream of men with smashed toes and bruised (even a couple of broken) legs from recoil, or who suffered from various degrees of rope burn and powder flash.

Tuesday's run of fast sailing—seven knots hour-after- hour—with the wind again east-northeast and course likewise south-southwest, was interrupted twice. At three bells in the afternoon watch the *Java* hove-to and sent a boat with provisions to the *William*, wherein they lost about an hour. Then, at three bells in the first watch of the night, the tow rope abruptly carried away. The convoy correspondingly shortened sail to match the *William*'s slow speed—only a little more than four knots—for Lambert decided to wait until daylight to reestablish the tow. Wednesday morning, unfortunately, opened with squalls, variable winds, and rain. Nevertheless, up-hammocks was advanced by half an hour, the *Java* and the *William* hove-to, and the tow rope was replaced with reasonably little trouble. However the weather remained problematic for the rest of the day as it allowed an average of only four and one-half knots. Maddeningly, Thursday was much the same. The squalls and variable winds kept the convoy to a miserable three knots, log cast after log cast.

Friday and Saturday, December eighteenth and nineteenth, brought an extremely welcome change. The light airs enabled no great speed—progress was only sixty-seven miles on Friday and ninety-four miles on Saturday—but at least the rain and squalls had given way to sunshine and fine weather. Friday was the more eventful day of the two. At three bells in the forenoon watch, all hands were called to witness punishment. Ordinary seaman Robert Place received forty-eight lashes and able seaman Christopher Wailing twenty-four for theft, while supernumerary ordinary Samuel Clarke, ordinary Samuel Warren, and ordinary William Harrison received twelve, six, and six respectively. Then, at two bells in the afternoon watch, all hands exercised the great guns and small arms. Today, Lambert authorized the firing of four rounds each from the cannon, and while there was again a quantity of relatively minor injuries, it was clear that the gun crews really were binding together as teams. Moreover, it was clear that the thunderous din and stabbing flames added immensely to the morale and increasingly high spirits of the men.

In contrast, Saturday saw almost nothing in the way of excitement. The moderate and cloudy weather had little to recommend it, particularly as the light airs neither helped with the heat and humidity of 1° 9' north latitude, nor drove the convoy forward at much more than five knots. However, the public knowledge of the observed latitude was the topic of considerable discussion, and indeed stimulated Captain Wood to once again press Mr. Robinson at dinner.

"Master, can you tell us something of this ceremony I understand we'll undertake in the next day or so?" asked Wood.

"To cross the equator—or cross the line—is a term generally understood to mean sailing across the line supposed to divide the earth into northern and southern hemispheres," replied Robinson as he pushed away his plate. "From time immemorial it's been a common custom with sailors, regardless of nationality and both in merchant services as well as navies, to perform the ceremony upon those who've never crossed before (or who cannot give a satisfactory account of their having done so). All persons who want to purchase their freedom from old King Neptune will bribe him with a few bottles of rum or a few pounds of sugar. Failing that, then they must expect to go through the whole of the operation."

"Surely you don't mean General Hislop?" interjected Wood, shocked.

"Surely indeed, Captain," Robinson grinned. "*All* persons are subject to my lord Neptune. Had Captain Lambert and Mr. Chads—or myself—not crossed many a time already, it'd apply to us too. However, I wouldn't recommend the general—nor yourself or the major for that matter—go through the ceremony. I recommend you pay out the bribe with some rum or even better spirits, and then just watch the spectacle."

Thus it was, on Sunday's hazy and muggy morning, the people quickly breakfasted and then began to prepare for the crossing. Most of the crew stripped to the waist and wore nothing but duck trousers. At noon Captain Lambert, Lieutenant Chads, Commander Marshall, and Mr. Robinson came to a formal consensus that the convoy was certainly in the latitude of 0° 15' south. So then, just an hour later, the foremasthead lookout hailed that he saw something on the weather-bow which he thought was a boat; soon after an unknown voice from the jib-boom hailed the ship. The officer of the watch, Lieutenant Herringham, made an answer to which the voice commanded him to heave-to as the monarch of the sea, King Neptune, intended to come on board. The *Java* was accordingly hove-to with care (though at the time she was sailing at the meager rate of only two knots, so it took no considerable effort to come to a stop), the mainyard was squared, and the head and after-yards braced up.

As soon as the ship was hove-to a young man (one of the veteran seamen), dressed in a smart suit of black, knee-breeches, and buckles, with his hair powdered and with all the extra finery and mincing gait of a fop, came aft and onto the quarterdeck. With a most polished bow he introduced himself as Mr. Neptune's gentleman's gentleman, and that he had been desired to precede his master and acquaint the captain of this here vessel with his intention to visit.

A sail had been extended across the forecastle by way of a curtain and from behind this King Neptune and his train, in full costume, now came forth. The car of the "god" consisted of a gun carriage. It was drawn by six black men—of course also part of the crew—who were tall and muscular fellows, their heads were covered green with seaweed, and they wore small pairs of cotton drawers. In other respects these men were perfectly naked, their skin was alternately spotted with red and white paint, and they had conch shells in their hands with which they made a most horrible discordant noise. Neptune was masked, as were many of his attendants, though most of the ship's officers could tell who was playing the god; nevertheless he was a clever hand and he played the part extremely well. He wore a naval crown which had been made by the *Java*'s armorer. In his right hand he held a trident, on the prongs of which there was a small dolphin. He wore a large wig made of oakum as well as a beard made of the same material which flowed down to his waist. He was fully powdered and his essentially naked body was also covered in paint.

Neptune was attended by a splendid court. His secretary-of-state had his hair stuck full of sea-bird quills; his surgeon carried a lancet, pill-box, and scent-bottle; his barber had a razor whose blade was two feet long cut off an iron hoop; the barber's mate carried a small tub as a shaving-box—the contents of which, by its terrible odor, likely had *not* come from Smith's in Bond Street, Mayfair.

Amphitrite followed Neptune on a similar carriage, drawn by six white men costumed much like the others. The goddess was played by an athletic-looking but singularly ugly seaman, terribly marked by having had smallpox, dressed as a woman with a nightcap on his head which was ornamented with sprigs of seaweed. "She" had a harpoon in her hand upon which was fixed an albacore, and in her lap lay one of the smaller ship's boys dressed as a baby with long clothes and a cap; he held a marlinspike which was suspended around his neck with a rope yarn. The baby's "nurse" attended him with a dirty bucket full of burgoo, with which she occasionally fed him out of the cook's iron ladle. Two more stout men were habited as sea-nymphs as attendants to the goddess. These carried a looking-glass, a birch-broom, and a pot of red paint (by way of rouge).

As soon as this august procession appeared on the forecastle, Captain Lambert came up the companionway attended by his steward, who bore a tray with a bottle of wine and some glasses. The cars of the marine deities, which had made the perilous journey down the narrow gangways, were carefully drawn up on the quarterdeck. Neptune lowered his trident and presented the dolphin to the captain, as Amphitrite did her albacore, as tokens of submission to the representative of the King of Great Britain.

"I 'ave come," said the god, "to welcome ye into me dominions h'and to present me wife h'an' child." Lambert swept off his hat and bowed low with a great flourish. "Sir," went on Neptune, "ha'low me to h'ask h'after me brother h'an' liege sovereign, the good old King George."

"He is not so well," replied Lambert, "as I and all his subjects could wish."

"More's the pity," said Neptune. "Then 'ow is the Prince o' Wales, pray?"

"The Prince is well," said Lambert, "and presently governs as regent in the name of his royal father."

"An' 'ow does the Prince get on with 'is wife?" pressed the inquisitive god with a grin.

"Bad enough," said the captain with a straight face, "they appear to agree together like a whale and a thrasher."

"Ah! Indeed, I thought so," said the king of the sea. "Well, 'is royal 'ighness should take a leaf out o' my book: never ha'low it t'be doubtful just 'oo is the commanding officer."

"Oh, indeed," replied Lambert. "Pray, what might be your majesty's specific to cure a bad wife?"

"Nothin' more than three feet o' the cro'jack brace athwart 'er arse every morning afore breakfast, fer a quarter of an 'our, and 'alf-an-'our on Sundays."

"But why more on a Sunday than any other day?" asked Lambert, scratching his head.

"Why?" said Mr. Neptune, "Why, because she'd been a-drinkin' Saturday night, to be sure. Besides, she 'as less to do of a Sunday an' more time to think of 'er sins an' do proper penance."

"But, my lord, you wouldn't have a prince strike a lady, surely?" objected Lambert.

"Oh, wouldn't I, Cap'n, just wouldn't I? No, yer in the right of it, t'be sure. If she be'ave 'erself as sich, on no account. But if she gives tongue an' won't keep sober, I'd sarve 'er out as I do Amphy—don't I, Amphy?" and he chucked the goddess under the chin. "We 'ave no bad wives at the bottom o'the sea, Cap'n, so if ye don't know 'ow to keep 'em in h'order, send 'em to us."

"But your majesty's remedy's a bit violent. We'd have a rebellion in England if the king were to beat his wife."

"Well, then, make the bleedin' lords in waitin' do it," said Neptune, somewhat surly, "an' if they're too lazy, which I dare say they are, send fer a bosun's mate from the old *Royal Billy*—'eed sarve 'er out, I do warrant ye, and fer 'alf a gallon o' rum would teach the yeomen o' the guard to dance the 'ornpipe into the bargain."

"Well, his royal highness shall certainly hear your advice, Mr. Neptune, but whether he'll follow it or not isn't for me to say. Now, sir, would you be pleased to drink King George's good health?"

"Why, with h'all me 'eart, sir. I been h'always loyal to the king, an' ready to drink 'is 'ealth, an' to fight fer 'im."

Lambert presented the god with a bumper of Madeira, along with another to the goddess.

"'Ere's good 'ealth an' a long life to h'our gracious king an' all the royal family," said Neptune. "The roads are uncommon dusty, h'an' we 'aven't wet h'our lips since we left St. Thomas on the line this mornin'. But, we 'ave no time to lose, Cap'n. I see many—oh, so many—new faces 'ere as requires washin' h'an' shavin'. If we h'add bleedin' h'an' physic—why, they'll h'all be the better fer it."

Lambert nodded his assent and formally backed away. Neptune struck the deck with the butt of his trident and commanded the attention of all. He then addressed his court.

"Hark ye, me Tritons, ye're called 'ere to shave, duck, h'an' physic h'all that needs, but I command ye to be gentle. I'll be 'avin' no ill-usage, fer if we gets a bad name, we gets no more fees. So, the first of ye as disobeys me orders I'll tie to a carronade h'an' sink ten-thousand fathoms deep—where ye'll feed on salt water h'an' seaweed for a 'unnert years. Now, begone to yer work!"

Twelve attendants, with thick sticks, immediately moved to the waist and sent down the enormous number of the crew who had never been initiated. At this point they guarded them strictly until they were called up one-by-one. The ship's remaining livestock—a few sheep, goats, and chickens—had been temporarily relocated from the manger up forward, and then the manger had been prepared for the "bathing" by being lined with double canvas and tarred so that it held water. It now contained about four butts, and was constantly renewed by a pump. Most of the uninitiated officers—ship's company as well as the passengers—took the master's advice and purchased exemption from the shaving and the doses of "medicine" with bottles of rum or fine wine from their personal stores. However, none could escape the spray of Neptunian sea water which was flung about every which way in great profusion. Even Captain Lambert and General Hislop accidently received a great deal more than their share, but with great good-nature and laughter, and they seemed to enjoy the sport. Then up forward, one by one, each candidate was seated on the side of the manger.

He was asked the place of his birth—and the moment he opened his mouth to reply, the shaving brush of the "barber," which was a large paint brush, was crammed in with considerable filthy lather. The lather was also liberally applied to his face and chin, and then it was roughly scraped off with the great iron-hoop razor. The "surgeon" now felt his pulse and then prescribed a pill, which was forced into his mouth. The surgeon's scent-bottle, the cork of which was armed with several short pin points, was next thrust against his nose and thus generally drew a little blood. Then he was thrown backwards into the bath, finally being allowed to scramble out the best way he could.

It was easy to perceive who were favorites with the ship's company by the degree of severity with which they were treated. The master-at-arms, the ship's corporals, and the purser's steward were handled fairly roughly—as might have been expected. The purser himself, who really should have bribed his way out of it, fortified himself in his cabin and with sword and pistol vowed death against any intruder. However, the younger midshipmen, who had already survived their own initiation, had him out regardless and dunked him soundly. Their justification was that thus far in the voyage he had refused to give them more spirits than their regulation allowance. He was paraded to the weatherdeck in great form with his sword held over his head and with his pistols carried before him at the bottom of a bucket of water. Then, having been duly shaved, physicked, and soused in the manger, he was allowed to flee back to his cabin, much resembling a drowned rat.

Finally, it was all over. Once again King Neptune thumped his trident on the deck which gradually stilled the considerable hilarity and mirth.

"Shipmates," he called out, "shipmates one h'an' h'all! Welcome ye to the Kingdom o' *Neptunus Rex*. From this point h'onward ye're now, h'as we say, *free of the equator*. We're now all members h'an' brothers together, and I 'onor ye fer it." He saluted Captain Lambert and then slowly and ceremoniously withdrew from the quarterdeck, onto the forecastle, and disappeared behind the curtain.

It was well that the line crossing on Sunday had delivered so much excitement, for the next six days settled into a rather dull pattern, appearing pretty much as peas from the same pod. The weather was uniformly hot and humid; the winds were moderate to light and reasonably steady from the southeast, southeast-by-south, and south-southeast; the ships' speeds averaged only around three to five knots; and the courses were steadily southwest, southwest-by-south, and south-southwest. There were, however, some occasional high points to break into the monotonous routine. Wednesday, December twenty-third, saw a little of this activity. Lieutenant Chads, more out of curiosity rather than necessity, had the deep-sea lead broken out. The first sounding discovered thirty-two fathoms of water with the bottom coral, fine sand, and shells; however two hours later another sounding found no ground at all with a hundred-fathom line. One bell in the forenoon watch saw the crew mustered by divisions, though this was no real surprise as this evolution appeared on most Wednesday mornings. Later in the afternoon the convoy hove-to for a half-hour while the *Java*'s blue cutter was sent to the *William* with a quantity of fresh water.

Most significant, however, the sunrise had disclosed to the lookouts the island of *Fernando de Noronha*, which bore northwest-by-north at fourteen leagues distance. This confirmed to Mr. Robinson his belief that the *Java* and her convoy were within 250 miles of the northeast coast of Brazil.

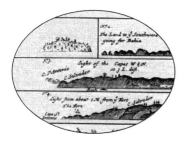

CHAPTER 19

COAST OF BRAZIL

Coast of Brazil
24 nautical miles S.E.-by-E. of Cape San Antonio
Vicinity 13° 10' S 38° 12' W
Christmas Day, Friday, December 25th, 1812
4:45 a.m.
Light breezes and cloudy

It was just after dawn that the USS *Hornet*'s lookouts sighted the USS *Constitution* to windward. They had previously lost sight of her a little before midnight. Captain Lawrence immediately tacked to the southeast in chase of the flagship, flashing out top-gallants, royals, staysails, jib, and flying jib. At eight bells in the forenoon watch, just as the Hornets were piped to breakfast, the commodore signaled, 'Captain and two officers to repair on board.' Thus, at six bells, the *Hornet* took in staysails, flying jib, and royals. She then wore ship, backed the main topsail, and lowered the gig. Ten minutes later Lawrence, Acting-Lieutenant John Newton, and Lieutenant David Conner—already hot and sticky in their full-dress uniforms—came through *Old Ironsides*' starboard entry port to the usual formal ceremony. Lawrence's gig immediately returned to the *Hornet*, whereupon she filled away in company with the *Constitution*. The weather was pleasant with light breezes, and Cape San Antonio bore northwest-by-west, distant eight leagues.

"Welcome, gentlemen, welcome," boomed out Commodore Bainbridge, smiling affably as he enthusiastically shook everyone's hands. "Dinner shall be served shortly. Thanks to you Hornets, and your fresh Brazilian supplies, our repast'll be a little more grand than ordinary ship's fare, but only a little. Nothing like we'd be having at home. But, hey, it's the company that makes your Christmas dinner, not so much the vittles, hey?"

The great cabin was soon augmented by a few of the *Constitu-*

231

tion's officers—Lieutenants Shubrick and Aylwin, Surgeon Evans, and the junior marine officer, Lieutenant Contee. Bainbridge's cook had indeed worked up a grand dinner for the most part based around the fresh provisions: there was roast pork in brown onion sauce with sage and onion stuffing, cold roast chicken, and—as a further acknowledgement of both the holiday and the South American heat—a pleasant display of sliced oranges, bananas, mangoes, and watermelon which complemented the small mince pies, plum-cake, and the obligatory Christmas pudding. The magnificent pudding had, of course, been made almost three weeks ago to ensure that it was properly aged. To wash it all down there was a variety of drink, which included some unusually welcome iced lemonade heightened with marsala.

The conversation ranged widely—the war, shipboard and nautical technicalities, prospects of prizes, the local Portuguese, past Christmases ashore—all unconsciously limited by Bainbridge and Lawrence who, by custom, were the only ones present who could speak without first being spoken to. Unsurprisingly, Lawrence soon came around to Thursday's lost British packet.

"We were this close," he said as he placed his glass of port next to his glass of lemonade, "within musket shot certainly, and almost within pistol shot. I could've taken her but, per the Commodore's orders, I didn't wish to violate the neutrality of the Portuguese." At this Aylwin and Evans thoughtfully and without expression studied their slices of plum-cake and pudding, but the amused lieutenant subtly nudged the surgeon with his elbow: on the day of the chase they had attentively watched it through Aylwin's glass, and had mutually agreed that the *Hornet*'s shots had been fired very much within three miles of the land—well inside Portuguese territory.

"I had a dream last night," said Bainbridge, abruptly changing the subject.

"Indeed, sir," inquired Shubrick after a startled moment. "A dream?"

"Yes. A confused, strange dream. I dreamt of fighting an action with an English frigate. It was quite severe, but of course I ultimately triumphed."

"Well, sir," laughed Lawrence, "thank God for that!"

"Yes," went on Bainbridge, frowning at him. "Yes. Well, that was not my point. Of course I—*we*—would triumph. But this's what's so strange: in my dream, as you might imagine, we took many prisoners from the defeated ship. Among those prisoners were several army officers, and one of 'em was a tall man—and he was a general."

"A general?" said Evans. "How strange. Sir, why would there be a general on board a frigate?"

"Well I'm sure I don't know, Doctor," replied Bainbridge, "but he was clearly a general officer. What can it mean? I've always found dreams to be puzzling." He fell silent for a moment.

"I've no great desire to meet an English general—though I would not mind at all meeting an English frigate!" There was an amused chuckle from around the table, and Lawrence raised his wineglass, immediately followed by the others.

"Gentlemen, may I?" he began. "To the Commodore's frigate: may we see her soon, with or without her general!" The toast was happily drunk, and as Bainbridge placed his glass back on the table he still smiled.

"A note of business, gentlemen, if I may. Upon reflection, if the wind permits, I'll take the *Constitution* into the harbor tomorrow. I'd very much like to talk to Mr. Hill—our esteemed consul—face-to-face, and I find we could stow even more provisions than what the *Hornet* brought out to us, prodigious though they were. Moreover, I believe it'd be prudent to bring our water to fullest capacity. Thus, Captain Lawrence, when you return on board the *Hornet* this evening, be so kind as to send over your sailing master. I'm sure he'll suffice to bring me in, which will eliminate the need for a Portuguese pilot. While I'm in port, the *Hornet* shall stay in the approaches, ever vigilant for any British shipping. Is that all clear? Good! Splendid!" Bainbridge pushed his chair back.

"And now gentlemen," he continued, "I fear we must bring this delightful dinner to a close. Before we do, however, shall we sing a hymn to mark the day? Splendid! I'll commence with one of my favorites, and those who know it may join in." Bainbridge cleared his throat and began, his singing surprisingly pleasant despite his usual rasp.

> *God rest ye merry, gentlemen,*
> *Let nothing you dismay.*

With a general nod of heads the other officers joined in; they all apparently knew the old English hymn.

Remember, Christ, our Saviour,
Was born on Christmas day
To save us all from Satan's power
When we were gone astray.
O tidings of comfort and joy,
Comfort and joy,
O tidings of comfort and joy.

Now to the Lord sing praises,
All you within this place,
And with true love and brotherhood
Each other now embrace;
This holy tide of Christmas
All other doth deface.
O tidings of comfort and joy,
Comfort and joy,
O tidings of comfort and joy.

At three bells in the second dog watch Lawrence and his officers returned to their ship. A half-glass later the *Hornet*'s sailing master, Mr. Sylvester Bill, came on board the *Constitution*, in anticipation of her entrance into San Salvador on Saturday. As Christmas day gave way to darkness the two ships wore to the north and filled away, with San Antonio light to the northwest-½-west, distant five leagues.

During the night both crews remained busy while they enjoyed the coolness, if perhaps not the wetness, that was brought by intermittent squalls of rain. At five bells in the middle watch the *Hornet* spoke a Portuguese brig from San Salvador. At six bells—having lost sight of *Old Ironsides*—Captain Lawrence came-to with the kedge, in twenty-five fathoms, after he decided to hold his position until daylight. So it was at two bells in the morning watch the *Hornet* ran up her kedge, tacked to the southeast and, despite the continuous showers of rain, sighted the *Constitution*. By eight bells in the forenoon watch the ships had drawn together, whereupon Lawrence went on board the flagship. Both ships then wore to the southwest and sailed in company. Cape San Antonio bore north-northeast, distant five leagues. During the early afternoon the squadron cruised farther southwest, then northeast, then south. They occasionally tacked and wore, taking full advantage of the light breezes and pleasant weather which had replaced the rain. At seven bells in the afternoon watch the commodore hung out the signal to speak, but when the ships drew close together it was not Bainbridge's voice but rather Lawrence's which floated across to the *Hornet*.

"Mr. Stewart; Mr. Stewart, there," he hailed. On board the *Hornet* Acting-Lieutenant Newton had the watch but Lieutenant Stewart—acting in command—was predictably on the quarterdeck.

"Sir!"

"The commodore desires I go with him into Salvador," called Lawrence. "So, I want you to cruise off the mouth of the harbor, if you please. If the flagship doesn't come out by tomorrow noon, then I'll—if the wind permits—come out to you in a boat."

"Aye aye, sir," replied Stewart, "cruise about in this vicinity and await the flag or your boat tomorrow."

So with light and favorable breezes, the *Constitution* left the *Hornet* behind and stood into the Bay of All Saints. Lawrence and Bill had just begun to point out the navigational features of the bay when the lookouts identified two boats coming out. These boats seemingly headed straight for *Old Ironsides*, with several civilians on board occasionally waving their arms. When they had approached within pistol shot they dropped their sails; the frigate correspondingly hove-to.

"The boat, ahoy!" came the hail from *Old Ironsides'* quarterdeck. A tall man in the closest boat carefully stood up, cupped his hands in front of his mouth, and called back.

"Sir, my name's Davis, master of the *Sally* out of Philadelphia. My associates and I bring you letters from Mr. Hill, and beg you—in his name—to *not* enter the port today."

A few minutes later Davis and two other American merchant captains came onto the *Constitution's* quarterdeck—to be met by a puzzled Lawrence and an angry Bainbridge.

"What's all this, sir?" he snapped, barely waiting for the civilities of introductions.

"Commodore Bainbridge, Mr. Hill sends his apologies for not coming out himself, but he's spent most of his time at the governor's palace these last three days." Captain Davis tried not to wilt under Bainbridge's red-faced glare. He cleared his throat and continued.

"The governor—as of course you know the Count dos Arcos—has reversed his earlier friendly attitude and now suddenly shows an unfriendly disposition toward the United States. He says he's much irritated at the *Hornet's* conduct in regard to the chase of the British packet the other day, as well as your close blockade of San Salvador. He says these acts on your part aren't only violations of neutrality, but he construes them as acts of hostility."

"Blockade! Hostility!" spluttered Bainbridge.

"Er—yes, sir," replied Davis. "Mr. Hill's hopeful that he might soon remove these newly found prejudices and erroneous sentiments on the part of the governor. Umm, prejudices which as of today include withholding from your squadron those civilities which were—and should be—due to you. Mr. Hill further promises that if he fails in negotiating these points with the governor, Mr. Hill will send out to the *Constitution* water and provisions in three or four days time."

"Hell and death!" fumed Bainbridge. "You say you have letters from Mr. Hill?"

"Yes, sir," replied Davis as he held them out.

"Gentlemen, pardon me for a moment," said Bainbridge. He took the papers and walked over to the railing. He riffled through them for a few minutes. At one point he pounded his fist upon the barrel of the carronade next to him, and at another he literally stamped his foot. After a while he strode back over to the merchant captains.

"Gentlemen, thank you for coming out to me with this important intelligence," he began. A cold rage had replaced his earlier heat. "When you return to the city, I wish that Mr. Hill informs the governor that I consider his remarks and letter as personal insults. He must be a strange person to think American cruisers won't patrol in this ocean just because the coast of Brazil is washed by its waves. He apparently has talked of hostilities. Pray ask Mr. Hill to inquire if the governor considers our countries to be at war. Then, inform me of his answer and I'll act accordingly."

"Mr. Parker," called Bainbridge. He turned towards the officers who stood by the binnacle.

"Sir," replied the first lieutenant as he stepped forward.

"Under the circumstances we shall not enter the port. Pray take us back out of the bay and rendezvous with the *Hornet*."

"Aye aye, sir," said Parker.

"Captain Davis," said Bainbridge as he now turned back to the civilians, "accompany me out to sea, if you please. Directly I draft a letter to Mr. Hill you will kindly take it in to him—most likely later this evening. You other gentlemen, I thank you again for your consideration and your efforts, and you may now return to your boat."

At eight bells in the second dog watch the *Constitution* ranged close alongside the *Hornet*. Captain Lawrence, Captain Davis, and Mr. Bill rowed over the smooth sea in Davis' boat. The *Hornet* filled away and stood in for the land, while *Old Ironsides* wore to the east-southeast. On board the *Hornet*, Davis clutched a folder wrapped in oilskin which contained a sealed letter from the commodore.

U.S. Frigate <u>Constitution</u>
In the approaches to Salvador
26th Decr 1812

My Dear Mr. Hill,

I was entering the Port of Bahia, with the frigate <u>Constitution</u> under my command, to receive a supply of Water when your communications of the 23rd and 25th instant were handed to me, containing the official correspondence between his Excellency the Governor of Bahia and yourself, relative to the Squadron under my command cruising along the Coast of Brazil.

It was with deep regret and great astonishment that I learned his Excellency had taken misconceptions of the Conduct of my Squadron on this Coast, and particularly the Act of Captain Lawrence, commander of the <u>Hornet</u>, in a chase of an English ship on the 24th instant.

Had his Excellency been correctly informed of the uniform good Treatment given by the Squadron under my command to all Portuguese vessels which it meets with; and in no instance does it molest in the least any coasting Vessel of his Nation, he certainly would not have breathed such sentiments of hostility towards us.

As to Captain Lawrence's conduct in chasing the English ship, the Fact must have been self-evident to his Excellency and every Person who witnessed the Chase, as to convince them that <u>nothing but respect for the neutrality</u> of this Coast prevented the <u>capture of that Ship</u>.

Please assure his Excellency that I shall not, <u>according to my Judgement</u>, violate the neutrality of Brazil, or do any Act to give just cause of offence. But, I shall strictly fulfill the Duties I owe to my own Country, to whom I am <u>alone</u> responsible for my Conduct.

I am very sorry his premature Opinion and hasty determination deprive me of the Pleasure of making his personal Acquaintance, as I had intended, but which his expressions of Hostility now prevent.

I shall take English ships wherever I find them without the jurisdiction of a Neutral coast.

My dear Sir, I thank you, again, for all your Aide and assistance, whilst I remain your humble and obedient Servant,

Wm. Bainbridge

As he stood by the *Hornet*'s wheel, Master Commandant Lawrence kept one eye on the trim of his sails while otherwise lost in thought. In his coat pocket was another memo—much less formal.

U.S.F. <u>Constitution</u>
26th Decr 1812

My Dear Lawrence,

Mr. Hill informs me that, having attentively observed the conduct of the British officers, it is his belief that it is the intention of Captain Greene to <u>run</u> to sea <u>unobserved</u> by us at the first favorable Moment.

Thus, I desire you remain in this vicinity off Salvador, viz. the approaches to the Bay. Watch close, but do <u>not</u> enter the Bay. I shall stand to Sea and run down the Coast, cruising for Prizes.

I shall keep off the Land to the northward of Lat. 12° 30', until Thursday next, when you will meet me there, except you have great reason to believe the <u>Bonne Citoyenne</u> is coming out. In that case, <u>watch close</u> and join me on Saturday next.

May Glory and Success attend you!

W. B.

CHAPTER 20
SOUTH ATLANTIC OCEAN

South Atlantic Ocean
110 nautical miles E.-by-N. of Recife, Brazil
Vicinity 33° 47' W 7° 43' S
Christmas Day, Friday, December 25th, 1812
Fine weather, winds S.E.-by-E

For the last five days, H.M. Frigate *Java* and her convoy had found themselves in steady and uneventful blue-water sailing. Even today—which was, after all, Christmas—saw little change to the basic morning routines. Captain Lambert decided not to hold any particular Christmas ceremony. He felt that an extra emphasis during the coming Sunday's divine services would suffice for the occasion. The galley did, however, produce a dinner for the crew considerably above the ordinary. Fridays were by routine "banyan" days, which is to say a meatless day of oatmeal and pease. Nevertheless, this Friday saw the galley come out with a double-ration of salt pork, a double-shotted plum-duff, and a double-issue of noon-time grog. The wardroom cook followed suit with a special dinner of roast pork and mince pies for the ship's officers. It was, however, the great cabin that really stretched out for a memorable dinner. General Hislop had thought this out far ahead, and had accordingly brought with him, from Portsmouth and Gosport, supplies for a sumptuous feast to which he planned to invite his own aides as well as the *Java*'s senior officers. Moreover, as he was bringing out to India a magnificent service of silver plate, befitting a royal governor who would give official dinners in a foreign land, he now had it roused up from a storeroom below for this occasion. So it was that he turned his Christmas victuals over to the captain's cook for cooking, and he turned his silver over to the captain's steward for polishing. With all this culinary activity from early-on, all-day long wonderful aromas wafted aloft from the

Java. The ship's company was piped to their dinner at noon; two hours later the wardroom officers sat down; and, finally, the great cabin a half-hour after that. This last period was a specific trial to those invited to the cabin who, terribly sharp-set, repeatedly stole occasional glances at their watches, while sniffing in particular the cinnamon, nutmeg, ginger, cloves, and currants as Hislop's Christmas pudding received its final two-hour steaming.

The crew, upon the whole, enjoyed the extra food and drink and made the best of the celebration, considering the distance from home, the absence of loved ones, and for most the un-Christmaslike hot weather. Bits of song and bursts of laughter erupted here and there among the messes. One group, particularly high-spirited, broke out in a Plymouth ditty which was, for the most part, carried by four seamen with singularly clear tenor voices.

'Twas at the landing-place that's just below Mount Wise,
Poll leaned against the sentry's box, a tear in both her eyes,
Her apron twisted round her arms, all for to keep them warm,
Being a windy Christmas-day, and also a snow storm.

> *And Bett and Sue*
> *Both stood there too,*
>   *A shivering by her side,*
> *They both were dumb,*
> *And both looked glum,*
>   *As they watched the ebbing tide.*
> *Poll put her arms a-kimbo,*
>   *At the admiral's house looked she,*
> *To thoughts that were in limbo,*
>   *She now a vent gave free.*
> *"You have sent the ship in a gale to work,*
>   *On a lee shore to be jammed.*
> *I'll give you a piece of my mind, Old Turk,*
>   *Port Admiral, you be damned.*
> *We'll give you a piece of our mind, Old Turk,*
>   *Port Admiral, you be damned.*

"I'd the flour an' plums all picked, an' the suet chopped up fine
To mix into a pudding rich for all the mess to dine.
I pawned my ear-rings for the beef; it weighed at least a stone,
Now my fancy man is sent to sea, and I am left alone.

Here's Bett and Sue
Who stand here too,
 A shivering by my side.
They both are dumb,
They both look glum,
 And watch the ebbing tide."
Poll put her arms a-kimbo,
 At the admiral's house looked she,
To thoughts that were in limbo,
 She now a vent gave free.
"You've got a turkey, I'll be bound,
 With which you will be crammed.
I'll give you a bit of my mind, Old Hound,
 Port Admiral, you be damned.
I'll give you a bit of my mind, Old Hound,
 Port Admiral, you be damned."

"A glass of sherry with you, gentlemen," offered General Hislop as he and his guests sat down in the great cabin. Captain Lambert, Commander Marshall, Major Walker, Captain Wood, Lieutenant Herringham, marine Lieutenant Mercer, and the captains of the two Indiamen all raised their glasses to their host. Hislop had been a little disappointed, but entirely understanding, that Lieutenant Chads had respectfully declined his invitation. As president of the wardroom mess, Chads was obliged to host that dinner and necessarily could not be in two places at once. Even without Chads' presence, the great cabin—the entire great cabin today because the temporary bulkhead which divided it had been removed for this occasion—was resplendent. The table and sideboards gleamed with Hislop's plate. The naval officers were strangely outnumbered by the marine and army officers, but their best blue-and-gold uniforms pleasantly set off the others' scarlet-and-gold. Each officer had a servant—a boy, a seaman, or a marine—who stood behind his chair, equally well-dressed in his finest. All looked splendid indeed, although in most cases the broadcloth of the elegant coats was designed more for the English Channel than the heat and humidity of the equator. The dinner did Hislop—and Lambert's cook—proud: smoked tongue, sucking pig, roast pork, mince pie, ratifia biscuit, apple pie (with Cheddar cheese), and that aromatic Christmas pudding. It was all helped down with glasses of sherry, claret, and burgundy. When the cloth was drawn, the king's health was drunk in a glass of port, which was followed by a toast to wives and sweethearts, and lastly one that wished considerable confusion to Monsieur Bonaparte. Despite the stifling air temperature and high humidity, the wine throughout the dinner was reasonably cool, for several of the bottles had been wrapped in wet blankets and slung from the crossjack yard to the shaded side (the wardroom had executed a similar wine-cooling tactic by using a net and a twenty-fathom line to tow two-dozen bottles deep behind the ship). Cups of coffee finally joined the glasses of port, further accompanied by comfortable noise, convivial talk, and generally good humor. Captain Lambert mentioned his now-firm intention to put in at San Salvador, particularly as the planned stop at Porto Praya had been so abruptly terminated. This was enthusiastically greeted by all, with the exception of the captains of the Indiamen.

"We certainly understand your desire, sir, to acquire additional water and provisions," said the older and thinner of the two, "particularly with your large crew and with so many supernumeraries. But with our small crews, my colleague and I are happy with our water and stores, and so prefer to shape our courses directly toward the cape. We thank you for your protection thus far, but we believe we'll now be relatively safe proceeding on our own. So with your permission, Captain, and winds permitting, we'll part company with you some time tomorrow."

"Certainly, gentlemen," replied Lambert as he raised his glass, "with all my heart I wish you fair winds and a very happy return."

A deck below, the wardroom's feast was much the same as the one in the great cabin, even though it was without the brilliant plate nor quite so many removes. By the time the similar toasts were drunk and the aroma of coffee filled that room, Lieutenant Chads was thankful for a party that appeared to be going well. With a smile he loosened his stock and listened to the talk and laughter, the riddles and poems, and the songs—though the last one replaced his smile with a look of nostalgia:

> *The first Nowell the angels did say,*
> *Was to certain poor shepherds in fields as they lay;*
> *In fields where they lay keeping their sheep*
> *On a cold winter's night that was so deep.*
> *Nowell, Nowell, Nowell, Nowell,*
> *Born is the King of Israel.*
>
> *They looked up and saw a star*
> *Shining in the East beyond them far,*

And to the earth it gave great light,
And so it continued both day and night.
Nowell, Nowell, Nowell, Nowell,
Born is the King of Israel!

This wardroom singing was clearly audible in the great cabin immediately above, perhaps unsurprisingly as it was around twenty voices strong, and this last song a carol everyone knew well.

"Nicely done," said General Hislop as it concluded, his eyes closed and his head cocked to the side. "Well done, indeed. The gentlemen below us picked one of my favorites. In fact, I was just about to suggest *we* try our voices here. After all, we cannot allow the wardroom alone to honor the day? Gentlemen, are you with me? *Adeste fideles, Laeti Triumphantes,*" Hislop began in a clear baritone, immediately joined by most of the others.

Venite, venite in Bethlehem:
Natum videte, Regem angelorum:
Venite adoremus, Venite adoremus, Venite adoremus
—Dominum.

Deum de Deo, Lumen ad lumine,
Gestant puellae, viscera:
Deum, verum, Genitum non factum:
Veneti adoremus, Venite adoremus, Venite adoremus
—Dominum.

"Excellent!" Hislop cried, "Superb! Thank you, gentlemen. I must tell you that for me it's just not a proper Christmas unless I sing that carol at least once." He paused for a moment, considering. "Now, I wonder if you'll forgive me if I speak—just for a few minutes I assure you—of matters that have to do with the war, particularly as we're now on *this* side of the Atlantic. I've much wanted to discuss—particularly with you, Captain Lambert and Captain Marshall—our maritime war with the Americans, yet thus far I've restrained myself, well aware it's an unpleasant subject. Yet, I'd like to know your thoughts. That is, if you'd be willing to share them with ignorant military men?"

"Certainly, General Hislop," replied Lambert. "It's, as you say, a subject of great irritation and frustration in the Navy, in the mercantile marine," he nodded to the East India Company officers, "and to the entire country, for that matter. Whether you choose to consider the shocking naval actions, or the similarly amazing commercial losses, it's a bleak and aggravating situation. Damned aggravating."

"Exactly, sir!" said Major Walker, his face a little more pink than usual after several glasses of Christmas cheer. "Exactly! The frigate actions in particular are astounding. We know that our *Guerrière* struck to their *Constitution* in August. Now we hear rumors that our *Macedonian* has struck to another of their big frigates. Gentlemen, these are occurrences which call for serious reflection. And the statement in that last batch of newspapers we saw—*Lloyd's List* contains notice of around 250 British vessels captured in six months by the Americans. Two frigates, a couple of lesser men-of-war, and some two-hundred fifty merchantmen, it would seem!"

"Sir," asked Captain Wood, "haven't we established any sort of plan to interfere with the cruises of their national ships or to sweep their damned privateers from the seas? Clearly we *are* carrying war to them. I dare say their trade suffers. But so's ours, and it suffers severely, I might add."

"Can these things really be true?" asked Lieutenant Mercer, the most junior officer present. It was somewhat of a surprise to hear him dare to speak out uninvited. "The British people can't hear them unmoved. It's my belief that anyone who had predicted such a result of an *American* war this time last year would've been treated as a madman—or a traitor. He would've been told, *if* his friends had even bothered to argue with him, that long before four months had passed the American flag would be swept from the seas, the contemptible little navy of the United States annihilated, and their maritime arsenals rendered a heap of ruins."

"Yet, gentlemen," interrupted Commander Marshall, "down to this moment not a single American frigate has struck her flag. They insult and laugh at our want of enterprise and vigor. They leave their damned ports whenever they damn well please, and return to them whenever it damn well suits 'em. They traverse the Atlantic. They beset the West India islands. They parade along the coasts of South America. Hell and death, they advance to the very chops of the Channel! Seemingly we can't manage to chase, nor intercept—and we apparently can't engage 'em but to hand *them* victory."

"I heard a remarkable thing," chimed in the elder East India Company officer, "the source of which was British mariners briefly held by the American frigate *President*. They said that some of the Yankee officers repeatedly expressed a wish to fall-in with an English 74-gun ship-of-the-line—if they can find one by herself. They are positive they could take one. And, when she fights, the *President* apparently hoists two large white flags with black letters, one which says 'No Impressment!,' and the other 'This is the HAUGHTY President—How Do You LIKE Her?'" These pieces of intelligence were met with a surprised silence, finally broken by Major Walker.

"What this means, my friends," he said as he reached for the bottle, "what this signifies is nothing less than our honor—the navy's honor, sure, but the nation's as well. The public shame is our shame at these seemingly unanswerable American naval victories."

"Well," said Lambert slowly as his finger traced a figure-eight on the table, "it seems to me that the two prime objects to be attained in successful warfare are to cripple the antagonist and to give heart and confidence to one's own side. We all know—don't we?—that the first object can't be attained by the little American navy. It's powerless to inflict appreciable damage to the colossal sea might of Britain. But it's that second object which troubles us all. The Americans can and are most certainly achieving that end. Thank God that on land the American attempts to invade Canada have resulted in humiliating disasters for them. But, damn it, the effects of their victorious sea actions are doubtless great as they offset the mortification and depression which those land disasters caused."

"In England," said Hislop, "and to us here, the news of these naval actions've brought forth at least as much excitement, but of a wholly different kind. Neither the British government, nor the British people, and least of all the British Navy I'm sure, had ever dreamed it possible that on sea we could possibly suffer any serious annoyance from America."

Walker slammed his fist on the table, making the glasses jump. "Gentlemen, it's this clear. The American navy must be destroyed. The Stars and Stripes must be swept from the seas—entirely swept, I say. The Americans must be taught—and, by God, the entire world must be taught—that no power whatsoever can venture to pit itself against the Royal Navy."

"Hear, hear! Hear him!" echoed several voices.

"Well, my friends," interjected Hislop as he gazed thoughtfully at Walker's red face. He was now a little sorry that he had brought up this particularly emotional subject at the Christmas table. "Let's pass the port one more time and give the loyal toast. Ah, all ready? Gentlemen, the King." Glasses in hand the officers rose, stooped slightly under the deck beams, and drank the sovereign's health.

"On that note, let's say good evening. Perhaps we might go on deck to see if there's any refreshing breeze at all. This's been an extremely pleasant gathering. I thank you, one and all, for your presence."

The day after Christmas presented moderate to fresh breezes and fine weather throughout, with the winds southeast and east-southeast. The *Java* and her small convoy ran south, south-by-west, and south-southwest, at an average of around five and a half knots. At eight bells in the second dog watch the *Cape Packet* and the *Atlantic* altered their courses to the southeast-by-east and parted company, in accordance with the intentions expressed the day before. Thus, the *Java* continued towards San Salvador; alone save her prize, the *William*, which faithfully dogged the frigate's heels at the other end of the tow rope.

Sunday was similar. The winds backed some, now more from the east-northeast and east-by-north, and the course altered slightly to the southwest and west-southwest. Mr. Robinson believed that Salvador bore to the southwest at less than 150 miles distance. At two bells in the forenoon watch the ship's company formally mustered by divisions. Captain Lambert read the Articles of War and performed divine services. For the latter he selected a lengthy sermon, again from his favorite resource (Dean Donne), and included several more hymns than usual to make up for the omission of services on Christmas.

The next day, December twenty-eighth, saw considerable change and more activity. Winds, speeds, and courses maintained Sunday's pattern, though considerable clouds had begun to form as the ship's company again mustered by divisions to witness punishment. Able seaman Armand Gullichsen received thirty-six lashes for mutinous behavior, while able seaman William Gardiner, marine private Benjamin Newton, and ordinary seaman John Russell received twenty-four, twenty-four, and twelve for disobedience of orders. By two bells in the afternoon watch the clouds became squalls with rain. This forced the disappearance of studdingsails and topgallants, and required first and then second reefs to be taken in the topsails. The *Java*'s speed fell to barely one knot—barely steerageway. At four bells, just as the officers sat down to dinner, the lookouts simultaneously discovered the land, bearing from west to west-northwest, as well as several small ships to the southwest. Around eight bells in the second dog-watch the squalls and rain gave way to light winds and clouds. At midnight the *Java* struck soundings in twenty-five fathoms—her leadsmen having tried every two hours, for the past three days, with no result.

"Finally!" said the master to himself as he turned-in. "We can hardly be ten leagues from Salvador. We'll signal for a pilot by 'hands to breakfast.'"

CHAPTER 21
COAST OF BRAZIL

Coast of Brazil
8 nautical miles to the east of
São Salvador da Baía
Vicinity 12° 58' S 38° 29' W
Tuesday, December 29th, 1812
8:00 a.m.
Sea nearly calm; light winds from the E.N.E.

HMS *Java*'s forty-eighth day out from England began with a spectacular dawn and singularly pleasant morning. After an uneventful night she continued to tow her prize as she approached the port of San Salvador. She had struck soundings at midnight, and as Mr. Robinson had predicted, now prepared to hoist a signal to request a harbor pilot. It was just after three bells in the forenoon watch when the lookout, in the *Java*'s maintop crosstrees, perceived a sail to the southwest.

"Come in," said Captain Lambert as he responded to the cabin sentry's announcement. Young Edward Keele, one of the midshipmen of the watch, raced in. "I beg your pardon, sir," he cried. "Mr. Chads' duty, and a sail off the larboard bow, royals up from the masthead."

"Thank you, Mr. Keele." said Lambert. "My apologies, General Hislop. I need to jump up on deck for a moment."

"Of course, my dear sir," said Hislop. Lambert tossed his napkin onto the table—abandoning his bacon, toast, and coffee—edged around Hislop's chair, and walked out of the cabin. He followed Keele up the companionway to the quarterdeck, though Keele had left him far behind.

"Don't run, Mr. Keele," said Lambert as he caught up to him. "It has a bad effect on the men, particularly if we're in action. Unless the mast is falling directly upon you, walk with dignity."

"Aye aye, sir. Sorry, sir."

Lambert stepped over to Lieutenant Chads, who smiled and touched his hat.

"Good morning, Captain."

"Good morning, Henry. Beautiful day. Have you found us something interesting, I wonder?"

"Something indeed, sir," Chads nodded towards the larboard bow. "'Royals up' says the masthead lookout, but Sanders, absolutely beside himself to be helpful, has also taken his glass aloft." As if on cue, Lieutenant Sanders' voice drifted down from the main royal yard.

"Deck there! A ship. Could be a warship. I can just see her tops'ls."

Lambert rubbed his chin, deep in thought. "Mr. Chads, Salvador beckons, and I want that run on shore. I want that fresh water too—but surely we can postpone for a few moments. Let's see what we've found. Cast off the *William*. Give her a hail and direct 'em to proceed into the port. We'll meet up with her later." He then turned to the master.

"Mr. Robinson."

"Sir?"

"Pray alter course, if you please. Bear down upon our unknown guest."

At this same time, the USS *Constitution* was running about twenty miles offshore when her foretop lookout, in turn, observed two strange sails on the weather bow, extremely close together. A few minutes later the lookout saw even more of interest.

"Sir," he called down, "one sail continues standin' in fer the land. But t'other one—the larger one—has come about an's a-headin' toward us."

As he pulled his chin in thought, Commodore Bainbridge came to a decision. "We shall about-ship."

The seamen, petty officers, and officers of the larboard watch stood ready. The off-duty starboard watch was not called, since this was a routine—albeit complex—evolution.

"Stations for stays!" roared the master. About seventy seamen—sail trimmers, topmen, waisters, afterguard, forecastlemen, and quarterdeckmen—ran to their stations and jumped to the master's next volley of orders.

"Ease down the helm...Helm's a-lee...Rise tacks and sheets... Mains'l haul! Of all, haul!" The *Constitution* passed from the one tack to the other, and as quickly as it began the considerable hub-bub on the weather deck and in the rigging subsided. She now headed east-northeast, towards the larger of the unidentified ships. The wind in the rigging played a pleasant symphony as the ship lay over in the light breeze, while the waves crashed and hissed as they flowed down her sides.

It fast grew hot, and the heat which poured down from the sun was intensified by the remarkable humidity. On board the *Java*, at around four bells, Captain Lambert pulled some sheets of paper from his coat and checked the information on them.

"Mr. Chads, if you please, throw out the private recognition signals—British, Spanish, and Portuguese—making them in suc-cession."

"Aye aye, sir."

None were answered by the unidentified ship, which was not necessarily alarming. On the other hand, since those signals would be meaningless to ships from any other countries but those—say France or the United States—it was neither particularly comfort-ing. The chase, in turn, did not seem to be alarmed by signals she apparently could not read, and continued to stand toward the *Java* on the starboard tack.

Commander Marshall and Mr. Robinson leaned over the rail-ing, studying the chase through their telescopes.

"I begin to think she's not large enough to be a ship of the line," said Marshall. "Perhaps she's a *razee* or a large frigate."

"I can't be sure, sir," replied Robinson as he wiped his eye. "Regardless, she's clearly under easy sail and comes directly to-ward us."

"Mr. Chads," said Lambert, standing by the binnacle, "we'll clear for action, if you please, and beat to quarters."

Like an ant hill disturbed, the ship burst forth in an uproar of activity. Many of the men jumped up from where they had been lying on the deck, having found strips of shade under the gang-ways or beneath the spread of the sails. Those off watch came pouring up from the berth deck.

The gunports were opened, the guns run out, fire buckets were filled and hoses were rigged to the pumps, the shot garlands were filled with roundshot and the scuttlebutts were filled with water, the decks were wetted down then sanded, wet "fearnought" screens were spread over the hatches which led to the powder magazines, the galley fire was thrown over the side, and a considerable number of cutlasses, tomahawks, pistols, and boarding axes were broken out and readied for use. Two boatswain's mates climbed into the rigging of the fore- and mainmasts. They led working parties to make fast chains and puddenings to the principal yards—reinforcement in anticipation of enemy shot striking the everyday slings, which likely would cause unreinforced yards to fall to the deck. Finally, with a rap-rap-rap of hammer and mallet the carpenter's mates knocked down the gundeck's interior cabin bulkheads and carried them below.

The task was made a little harder due to the embarked passengers—the army officers as well as the naval supernumeraries—whose extra numbers and additional baggage measurably added to the material that had to be struck down into the hold, which also measurably added to the time and effort to do so. Of course, the many tons of shipbuilding supplies destined for Bombay, although previously stowed below, complicated the problem as they took up considerable space.

Mr. Jones called for his assistant surgeons, surgeon's mates, and loblolly boys, and led them from the sick bay to the cockpit.

"Gentlemen, it's time. Bring our instruments and accouterments, if you please."

The sick bay was forward on the berth deck, where the medical men usually presided over their routine charges. These sick and injured men they kept close at hand in swinging cots, and those men benefited from the proximity to the privies at the ship's head. From the sick bay they also had a chance at reasonably fresh air which came from above.

The sick bay, however, was not utilized when the ship came into action. The surgeon and his associates set up in the after part of the orlop deck, down in the cockpit, significantly below the waterline and thus safe from shot and splinters. The operating table, and other necessary pieces of side furniture, were created from materials at hand. Several midshipmen's sea chests were pulled out and lashed together, and then covered with tightly drawn sailcloth. Brought down from the sick bay were the instrument and medicine chests, and from them were laid out the necessary materials and implements: on the one side were the probes, forceps, knives and saws, needles and sutures, tourniquets and dressings; on the other the leather-bound chains, catlings, retractors, splints, sedatives (rum, laudanum), aprons (for the surgeon and attendants), and multiple coils of bandages. Several buckets, swabs, and two boxes for severed limbs completed the setup.

On the quarterdeck the various officers made their reports to Chads, who then stepped up to Lambert and touched his hat.

"A clean sweep fore and aft, sir, and hands to quarters."

"Thank you, Mr. Chads," replied Lambert. "Would you be so kind to ensure that Mr. Herringham has slow matches in the tubs?"

"Certainly, Captain. It's already been done, for we knew you were going to order that." Lambert laughed.

"Well, I know you're a progressive thinker in regards to gunnery, and believe I'm old fashioned. But until the guns grow hot, and with the chance of spray flying aboard, we may need to use the old-fashioned method in case we have trouble with the flintlock mechanisms."

The frantic activity and bustle was over. The *Java* bore down toward the other ship in relative silence, aside from the creak of woodwork, the occasional flap of sail, the clatter of blocks, and the whispers of wind in the rigging. The seamen stood by their great guns, and each weapon's powder boy sat behind it on his leather cartridge case. For the most part the gun crews were grim, or anxious, or both.

"Ben...Ben!" hissed eleven-year-old George Herue, one of the gundeck's powder boys, as he sat behind his gun. He cringed at the sound of his own voice in the relative silence, but needed to talk to his friend who sat behind the neighboring cannon.

"Wot h'is it, Georgie?" replied Benjamin Pauling, his whispered response barely audible.

"Ben, are we goin' to be kil't?"

"No, Georgie."

"H'is you certain? I 'eard lots was kil't on the *Guerrière*."

"Yes, George, certain. Why, lookee, we're too small to get 'it by anythin'. H'it's the big buggars what'll cop it—them an' the officers, all showy in their fancy uniforms."

"Really?"

"Yes, Georgie. Now pipe down an' wait fer orders. Don't you worry. When the action starts you'll be too busy t' be thinkin'."

The second lieutenant, Mr. Herringham, had charge of the main deck guns. Under him, Mr. Buchanan, the third lieutenant, had the after guns. Lieutenant Chads and Mr. Robinson stood by Captain Lambert on the quarterdeck, just to the side of the binnacle. General Hislop, his aides Major Walker and Captain Wood, and Commander Marshall also took positions on the quarterdeck, prepared to assist in any way possible. The other two supernumerary naval officers, Lieutenants Aplin and Sanders, took positions on the main deck and forecastle respectively, ready to contribute leadership and expertise.

"General, gentlemen," said Lambert, addressing the army officers. "At times like these we generally write brief letters to our wives or loved ones, and then exchange those letters with one another. That way, if any of us are killed or knocked overboard, it's more likely that such letters will reach those to whom they're addressed. We'll be at leisure for a while yet. You may wish to take advantage of this custom."

He continued after a moment, looking grave. "I thank you for sharing my quarterdeck this afternoon. I'd recommend that when the dust begins to fly you walk about and try not to stand in one place for too long a time. Even more than my blue, your fine scarlet uniforms will make splendid targets for the enemy's marksmen." General Hislop smiled at this and shrugged his shoulders. It was the duty of an officer and gentleman to stand tall and dignified, particularly under fire, and set a proper example for the men.

"Captain," he said as he took Lambert's arm, "I wish you the best of good fortune in this encounter. I'm confident that you and the *Java* will meet with the success you both deserve."

For their part, the American officers began to think their challenger might be a 74-gun British ship of the line, perhaps the *Montagu*—flagship of Lord Nelson's old friend Rear Admiral Manley Dixon—which they had recently been informed could be in these waters. Accordingly, just after six bells, Bainbridge beckoned to his first lieutenant.

"Parker, I'd be obliged if you'd haul up the mains'l and take the royals off her. I've no desire to be confined by a larger adversary while in neutral waters." He paused and looked at the coast which was still plainly visible. Parker executed those orders and tacked the ship to the southeast to head farther seaward. Bainbridge continued to speak as the sail trimmers and topmen finished their work and as the activity subsided.

"As we've discussed, the Portuguese are, strictly speaking, neutral. But as Portugal's strongly allied with Britain against France, I don't really think they're neutral at all. The last three days have certainly shown us the local Portuguese are extremely sensitive and, perhaps, even hostile."

At seven bells the *Constitution* hoisted the private American recognition signal, which of course made no sense to the British and therefore they made no answer. Since there was no answer, Bainbridge became certain that the strange sail was indeed the enemy, particularly as the other ship had earlier thrown out signals that made no sense to *him*.

"Parker, I'll have the mains'l and the royals reset. I want to continue generally to the east to draw the enemy farther from the coast."

"Aye aye, sir," said Parker, who then turned and raised his voice. "Stand by to make more sail...Set the mains'l and the royals!"

"Lay aloft, royal yardmen!" Parker continued. "Lay out and loose! Man the royal halyards, sheets, and weather royal braces...Haul taut! Let fall...Sheet home! Hoist away royals!"

At the same time the master, Nichols, attended to the main course. "Lay aloft and loose the mains'l! Man the tack and sheet... Let go clew-garnets, buntlines, and leech lines...Let fall! Get the tack aboard...Haul aft the sheet! Haul out the bowline!"

As the sails filled and were trimmed, Bainbridge pulled at his collar. He was sweating heavily which caused his shirt to stick and chafe. He refocused his glass upon the enemy.

"Nichols, at what distance are they, do you estimate?"

The master carefully studied the approaching ship through his own glass. "All of four miles, I believe, Commodore."

"I agree," said Bainbridge, and shut his telescope with a pronounced click. "No point in further delay. Parker, clear the ship for action and beat to quarters." The Constitutions cleared ship and ran to their quarters with apparent high spirits, judging from some spontaneous cheering, widespread chatter, and laughter. The lieutenants were surprised that the usually tyrannical commodore did not order "silence," or check the undisciplined noise in any way. Perhaps he does not notice, wondered Lieutenant Aylwin.

The *Java* hauled up and made sail on a parallel course, with the *Constitution* bearing about three points on her lee bow. The British frigate gained rapidly, she was measurably faster—and now ran at fully ten or eleven knots, a prodigious speed for any ship, even in such fine weather.

At noon the hands were piped to dinner and the drums simultaneously beat for the officers' repast as well. This was true in both ships. In 1812, the customs, traditions, and routines of the United States Navy and the Royal Navy were remarkably similar. As both ships had already cleared for action, which meant that the galley fires had been extinguished, the meals today were served cold. But dinner time it was, imminent action or not, and in any event both British and American officers were generally in agreement about their men going into action, if at all possible, with full bellies.

It was also around noon that the British were now able to discern, flying from the chase's main-topmast head, not a long, narrow commissioning pendant, but a short, broad pendant.

"Henry, I think we pursue a commodore," said Lambert to Chads. "And, in these waters, that likely means an American."

This was confirmed a few short minutes later as the chase hoisted her colors, showing the U.S. jack at the foremast, that just-observed broad pendant at the main, and the American ensign at both the mizzen-topgallant masthead and the end of the spanker gaff. The jack was impressive even at this distance: a large blue flag, with a constellation of fifteen white stars arranged in an irregular rectangular pattern.

On board the *Java* most of the officers were below as they took their meal. However, unwilling to quit the deck even for a moment, Lambert, Chads, Robinson, Marshall, and the army officers were served sandwiches and small beer, carried up by the captain's steward and the wardroom servants.

Thus, standing against the rail with his glass fixed upon the American, Mr. Robinson—between bites—described the tactical situation to Hislop, Walker, and Wood. The naval and nautical scenario was far different from anything the soldiers had seen in their military careers.

"Gentlemen," began the master, "as you can see the situation's extremely fluid—I beg your pardon for the apparent pun—with both ships moving much faster than infantry could ever hope. This far out from the shore we needn't be concerned that any features of terrain nor underwater obstacles will influence or impede our progress. And, the sea's pretty smooth today. Nevertheless, I can't emphasize enough how everything—gentlemen, *everything*—we and the enemy do is going to be completely governed by the *wind*. It's true that the modern square-rigged ship's a prodigiously capable, flexible, and maneuverable machine, but it has limits, and those limits are much prescribed by the elements."

Robinson swallowed the last of his beer, which had quickly become too warm in the weather deck's heat. He made a face. "Sure, as it is with you soldiers, we must be concerned with how and when we apply our weapons upon the enemy—and if, how, and when we approach, board, and engage him in close action, fighting hand-to-hand. But, in addition, we must constantly keep our minds—and a goodly number of our men—*actually sailing the ship*, for the wind and the sea are constantly in play, and a moment's inattention can make all the difference in success or failure. So, we must continually work to build upon any advantage the forces of nature may offer, and guard against those same forces offering us disadvantage. You'll no doubt see, during the course of the action today, the sail handlers—or trimmers—called away many times from their duties at the guns. This is because the ship must be handled well and smartly in order for any gunnery to be satisfactory."

He paused for a moment, fingering his telescope in the scorching sunlight. "You'll also see that with our great guns we'll endeavor to hurt the enemy in his masts, sails, and rigging, in order to aid nature to provide him with disadvantage. Alas, the enemy will also offer us the same favors in turn, for the very same hope. Indeed, and you must always bear this in mind, whether it be in action or in plain sailing, the wind and the sea are *profoundly* unforgiving of any carelessness, inattention, or incapacity." He again paused as he gazed at the approaching warship.

"Many thanks, Mr. Robinson," said Major Walker. "As always, your insights are astonishingly helpful. I confess to a burning question, though, which isn't specifically one of seamanship. Have you any notion of who our enemy is? That is to say, which Yankee ship this might be?"

"Well, Major," replied Robinson, "I've just overheard one of our officers state the conviction that she must be their *Essex*, and indeed this idea can't be too quickly dismissed as we have some intelligence that the *Essex* was bound for these very waters. To my eye, however, I rather think that this vessel is *not* the *Essex*. See the impressive length, see how tall she is, the apparent heavy and stout build, the steady—not exceptionally fast, but steady—progress, the stiffness she exhibits as she cuts through the water, how little she leans while carrying considerable canvas. The *Essex* is a 32-gun ship, and though I can't quite count their ports from this distance and at this angle, it seems there are more than sixteen in yonder ship's broadside. I could *wish* she were the *Essex*, for that vessel's said to be armed with carronades only—the short-barreled weapons like those beside you here on our quarterdeck and fo'c'sle —and while a carronade throws an extremely heavy ball that does considerable destruction, its fire's only effective at pretty short distances. In such a case we could stand off outside the range of their carronades, and do for them with our main deck long guns."

"But, gentlemen," Robinson continued with a grave look, "I fear this particular ship's one of their large ones, which can only be the *United States,* the *Constitution*, or the *President*. Thus, she'll carry a goodly number of long 24s on the gundeck—heavier metal than our own 18s."

"Well, then," interjected Wood, "if this ship indeed turns out to be our superior, are we justified to engage her?"

"Oh, Captain Wood," replied Robinson. He shook his head and smiled as if responding to a child's question. "I must preface any answer to that by observing that it's a rule laid down in our Service, and always acted upon as a point of honor, that if *any* frigate of ours falls in with *any* frigate that belongs to an enemy, such frigate must if possible bring her enemy to action. And this is true even if that enemy evidences infinite superiority."

"I dare say, Master, you've seen much action at sea?" asked General Hislop.

"Yes, sir. More than enough to suit me." Robinson mopped his face with his handkerchief as he perspired freely in the blazing sun.

Lambert and Marshall stood few feet away from Robinson and his retinue. They, likewise, observed the enemy and considered options and—despite themselves—listened to his remarks.

"Sir," said Marshall, "I find myself entirely in agreement with the master. This's one of the big Americans. See how much higher she carries her guns than we do? I conceive, therefore, that she'll be superior in the weight of her metal, and no doubt in the number of her men."

Lambert nodded thoughtfully and turned to give direction to the signal midshipman. "Colors, Mr. West, and the recognition again to the maintop."

The *Java* raised her red ensign and repeated the signal flag recognition—red-yellow-red. There was no reaction from the American ship.

Lambert was to windward of his opponent and as a result held the weather gage. He thereby controlled the next move in this game. He could refuse action and easily fall back into neutral waters, to include the Portuguese harbor. Or, just as easily, he could take advantage of his ship's superior speed and force action. As he watched the American frigate through his glass, Lambert thought hard about the events of the naval war with the Americans thus far, dwelling on the real and painful details of the *Guerrière's* fate at the hands of the *Constitution* last August. He was also aware of the unsettling rumors about the capture of HMS *Macedonian* by the USS *United States* just two months ago. Although he could not know it, the big frigate he now studied was, of course, the very one that had destroyed the *Guerrière*. But even without that specific knowledge, it was clear to Lambert that this ship—a tall, stiff, heavy frigate—must be of the same class.

In reality, there was no decision to be made. Robinson had clearly stated the issue a moment ago: no British frigate captain would or could decline an encounter with an enemy frigate. Moreover, *no* British captain could possibly turn away from *any* American. The rumored defeat of the *Macedonian* and the too-well-known defeats of the *Alert* and *Guerrière* demanded redress. The wounded pride of the Royal Navy and, for that matter, the whole British nation desperately needed to be avenged.

Lambert was physically uncomfortable as he stood in the glaring sun. The enormous heat struck him from both above and below, since it was also reflected from the shimmering deck. He was uncomfortable in his thoughts as well. Something in his demeanor betrayed it to Marshall, who stood next to him on the quarterdeck, glass in hand, and likewise studied the enemy. Marshall was about to speak when his attention was taken by a seaman who approached the officer of the watch.

"If you please, sir, I'm an American. Please, sir, mayn't I not fight against my countrymen?" In fact, since the moment where the chase had been identified as American, there had been a succession of men who came onto the quarterdeck with the same request. Lambert called Chads over.

"Henry, that's enough of that. Damn it, I can't stand it," he said irritably. "Pass the word for any Yankees in the crew to go below and help the surgeon. I won't make 'em fight against their own, but they need to make themselves useful, none-the-less."

Marshall perceived in Lambert considerable agitation, and knew it had more behind it than a few American seamen among the gun crews. He attempted to cheer him.

"Captain Lambert, I give you joy. You now stand in the proudest situation, ready to rectify these wrongs of the past few months, and to show the world the true merit of the British Navy."

Lambert thought for a moment before he replied. "My friend, the captains of the *Alert*, *Guerrière*, and *Macedonian* no doubt likewise rejoiced. Of the outcome of the events I'm sure *they* were completely confident, yet consider the results. Were all other things of a piece I'd be content. But you know that we have little reservoir of experience. I don't wish to speak despondently, or infer that my thoughts are grounded in any fears about the crew's efficiency. On the surface of it we're well manned, but as we've discussed any number of times since we left Spithead, it's an illusion. We have seven non-combatants, twenty boys and reefers eleven years old and younger, and the rest of the crew chiefly new-raised men, the greater part of whom know little of gunnery or close action. Upwards of one hundred have never been at sea before. As you and I've observed, we've never seen a ship so miserably off for right seamen, and the ship's been only six weeks at sea since she was commissioned. Crowded as we are with supernumeraries, passengers, baggage, extra stores, and tons of shipbuilding materials, it's been difficult to apply effective instruction. In the course of the voyage so far, we've only exercised the great guns five times—which for many was the first time ever. How I wish we'd done more."

Marshall knew too well that Lambert's points were gravely accurate, and groped wildly for a positive response, a response of substance and not just mere enthusiasm. He was pleasantly forestalled, however, as Lambert turned to him with a smile.

"Still, you're in the right of it," Lambert continued with new demeanor. "For all the reasons you've just named, this's a golden opportunity. I'm gratified to have this chance to set things to rights. The Yankees and their ships are most certainly not the low, insignificant creatures most of us have assumed. At the same time they can't be the indefatigable giants that some of us have begun to think. We are, as a ship's company, not quite what we might like to be, but we're true British sailors none the less, and this ship's swift, sound, and true in her own right. We'll take nothing for granted, we'll assume the enemy is capable, and we'll make every effort to maneuver effectively and take every possible advantage. And, surely, the enemy'll have his own shortcomings. This war's only a few months old. Can they really have created efficient fighting crews and brought forth nothing but crack ships in so short a time?"

"No, Captain Marshall," said Lambert as he clapped him on the shoulder. "We won't have fear for ourselves nor for our conduct today. The *Java* and her people—and her captain—are formidable foes. 'We'll rant and we'll rave' as the song goes, and depend upon it, the Yankees will know they've been in a fight."

On board the American ship, Commodore Bainbridge had concluded that the British ship was too small and too quick to be a ship of the line. No line-of-battle-ship, not even a fast French-built one, could close on the *Constitution* this rapidly.

"Though speaking of French built," Bainbridge continued his thoughts aloud to the master, "this ship certainly has that look even if she ain't a liner."

Bainbridge now felt comfortable that he was as far offshore as he needed to be in regard to any issue of Portuguese neutrality. Thus, at three bells in the afternoon watch, he again called over the first lieutenant.

"Parker, luff up if you please, and take in the mains'l and royals. Come about onto the larboard tack. Let's stand toward the enemy." Those orders were executed with alacrity, and when about one mile separated the ships, he had the ship tacked again, so she now ran under topsails, topgallants, jib, and spanker.

What a grand prize you'll make, my pretty, thought Bainbridge to himself, eye to his glass once again. We'll all be stinking rich, and you'll make me a hero.

The *Java* also reduced sail, taking in her mainsail and royals. She continued to bear down on the *Constitution*. A few minutes before four bells rang out, both frigates were heading southeast, with the *Java* to windward as she rapidly came down on the American ship's weather quarter. As they neared, both captains were completely engrossed with complex mental assessments and equations of distance, wind direction and strength, speed, materiel, and the force of the water. They tried to read each other's minds, of course, as each skillfully wrung every possible advantage from his respective ship, crew, and relative position. The *Java* remained to windward and continued her rapid approach. She showed every intention of trying to open an action with a raking maneuver, which the *Constitution* early forestalled as she wore ship—and thus altered the distance and bearing.

On board the *Java*, Captain Lambert clicked shut his telescope and caught Lieutenant Chads' eye.

"Henry, we still have a moment. Send the hands aft to me, if you please." Lambert walked over to the break of the quarterdeck. He waited for a few minutes while the crew came aft. The men at their stations on the quarterdeck remained there, those on the forecastle—and the marines—drew up along the gangways on both sides. Those on the gundeck crowded under the open waist and peered up at him through the booms and spars lashed across that wide space.

"Men!" he began. "Javas! Over there approaches the enemy. They wait for us. They are, as you already know, Americans. You also know that on several occasions, lately, American ships have triumphed over British ships."

He paused for a few seconds as he studied the faces of his men, and wondered how many he would see at the end of the day. How bad would the "butcher's bill" be? Who would live and who would die? Who would suffer shocking wounds, face the further agonies of surgery without anesthetic, and then be discharged without a pension— maimed and crippled? What, for the love of God, might happen to him, to Henry Lambert? He scowled and shook his head as he pulled himself together.

"Javas, it does not matter! Today we will let *these* Yankees know that Britons still rule the waves, and that we indeed know how to fight. I know that many of you are new to the sea and have never been in a sea battle, but I tell you—it does not matter! We have drilled earnestly at sail and gun. You have acquired considerable skill with the great guns. Today will put that skill to the test.

"It's our common duty to fight today. We'll fight for our king and our country. We'll fight to protect ourselves and our shipmates. We'll fight out of fear, perhaps, and perhaps out of hatred, too. Of course, we shall fight for the *Java*—for our ship! Thus, remember your drill. Work steadily. Keep cool. Listen to the commands of your officers. As a team of horses draws a cart, we must work together and fight as a single unit.

"If we board them—or they board us—again, work steadily, work together, *do not falter*. Remember our comrades who've fallen. Remember the *Alert*. Remember the *Guerrière*. Remember the *Macedonian*. As you do so, then strike *true* at this enemy, and strike them *hard*. If we do so, then I have no doubts that *we shall triumph!*"

A few of the men began to cheer. Just a few at first, but it caught and grew. It swept across the gundeck and around the weather deck. Lambert turned and saw both Chads and Marshall as they nodded with satisfaction at the men's reaction. Lambert smiled faintly.

"Perhaps it's just as well so many are ignorant of how rough this day might be."

"They seem keen to fight, Captain," said Chads.

Lambert's smile faded entirely. "Yes. Well. Right. Please get them back to their stations, Mr. Chads. Let's get down to business."

As four bells rang out the *Java* was within a half-mile of the *Constitution*. The British frigate had earlier hauled down her large ensign in order to dip her gaff—and then had overlooked its re-hoisting. Although she continued to clearly fly a smaller union flag at the mizzen, the American commodore on board *Old Ironsides* chose to be affronted.

"Mr. Aylwin," Bainbridge called to the lieutenant in charge of the forecastle division's guns. "I'll see his colors again. Fire the chaser across his bow."

CHAPTER 22

COAST OF BRAZIL

Coast of Brazil
30 nautical miles to the southeast of
São Salvador da Baía
Vicinity 13° 12' S 38° 5' W
Tuesday, December 29th, 1812
2:05 p.m.
Sea nearly calm; light breezes from the E.N.E.

Upon the main gundeck of the U.S. Frigate *Constitution* resided thirty long 24-pounder cast-iron cannon—fifteen each to a side. They were massive, ungainly brutes, nine and a half feet in length. They nestled in sturdy wooden carriages that could bear their considerable weight—about six thousand pounds each—and move them back and forth on four fourteen-inch wooden wheels called trucks. On the weather deck above stood another set of seagoing artillery—another twenty-two guns—but aside from the long 12-pounder bow chasers, these weather-deck guns were carronades, cannon of large caliber—32-pounders—short-barreled and thus short-ranged. The carronades were mounted on slide carriages attached to the lower sills of the gunports, which allowed a quick pivoting motion to reload and thus far fewer men to crew.

At this moment each gundeck 24-pounder was run out of its individual gunport, with its carriage's curved facepiece jammed against the ship's inside bulwark. The captain of each cannon was bent forward, slightly behind and to the side of his gun. From there they each peered along the top of the weapons, out across the sea, for a glimpse of the enemy. The British frigate remained to windward and was now about a half-mile distant. She was clearly visible through the gunports. The *Constitution*'s gun captains each held a lanyard, loosely, which connected their fingers to the flintlock firing mechanisms mounted on the guns. From these flintlocks small amounts of fine-grained gunpowder ran through slender tin priming tubes; these tubes had been inserted into narrow holes and thus went through the thick iron sides of the guns and down into the cartridges. The cartridges were nothing more than sized and stiffened flannel bags, each filled with seven pounds of course-grained gunpowder. These cartridges had been shoved into the muzzles, down the entire length of the barrels, and hard pressed into the breeches. A twenty-four-pound solid-iron round-shot had been rammed down tight upon each cartridge, and a wad—a compressed mass of oakum bound with twine, three to four inches thick—had been pressed in on top of that. When the loading and priming process had been completed, each twelve-man gun crew clapped-on to the side tackles and ran their guns out. The barrels reached well beyond the ship's side, ready for action.

As with many warship crews world round, the *Constitution*'s crew had named their cannon, fanciful bellicose names for the most part. These names generally reflected the fancy, or literacy, of their handlers. They were carved into the carriages, or carved into the ship's side over the gunports, or both. The aftermost larboard side 24-pounder, No. 30, which resided in the commodore's day cabin, was called *Willful Murder*. The next one forward was *Rattlesnake*, the next one *Liberty*, then *Sudden Death*, then *Defiance*, and so on.

A shout was heard as it came down from the quarterdeck.

"Stand by the chase gun. Point wide across her bows. Fire!"

The crew of the long 12-pounder bow chaser, all the way forward on the weather deck, had been heaving with handspikes and crowbars against its carriage. They steadily adjusted their aim, as best they could on the moving deck, as they anticipated an order to fire. The gun was manned, on the occasions when it was needed, by the same men stationed at carronade No. 1 on the forecastle. Tom Coursey, the forecastle quarter-gunner who also acted as gun captain, cursed and had his men slew the gun—which they called *Doomsday*—around, so that it now aimed at the empty ocean well forward of the *Java*.

"Dammit," Coursey swore again as he yanked the lanyard. "Throwin' this shot away. I was right true on her mainmast." Whatever else he said was completely muffled by the firing of the chaser—the report sounded flat in the heated air and heavy humidity—and by his practiced sideways arch as *Doomsday*'s 3,800 pounds flew back right past his toes and then jarred to a stop when it hit the end of its breechings.

As he leaned over the hammocks stowed in the *Java*'s starboard quarterdeck netting, Lambert stared across the sparkling sea at the American ship. Aside from the routine sounds of the wind, the sea, and the ship's fabric in motion, the *Java* was silent. The crew remained grave and pensive, as men often are before mortal combat.

In response to the American chaser's smoke and report, and its ball's quite visible splash off the *Java*'s bow, Lambert looked up at his pendant and jack. He knew he had just reached the point of no return.

So be it, he thought.

"Mr. Chads," he called. "If you please, I'll have colors at the peak and weather main rigging."

On the *Java*'s forecastle, from where watched the American, Surgeon Jones waved at his associates. "Come, gentlemen, we'll be busy directly. Bring along two or three more lanterns, and let's get below."

As the two red ensigns rose on board the *Java*, Bainbridge called for a broadside of gundeck 24-pounders only. Once again the crews of the main battery heard a shout from the quarterdeck above. However, this time the cry was echoed on the *Constitution*'s gundeck by Lieutenant Hoffman, who commanded the First Division of guns—as well as the entire deck—during action.

"Stand by, larboard guns...ready...fire!"

The gun crews had been constantly busy, these last fifteen minutes, as they adjusted their aim with crowbars and handspikes—and thus were ready and anxious. Now the gun captains jerked their lanyards in succession about half a second apart. They started with *Willful Murder* in the commodore's cabin and moved forward, a fine rolling broadside, with no noticeable gap between the boom of one gun to the next.

As the flintlocks snapped, the white sparks flashed down the priming and into the cartridges. Inside each gun the powder ignited and burned, producing gas that instantaneously expanded to 300 times the cartridge's original volume, the pressure of which hurled the shot out of the barrel. The guns recoiled brutally, leaping almost five feet straight backward. They abruptly stopped, violently halted by the stout rope breechings which fixed them to the ship's side. The thunder of the guns was deafening. Trapped by the bulkheads and the low overhead decking, the sound was physically staggering. The ship shook from keelson to maintruck. She vanished, momentarily, behind the yellowish orange flashes as well as the clouds of dense, acrid, white-gray smoke, which then drifted in blankets across the weather deck. In fact, a good deal of the smoke also blew back into the wide-open ports and swirled around the gundeck, burning the eyes and lungs of all.

The deadly iron shot—fifteen solid spheres which totaled nearly 400 pounds—burst from the guns' muzzles at almost 1,200 feet per second, flying toward the *Java*. With a sound much like ripping cloth, the roundshot took hardly more than two seconds to hurtle across the half-mile of sea between the ships, each ball more than able to punch through two and a half feet of solid oak. The distance was about the maximum effective range of the American 24-pounders. It was certainly beyond the effective range of the 32-pounder carronades, and a little past that of the long guns on the British ship. The time was ten minutes past four bells in the afternoon watch— just a little after two o'clock.

Three decks below, in the *Constitution*'s cockpit, Surgeon Evans and his assistants calmly waited for the first of the wounded to appear. Not far from them the gunner, Mr. Darling, and two of his mates looked out from the powder magazines and shot lockers. They similarly waited for the rush of boys who would come to draw more of both. Now, for no logical reason at all, neither medicos nor gunners spoke in more than whispers.

The *Java* had been in position to windward of the *Constitution*, on her port side, a little farther forward at about two cables' length distance—but not quite to Commodore Bainbridge's satisfaction. The fact that every shot of his broadside had fallen short was not quite to his satisfaction, either.

"Dammit, he's much farther out than I'd like," he said under his breath as he stared hard at the *Java*. Bainbridge, the sailing master, Nichols, and the principal master's mate, Carlton, stood next to the wheel as they watched the enemy off the larboard beam. The *Java* had not returned any fire. Bainbridge leaned over and shouted down the hatchway.

"Hoffman, give him another, if you please. And try to hit him this time, will you?"

The larboard battery finished reloading and ran out.

"All right, lads," called Hoffman. "That's right. Fire at the word. Fire steady from aft forward. Ready . . . fire!"

The first broadside, well aimed and grouped together, had torn up the water in perfect alignment with the enemy, but was too short. The second broadside was again well aimed and grouped, but the shots passed between—and even over—the *Java*'s masts, doing no appreciable damage. Bainbridge kicked at the binnacle, cursing.

"Oh, for the love of God," he said to no one in particular. "Must I come down there and lay the guns myself?"

Still, the British withheld fire as they tried to edge the *Java* closer onto the *Constitution*'s weather bow. Finally, Captain Lambert decided it was time.

"Mr. Herringham," he called.

The captain's voice caught Lieutenant Herringham deep in reverie. In the quiet after they had cleared for action, his mind had taken him back seven years to the Battle of Trafalgar and partially forgotten memories of the many wounded and maimed, the dead and the dying, and the blood. He realized that while he certainly feared death, he feared being crippled or mutilated even more. Months after Trafalgar he had gone to Gosport to visit the Royal Navy's hospital, Haslar. He found the friend he was there to see, surrounded by other men missing hands, feet, legs, arms. His friend was missing his nose and most of his left cheek, horribly disfigured and in unbearable, constant pain. He shuddered at the specter.

"Mr. Herringham, there!"

"S-sir?"

"Pray commence fire, if you please."

"Aye aye, sir," Herringham replied, shaking off his memories, glad to spring into action.

The *Java*'s broadside burst into thunder, flame, and smoke. She opened fire with her lee, or starboard, 18-pounder long guns as she at last began the action in earnest. The ships were now within effective cannon-shot distance of each other, but at what was called "long bowls"—good for roundshot but still a little far for grape and definitely far for canister. The *Java* was to windward, constantly using her greater speed in an effort to turn and rake the *Constitution*. The cannonade was spirited on both sides, at this point the ships suffering about equally. From both sides grape and roundshot howled overhead, raised fountains in the sea, and smashed into the hulls. Blocks fell, ropes parted, and—blasted from the ships' fabric—jagged splinters of wood tore whistling across the decks. Dust from shredded wood and paint drifted everywhere, before becoming lost in the enormous clouds of powder smoke. The ships struggled to obtain advantageous positions. Both vessels made many skillful maneuvers as they tried to rake each other and, more important, to avoid *being* raked. The *Constitution* deliberately stayed clear of close action and fired most of her guns at the enemy's masts, trying to disable the *Java*'s spars, sails, and rigging. But the Americans were unsuccessful with this intention to wreak havoc with the *Java*'s masts and achieved no success in slowing her, to say nothing of stopping her.

The initial broadsides of the *Java,* carefully loaded and carefully aimed, were respectably destructive. They hit the *Constitution*'s hull, cut rigging, wounded spars, and dropped a few of the crew. One of these was the American commodore himself, who was standing on the larboard side, next to No. 16 carronade, facing the enemy.

With a cry, Bainbridge spun and fell to the deck. A chunk of copper, torn by shot from the companionway coaming, had buried itself in his right leg just above the knee. Startled and confused, he found himself prostrate by the binnacle. His telescope rolled across the deck from where it had flown from his fingers and his white trousers reddened from seeping blood. Midshipman Gordon, stationed at Bainbridge's side as *aide de camp* and messenger, knelt down.

"Sir, sir! Are you badly hurt?"

"Dammit!" roared Bainbridge in reply. "God damn it! Help me up, Gordon, damn you."

The midshipman pulled his commodore slowly to his feet and then remained, supporting Bainbridge as he regained his bearings.

The ship's structure had suffered in addition to losses among the crew. Among several pieces of the *Constitution*'s rigging which had been cut were the flying jib halyards. Foretopman Asa Curtis instantly comprehended the situation from his position high in the mast. He was acutely aware of how critical the flying jib was to the ship's maneuverability. He glanced at John Day, the master's mate who sat with him. Seeing no indication of any orders forthcoming, Curtis clenched his teeth, sprang for the foretopgallant stay, caught hold, and began sliding down its length.

"Oh, God," he said, almost in a chant. "Help me, help me, help me." He was terribly exposed to the enemy's fire, wincing repeatedly as grapeshot continually screamed past him. He almost fell, twice, but with great difficulty Curtis managed to re-bend the cut halyards, preventing that key headsail's loss.

The *Java* continued to close, edging down. The action continued with roundshot and grape, then, as the distance decreased, musketry and occasional rounds of canister. The shriek of their slides, as well as the different pitch of their reports, clearly indicated that carronades had joined in the battle. Iron and lead screamed overhead and crashed into both ships. Thick, greasy smoke trailed about the ships and hung in the air between them, more solid than a London fog. It became difficult for either captain to see individual men on their respective forecastles, and neither captain could see much of his enemy aside from masts jutting above the gray clouds.

"Hot work, this, sir!" shouted Chads.

The swifter British ship began to forereach. She forged ahead as she clearly still pursued the intention of wearing across the slower *Constitution*'s bow and raking her at point-blank range. However, as the American ship fired another full broadside—which considerably added to the already dense smoke and thus screened her movement—she simultaneously filled her headsails and put before the wind, wearing around.

As soon as Lambert realized what was happening, he roared out orders.

"Wear ship! Wear the ship!"

The *Java* efficiently wore after the American ship with creditable speed, but she was not quite able to catch and rake the *Constitution* on the turn. Both ships now ran off to the west, the British still to windward, but now to starboard of the Americans. The action went on at pistol-shot distance. The *Java* drew alongside, but after a few minutes she again forged ahead, out of the full weight of her adversary's fire, again trying to cross her bow.

But the *Constitution* again wore and she was again obscured by the thick smoke. Once more Lambert shouted out a series of commands, his voice rising in pitch, which betrayed his frustration and anxiety. The *Java* came around, very quickly. Now both ships were heading to the southwest, *Java* still to windward, *Constitution* still to leeward. Indeed, the *Java* tenaciously kept the weather gage, forereaching a little, and whenever the *Constitution* luffed up close the former tried to turn and rake her.

For the third time the *Java* drew alongside the *Constitution* and appeared to move ahead. Lambert leaned against the railing, both hands gripping the mizzen shrouds. He alternately looked at the enemy and up at his own sails. He gauged it carefully and then abruptly called out to the sail trimmers.

"Let fly the tops'l sheets...take stations for wearing ship!" Many of the seamen instantly jumped, casting off from the belaying pins, all the quicker because they stood poised and ready for any such orders in this battle of maneuvers. As the three topsails flew loose they spilled their wind; the *Java*'s speed was checked sharply. Again, gauging it carefully, Lambert rapidly spat out his next commands.

"Up mainsail and spanker! Clear away the after bowlines... brace in the afteryards...up helm!" Smoothly and rapidly the *Java* started to wear, swinging around.

"Overhaul the weather lifts!" Lambert continued, as the swing of both the yards and the ship herself increased. "Man the weather headbraces...rise fore tack and sheet!" The wind was now coming from directly aft. "Clear away the head bowlines...lay the head yards square...shift over the head sheets!" The maneuver continued, though this time with feverish anxiety that it would be quick enough to catch the Yankees.

"Man the main tack and sheet...spanker outhaul! Clear away the brails...hard aboard! Haul out!" The sail trimmers rushed about their tasks. The spanker was set and filled, the main tack got down, and the main sheet brought aft. The *Java* now came rapidly into the wind. The head yards were braced up, the jib sheets were hauled aft, and the helm was righted. Finally, Lambert called out, "Overhaul weather lifts...hard aboard! Steady out the bowlines... haul taught the weather trusses, braces, and lifts! Clear away on deck!"

On board the *Java*, almost eighty seamen worked together with commendable precision. She abruptly slowed and wore around. *Java* shot under *Constitution*'s stern and finally achieved the long-sought rake. The British ship's entire larboard broadside fired, with many rounds crashing into the American ship. Some of the cannonballs flew through the *Constitution*'s entire length, all the way from stern to stem.

As the *Java*'s last gun boomed out, and she sailed past the *Constitution*'s now-battered stern, the British crew roared out in thunderous cheering. Lambert found himself swept up in the excitement. He repeatedly pounded his fist into his hand and barely restrained himself from jumping up and down. The crazy exaltation of battle momentarily blanked the earlier fears he had faced—of defeat, death, and mutilation.

The wind quickly pushed the smoke to the southwest, which revealed that the American ship had been hard hit. While the accuracy of the ill-trained British crew could have been much better, and therefore considerably more damage could have been done, this still was the kind of raking broadside that won battles. The *Constitution*'s big double steering wheel was shot entirely away, disintegrating into splinters and sawdust. All four American helmsmen had been cut down, as well as eleven men among the quarterdeck carronade crews. Midshipman Gordon forced himself to look away from the bloody mess of wood splinters and tangled flesh, trying not to vomit. Here and there he could see pieces of bone which shined whitely through the carnage.

"My God," exclaimed Robinson as he intently stared at the American ship through his glass. What was now revealed to the British, as they crossed the *Constitution*'s stern, was her name in foot-high letters, boldly displayed below her great cabin's windows. Besides the master's, several telescopes and naked eyes alike picked out the letters from behind the smoke and despite the damage. Like Robinson, many of the British officers paused, with thoughtful expressions on their faces, as they realized they were engaged with the very ship that had demolished the *Guerrière* just four months earlier.

On board the *Constitution*, Commodore Bainbridge was among the quarterdeck casualties. He *again* had been struck down, dropped to the deck, wounded for the second time in less than twenty minutes. This time he was hit by flying wreckage from the shattered wheel, which knocked his left leg out from under him. Face down on his quarterdeck, flung there among the blood, bodies, and splinters created by the *Java*'s broadside, Bainbridge fought off the pain of his wounds as well as panic and despair. He turned his head and stared into the dead eyes of John Allen, one of the junior helmsmen, who lay next to him. As he studied the surprised expression on Allen's face, the recollection of his three earlier failures, while in command of American ships, flashed through Bainbridge's mind.

'Hard Luck Bill' now confronted the very real specter of a *fourth* disaster. Clearly, with one stroke, the British had gained the advantage in this battle. Surely, *surely*, he would not have to surrender a *fourth* American ship to the enemy. Was he cursed? he wondered. Doomed to be constantly defeated and disgraced?

"Oh, God. Oh God, no," he moaned as he rocked back and forth. Hot tears of pain and fear coursed down his face. At this moment he did not fear death. He did not even fear disfigurement. He feared defeat. *Another* defeat and the pitying contempt of his colleagues, if not the entire country.

But Bainbridge's despair, and hesitation, were only of a few moments. He rapidly mastered his thoughts as he tried to get up.

"God damn your eyes, Gordon, you useless bastard, help me up!" With grim determination, he pulled his thoughts together as he once again pulled himself to his feet with his midshipman aide's help. He wiped blood and tears from his face, and stepped over the unconscious body of Woodbury, the quartermaster. Bainbridge looked about, assessed the situation, and then began roaring out orders.

"Parker, send all hands to the weather rail! We've got'ta lessen the pressure under the lee bow 'til we can rig relieving tackles on the tiller."

"Aye aye, sir!" As Parker moved forward, shouting orders, Bainbridge turned his attention to the master.

"Nichols, call the sail trimmers! You need to steer the ship by trimming the sails—handsomely, oh so *handsomely*—'til we make repairs. We can't heave-to under the enemy's guns. Keep her thus. For God's sake, we mustn't let the rudder beat side to side, nor turn us into the enemy."

"Aye aye, sir!"

Bainbridge then focused upon trying to improvise a jury-rigged steering system in lieu of the destroyed wheel. He leaned heavily on Midshipman Gordon's shoulder and called the boatswain to his side.

"Adams, get your mates and jump below. Hook relieving tackles onto the tiller and man 'em with hands from the after guns. Chearly, Adams, damn you, we've no time to lose!"

"Aye aye, sir!" Shouting to two of his mates to follow him, Adams raced two decks down to the storeroom on the berth deck just abaft the wardroom. This was where the ten-foot-long tiller swung as it controlled the ship's huge rudder. The wheel ropes, starboard and larboard, ran from where the wheel had been on the weather deck, down through channels in the captain's pantry on the gundeck, across the overhead decking of the wardroom through sleeves bored through two beams, across the overhead decking of two officers' cabins, and finally into the tiller room. While the ropes remained intact, the destruction of the wheel had made them useless.

"Damn and blast this infernal baggage!"

The boatswain and one of his mates cursed and kicked boxes of stores out of their way. They cut loose the ropes from the tip of the tiller, while in their place three other men rove relieving tackles and attached them to the tiller. Four seamen were stationed on either side of the room. They clapped on to these tackles as they continued to kick and push various boxes, baskets, crates, and trunks out of their way and particularly out from underfoot.

At the same time, two midshipmen sent by Bainbridge took up positions at the forward end of the wardroom, as well as under the after hatch grating between the gundeck and the quarterdeck. With the midshipmen in place to relay orders, and the men in place to manhandle the tiller, Bainbridge could now steer by shouting orders down through the gratings. It was by no means an ideal or efficient solution, but it was workable. In what had developed into a battle of precise maneuvers, the *Constitution* was clearly handicapped by the loss of her steering wheel. The rudder itself was unharmed. It fortunately survived the raking broadside, but steering the ship by relieving tackles as a substitute for the wheel was going to be neither quick nor precise.

While this new steering system was being arranged and other repairs were made, the *Constitution* sailed steadily forward, the rudder angle and sail trim essentially unaltered, due to Nichols' superb seamanship.

The British did not realize they had crippled the Americans' steering. "Why the devil don't they turn to starboard? Why don't they range alongside?" muttered Lambert to himself.

Since the Americans made no turns at all, it appeared that the *Constitution* had disengaged from the action.

"I think they've got enough of it," cried petty officer Charles Speedy, the 'captain of the forecastle.' He addressed his fellow Javas quartered at the foremast carronades. "Lads, they're making off from us!" After a couple of minutes' observation, Captain Lambert drew the same conclusion.

"Mr. Chads, we'll come about."

The *Java* tacked across the *Constitution*'s wake and fired another raking broadside, this time from the starboard guns, at the Americans' stern. However, because they had hesitated, the British had allowed the distance to widen considerably. As a result this broadside, at longer range, was far less destructive than the previous one. It was also less effective because the novice British gunners had failed to reload many of the starboard guns before they left them. In the confusion of battle they had been thrown off the needed rhythm as they ran from side to side, manning starboard battery—then larboard battery—then starboard again. As a result only a few guns fired, and not many of those struck the *Constitution*.

"Dammit...God dammit," fumed Lambert. "Again, Mr. Chads, come about—quickly!"

The *Java* reassumed the weather gage, then quickly hauled forward to come up on the *Constitution*'s larboard quarter.

Bainbridge dispassionately watched the *Java* approach, at this point confident that he had regained effective control of his ship. However, the British ship's superior speed continued to be plainly evident. It presented the constant threat of her crossing the *Constitution*'s bow or stern again with another raking broadside.

"God dammit, Parker, we've got to be mindful of their speed—not to mention their potential to quickly tack or wear," said Bainbridge. "I want to force closer action. Set the fore and main courses, if you please."

This was an unusual move, for long experience in most navies dictated that, for a number of reasons, the huge courses would be clewed up during action. As a general rule engagements were fought with a minimal spread of canvas—the "fighting sails." But, there are always exceptions to rules. The enormous courses were set, filled, and skillfully trimmed, and so the *Constitution* picked up speed and allowed herself to be steered even more closely to the wind.

"Ha! That's done it," said Bainbridge as he grinned with satisfaction. "Now, Parker, damn it, luff up close to him."

"Let her luff!" shouted Parker, and then a moment later to the sail trimmers, "Ease off main and spanker sheets . . . spanker outhaul!"

As *Old Ironsides* increased in speed the *Java* no longer

reached on her. By setting her courses, fore and main, she got up close on the *Java*'s lee beam, from where the *Constitution*'s ensuing heavy fire became very effective.

Indeed, the whole of the *Java* shook and trembled to the jarring impact of the *Constitution*'s shot, and British seamen were cut down left, right, and center.

On the quarterdeck, Captain Wood caught General Hislop's eye. "General, sir, I don't think I can stand this. This's madness! We're all of us going to be cut down any minute now, like these poor sailors." He was white as a sheet. He clasped both hands together to keep them from shaking, and watched a screaming man being carried below.

"Wood," replied Hislop, stepping close to him. He tried to ensure they were not overheard, though in the staggering noise of the battle that was unlikely. "Wood, recollect yourself. An officer must always set an example, which includes calmly facing the enemy's shot. I grant you this's completely unnerving, even frightening, but there's no help for it. I wish we had something useful to do, to occupy us, but unless we board the enemy or are boarded by them—in which case we'll draw our swords and jump into the fight—we must remain here and stand tall." Hislop grasped Wood's shoulder, to force him to look at him.

"We surely can't go below decks," the general continued, "and we can't go below the waterline and hide. How could we abandon Captain Lambert and his men? We'd dishonor ourselves as well as the Army."

"Yes, sir," replied Wood, heartened a little by both Hislop's words and kindly demeanor.

"That's my lad," said Hislop. "You can do this. We all can. And I daresay we'll never again see our bravery tested like it's being tested *today*."

On board *Old Ironsides*, it suddenly occurred to Lieutenant Parker that thus far this battle had not been, and was not going to be, a mere pounding match. It was more a complex combination of skillful maneuver and artillery duel. He realized the two ships were much like fencers or boxers, with a succession of evolutions which resembled those kinds of changes of position—parries, lunges, ripostes, retreats, and advances—all accompanied by a continual play of the great guns, answering to the thrusts and blows of each individual movement.

Charlie Speedy, the captain of the *Java*'s forecastle, was enraged by the quantities of round and grape that the Americans kept firing his way. He was also irritated with the enemy's clear determination to cripple the *Java*'s masts by using dismantling shot. From various places on the deck he picked up five American bar shot. As the ship rolled these had fallen out of the foremast rigging and sails, their force spent, having been caught there after being fired at the *Java*.

"Mother of God, will you look at this?" he said, his arms full. He handed some of the shot to his men who rammed them down the barrels of their carronades, then fired them back with fresh powder.

"That's it, lads," he said. "Send the bloody things back to their rightful owners, 'cause we refuse to pay the postage!"

Farther aft, on the *Java*'s quarterdeck, Commander Marshall was also concerned about that bar shot. He turned to the army officers with a remark. It was not particularly important that the redcoats understood everything that was going on, but under the circumstances Marshall felt considerable sympathy for them. With no assigned duty during this battle other than bravely trying to face the enemy's fire, their minds were unoccupied except for thoughts of imminent death as shot and splinters flew around them. Thus, Marshall thought a discussion of technicalities might distract them.

"Gentlemen," he began in a loud voice. "Almost a year ago the Navy's Board of Ordnance stopped supplying dismantling shot— since, as they put it, 'it has not recently been much used.' Well, I fear the Yankees take a different view on the subject and are *extremely* happy to use it."

"That's the ordnance intended to cripple a ship's ability to sail?" asked Walker.

"Indeed, Major, it is," Marshall replied. He cleared his throat to pitch his voice above the roar of battle. "I've heard *Guerrière* and *Macedonian* were terribly hurt by bar shot—much as *we* suffer today. I'm also told that, of their total ammunition allowance, U.S. Navy ships often carry 25 percent in dismantling shot of various kinds—predominantly the bar shot we're seeing right now."

The *Constitution* kept up a remorseless, steady fire. Considerable quantities of iron and lead shot, as well as frequent showers of wood splinters, shrieked across the *Java*'s decks. Many of the splinters were tiny, trifling, of no account—but some were jagged, large, and deadly.

Five bells sharply rang out, startling Major Walker in spite of the pervasive din of battle. He noticed that neither the marine who had struck the bell, nor the two quartermasters at the wheel, were the same as those who had begun the battle. Walker shook his head in admiration for the naval discipline which unfailingly kept the wheel manned, the hour glass turned, and the bell rung in the midst of such noise, death, and destruction.

It was just after those five bells rang out when some of *Old Ironsides'* roundshot tore away the end of the *Java*'s bowsprit, as well as its cap and jib boom. Significantly, with her headsails (jib, outer jib, and flying jib) now dangling and useless, this event left her ability to turn horribly degraded. The *Constitution* forged ahead and, repeating her former maneuver, wore in the heavy smoke. Barely seeing this movement through the gray smoke clouds, Lambert once again attempted to tack across the wind in order to remain engaged. In lieu of employing her now useless headsails, he tried to use the *Java*'s spanker to drive her stern into the turn. Unfortunately, the maneuver failed. The ship hung in stays—hung up heading into the wind—hung 'in irons' to use the common sailors' expression. She was unable to complete the turn without the leverage of those headsails to force her around; unable to drive her bow off the wind. Now, because she had picked up sufficient speed to bear down on her larboard quarter, the *Constitution* took immediate advantage of the *Java*'s temporarily helpless condition. *Old Ironsides* came within musket shot and poured a careful broadside into the British frigate; a heavy, raking broadside, into her stern.

"That's given him a bellyful!" shouted Bainbridge. "Give it to him *again*, boys! Give it to him!" In his excitement, Bainbridge would have capered about his quarterdeck had he not been wounded in both legs. As she fell off, the *Java* could only reply with a few of her larboard guns. On board the *Constitution*, the commodore caught the master's eye.

"For Christ's sake, Nichols," Bainbridge swore, "you might bother to notice we're about to miss stays. Let *us* not get caught in irons. I'd rather leave that sort of thing to the English, so wear to larboard directly."

"Aye aye, sir," said Nichols, flushing. He turned to begin the series of commands. "Take stations for wearing ship!"

As she successfully completed the complex maneuver, the *Constitution* swung around until she headed south. The *Java* shortly followed when she finally succeeded in forcing her bow around. Now, both ships ran free, the wind on the port quarter, the *Java* abreast and again to windward of her antagonist, both with their heads a little east of south. The ships were less than a cable's length apart and the firing was again heavy. But, now, the *Constitution* was noticeably inflicting great damage while suffering relatively little herself. Broadside after broadside, the *Java*'s engaged side rose up to the recoil of her own guns—and then leaned over even farther from the impact of the *Constitution*'s return fire striking that same side. And, by this point, the *Java*'s gunnery was seriously deteriorating. It was far less accurate now than it had been during the first exchanges.

"I fancy his fire's slackening, sir," shouted Nichols on *Old Ironsides*' quarterdeck.

"They're feeling our fire," agreed Bainbridge. "Yes they are, damn them! And they fire wild. Look at that!" Bainbridge pointed at a section of the sea, torn up by a dozen British shot, which had missed *Old Ironsides* by a good fifteen yards.

The *Java*'s growing inaccuracy meant that most of the loss the Americans were to suffer this day had been confined to the early part of the action, and thus, unknown to any of the participants, had already occurred.

On the *Java*'s quarterdeck, Commander Marshall again thought of something to distract the army officers. "Sir," he addressed General Hislop, "as you know, the big American frigates were in part constructed with live oak, the hardest and most dense wood known." He was silenced for a moment by a shriek of round-shot overhead. "Do you notice that too often our shots don't even pierce her side, while many of her shots not only go through *both* our sides, but also drive in large portions of timber?"

Indeed, the advantage had clearly shifted toward the Americans. Even if Marshall (who many years later would become an admiral) could see it, most of the other British officers and crew did not—or did not yet so choose. Although the standard British 18-pounder long gun was a remarkably hard-hitting weapon, and notwithstanding the serious effect of the weather deck 32-pounder carronades on both ships, there was a difference between 18s and

24s, and it was beginning to tell. Again Marshall caught Hislop's eye.

"General, three critical factors work against us, if I may name them."

"Please do," replied Hislop, trying to speak over the roar of the guns, the shouts of orders, and the cries of the wounded.

"First, the heavier broadside weight of the *Constitution*. Second, the superior gunnery of the American gun crews, who—unsurprisingly—appear much better practiced than we. Third, the enhanced protection afforded those gunners by the *Constitution*'s thicker scantlings. And as I mentioned, sir, several inches of those scantlings are constructed of live oak."

"Though no seaman," said Hislop, "I know a little about artillery. I fear the scales have tipped in this action. The enemy now inflicts more damage on us than we inflict on him."

"Yes, sir," replied Marshall. "And the more damage inflicted over time, the greater will be the disproportion."

In addition, losses among the gun crews, among the division officers (already the *Java* had suffered four midshipmen killed and three wounded), and, most important, among the powder boys (who valiantly struggled to keep the guns steadily supplied with powder and shot from the magazines) all critically degraded the *Java*'s speed and accuracy of fire.

"Captain," shouted Chads, on the other side of the quarterdeck, "we've been—and are—damaging the enemy's rigging, but we infrequently hit her hull."

"I see it, Henry," responded Lambert. "And the poor *Java* suffers heavily both alow and aloft, while her decks look like a butcher's shop."

In fact the *Java*'s surgeon, Mr. Jones, was extraordinarily busy far down below deck, below the waterline in the dim cockpit. He worked with his assistant surgeons, his surgeon's mates, and his loblolly boys; all working in the poor light coming from the swinging lanterns.

"It's essential we operate quickly," Jones called for the second or third time to his assistants, "while their minds—and bodies—are in shock. The pain and bleeding are significantly lessened."

They treated case after case, a constant stream of wounded with injuries of all types and degrees, from the mortal to the slight, from the relatively complex to the quick dressing—a tot of rum—and the man back up on deck. The instruments were constantly in play, particularly the knife, saw, and tourniquet. The same instruments were used and reused with barely a wipe on the sleeve or on a piece of bandage between cases, for there was no time for sanitization and, in the year 1812, no fully perceived need.

"Mr. Jones," cried Capponi, "the tubs overflow with amputated limbs, and still more wounded come. My God, it's an endless stream!" Capponi had never before been in such intense action.

"Aye, Mr. Capponi," replied Jones as he ducked under a jet of blood from a severed artery. "Cut and saw, bind and bandage—it is our lot. Stay with me, now, do not falter."

The British were losing many men from the musketry of the American seamen and marines in the fighting tops. They were losing still more from the round and grapeshot which flew across from the great guns, particularly on the forecastle. Iron hail swept the *Java*'s decks. Dead men continued to be piled around the masts so as to be out of the gun crews' way. A steady stream of wounded staggered on their own or were dragged across the deck and down the ladders, on their way to the new horror of the cockpit.

In fact, men in a ship which suffered to the degree that the *Java* suffered might well be shaken by the immense death and destruction all about them, just as the enemy who inflicted that damage might well be uplifted by the sight. But there was no noticeable faltering on the part of the British crew—with one exception. Lambert suddenly found Lieutenant Herringham standing before him, touching his hat.

"Captain, some of my men on the main deck are disheartened, have laid down between the guns, and want us to strike our colors. It *is* rather horrible—reminds me of Trafalgar, on board the *Colossus*." Lambert, as well as the army officers, had been momentarily mesmerized as they watched some blood from the quarterdeck drip down—like scarlet rain—upon the gunners below the gangway. Lambert tore his gaze away from the sight and stared at Herringham, briefly at a loss. Then, rubbing his eyes, he turned and spoke to the first lieutenant who stood next to him.

"Mr. Chads, please accompany Mr. Herringham below—take old Smith there with you. See if you might rally those men to their duty. It's hellish work, to be sure, but tell 'em they mustn't falter." Chads nodded, touched his hat, clapped Herringham on the shoulder, and made for the main deck ladder. They walked upright and rapidly, mindful of the need for haste, yet refrained from actually running; the sight of officers running below decks, during the height of action, could have an unsettling effect upon the sea-men. On the way they collected the ship's cook, who was pointing one of the quarterdeck carronades.

"Come, Barbecue, I need your help," Chads shouted.

"Aye aye, sir."

The cook, John Smith, was an old shipmate and had formerly served with Chads and Lambert on board the *Iphigenia*. Like his captain and the two lieutenants, he had many times smelled gun-powder in earnest and he knew, from the seaman's point of view, just what to say to the tired and frightened men.

This incident aside, the British sailors fought valiantly, veteran and novice alike, many stripped to the waist in the oppressive equatorial sun. Their half-naked bodies were blackened by powder smoke and shown with sweat. Casualties among them continued to mount. Those who were killed outright were immediately dragged out of the way into piles, as was the custom, or were thrown unceremoniously overboard, as was expedient. On the forecastle one man, effectively cut in half by a shot, was caught as he fell by two of his shipmates; as the last flicker of life left him they tossed him into the sea.

Below decks, the boatswain came into the cockpit cradling his arm. His hand was gone and his forearm torn open up to the el-bow, likely the result of being hit by grape. He tightly wrapped his wrist in a dressing and held it up. He then waited his turn for treatment among the scores of screaming or moaning men already there, and which continued to flow in behind him. Jesus, he thought, I've traded one circle of hell for another. A surgeon's mate finally attended him; all he could do, temporarily, was apply a tourniquet and tie the artery. He also handed him a tiny glass which contained a little less than a teaspoon of laudanum—the al-coholic tincture of opium. This was to deaden the intense pain which would soon come as the shock of the wound wore off.

"That'll have to suffice for now, Mr. Humble," said the medico. "After the action we'll have another look at you, and Mr. Jones'll finish it off elegant."

"Much obliged to you. You've put it some to rights. Thankee kindly."

"How goes the action, will you tell me?"

"Well, mate," said Humble, "we're much disabled aloft, espe-cially in the foretop—in fact, I saw two large planks shot out of it which then lodged in the bunt of the fores'l. The fo'c'sle's suffered much from round, grape, and musketry. But, our shot's carried away their wheel, and the Americans have got a good touching-up about *their* fo'c'sle and quarterdeck, and they seem very sick upon it, too."

With that he tucked his arm into the bosom of his shirt and went slowly back up to the battle. He was glad to escape the gloom of the cockpit, oppressively lit by lanterns which flickered in the foul air, and he was starting to feel some pain as well as the high of the drug. On the ladder leading to the gundeck he momentarily stood aside, to allow two of the army officers to come down past him. Major Walker half supported and half carried Captain Wood, who, though conscious, bled profusely from a gash in his head.

On both gundeck and weather deck the officers moved among the seamen, trying to guide, encourage, and lead. Lieutenant Chads, in particular, appeared to be everywhere with directions and orders. He had just regained the quarterdeck when he felt a violent push of air, and he was deafened by an enormous tearing noise that vibrated right through him. A twenty-four-pound roundshot had passed close behind his legs, almost touching him. It sheered off the tails of his coat and violently threw him into the capstan. He then fell hard onto the deck.

"God's my life—!"

He slowly pulled himself up, with the help of Lambert and Hislop, and was relieved to find he was unbloodied. Nevertheless, he was a bit dazed and in considerable pain in his back and arm. Two carronade crewmen steadied him and brought him to the cockpit. But as soon as his arm and lower back were tightly bound, he returned to the deck—shouting encouragement to the men.

It was just after six bells, and the *Constitution*'s heavy, remorseless fire continued. The *Java* showed a great many hits between wind and water. In addition, with her fore and main masts having been severely hit and with considerable rigging cut to pieces, Captain Lambert reluctantly came to the conclusion that he was being beaten—soundly beaten—in the gunnery duel. The *Constitution* certainly continued to experience difficulties due to the loss of her wheel, and remained generally slower. However, the *Java*'s loss of jib boom and headsails meant she continued to have even more difficulties in maneuver and in preserving the weather gage.

From the beginning of the action Mr. Robinson had been at Lambert's side, advising him in the handling of the ship. Coincidentally, at this point, the master was fixed upon the same thoughts that were going through his captain's mind. Pocket watch in his hand, he stepped in close to Lambert.

"Captain, it's been one hour since the action began. Our rigging's much cut up, the slings of the mainyard are shot away, and the head of the bowsprit's gone. Sir, as it stands, I don't see any favorable prospect of this action ending to our advantage." The words were scarcely out of his mouth when another blast of grape screamed across the quarterdeck. Robinson was hit and fell violently to the deck. Some of his blood spattered onto Lambert's uniform. Major Walker instantly caught the attention of two marines as they fired their muskets from the railing, and the three of them carefully picked up the master and carried him to the cockpit. Lambert stared after them as they proceeded below, while he continued to cast about for alternative tactics.

Boarding an enemy ship with a quantity of desperate, hard-fighting men had often pulled victory from defeat, and in any event such an attempt could bring no worse defeat than what Lambert now faced. The day is lost, he thought to himself, unless we board the American and carry her by fighting on her decks. No doubt he was aware of Lord Nelson's maxim, 'Desperate affairs require desperate remedies,' and was taking a page from the great admiral's book. In an instant Lambert made up his mind. He would lay the *Java* on board the enemy, who was at present on her lee beam.

"Mr. Chads, let's run the ship alongside the American."

"Aye aye, sir."

Chads had the helm put over such that the British frigate rapidly came down for the *Constitution's* larboard mainchains. The *Java* moved forward towards *Old Ironsides* with hardly more than one gun able to bear from the bow, and received considerable musketry, particularly from the American marines and seamen shooting down from the *Constitution's* mizzen and main fighting tops. Musket balls smashed and thudded into the deck, seemingly as thick as hail to those men who had not been in action before.

"Lieutenant Mercer," Lambert called the marine to his side. "It's my intention to board. Prepare your men, if you please."

"Aye aye, sir." Mercer was off, rushing twenty of his remaining marines forward from their stations on the quarterdeck, who now joined the ten already on the forecastle. Coming from all parts of the ship, thinning the gun crews considerably, a large number of seamen and marines gathered on the forecastle and the gangways.

They armed themselves with muskets, pistols, cutlasses, swords, tomahawks, and pikes.

On the quarterdeck by the binnacle, just a few feet behind Captain Lambert, General Hislop looked hard at his two *aides-de-camp*. "Major Walker, Captain Wood," He flashed a smile. "Finally! Here's an opportunity to be of help." He drew his sword and began to walk forward. "Follow me." The two younger officers also drew their swords and strode forward in their superior's wake. All three were quietly elated with this chance to cease observation and actually join the battle, even Wood, who visibly felt his heavily bandaged head wound.

"Mr. Humble," called Chads to the boatswain; both moved forward down the larboard gangway. "Please cheer up the men—if your arm allows."

So the boatswain came to stand at the head of the massing boarders, his silver call at his lips, 'cheering up' the men as they prepared to spring aboard the enemy. He succeeded in this tolerably well despite the loss of his other hand. His tourniqueted arm, still stuffed into his shirt, throbbed with pain, but the laudanum was keeping it bearable.

The British plan was certainly apparent to those on the *Constitution*'s quarterdeck. The Americans could clearly hear the orders which the British officers shouted to their men.

"Hands to repel boarders!" called Lieutenant Parker. Even before he spoke, many of the quarterdeck gunners and sail trimmers had already started to move from their stations. They picked up whatever small arms and edged weapons they had earlier laid aside. Other than those up in the fighting tops, who were frantically busy firing down on the *Java*'s deck, the rest of the American marines were surging from all parts of the ship toward the stern. Likewise, Lieutenant Aylwin led aft most of the men from the forecastle. As he raced through the billowing smoke, he shouted all the while.

"Come on! Come on with me!"

The men bunched tightly together. They all tried to anticipate the point of impact, which therefore would be the place where the British boarders would likely surge over the side. But in so doing at this extremely close range, they presented a dangerously tempting target for any high-initiative British gunners to spot. This was particularly worrisome since those Javas might fire into them the terribly effective flesh-rending grapeshot or canister. Of course, high-initiative American gunners were trying to do this same thing to the Javas massed on the British frigate's bows, but so far were having no luck.

"Spread out, spread out," shouted Aylwin to the American seamen and marines. Everyone slipped, jostled, and struggled.

As he rushed across the *Constitution*'s deck, Aylwin quickly broke up the pack and spread out the men as much as the circumstance would allow. Then he turned to face the enemy, stepped to the rail, drew his pistol—and upon that instant was grazed by a three-pound grapeshot. Ironically, he was hit in the same shoulder that had been torn open by a musket ball, in the battle with the *Guerrière*, just four months earlier. He spun around as he dropped the pistol to the deck. He cradled his arm and held his hand over the profusely bleeding wound. He shook off two seamen who sprang forward to take him below to the surgeon.

"Get away, damn you! I'm all right." He certainly was not, but he ground his teeth against the pain and continued to marshal the men, awaiting the British attack.

On both ships the preparations for boarding—and to repel boarding—had hardly been completed when the *Constitution* let loose another broadside into the *Java*'s bows. This broadside raked her with terrible effect, but surprisingly did not cut down very many men. However, the broadside did cut through the *Java*'s foremast near the catharpins, breaking it through just below the fighting top.

"Deck there, stand clear! Stand from under!" came a shriek from that top. The whole mass swayed and tottered.

"Commodore, see their mast!" shouted Lieutenant Parker from the *Constitution*'s quarterdeck.

As it fell, the *Java*'s foremast slammed down through the forecastle and main deck. A shocking amount of spars, sails, and rigging came down with it; a considerable amount massed on the bulwark and an equally amazing quantity trailed over the side. Most of the men, who had been massing to board the *Constitution*, managed to scramble out of the way—including the three army officers. But a considerable number could not, and were crushed into the splintered deck or swept right over the railing and into the sea.

The *Java*'s rush ahead, to board the enemy, had faltered. Yet, despite the drag of the trailing wreckage, the momentum of that rush still carried the *Java* slowly forward. The remains of her bowsprit passed over the *Constitution*'s taffrail.

"Captain!" shouted Chads from the forecastle. "The bowsprit's stump's caught in their mizzen rigging." But nothing could come of it, for the *Java* continued to swing, hardly manageable.

When the bowsprit's stump finally tore loose and the ships separated, they both slowly resumed an eastward heading, but this time the *Constitution* held the weather gauge. The *Java* moved slowly, crippled by both the loss of the foremast and the foremast's wreckage as it dragged through the water. The *Constitution* fore-reached on the British frigate, moved down her larboard side, then wore across her bow, raking her with thunder and flame. *Old Ironsides* continued to wear, moving southwesterly down the *Java*'s starboard side. The normally beautiful American ship now appeared black and wicked with menace. This prolonged wearing maneuver, left unchecked, allowed the Americans to almost circle the *Java*, such that at fifteen minutes past eight bells the *Constitution* came to a northerly heading, whereupon she savagely raked the *Java*'s stern with her starboard guns. At this close range the American gunners tore into the helpless British frigate, raking her from aft forward. The Constitutions cheered from the gundeck through the roar of the cannonade. The half-naked men poured with sweat as they wrestled with their massive pieces of artillery. As she now sailed directly into the wind, the *Constitution* was unable to quite complete the circle around the British frigate, and was close to being caught in irons. In any event, Bainbridge actually had no wish to complete the circle, nor hang in stays, and he saw an obvious, better tactic.

"Nichols, you fool," he cried. "What the Goddam hell are you about? Fall off to larboard and come tightly back around."

This allowed the *Constitution*'s larboard broadside to rake the *Java*'s battered stern once again. She thus essentially achieved a double-rake in a short few minutes' time. Lambert winced as he felt, transmitted up through his feet, the impact of American shot as it struck home deep into the *Java*'s hull.

At this point the *Constitution* slowed. She slowed and in fact tried to come to a stop, in order to maintain a position on the *Java*'s starboard quarter.

"Shorten sail, God damn it!" Bainbridge shouted. "In royals...Down the flying jib! In spanker! Ease away tack and bowline! Now—fire as you will. Pour it into him, boys, pour it in!

The American gun crews began firing as rapidly as possible while the *Java* could bring no guns to bear in return. Again, the thick smoke instantly billowed up, the enormous din rose even higher, and the *Constitution's* entire fabric throbbed with every gun on her engaged side in action. The tremendous concussion was not heard with the ears alone, but every man felt it through his entire body. After just a few minutes of this treatment the British frigate's gaff, spanker boom, and spanker were shot completely away. They fell to the quarterdeck and then down into the sea. The *Java* immediately came off the wind and slowed appreciably. For her part, due to her own cut-up rigging, the *Constitution* was unable to trim her sails quickly enough to avoid shooting ahead. This brought the two ships broadside-to-broadside. Both now fired as steadily as possible—but only a few British guns answered many American.

Unfortunately, for the British, a considerable amount of tangled wreckage—sails, spars, rigging, and blocks—lay on and over the *Java's* starboard side. As a result, the few guns on that side that were still firing set this mass of extremely flammable material ablaze with every detonation. Commander Marshall could see no ship's officer available to handle this problem, so he ran from the quarterdeck and onto the gangway—in so doing he passed the army officers who were making their way from the forecastle back to the quarterdeck.

"Quarterdeckmen!" he shouted, "Larboard-side gunners! Afterguard! Axes, here! Tomahawks! Fire buckets!" Following his directions, British seamen and marines swarmed over the starboard side—heedless of the murderous American shot pounding into their ship. They desperately alternated between cutting the wreckage away and throwing buckets of seawater onto the flaming material that remained. As he wiped spray from his eyes, Marshall tried to cheer the men. He assumed a smile and called out in a reasonably calm voice.

"Never mind the bloody God-damned *Constitution*, men. Let's cut away this wreckage and *then* we'll take care of the Yankees!" He felt the *Java* tremble as more American shot struck home. He heard a musket ball scream past his cheek. A flying twenty-inch splinter tore open his sleeve, lacerating his arm. "Hurry up!" he shouted to the axemen, who were making good progress in clearing a few of the guns.

Just then, on the *Constitution*'s quarterdeck, Lieutenant Parker gave a shout. "Commodore! Their main topmast—it's coming down."

The *Java*'s main topmast indeed fell, shot away just above the cap. This left the *Java* totally unmanageable, and with many of her starboard guns once again rendered useless as more wreckage fell upon them. From this time on the *Java* could not fire more than two or three guns in any one direction. The slaughter of the crew continued, terribly. It was clear that the British frigate was now beaten, beaten beyond any recovery. She still sailed, but she sailed low and heavy. Chads stepped close to Lambert's side.

"Captain, I fear she can't take much more."

The barrel of the carronade beside them suddenly rang like a bell, struck by a thirty-two-pound roundshot.

"Henry," cried Lambert in response. "She *must*." Lambert winced as he continued to feel, transmitted up through his feet, the impact of American shot striking home deep into the *Java*'s hull. He coughed in the thick, acrid smoke. He felt the sick fear of defeat rise from the pit of his stomach. He looked around and took some heart in that the colors waved bravely and the remainder of the crew stubbornly fought and struggled on with repairs. Lambert walked the deck, accompanied by Chads, Hislop, and Walker. He heard the constant scream of splinters and felt the steady wind of shot flying past him. The deck was heaped with dead men as well as pieces of men. He idly wondered how it was that he could move through this typhoon of shot and survive.

For some time the white, blue, and particularly the gold of Captain Lambert's uniform—to say nothing of the scarlet and gold uniforms of the army officers close by him—had caught the eye of Sergeant Adrian Peters, U.S. Marine Corps. Peters, born and raised in Holland, had served as a marine for the last four years. Today he was stationed in *Old Ironsides'* main fighting top, from where he had been firing steadily at the *Java*'s quarterdeck, thus far with no success. The unsophisticated weapons, and the incessant movement of both shooters and targets, made this type of marksmanship extremely difficult. However, with indefatigable determination, Peters once again loaded, primed, and cocked his sea-service flintlock musket, braced it against the platform's edge, took careful aim, and squeezed the trigger. Despite the inaccuracies of the standard late-eighteenth-century smoothbore musket, the motion of the *Constitution*'s mast, the motion of the *Java*'s deck, and the fact that Lambert himself was in motion— walking across his quarterdeck as he talked to Chads—Sergeant Peters' incredibly lucky shot hit Lambert squarely in the chest. He fell, heavily, though his head was spared the hard deck, fortuitously cushioned by Chads' foot.

"Captain!" shouted Chads. Chads and the army officers instantly knelt down on the deck beside Lambert and viewed with dismay the shocking wound. They tried to ease his position. "Steady, sir. We'll get you to the surgeon directly."

Oddly, Lambert felt no particular pain. Not surprisingly he was disoriented and confused. He looked around and tried to comprehend what had happened. His gazed fixed upon the crew of the *Java's* No. 14 carronade, starboard side, fairly close by. To his dazed mind they were no longer a rapidly moving team, smoothly loading and firing; rather, they seemed frozen in place, as if they were part of a painting or a *tableau vivant*. He studied them with great intensity. To the left of the gun, against the bulkhead, stood the sponger, a blond man in torn brown trousers and a dirty blue-striped shirt. He leaned away from the muzzle, having just finished the loading process by ramming a wad down the barrel on top of a new thirty-two-pound roundshot. To his side was a marine, musket lying on the deck, hat nowhere in sight, his scarlet jacket torn across the front and his white breeches stained with gunpowder and blood. The marine leaned over, far over, his forehead almost touching the gun's breeching loop. He wedged his handspike against the carriage, which forced the gun to move as it swung from the loading to the firing position. His counterpart on the other side of the gun, a seaman dressed in off-white trousers, sweat-stained white shirt, and blue neck cloth, pushed back with his own handspike as the carronade resumed pointing straight out its port. Outboard from him was the loader, his dark blue shirt contrasted with his mate's white one and his red neck-cloth was tied around his ears. He was straightening up, as moments before he had tipped a shot into the muzzle. The second gun captain, blond and naked to the waist, stood three feet behind the gun and to the right; his left foot almost touched Lambert's. The blond seaman leaned forward while both hands securely gripped the side tackle. All of the men, save the sponger, looked intently at the first gun captain, who stood behind the gun to the left. His feet straddled a deep, furrowed gash in the deck where an American shot had skimmed across it. Despite the oppressive heat and humidity, he wore his short, blue jacket trimmed in white, and though it was now torn and dirty, he was still rather more resplendent in dress than his gun crew. His cutlass dangled at his left side. His right hand held, loosely, the lanyard which was attached to the carronade's flintlock. He glared along the gun's barrel and out the port, his left arm stretched out. His hand motioned for the handspike men to force the gun to point farther forward, as he tried to achieve the best possible shot at the *Constitution.*

Lambert's gaze shifted slightly up and focused upon the shrouds reaching towards the maintop. They were rather cut up, he thought, growing alarmed as he realized almost half of them were shot through. But his thoughts were interrupted as he began to be lifted from the deck. General Hislop and Major Walker had called over two of the gunners from the currently disengaged larboard carronades. These men joined the army officers as they carefully picked Lambert up, and once situated, they carried him below decks to the cockpit.

As they passed through the gundeck, Lambert noticed that many of the dead piled around the mizzenmast were decapitated. Is it the raking fire that took off so many heads? he asked himself. How curious. Then he noticed a number of marines carrying powder and shot. How strange, he silently continued. Where are the poor powder boys? Surely they're not all dead? Finally, after what had seemed an eternity, they reached the orlop deck.

"Make a lane, there, dammit, make a lane for the Captain!" The surgeon, just finishing an amputation, turned and cleared a space on the table as the four men from the quarterdeck approached, gently bearing Lambert's weight. At the moment he was conscious. Jones wiped his hands on his apron and quickly examined his commander. He concentrated against the bedlam in the overflowing cockpit, the constantly changing motion of the ship, the steady and extremely loud vibrations as the ship's cannon fired at the enemy, and the continual thunderous jarring as enemy shot struck the *Java* in turn.

Jones' clothes were almost completely soaked in blood; his outer apron had been fully saturated in the first twenty minutes of the action. His face was pale and drawn with exhaustion and stress. After a couple of minutes he cleared his throat.

"Ha—hmm. Captain, it appears that a musket ball's entered your left side under the clavicle, fracturing the first rib—the splinters of which have severely lacerated your lungs." He put his finger in the wound and carefully detached and extricated several pieces of bone. Lambert winced.

"Oh, sir, I'm sorry! I hope I didn't hurt you too much."

"No, no, Mr. Jones," whispered Lambert. "In fact I feel virtually nothing from the wound in my breast. But I've a good bit of pain which extends the whole length of my spine."

"Well then, your honor, I'm going to give you a draft of laudanum, bandage you, and have you lie quiet, for there's not much more I can do for you right now." Stoically, Lambert took the draft and the bandaging, and then Jones, Capponi, and two loblolly boys carefully moved the captain to a cot. They wedged it against the bulkhead, to minimize motion, and covered him with a blanket.

"Thank you, thankee kindly," he said softly, the laudanum taking effect. "I beg you go back to your work. Oh, Lord, there are so many wounded..."

Even without knowing the surgeon's diagnosis of the wound, it had been instantly apparent on the quarterdeck that Lambert's injury, even if not mortal, was completely incapacitating. Accordingly, as first lieutenant, Chads assumed command, though he suffered from the considerable pain of his own injury.

Success for the *Java* was no longer within reach. She was powerless against the precision, volume, and accuracy of the Yankee fire. And it was all accompanied with incredible noise which was pervasive, continuous, and physically staggering. It deafened the ears, drove through the mind, and shook the body. The rolling waves of concussion were shocking on the weather decks, and in the confined spaces of the gundecks they were almost unbearable.

The *Java* continuously vibrated with the impact of the *Constitution*'s shot. Some of that shot now carried away all but a short stump of the *Java*'s foremast. The remaining ensign was cut away. Then, right before two bells in the first dog watch, the mizzenmast fell, cut through no more than fifteen feet above the deck. At this point all that the *Java* had left standing, which could support any sail at all, was the main yard on the lower part of the mainmast—and that was tottering. Thus, the virtually dismasted *Java* could do nothing to save herself. Most of the men were, at the least, faint with fatigue; even those not significantly wounded suffered from innumerable small splinter bites, smoke inhalation, tinnitus, rope and flash burns, and various bruises and contusions. Few guns would bear even if serviceable. Finally, the British fire stopped entirely.

On the *Constitution*'s quarterdeck, Bainbridge fought against his own weariness and pain. He roused himself and took another assessment.

"Cease fire! Cease fire, all."

Thus, at ten minutes after two bells, the afternoon fell silent. The first lieutenant approached the commodore.

"Sir, I suppose they've struck? We've apparently silenced her fire, and her colors are down in the main rigging. She's quite low in the water, too."

"It's apparent they're beaten, Parker," replied Bainbridge as he stiffly turned, "but whether the English or their commander can accept it remains to be seen." He staggered, stupid with fatigue and the pain in both his legs. He leaned upon Midshipman Gordon even more heavily than before. He tried to think clearly. "Pray alter course and move ahead of the enemy. Our own rigging's extremely cut up. We'll make some repairs. Then we'll close and take possession."

"Aye aye, sir."

Leaving the *Java* an unmanageable wreck, the *Constitution* hauled about and moved ahead out of gunshot. Lieutenant Parker made a quick tour of the ship and was delighted to find less damage than he had feared. He then nerved himself to visit the cockpit. As he entered the cramped space he was pleasantly surprised to see fewer wounded men than he had expected.

"Ah, Mr. Parker," exclaimed Surgeon Evans in greeting, walking over to the lieutenant while he dried his hands on a piece of bandage. "The guns are silent, I find. Would this be a good sign, at all?"

"Good afternoon, Mr. Evans," replied Parker. "A good sign, indeed, for I believe I can fairly say the battle's over. We move away from the enemy to make some quick repairs. More significantly, we actually wait upon the British. Their ship's a dismasted and smoking hulk, and so we expect them to strike momentarily." He hesitated for a moment. "Dare I ask you the butcher's bill?"

"Sir," said Evans thoughtfully, "in no way do I wish to make light of the suffering I've seen today, but if you say the battle is truly over after some three hours of heavy fire, then I think we've come off pretty well. At this point I'm aware of only nine poor souls who've been killed. Of the wounded, there are about thirty whom we've treated. Sixteen of those are what I'd call severe or serious, which includes four limb amputations and a couple of shocking burn cases." Evans walked Parker a few feet aft from where they had been talking, to gaze upon a pale, heavily bandaged officer in a laudanum-induced sleep.

"I much fear for my friend Mr. Aylwin," Evans continued. "He's sustained a severe wound to the same shoulder which was so badly torn open during the action with the *Guerrière*. So far so good, but shock, loss of blood, and infection sit so closely around his cot that I can't predict the outcome." Parker looked down upon Aylwin; his expression of deep concern mirrored the surgeon's.

"On a lighter note," said Evans, trying to cheer himself as well as the first lieutenant, "about nine of the slightly wounded have already been returned to duty. I'm told the commodore's to be counted as one of these, since he refuses to come see me and's kept the deck all this while." Parker laughed and clapped Evans on the shoulder.

"Yes, Surgeon, the commodore's hurt in both legs, and can't stand upright without using poor Mr. Gordon as a crutch. I trust his aren't serious wounds, and that he'll allow himself to be looked after as soon as the enemy strikes."

Old Ironsides shortly hove-to, to windward of her enemy, while her topmen furiously raced over her rigging. They found that one eighteen-pound ball had gone right through the mizzenmast, and that the foremast, maintopmast, and several spars were damaged to various degrees. The most serious issue was that the running rigging and shrouds were, indeed, a good deal cut up. However, the crew exerted themselves massively; they spliced lines, replaced lines, and rebent sails, and in just under an hour *Old Ironsides* was again in effective fighting trim.

For their part, the British certainly had *not* surrendered, though the prospect was very much in mind. As the *Constitution* moved off, Lieutenant Chads and Commander Marshall paused for a moment to study the American ship, and to converse.

"Our situation appears pretty desperate," said Chads. "In truth, sir, at this point there's not much hope left for us. How can we successfully resist the overwhelming power of our opponent? Yet, I'm loath to surrender the ship. May I beg your opinion?"

With the cessation of fire the heavy smoke dissipated in the light breeze, and as a result the early evening's sunshine flooded down upon the torn deck.

"Mr. Chads," replied Marshall, after a moment's thought. "Due to Captain Lambert's unfortunate incapacitation, command has fallen to you, and the responsibility that you bear for our country's considerable. In my view, your actions today have been very officerlike and noble."

"Yes, sir, thank you."

"So, since you ask it," Marshall continued, "allow me to make an observation. I can only acknowledge our hopeless situation. However, it's not inconceivable that we might still dismast the enemy, or even still contrive to board him, if he'd return alongside. We're yet strong at our guns if we can clear away more of the wreckage. And, it's just possible that some accident might force the enemy to decline any further contest—or possibly some friendly sail might heave into view at any moment." He rubbed his forehead with his powder-blackened hands.

"I don't like to merely advise," Marshall went on, "and yet that's all I *can* do. As you know, though I'm senior to you in rank, I'm legally but a passenger. You must carry this burden. But know this: whatever you decide, I'll attest to the honorable and gallant conduct of you and every officer on board during this action." He again rubbed his forehead.

"Having said that, I recommend that we play this out to the end. Let's not give up too soon. So, I advise you to *not* strike our colors."

"Thank you, sir," said Chads as he nodded his head with satisfaction. He turned to the officers who stood behind him, awaiting orders. "I hoped that you'd so advise. I'm entirely in agreement with your thinking."

Thus, the Javas began to work—feverishly—trying to make their own repairs during this unexpected break. Many made repeated short stops at the scuttlebutts to drink and throw water in their faces—small comfort in the staggering heat and humidity. Since they anticipated that the action would be renewed momentarily, during this interval the Javas made every exertion to bring some sort of order and capability out of the chaos that reigned on board. The carpenter, Mr. Kennedy, came up on deck. He blinked in the now bright sunlight and coughed in the remainder of the smoke. He knuckled his forehead, ready to report, but Chads spoke first.

"Chips, what's the damage?"

"Thirteen shot 'oles, sir, below the waterline, h'all around the 'ull."

"Christ," responded Chads. "Well, if any're grouped together we'll fother a sail under the bottom—if we can gather enough men. In the meanwhile try your best to plug the worst."

"Aye aye, sir."

The Javas succeeded in clearing most of the debris of the masts from around and in front of the guns. They also cut away the enormous amount of wreckage that trailed in the water. Lieutenant Sanders, bloodied from a falling block which had struck him when the foremast collapsed, found a surprisingly undamaged spare topgallant mast in the clutter of the booms. Despite the extremely heavy pitch and roll of the ship, which worked—maddeningly—against their every move, Sanders and some forecastle hands managed to fish it to the stump of the foremast. Then, with further great difficulty, they rigged a staysail between it and the remains of the bowsprit. The sail filled and miraculously the *Java* moved forward. She actually picked up enough speed for the rudder to bite and the helm to answer. She turned slightly, bringing the wind a little abaft the beam, pointing more or less toward the *Constitution*.

Happily, the weather-half of the mainyard remained aloft, thus Chads envisioned a further opportunity to get the *Java* solidly before the wind and ensure steerageway—particularly since the helm, tiller ropes, and rudder were undamaged.

"Mr. Humble," he called to the boatswain. "Get the main tack brought forward and see if it can be set."

"Aye aye, sir."

In fact, it was possible to set, fill, and trim it. But the damaged mainmast—that is, the remaining lower mast—was unstable and even appeared to sway. It had been hit several times and had most of its stays and shrouds cut. Because so much of the *Java*'s top-hamper was gone, the stability it provided was also gone, which allowed the poor *Java* to roll—and to roll heavily. This radical motion made the stress of even the little bit of sail on the wounded mainmast too much to bear. The British officers realized that it was not going to work, and with every second the realization increased that the mast was going to fall—and, with the ship before the wind, it was going to fall onto the deck.

"Bloody hell!" Chads cursed. "Helm a-weather! Mr. Humble, get your mates and cut those remaining weather shrouds away right now!" Instantly both orders were carried out and the mast fell, not onto the deck but over to leeward, covering the sea and the starboard side with more wreckage. Once again a party of men swarmed over the side with axes, tomahawks, and even cutlasses and swords. They frantically cut things away, trying to clear the guns. Unfortunately the *Java*, which was in effect now completely dismasted, now rolled even more wildly—sickeningly so—even for men long accustomed to the motion of the sea, and in so doing created another challenge for the weary working parties.

A small ship's boy nervously approached Chads and knuckled his forehead. "Sir, the carpenter, 'e sent me. The larboard chain pump's h'all knocked to pieces. 'E says the water's gaining bad. 'E says there's four foot o' water in the well, an' nearer five. An' 'e says 'e's tryin' to plug what 'oles 'e can."

"Thank you, youngster," replied Chads, who smiled to hide his despair from the boy. "Run back and tell the carpenter I know he'll do his best."

A few minutes later, Chads called together the *Java*'s surviving officers on the quarterdeck. Out of courtesy he also included Marshall as well as the general and his aides. He cleared his throat and flashed a tight smile.

"General Hislop, Captain Marshall, gentlemen. It's now my duty to give you my assessment of the ship's situation. Clearly, we're in a pretty serious state of affairs. The enemy's disengaged for the moment and has left us a perfect wreck. They've moved ahead, out of gunshot, where they've remained for upwards of an hour effecting repairs to *their* damages. We've mustered at quarters and have found missing at least 120 men. Six quarterdeck guns, four fo'c'sle, and many of the main-deck guns are disabled, some with wreckage laying over them. The hull's quite knocked to pieces, all three masts and bowsprit are gone, and the foremast in falling has passed through the fo'c'sle and main deck. And, with many shots below the waterline, the ship makes considerable water, particularly with one of the pumps shot away."

He paused for a moment and looked at the *Constitution* in the distance.

"I've just received reports from Lieutenants Herringham and Buchanan for'rard. The master, as you know, is below decks severely wounded. Taking everything into consideration, I've decided that we'll engage the enemy again if he gives us *any* opportunity of doing so. We've made every preparation to receive him when he chooses to renew the action. Accordingly, we've reloaded the guns with round and grape. If he gives us that chance I'm determined to engage with a view to possibly disabling him, which is now my sole object." He again paused and toyed with the bandages that bound him.

"However, having said all that, I much fear the enemy'll renew the action. I estimate he'll assume a raking position, whereupon none of our guns will bear upon him. In that case I believe a continuation of the action would be fruitless—and that it'd be wasting lives to resist any longer." General Hislop had been listening carefully, barely able to retain his balance with the shocking roll of the ship. As Chads talked, Hislop had kept his own eyes fixed in the distance upon the American.

"Mr. Chads, as far as it can be supposed that as a military officer I can be any judge of a naval action, I'm fully satisfied that everything's been done for the defense of His Majesty's ship. If the enemy does choose to stand off and rake, I agree further resistance would be quite useless."

Down in the cockpit, Surgeon Jones paused for a moment as he finished the stitches on a severe splinter wound. The heavy, humid air of the entire orlop deck was thick with the stench of gunpowder and blood. Grateful that the pounding of the guns—both British and American—had stopped, and even more grateful that the stream of casualties had proportionally diminished, he surveyed the cockpit full and overflowing with wounded. There had been well over 100 brought below, and although many of those had died—expiring before they could be treated or in spite of his, Mr. Falls', or Mr. Capponi's best efforts—he had also been able to return around 30 of the lesser-wounded to duty. Jones prayed that the 70 or so who remained might pull through. Statistically, he knew that this many wounded meant there could be as many as forty or fifty who had been killed where they had fought. He dreaded going on deck and seeing the piles of bodies stacked around the masts, though even that would not tell the whole tale. He knew that a number of the dead would have been immediately thrown overboard by their shipmates during the action. Win or lose, tomorrow's accounting for personnel would be difficult.

It was not hard to account for the brothers Keele, however. Both were midshipmen from Southampton, one aged sixteen and the other eighteen, and both lay severely wounded on the canvas-covered deck. The younger boy, Edward, had needed to have his leg amputated and was in critical condition; Jones hoped for his recovery, but the next day, unfortunately, would see that hope dashed. The older brother, acting as a gundeck division officer with great coolness and bravery, had been severely wounded by a grapeshot passing between his arm and his side. As Jones walked over and looked at them both, Edward spoke in a soft whisper.

"Pray, Mr. Jones, is the action over? Have we struck?"

"I don't know, Mr. Keele," replied Jones. "I think neither, for in either case they'd send us word. Please lie still and be as calm as you can. Your wound's quite serious and you need to conserve your strength." Jones moved back toward the operating table.

"Come, gentlemen," he called to Falls and Capponi. He raised his voice above the pitiful moans and cries which filled the area. "Rouse the mates. I don't know if the action's over or if it'll directly start again, but let's re-examine our patients. Look closely at sutures and bandaging, particularly among the amputees. And we've laudanum to spare for those who particularly suffer, so let's not be stingy with it."

Exactly at three bells in the first dog watch, as if her crew watched a clock and respond to a cue, the *Constitution* wore and stood toward the *Java*, moving in to administer a *coup de grâce*. She came within hailing distance.

"Parker," said Bainbridge, "we'll lie across her bow and rake her from there if she don't strike."

"Aye aye, sir."

The Americans observed that, during the last hour, the British had hoisted a new ensign to the stump of their mizzenmast. Bainbridge leaned against the *Constitution*'s railing and braced himself against a newly re-rove shroud. He thought the flag's seemingly defiant waving an odd contrast to other things he could see.

"Sweet Jesus," he exclaimed, staring at the *Java*'s side, shockingly riddled with shot. "Parker, look at the dark red streaks which run down to the water. That's blood, dribbling from their scuppers."

"Yes, sir," replied Parker, similarly unable to tear his gaze from the British ship. "And did you see them throwing dead men over the side? Do you see the trail of dead in her wake?"

Old Ironsides got relatively close to the *Java*, athwart her bows, in an extremely effective raking position. She was close, but far away enough to preclude any chance of collision—and any opportunity for the anxious British crew to board. The lone staysail, which the *Java* wore on her jury-rigged foremast, could not pull her forward fast enough to run down and close the *Constitution*. With this single sail the *Java* could not effectively move into the wind; thus, she could not really even continue moving toward the *Constitution*. All the British could do is turn, slowly, in an effort to bring their few remaining broadside guns to bear, but even that would be pointless—the Americans would not just passively wait for it, but would shift their own position. And, clearly, the Americans would commence that threatened, dreadful full-broadside raking fire while they shifted. Indeed, the *Constitution* shivered her topsails and came virtually to a stop, under perfect control. She rocked gently, with every gun of her essentially undamaged starboard broadside bearing on the *Java's* defenseless bow.

Bainbridge intently studied the enemy ship. He waited for the British to act; he hoped they would bow to the hard logic of the situation. She must strike, he thought. Why don't she strike?

Seconds dragged into minutes. Bainbridge was not a patient man by nature, and right now the pain of his wounds nagged at him and acted as spurs. He at last opened his mouth and began giving the commands to fire.

"Cock your locks!" he called to the division officers. "Take your aim!"

But just then the *Java* did strike those colors on the mizzen-mast. Lieutenant Chads yielded to the inevitable and even lowered the colors himself. Had Chads imprudently allowed that broadside to have raked the *Java*—and the subsequent broadsides that were ready to come—her additional loss of life would have been terrible, lying as she was like a log upon the water, perfectly unmanageable and perfectly indefensible. The *Constitution* could have raked her again and again, for the rest of the day, without being exposed to more than two or three British guns—if even that.

On board the *Java*, Chads called to Marshall.

"Sir, could you please help me below for a minute?" They ran below to search for the ship's vital documents: official letters; Admiralty orders; dispatches for the Cape of Good Hope and Bombay; signal book and codes; log book; muster book—even the punishment book. In Lambert's cabin, amid the indescribable wreckage, they rifled his shattered desk and they searched through his dispatch box—a bulky piece of baggage covered in Russian leather, its distinctive key fortunately in the engraved brass lock. Elsewhere there were other documents, dispatches, and official mail that also should be kept from falling into enemy hands, but these first items were the most important and held Chads' attention. The signal book had lead bound into its covers and thus could be depended upon to sink instantly once thrown overboard. Chads kept some things he would need in captivity. He thrust the other books and papers into the captain's heavy iron box, which was weighted with lead and featured several holes in its sides, designed for just this purpose. They climbed back on deck and strode purposefully to the rail.

"Ready, sir?" asked Chads. "One, two, heave!" With Marshall's help Chads pitched the box and the loose signal book as far from the ship's side as possible, where they sank at once, beyond any recovery.

Chads then ran back below and down to the cockpit. Before the Americans came on board he wished to see Lambert for a moment. Lambert was conscious and, despite his wound, gave a wan smile in greeting.

"You've struck, I fear."

Chads nodded. "Sir, the dear *Java*'s destroyed. We're completely dismasted and—" he stopped as Lambert winced as he tried to raise his hand.

"I understand, Henry. It's all right." Wincing again, he said, "Underneath the cot—my Dolland glass. I beg you take it and keep it as a remembrance of me." He paused for a moment. "Mr. Chads, if I live, I'll be damned if I don't impeach Lord Melville. I had a high character in the service. Yet, notwithstanding my remonstrances, he forced me to go to sea with an insufficient and inefficient crew, and this's been the result." Chads nodded again and took his captain's hand.

"Sir, you certainly will live, and your high character remains sterling—sound as a pound. But I must leave you right now. I must regain the deck. The Yankees'll be on board directly. Please compose yourself and rest. I'll see you again, soon." Lambert smiled, closed his eyes, and released his hand. For a brief moment the twenty-four-year-old lieutenant gazed upon his twenty-eight-year-old friend—his dying captain—and then walked out of the cockpit.

Upon seeing the British colors struck, the Americans—almost as one man—began cheering, which echoed the cheers they had given when the *Constitution* had first beat to quarters. In fact, the entire ship cheered, cheering madly, the pervasive exultation radiating from maintruck to keel and bowsprit to spanker boom. It was clearly heard on board the *Java* only a hundred yards to leeward. In the fighting tops, from around the guns on the weather deck, and leaning out of the ports on the gundeck, the Constitutions capered and danced and shouted. Forward on the gundeck, Seaman John Chevers of Marblehead, Massachusetts, who had been No. 9's second sponger, lay mortally wounded only a few feet from the dead body of his brother Joseph, who had been No. 5's second loader. When he heard the cheering, he begged to know the reason.

"Why, John, the enemy's struck, damn them!" Chevers raised himself on to his elbow and, with considerable effort, joined the din by croaking out three cheers of his own.

Bainbridge slowly and softly clapped his hands together, partially in satisfaction and partially in relief.

"Take stations for wearing!" he ordered. "In spanker...Up mains'l...Brace in after yards...Helm up...Brace headyards square!" The ship wore and moved closer to the *Java*.

"Mr. Nichols," said Bainbridge, "kindly put the main tops'l to the mast." With the ship thus hove-to, once again essentially motionless, the Constitutions turned their attention to the small boats.

After he discovered that only two of the ship's eight boats had survived the action and would actually swim, Lieutenant Parker ordered one of them, the larger cutter, hoisted out.

The boatswain, Mr. Adams, made it ready. "Quarterdeckmen, muster aft! Clear away the No. 3 cutter! Let go the gripes...Stretch along the falls...Walk back the falls...Lower away aft...let go aft! Lower away forward...let go forward!"

While the cutter was being lowered, Parker rapidly assembled a boarding party to take possession of the *Java*—himself, Midshipman Henry Gilliam, ten seamen, and ten marines. They crowded into the boat, cast off, and rowed across to accept the surrender. The time was approximately four bells in the first dog watch—six o'clock.

As it approached the *Java*, the cutter was obliged to steer carefully through a considerable amount of wreckage which floated in the sea around that unfortunate ship. Flotsam aside, the boarding party was mindful of many mangled bodies in the water—bodies of British crewmen, which also lay exposed on the floating wreckage of the masts.

"Jesus, Mary, an' Joseph," whispered one of the marines. "Would ya' look at that, fer the love a' God."

As the Americans clambered up the *Java*'s accommodation ladder, and came onto her weather deck, they were greeted by an awful, bloody scene. As he quickly surveyed the *Java*'s deck from her starboard entryway, Lieutenant Parker recalled Surgeon Evans' horrifying report from when Evans had boarded the shattered, bloody *Guerrière* just four months earlier. He then became aware of a strange, low sound, an indistinct undertone beyond anything expected. He suddenly realized it was the helpless murmuring of wounded men, who seemingly were cached all around the ship as well as down below decks.

Following the first lieutenant, Midshipman Gilliam silently reflected upon what he himself had said when he stepped upon the *Guerrière*'s deck—which had been all too similar to this one. "Oh, God. Pieces of skulls, brains, legs, arms, and blood lie in every direction."

A number of men lay heaped at the base of each mast, their bodies bloody mounds of flesh. Gilliam had volunteered to board the *Java* with the notion that his experience on board the *Guerrière* had hardened him, but he was mistaken. He suddenly put his hands to his mouth, vainly, for there was no holding back the vomit which spurted between his fingers.

Parker left the incapacitated Gilliam behind by the entry port, and walked onto the quarterdeck. He stepped carefully as the *Java* rolled wildly, feeling his shoes slip in blood. He noticed that everywhere the deck was heavily ploughed up by shot, with the furrows lined by fringes of vertical splinters. He focused upon a tall and slender officer who appeared before him, his blue coat torn in several places, his white breeches considerably splattered with blood, his torso and lower back bound with stained bandages. The American drew himself up to speak formally.

"We're come aboard, sir. I'm Lieutenant George Parker of the United States Ship *Constitution*. It's my understanding that you've struck your colors, and if so, I'm here to take possession of this ship as a prize of the *Constitution*."

"Good evening, Mr. Parker. I'm Lieutenant Henry Chads, in command of His Britannic Majesty's Ship *Java*. I'm in command as my captain, Henry Lambert, has been severely wounded. I regret that you're correct in your understanding of the situation. We've indeed struck our colors."

Chads stepped aside and drew Parker's attention to several officers standing behind him, one in blue naval uniform and three in red coats.

"General Hislop, Captain Marshall, Major Walker, Captain Wood, may I present Lieutenant Parker, United States Navy, and his party. Mr. Parker, these gentlemen—as well as a number of others on board—are passengers being transported to India."

"Gentlemen," responded Parker, "I'm honored to make your acquaintance. I- I'm extremely sorry our meeting couldn't be under different circumstances." He was hoarse from shouting throughout the battle and paused to clear his throat. His own fatigue and the horrible sights of the *Java*'s deck oppressed him heavily.

"Mr. Chads," he finally went on, "I must beg you to come aboard the *Constitution* and formally surrender to my commanding officer, Commodore Bainbridge. I see you've no boats left in serviceable condition. We've only two ourselves, and thus we'll have to make do. I can also see, by the shocking condition of your deck, that you must have very many wounded. Our wounded have already been cared for, so I believe our surgeon could come aboard if you'd find his assistance of use." As he said these last words, his gaze rested on Captain Wood, who looked remarkably pale and whose head was tightly wrapped in a frighteningly bloody bandage. Its darkly stained red clashed unpleasantly with his scarlet uniform coat.

"I daresay your surgeon's assistance would be invaluable," Chads replied. "That's kind of you."

"Then, gentlemen," said Parker, "if you'd be so kind as to enter my cutter, we'll go."

"Mr. Parker," said Marshall, "I beg your indulgence that I might stay on board and remain with our unfortunate captain. I'd like to keep him company and provide whatever aid to him possible."

"Of course, sir, certainly," replied Parker, and with courteous gestures the remainder of the group ushered itself to the entry port. With no ceremony whatsoever Wood, Walker, Hislop, and lastly Chads and Parker climbed down the *Java*'s side and into the *Constitution*'s boat, a feat which required some skill as the *Java* continued to roll dreadfully At times the muzzles of the gundeck 18-pounders nearly touched the water. Midshipman Gilliam and the ten U.S. Marines remained on board, symbolizing the *Java*'s new possession by the U.S. Navy.

It took the weary American boat crew only a few minutes to row back to the *Constitution*. It was a fairly silent trip, for although Lieutenant Parker tried to think of some appropriate pleasantries, turning a number of potential remarks over in his mind, he found them all wanting under the circumstances. Moreover, Parker had never before been on board a beaten ship, and his thoughts were filled with the horrifying things he had just seen. His heart went out to the Javas in their helplessness and misery.

For their part the British officers were quiet, all seemingly lost in thought. Captain Wood sat stonily silent, eyes closed. He swayed with the motion of the boat—which was a good deal less than the motion last felt on board the *Java*. The army officer was clearly trying to deal with the pain of his head wound.

Lieutenant Chads sat and stared fixedly at the nearing American frigate. His chin rested on his hand, which was folded over the hilts of two swords held upright between his knees. Parker assumed that the one sword, which Chads had been wearing, was his; it was straight and fairly plain. The other one must likely belong to the wounded British captain who remained in the *Java*'s cockpit. This second sword was particularly striking, and surely had been a presentation sword awarded for valor. It was about thirty inches in length and slightly curved, with a red, white, and gold knot attached to the hilt. The belt was also attached, trimmed with a double row of exquisite oak leaves embroidered in gold on a blue background.

Commodore Bainbridge stood by the railing on the *Constitution*'s quarterdeck as he watched the boat come closer. Suddenly he stiffened and brought his glass to his eye.

"See there, Shubrick," he cried as he elbowed the lieutenant standing next to him. "See the red-coated officer next to Parker? Remember the dream about which I told all of you at Christmas dinner, the part where we would capture some army officers, including a general? That is the identical officer I saw in my dream. Damn it, see him! That's the general!"

The *Constitution* suffered the boat to come alongside without a hail. Parker's coxswain skillfully reached the mainchains with his boathook and drew them close in. Parker stood up.

"Gentlemen, if you'll allow me..." He quickly climbed the accommodation ladder. The British officers followed, Hislop first and Chads last. The small group stood assembled at the entry port on the *Constitution*'s weather deck. They arrived with the same lack of formal ceremony with which they had left the *Java*.

With another courteous gesture, Parker led the British party aft onto the *Constitution*'s quarterdeck, where he stopped in front of a senior American officer. To the British he appeared a tall, beefy man whose extremely pale face appeared in sharp contrast to his black hair and side whiskers. His trousers were torn and blood-soaked, particularly below the knees, and he leaned heavily upon the shoulder of a young midshipman. Two powder-blackened and weary lieutenants stood to his side.

"Commodore," began Parker, "may I name Lieutenant Chads, in command of his Britannic Majesty's frigate *Java*. Mr. Chads, this is Commodore Bainbridge, commanding the United States frigate *Constitution*."

Chads cleared his throat.

"Commodore Bainbridge, may I present Lieutenant General Hislop, the governor-designate of Bombay, as well as his aides Major Walker and Captain Wood." Each officer bowed slightly as Chads introduced them, while Bainbridge, clearly unable to bow, nodded to each individual in turn. His gaze lingered for a moment upon General Hislop.

"Sir, as Mr. Parker just informed you, I'm Lieutenant Henry Ducie Chads, in command of the *Java* because my captain, Henry Lambert, remains on board, grievously wounded."

Chads started to say something else but then simply stepped forward. He held out both of the swords which he had brought from the *Java*. Bainbridge nodded at Parker, who, confused, was slow to react. The commodore's nod turned into a glare, which jarred Parker to reach out with both hands and take the proffered swords. Bainbridge smiled in satisfaction and then addressed the British lieutenant.

"Mr. Chads, you, your captain, your men, and your ship have fought well, and have defended the honor of your flag with considerable bravery and resolution. You've done all that brave and skillful officers can do, and I know that you've surrendered only when it was clear that further resistance would've been a wanton effusion of human blood. I hope soon to meet your captain upon what I pray will be his rapid recovery." He paused for a second, as if he were going to say something else, but merely cleared his throat and looked down.

Lieutenant Parker exchanged a quick glance with Lieutenants Shubrick and Morgan, then also looked down. Four months earlier, Captain Hull had courteously refused to accept Captain Dacres' sword, on this very deck, when Hull and the *Constitution* had defeated the *Guerrière*. Today all three lieutenants were surprised that Commodore Bainbridge was not similarly generous or chivalrous. Why did he not give the swords back to this impressive British officer? Did the commodore not appreciate that the *Java* had put up a much longer and more respectable fight than had the *Guerrière*? Did he not care?

For his part, Mr. Chads gave no hint of surprise or disappointment. He simply nodded and looked out past the American commodore and across the dark sea. He looked at his dismasted, smoking *Java* as she drifted through her considerable flotsam and debris, a perfect wreck.

EPILOGUE

Commodore Bainbridge listened to Lieutenant Parker's report and carefully studied the *Java* through his glass. He then, briefly, considered three options. Above all, he profoundly desired to sail or tow the *Java* home to Boston, *à la* Commodore Decatur and the *Macedonian*, to increase the effect of his victory in the eyes of the public. (At this time Bainbridge was actually unaware of Decatur's achievement, but the same notion certainly crossed his mind as it had Decatur's). It was pretty clear, however, that the *Java* was damaged beyond any hope of repair at sea. And, even if some repair could be made, Boston was a long 3,800 miles away—a formidable distance, which would also require *Old Ironsides* to dodge the many cruisers of the growing British blockade outside each U.S. Atlantic port. He could, perhaps, bring the *Java* into San Salvador for repair or salvage, but the last several days' evidence of considerable Portuguese unfriendliness made that alternative probably unrealistic and certainly unpalatable. That left nothing but the third and obvious option: remove the crew and burn the *Java*—*à la* Captain Hull and the *Guerrière*.

It took Mr. Bainbridge all of fifteen minutes to decide on his course of action. It took the *Constitution*'s two surviving boats all night and all the next day to transfer the *Java*'s officers and crew, as well as some of their stores and baggage, from the one ship to the other. The unwounded men, excluding the officers, were placed in manacles. It was not an unknown phenomenom for a ship to be seized by captives held on board, and William Bainbridge was not about to risk any such thing. The Americans also spent some of that following day, December thirtieth, in making additional repairs to their own battle damage. This included detaching the *Java*'s undamaged steering wheel and moving it to the *Constitution*'s quarterdeck, where it replaced the one shattered early-on in the battle.

The transfer of the wounded prisoners, from the *Java* to the *Constitution*, was particularly difficult and time consuming. With no special equipment, the journey from the *Java*'s cockpit, orlop-deck and berth-deck, down her side into the small boats, across the sea, up the *Constitution*'s side, and then down below was dreadful at best. For the many severely wounded, it was absolutely unspeakable.

Captain Lambert was one of those, secured to a couch, moved at the last moment as gently as possible. When carefully hoisted to the *Constitution*'s weather deck he was met by Commodore Bainbridge. The American commander suffered considerable pain and inflammation himself, since he had been continuously on his feet for almost three days and nights, and had yet to have his leg operated upon to extract the piece of copper. Supported by an aide, he limped over to Lambert's side and spoke to him.

At three o'clock p.m. on Thursday, December thirty-first, after all the prisoners and baggage had been brought on board, the *Java* was set on fire. She blew up when the flames reached her smaller powder magazine. Most of the captives could not bear to watch. The American surgeon, Mr. Evans, did watch. He had also viewed the final moments of the *Guerrière* four months earlier, and he now confided to his journal that *the explosion was not so grand as that of the* Guerrière. Nevertheless, even at some distance, the detonation assaulted the already strained eardrums of everyone—British and American alike. Then, as the last of the smoke drifted away, the *Constitution* stood in for the land.

Early the next morning—Friday, New Year's Day, 1813—the lookouts sighted the land which surrounded the "Bay of All Saints." They also sighted an unidentified sail. Bainbridge immediately cleared for action and beat to quarters, and with considerable effort packed all the prisoners, including the wounded, into *Old Ironsides*' berth deck and holds below. There they suffered considerably from overcrowding, relentless humidity, and 120° heat. Some criticism later came to Bainbridge for this last, with suggestions of malice, but it is hard not to recognize the obvious military necessity; for all he knew the strange sail was the British line-of-battle ship *Montagu* finally up from Janeiro—thus he needed his gundeck and weather deck clear. As it turned out, the sail was not a threat, nor was the next, which actually proved to be a friend. Just outside the bay the USS *Hornet* ran alongside, her crew wildly cheering the crew of the *Constitution* the instant they heard the news. Shortly after 1:00 p.m. *Old Ironsides* came to anchor in San Salvador; the *Hornet* remained offshore, ever hopeful that HMS *Bonne Citoyenne* would come forth to do battle.

Based upon the high tensions of the preceding week, the Americans were extremely concerned about their reception in regard to the Portuguese authorities. Surprisingly, they found a different attitude and a reasonably cordial welcome. For whatever reason—it may have been nothing more than the news of the *Constitution*'s remarkable victory—the *Governador da Bahia*, the Conde dos Arcos, left off his bellicose rhetoric and offered the Americans everything that a national ship of a recognized country could expect. Thus, with civilized accommodation, *Old Ironsides* landed her prisoners, took on water and provisions, and hired ten local carpenters to make additional repairs.

What was the true extent of the *Constitution*'s injuries? In the official letter he would shortly write, Bainbridge confined himself to a single sentence which focused upon her sails and rigging being "very much cut" and "many of her spars injured." But in a private letter he went into more detail and stated that while her damage was nothing "to *the perfect wreck* we made of the Enemy,"

the *Constitution* [is] a good deal cut—some Shott between wind & water—Her upper bulkworks considerably Shott—Foremast and mizzen mast shott through—Main and mizzen Stays shott through, Eight lower Shrouds cut off—Foretopmast Stays & every Topmast Shroud—All the Braces standing and Preventers, and Bowlines were three times shott away during the Action—[6] Boats out of 8 destroyed by Shott—Our Sails extremely cut to pieces—the Main Topmast, main TopSail yards, Jib Boom, Spanker Boom-Gaft & Trysail mast were all so shott as to render them unserviceable—

So, the plan to take the *Constitution* home was perhaps motivated by more than Bainbridge's strong desire for immediate personal recognition, as some historians later would suggest. Perhaps *Old Ironsides* was too weakened and unfit to continue with her orders. Indeed, if she finally did make a *rendezvous* with the *Es-*

sex, and sailed with her for the South Pacific, she may well have been overwhelmed by the extremely rough seas found when attempting to round Cape Horn. Moreover, when the *Constitution* did at last reach Boston in mid-February, she underwent an extensive overhaul to include the replacement of beams, decking, waterways, ceiling, and copper sheathing—things certainly not all caused by the *Java's* fire, but legitimate maintenance and repair requirements none the less.

In any event, by January sixth Bainbridge felt *Old Ironsides* was ready to sail from San Salvador, and so she did. She also took with her two prize ships just captured by the *Hornet.* On the eighteenth of February, the commodore landed at Boston's Long Wharf to face an avalanche of honors and recognition—just as had Isaac Hull and Stephen Decatur in the past few months. At last "Hard Luck Bill" Bainbridge had found absolution for his previous string of naval disasters. The commodore's professional career was now at its zenith, though with his pessimistic nature and out of balance self-image, it was something he apparently could not properly recognize, nor fully relish.

While *Old Ironsides* had been busy with the *Java,* the *Hornet* had continued to be quite active (as one might have expected with the zealous Master Commandant Lawrence in command). She captured two vessels on the last two days of December. The first one was the poor *Java's* prize, the terribly slow and salt-laden *William.* She was caught by the *Hornet* while heading into San Salvador—not long after she parted from the *Java.* The second was a British schooner named the *Ellen,* which carried a cargo later assessed to be worth £34,000.

Before and after the *Constitution* departed for Boston, Captain Lawrence and Consul Hill—certainly with Commodore Bainbridge's help—continued the campaign to entice or shame the *Bonne Citoyenne* (and her hold full of gold) to come out of San Salvador and fight the *Hornet.* However, on January twenty-fourth, Lawrence was forced to abandon this project due to the appearance of the 74-gun HMS *Montagu,* which had *finally* come up from Rio de Janeiro to check on reports of American activity around San Salvador. So, Lawrence moved the *Hornet* up the coast to the north, and on February fourteenth captured the brig *Resolution* with a cargo of foodstuffs and about $23,000 in specie on board. Ten days later, off the mouth of the Demerara River, Lawrence found, engaged, and actually *sank* H.M. Gun-Brig *Pea-*

cock in an action that barely lasted fifteen minutes. At that point he decided it was now the *Hornet*'s turn to go home.

After he repeatedly missed—through no fault of his own—the various *rendezvous* with the *Constitution* and *Hornet*, at the end of January Captain Porter took the U.S. Frigate *Essex* around Cape Horn. She survived the Horn's terrible gales and extremely heavy seas before finally reaching the Pacific Ocean. Then, during the next several months, the *Essex* captured thirteen British whalers. She had particular success in the vicinity of the Galápagos Islands. In January 1814, the *Essex* was trapped in the neutral harbor of Valparaiso, Chile; after blockading her there for six weeks, H.M. frigate *Phoebe* and sloop *Cherub* ultimately disregarded Chile's neutrality, entered the harbor, and attacked. The engagement lasted around two and one-half hours; Mr. Porter finally surrendered after he sustained 155 casualties. (In one of those interesting historical coincidences, it had been in May 1811 that this same HMS *Phoebe* and her captain, James Hillyar, helped capture the French frigate *Renommée*—which of course became HMS *Java*.) For her part, after repair, the *Essex* served the British for many years. She finally finished her days, in the 1830s, as a prison ship at Kingston.

Upon the *Constitution*'s arrival in San Salvador, on the first day of 1813, Lieutenant Henry Ducie Chads transformed himself. He instantly found that he had traded the awful responsibility of commanding a stricken ship, during desperate fighting, for the incredible challenges of caring for a shipless crew and passengers—almost 350 souls—in a foreign port. Sadly, one of those souls was not to be his dreadfully injured captain, for though he had survived the battle, the move to the *Constitution*, and the move ashore to a hospital, the noble Henry Lambert passed away on the evening of January third.

Working with Commodore Bainbridge, General Hislop, U.S. Consul Henry Hill, H.M. Consul Frederick Lindeman, and Captain Greene (of the *Bonne Citoyenne*), Mr. Chads quickly negotiated an arrangement by which all the British prisoners-of-war were paroled. The terms of this agreement were fairly standard. The men were to return as soon as possible "to England and there remain until formally exchanged, not to serve in their professional capacities in any place, or in any manner whatsoever against the United States of America, until said exchange shall be effected."

Simultaneously, Chads arranged accommodation and victuals for his people as they were landed from *Old Ironsides*, and found additional medical treatment and medicines for his many wounded. He also found a lot of money, greatly facilitated by Consul Lindeman and several local British merchants, to hire two ships as cartels to carry himself and his charges to England. After almost a month of bureaucratic, administrative, financial, and logistical frenzy, these ships (*Mercury*, a British merchantman, and *Albuquerque*, a Portuguese brig) departed San Salvador on January twenty-seventh. They endured a longer voyage than they had expected or wanted, mostly due to contrary winds, and ultimately arrived at Spithead on the evening of April eighteenth. As the regulations and custom demanded, Mr. Chads and the other sea officers were immediately brought to court-martial for the loss of the *Java*.

— — — — —

The Lamentable War with America Continues; H.M.S. *Java* Captured"

We have still to regret the disastrous progress of the naval war between this country and America. Another frigate has fallen into the hands of the enemy! — The subject is too painful for us to dwell upon.

Captain Henry Lambert, the commander of the Java, had often distinguished himself in action. He commanded the St. Fiorenzo in February, 1805, when that ship captured the French frigate Psyche, commanded by the active Captain Bergeret. He also commanded the Iphigenia frigate in the attack of the French frigates at Port South East, Isle of France. He was brother to Captain Robert Lambert of H.M.S. Duncan. The supernumerary officers on board were: one commander, two lieutenants, one marine officer, four midshipmen, one clergyman, and one assistant-surgeon.

— "The Naval Chronicle" (Britain), February-March 1813

— — — — —

On Friday a Court-martial was held on board the Gladiator,

Admiral Graham Moore, President, on the surviving officers and crew of his Majesty's late frigate <u>Java</u>. The Court, after duly weighing the circumstances attending the capture and destruction of that vessel, were of opinion that the surrender of his Majesty's ship was unavoidable, and that nothing more could be done with prudence and effect in her defence, and did fully acquit them.

— "The London Times," April 28, 1813

SENTENCE.

AT a Court Martial aſſembled on board His Majeſty's Ship <u>Gladiator</u>, in Portſmouth Harbour, on the 23ʳᵈ April 1813.

PRESENT:

GRAHAM MOORE, Eſquire,

Rear Admiral of the Blue, and Second Officer in the Command of His Majeſty's Ships and Veſſels at Spithead and in Portſmouth Harbour,

PRESIDENT.

Rear Admiral EDWARD J. FOOTE.

Captain JOHN COCKET.	Captain SAMUEL BUTCHER.
Captain BENJAMIN WM. PAGE.	Captain LUCIUS CURTIS.
Captain GEORGE FOWKE. Captain	EDW. HENRY A'COURT.
Captain Sir CHRISTOPHER COLE.	Captain THOMAS COE.

Purſuant to an Order from the Right Honourable Lords Commiſſioners of the Admiralty, dated the Twenty-ſecond Day of April inſtant, and directed to the Preſident, ſetting forth, That Rear Admiral Manley Dixon had tranſmitted to their Lordſhips a Letter, dated the 31ſt of December 1812, addreſſed by Lieut. Henry Ducie Chads, Firſt Lieutenant of His Majeſty's late Ship <u>Java</u>, to their Lordſhips' Secretary, detailing the particular Circumſtances attending the Capture and Loſs of that Ship, after a ſevere Action for ſeveral Hours with the United States Ship the <u>Conſtitution</u>, on the 29th of the ſame Month, a few Leagues off the Port of Bahia; the Court proceeded to enquire into the Cauſe and Circumſtances of the Capture of His Majeſty's late Ship <u>Java</u>, and to try her ſurviving Officers and Ship's Company for their Conduct upon that Occaſion; and having heard the Witneſſes produced, and completed the Enquiry, and having maturely and deliberately weighed and conſidered the whole: The Court is of opinion, That the Capture of His Majeſty's ſaid late Ship <u>Java</u> was cauſed by her being totally diſmaſted, in a long and ſpirited

Action with the ſaid United States Ship the <u>Conſtitution</u>, of conſiderably ſuperior Force; in which the Zeal, Ability, and Bravery of the late Captain Lambert, her Commander, was highly conſpicuous and honourable, being conſtantly the Aſſailant, until the Moment of his much-lamented Fall; and that ſubſequently thereto the Action was continued with equal Zeal, Ability, and Bravery, by Lieutenant Henry Ducie Chads the Firſt Lieutenant, and the other ſurviving Officers and Ship's Company, and other Officers and Perſons who were Paſſengers on board her, until ſhe became a perfect Wreck, and the Continuance of the Action would have been a uſeleſs Sacrifice of Lives; and doth adjudge the ſaid Lieutenant Henry Ducie Chads, and the other ſurviving Officers and Ship's Company, to be moſt honourably acquitted: And the ſaid Lieutenant Henry Ducie Chads, and the other ſurviving Officers and Ship's Company, are hereby moſt honourably acquitted accordingly.

Graham Moore

Edward J. Foote	John Cocket	Samuel Butcher
Benjamin W. Page	George Fowke	Lucius Curtis
Christopher Cole	Edward H. A'Court	Thomas Coe

M' . Greetham, Jun.
Deputy Judge Advocate of the Fleet.

— — — — —

History reclaims the lives of the characters in this story; what actually became of some of them is as follows:

Captain Henry Lambert, Royal Navy (1784? – 1813). Lambert had first joined the navy in 1795 and had been posted as a captain in 1805. As mentioned in the text, he had previously commanded the troop ship *Wilhelmina*, the frigate *San Fiorenzo*, and the frigate *Iphigenia* prior to his commission in the *Java*. He had married in 1811. He and his wife, Caroline, had one child who, unfortunately, died sometime in 1812—I don't know if this sad event occurred prior to the *Java*'s departure from England or not. Since Lambert refers to his "family" rather than merely his "wife" in a letter dated eight days before the *Java* sailed, I hope he never learned of it. In any event, Lambert's gunshot wound to the chest was unfortunately mortal—certainly beyond recovery via 1812 naval medical care if not the care of any age. He survived the transfer to the *Constitution*, and survived being landed at São Salvador on January 3, 1813, but he passed away the next day. Strangely, or at least strangely to me, none of the *Constitution*'s officers attended his funeral service—although Commodore Bainbridge did send the British officers a nice note which praised Lambert as a brave and valiant foe.

Captain Sir Nesbit Willoughby, one of the Royal Navy's bravest—and most eccentric—combat officers during this period, later wrote the following about his old friend, "the noble-minded Captain Henry Lambert. No man was ever more beloved by all classes in the Service—whether by his Brother Officers or those of his own Ship and Men; and for the most simple reason, because he himself loved everybody. With an endeared Wife, Child, and Family and numerous and firm friends, rank, youth, and health, it is natural to suppose that he looked forward to many happy years. But, it pleased the Almighty, the Great Controller of Events, to order it otherwise. He fought more single Frigate battles than any Officer in the British Navy. In his first and finest Action he saved his ship by a most gallant defence against an Enemy double his force in every respect. In the second Action he took his Frigate; in the third he was obliged to surrender the *Iphigenia* under the most distressing and afflicting circumstances. In his fourth Action he was wounded unto death and again captured. Had *I* been called to render up my soul when my friend Lambert and I were in battle together—and when *I* partook of neither faith, hope, nor charity in the slightest degree—where should I have been? But *Lambert* was a very different character, and I have every reason to believe and hope that he was better prepared for the awful change than most men."

Commodore William Bainbridge, U.S. Navy (1774 – 1833) received a hero's welcome in Boston when *Old Ironsides* returned there, on February 17, 1813, with the news of her second tremendous victory. Bainbridge's next assignment was the command of the Navy Yard in Charlestown; he saw no more active service in the War of 1812. From July-December 1815 he embarked as commodore onboard the first American ship-of-the-line, the *Independence*, for Mediterranean duty. During the period 1816-1819 he was on shore duty at various stations. From 1819-1821 he sailed as commodore onboard the *Columbus*, again to the Mediterranean. From 1821-1823 he commanded first the Philadelphia and then the Boston naval stations, and then from 1824-1827 he served on the Board of Naval Commissioners. He again commanded the Philadelphia station from 1829-1831, and then again was in command at Charlestown until November 1832, when he was granted leave. His health failed and his death occurred in Philadelphia in 1833.

Many historical accounts promote the idea that Bainbridge formally, courteously, and kindly returned Captain Lambert's sword to that poor man as Lambert was taken ashore to die in Brazil. This certainly would be in keeping with the actions of Captains Hull and Decatur, who chivalrously refused to accept the swords of Captains Dacres and Carden—and such grace and magnanimity would particularly make sense, as the *Java* fought a much better and more creditable battle than did the *Guerrière* or the *Macedonian*. However, the unvarnished truth is that Bainbridge *kept* the beautiful presentation sword, had Lambert's inscription buffed off, and had it re-engraved with an inscription of his own (in Latin): *In fighting between the American Vessel Constitution and the British vessel Java, December 29 1812, William Bainbridge, praised by his country and his vanquished foe.* The sword has remained in the United States ever since, and is currently held by the U.S. Naval Academy Museum.

For the most part, "Hard Luck Bill" Bainbridge's career was essentially a series of frustrations—if not actual defeats—in his earlier years, which apparently soured him and made him prone to hold decades-long grudges against his contemporaries who had had more success. Strangely, the considerable glory he acquired after the *Java* action didn't seem to satisfy him. For example he tried, unsuccessfully, to discredit Captains Isaac Hull and Charles Stewart (fellow victorious combat commanders of *Old Ironsides*); but, fortunately, the courts of inquiry he brought against Stewart in 1814 and Hull in 1822 failed to recommend the courts-martial he desired. And, although he won the respect of the Constitutions through the victory over the *Java*, as a whole they could never much like him—in remarkable contrast to Isaac Hull, he was particularly moody and often an unrestrained tyrant.

Another problematic issue, to me hard to dismiss, is Bainbridge's role as the "second" to Commodore Stephen Decatur in the latter's 1820 duel with Commodore James Barron, in which Decatur—truly a national hero of considerable stature—was killed. Barron's second was Captain Jesse Elliott, who was known for antagonism toward Decatur. Bainbridge *also* had some professional jealousies *vis-à-vis* Decatur and the two had a history of not getting along; thus, it is remarkable that Decatur would choose him as his second. One of the many roles of the second, in a duel during this period, was to try to work out an arrangement with the other second—trying to prevent the actual fighting—as long as both principals' honor could be maintained. Elliott and Bainbridge appear to have been singularly uninterested in any such activity; in fact, right before the shots were fired on the infamous dueling field of Bladensburg, Maryland, Decatur and Barron actually (and unusually!) exchanged some conciliatory words. Upon hearing such words, both seconds should have leapt forward and brought an immediate end to the proceedings. However, to the contrary, it's said that Elliott hurried those proceedings on to their unfortunate outcome, with Bainbridge rapidly calling out the commands to fire and then looking away. In multiple historical accounts of this incident the behavior of Elliott and Bainbridge doesn't look good at all. Indeed, Decatur's widow, Susan, slowly came to think that Barron was merely a misguided fool led on by the other two; subsequently she referred to Elliott and Bainbridge as "my husband's murderers" and "his assassins."

In any event, I hope in *this* specific story of his triumph over the *Java*—truly the genuine highlight of Bainbridge's career—I've been fair to old "Hard Luck Bill." I confess that (parallel to his Constitutions) in some points I can certainly respect him, but I really can't bring myself to like him.

Lieutenant General Thomas Hislop, British Army (1764 - 1843) returned to England with the rest of the *Java's* survivors. Shortly after the action, Commodore Bainbridge restored to Hislop a chest with a considerable set of silver plate, which had initially been seized as the *Java* was abandoned, and which Hislop valued more for sentimental reasons than for its monetary value. Hislop was particularly grateful for this as well as for the generally "handsome and kind treatment" the Americans showed toward their British prisoners. In turn, Hislop presented Bainbridge with a "splendid gold-mounted sword" which Bainbridge treasured for the rest of his life. After bearing witness at Lt. Chads' court martial in England, in May of 1813 Hislop was appointed commander-in-chief at Madras. He was also created a baronet that same year, and made a Knight Commander of the Bath in 1814. He saw significant action in the Third Anglo-Maratha War of 1817-18, after which he was made a Knight Grand Cross of the Bath. He held command at Madras until 1820. There was some controversy over his severity at the Fort of Talnar in late 1817 (he hanged the governor as a rebel, and *executed* the garrison of *300 men*!), as well as the division of some prize money, but both issues were resolved partially due to his defense by the Duke of Wellington. In 1823 he married Emma Elliot, and they had one daughter. He served for many years as equerry to the Duke of Cambridge. In addition, for many years, he remained a relatively frequent correspondent with his one-time captor, Commodore Bainbridge, which lasted until the latter's death in 1833.

Master and Commander John William Phillips Marshall, Royal Navy (1785 – 1850), returned to England with the other paroled British crew, and testified at the court-martial. Disappointed that he could not take command of the sloop *Procris* on the East India Station, to which he had been appointed, he was pleased to be made commander of the brig *Shamrock* in November 1813. He and the *Shamrock* subsequently operated off Cuxhaven and in actions up the Elbe at Gluckstadt, Hamburg, and Haarburg, where his previous North Sea and Baltic experience proved extremely useful. His services were recognized by promotion to post captain in June 1814, and in 1815 the award of Russian and Swedish knighthoods, as well as the British Companion of the Bath. He became inactive after the demobilization, but in 1826 was selected to be Superintendent of Lazarettos at Milford, and then in 1827 as commander of the quarantine establishment at Standgate Creek. In 1832 he was created a Knight Commander of the Hanoverian Royal Guelphic Order by King William IV. His last appointment was in 1841, to the *Isis*, 44. The *Isis* served off the Cape of Good Hope and then returned in 1845. He was promoted Rear Admiral of the Blue in March 1850. Having survived the iron and lead hail of *Old Ironsides*, and much more during his long career, he died in September 1850 from injuries sustained in—of all things—a *carriage accident*.

Master Commandant James Lawrence, U.S. Navy (1781 – 1813), captain of the U.S.S. *Hornet*. He had earlier served with distinction in the war with the Barbary States, particularly in Tripoli Harbor at the destruction of the captured *Philadelphia*, and in the subsequent gunboat attack on the harbor in August 1804. Commanding the *Hornet* at the outbreak of the War of 1812, he had cruised with Commodore Rodgers' squadron before sailing with Commodore Bainbridge. After the *Constitution* had defeated the *Java* and sailed back to Boston, Lawrence continued his attempts to engage H.M. Sloop *Bonne Citoyenne* at Salvador. Forced to abandon this project by the appearance of the 74-gun HMS *Montagu*, Lawrence moved to the north, and on February 14th captured the brig *Resolution* with $23,000 in specie aboard. A week later, off the mouth of the Demerara River, Lawrence engaged and sank H.M. Brig *Peacock*. Upon his return to the United States, Lawrence was promoted to captain and given command of the frigate *Chesapeake*, at Boston. Scarcely ten days later, with a new captain and a crew of veterans (yet were new to each other), the *Chesapeake* sailed just outside the harbor to meet the challenge of HMS *Shannon*, a well-seasoned and trained-up frigate which was looking for trouble. In a remarkably short but extremely violent action, the *Chesapeake* was captured and Lawrence was mortally wounded. By all accounts he was a brave, capable, and energetic officer, though his eagerness and decision to engage the *Shannon* were somewhat rash. His dying words, "Fight her 'til she sinks!" and "Don't give up the ship!" became watchwords in the U.S. Navy.

Lieutenant Henry Ducie Chads, Royal Navy (1788 – 1868), First Lieutenant of the *Java*, was tried by court-martial (along with the *Java*'s other surviving officers) for the loss of the ship; as stated earlier they were all honorably acquitted—and even complimented—by the president of the court. Chads was further complimented by immediate promotion to the rank of commander and by being appointed commanding officer of the sloop *Columbia*. The *Columbia*, after some active service, was paid off in November 1815, during the demobilization when both the War of 1812 and the Napoleonic Wars ended. He married Elizabeth Townsend, with whom he had two sons and two daughters (the eldest son became Admiral Sir Henry Chads (1819 - 1906)). Lt. H. D. Chads had first entered the Royal Naval College in 1800, and was commissioned as a lieutenant in 1806. He was assigned to the *Iphigenia*, under Henry Lambert, in 1808, and then served in the *Semiramis* for nine months before rejoining Lambert in the *Java*. He later resumed his active career after the Napoleonic Wars. In 1823 he commissioned HMS *Arachne* and operated in the East Indies. Promoted to captain in 1825, he commanded the frigate *Alligator* in the First Anglo-Burmese War. In 1826 he was made a Knight Companion of the Bath. From 1834 - 1837 he commanded the *Andromache* in the East Indies, and then the *Cambrian* from 1841-1845 on that same station; he was senior officer at Chusan and Amoy towards the end of the First Opium War. (It was during this last command that he encountered *Old Ironsides* that one final time at Singapore). From 1845 - 1853 he commanded the naval gunnery school at Portsmouth, turning down several other opportunities, including a seat on the Admiralty Board. In 1848 he briefly commanded the *Blenheim*, the first screw-propelled ship-of-the-line, and also commanded a small squadron off Ireland. In 1854 Chads was promoted to rear admiral and served in the Baltic. Recognized as the Royal Navy's leading gunnery expert, he was made a Knight Commander of the Bath in 1855. He was commander-in-chief at Cork 1856 - 1858. He was promoted to vice admiral in 1858, and then to admiral in 1863. Made a Knight Grand Cross of the Bath in 1865, he later died in 1868. He appears to have been a truly outstanding seaman, leader, and innovator.

Lieutenant William Allen Herringham, Royal Navy (1790 – 1865), was the *Java*'s Second Lieutenant, stationed on the main deck during the battle. As a midshipman he had been wounded at the Battle of Trafalgar, in 1805, on board the 74-gun HMS *Colossus*. Thus, the *Constitution-Java* action was the second terrible sea battle for Mr. Herringham—for at Trafalgar the *Colossus* sustained losses greater than any other British ship, 40 killed and 160 wounded. In 1810 Herringham had served in the boats of the *Caledonia* at the storming of batteries at *Pointe de Ché*, Basque Roads, and was also promoted to lieutenant that same year. After the *Java* court-martial he served four years in the frigate *Tigris*. He was promoted to commander in 1818, and then to captain in 1837. Subsequently, on the retired list, he was promoted to rear admiral in 1857 and finally vice admiral in 1862.

Lieutenant George Buchanan, Royal Navy (? – 1833), was the *Java*'s Third Lieutenant, stationed at the after guns on the main deck. I can find little about Mr. Buchanan, other than he was commissioned as a lieutenant in March 1812.

Lieutenant George Parker, U.S. Navy (? – 1814), was the First Lieutenant of the *Constitution*, and was on the quarterdeck next to Commodore Bainbridge during the battle with the *Java*. He had been made a lieutenant in 1807. He was promoted to Master Commandant in July 1813; he and William H. Allen (the first lieutenant of the USS *United States* when she defeated the *Macedonian*) were promoted significantly ahead of their peers—as compliments to themselves, their ships, and their captains (Charles Morris, first lieutenant of the *Constitution* when she sank the *Guerrière*, had also been early promoted in August 1812). Parker died on March 11, 1814, while in command of the brig USS *Syren*, but I don't know the particulars.

Lieutenant Beekman Verplanck Hoffman, U.S. Navy (1789–1834), originally from New York, was the *Constitution*'s Second Lieutenant, and commanded the First Division of 24-pounders, as well as the overall gundeck during the action with the *Java*. He had fought onboard the *Constitution* against the *Guerrière*, and he was still serving onboard *Old Ironsides* in February 1815, under Captain Charles Stewart, and thus was also present at the *Constitution*'s famous and remarkable double-victory over H.M. Ships *Levant* and *Cyane*. Towards the end of this action, Lieutenant Hoffman and fifteen Marines were sent over and took possession of the *Cyane*, a light frigate rated at 24 guns. One probably shouldn't read too much into it, but it's interesting to note that in late 1810 Midshipman Hoffman had been court-martialed and reprimanded for striking a marine sergeant with a cane for alleged insolence, as well as knocking down and kicking a marine private for disrespect. In any event, he was promoted to Master Commandant in March 1817, and then later to Captain in March 1829.

Lieutenant John Templar Shubrick, U.S. Navy (1788-1815), originally from South Carolina, served as the *Constitution*'s Third Lieutenant, and was in charge of the Second Division on the gundeck. He had been present onboard *Old Ironsides* in the action with the *Guerrière*, where he had been commended by then-Captain Isaac Hull for his coolness and courage. He was transferred to the *Hornet* shortly after the action with the *Java*, and took part in the battle when the *Hornet* defeated HMS *Peacock* barely two months later on February 24, 1813. On June 20, 1813, he commanded a gunboat against the British as they attacked Norfolk, Virginia. Later serving under Commodore Decatur, Shubrick was captured when the USS *President* was taken by a British squadron on January 15, 1815. In June, 1815 he fought in the brief conflict with Algiers. Later that summer, in his first command (USS *Epervier*), he was drowned when that ship foundered with all hands while proceeding from the Mediterranean back to the United States.

Lieutenant Charles W. Morgan, U.S. Navy (1790 – 1853), originally from Virginia, served as the *Constitution*'s Fourth Lieutenant, and was in charge of the Third Division on the gundeck. He had been present in the *Constitution*'s action against the *Guerrière*. In 1817 he served as a lieutenant on board the 74-gun

Franklin. He was promoted to Master Commandant in 1820, and in that rank commanded the 74-gun *North Carolina* in 1824. He was promoted to Captain in 1831, and served as the Commodore of the Mediterranean Squadron in 1850. Morgan died in Washington, D.C. in January 1853.

Lieutenant John Cushing Aylwin, U.S. Navy (1778 – 1813), was the Fifth Lieutenant onboard the *Constitution*, and was in charge of the Forecastle Division of 32-pounder carronades. He was wounded during the battle, dying from that wound on January 28, 1813. He had entered the navy from the merchant service around the time that the war began, as a sailing master; in fact, his extraordinary seamanship as Sailing Master of the *Constitution* was a significant contributor to her narrow escape from a British squadron during July 17-18, 1812. Aylwin was promoted to lieutenant in September 1812 for his gallant conduct in the action against the *Guerrière*. In that battle he was preparing to board, as the two ships came together, but was wounded in the left shoulder by a musket ball. In the subsequent action with the *Java* he commanded the forecastle division, where his activity, bravery, and marked coolness gained him Commodore Bainbridge's admiration. When all hands were called to repel boarders as the *Java* attempted to come alongside, he left the forecastle and had mounted the quarterdeck hammock-nettings, and was in the act of firing his pistol when he was again hit in the same shoulder. Badly wounded, he kept the deck until just before the *Java* surrendered. He suffered almost a month, under great pain, until the end. All who knew him maintained that he was a congenial man, and an officer of extraordinary merit, and thus held him in high esteem.

Surgeon Amos Alexander Evans, U.S. Navy (1785 - 1848). Originally from Maryland, he had come aboard the *Constitution* in March 1812. He had studied medicine in Maryland, and also with the famous Dr. Benjamin Rush. In 1808 he joined the Navy as a Surgeon's Mate, and after some service was appointed a Surgeon in 1810. After sailing onboard *Old Ironsides*, he served ashore in the Charlestown Navy Yard, and in 1814 completed a medical degree (that is, an M.D. which *legally* changed him from being *Mr.* Evans to *Dr.* Evans; from being a surgeon to being a physician) at Harvard College. In 1815 he was fleet surgeon in the Mediterranean onboard the USS *Independence*. Later he served again at Charlestown, then went with permission into private practice. He fully resigned from the Navy in 1824. His journal was hugely important to fleshing-out much of this story, and I grew to like him very much.

The **United States Ship *Constitution***, *Old Ironsides*, was launched at Boston, Massachusetts in 1797; one of the "original six frigates" of the U.S. Navy (versus the Continental Navy) provided for by the Naval Act of 1794. She is named after the Constitution of the United States of America (the names of the six frigates were selected by President George Washington). Innovative architect Joshua Humphreys designed these frigates to be the young Navy's capital ships (the U.S. then in no position to afford ships-of-the-line), and so the *Constitution* and her sisters were larger, more heavily armed, and more stoutly built than the standard frigates of the 1790s. Built at Edmund Hartt's Boston shipyard, her first duties were to provide protection for American merchant shipping during the "Quasi War" with France and to fight the Barbary pirates in the First Barbary War. The *Constitution* is most famous for her actions during the War of 1812 when she captured numerous merchant ships and defeated five British warships: *Guerrière*, *Java*, *Pictou*, *Cyane*, and *Levant*. The battle with the *Guerrière* earned her the nickname of *Old Ironsides*. Sustained public adoration, over the years, repeatedly saved her from being broken up when deemed obsolete or beyond cost-effective maintenance. She continued to actively serve the nation during the nineteenth century, including as flagship in the Mediterranean and African squadrons. During the American Civil War she served as a training ship for the U. S. Naval Academy; later she carried artwork and industrial displays to the Paris Exposition of 1878. Retired from active service in 1881, she served as a receiving ship until designated a museum ship in 1907. In 1931 she started a three-year 90-port tour of the nation during which she received millions of visitors. In 1997 she finally sailed again under her own power to mark her 200th birthday. Today she is the oldest commissioned warship afloat in the world, open to visitors year-round in the former Charlestown Navy Yard, her pier hardly more than three cables' lengths from the site where she was built.

The **United States Ship *Hornet*** was launched at Baltimore, in 1805, as a brig of 440 tons. She was 107 feet long and 32 feet across the beam, had a draft of 14 feet, carried 18 great guns, and had a complement of around 144 men. She was the third of eight ships in the U.S. Navy to bear this name. Prior to the War of 1812 she saw various service, and then in 1810-1811 was rebuilt and ship-rigged in the Washington Navy Yard. After the start of the war she cruised in Commodore John Rodgers' squadron, capturing the British privateer *Dolphin* in July 1812. Sailing as part of Commodore Bainbridge's squadron, she cruised independently after the *Constitution* returned to Boston subsequent to the *Java*'s sinking. Abandoning her blockade of HMS *Bonne Citoyenne* at Salvador, she took the brig *Resolution* with $23,000 in specie on board, and then she later sank HMS *Peacock* after a short engagement off British Guiana in February 1813. For several months in 1813 and for most of 1814 she was blockaded in New London, Connecticut; finally escaping out to sea, she later took H.M. Sloop *Penguin*, off the island of Tristran da Cunha, in March 1815—unaware that the war had already ended. After several European cruises, the *Hornet* became based in and around the Caribbean Sea, mainly working against piracy, for almost ten years. There is some evidence that she foundered with the loss of all hands, in a gale off Tampico, in September 1829.

Appendix A

Extract from the Journal of
Commodore William Bainbridge,
U.S. Navy

Tuesday 29th December 1812

At 9 AM, discovered two Strange Sails on the weather bow, at 10. AM. discovered the strange sails to be Ships, one of them stood in for the land, and the other steered off shore in a direction towards us. At 10.45. We tacked ship to the Nd & Wd and stood for the sail standing towards us, —At 11 tacked to the Sd & Ed hauld up the mainsail and took in the Royals. At 11.30 AM made the private signal for the day, which was not answered, & then set the mainsail and royals to draw the strange sail off from the neutral Coast.

Wednesday 30th December 1812, [Nautical Time] Commences with Clear weather and moderate breezes from E.N.E. Hoisted our Ensign and Pendant. At 15 minutes past meridian, The ship hoisted her colours, an English Ensign, —having a signal flying at her Main Red Yellow-Red At 1.26 being sufficiently from the land, and finding the ship to be an English Frigate, took in the Main Sail and Royals, tacked Ship and stood for the enemy

At 1.50. P.M, The Enemy bore down with an intention of rakeing us, which we avoided by wearing. At 2, P.M, the enemy being within half a mile, of us, and to wind ward, & having hawled down his colours to dip his Gafft, and not hoisting them again except an Union Jack at the Mizen Mast head, (we having hoisted on board the <u>Constitution</u> an American Jack forward Broad Pendant at Main, American Ensign at Mizen Top Gallant Mast head and at the end of The Gafft) induced me to give orders to the officer of the 3rd Division to fire one Gun ahead of the enemy to make him show his Colours, which being done brought on afire from us of the whole broadside, on which he hoisted an English Ensign at the Peak, and another in his weather Main Rigging, besides his Pendant and then immediately returned our fire, which brought on a general action with round and grape.

The enemy Kept at a much greater distance than I wished, but Could not bring him to closer action without exposing ourselves to several rakes. —Considerable Manoeuvers were made by both Vessels to rake and avoid being raked.

The following Minutes Were Taken during the Action

At 2.10. P.M, Commenced The Action within good grape and Canister distance. The enemy to windward (but much farther than I wished).

At 2,30. P.M, our wheel was shot entirely away

At 2.40. determined to close with the Enemy, notwithstanding her rakeing, set the Fore sail & Luff'd up close to him.

At 2,50, The Enemies Jib boom got foul of our Mizen Rigging

At 3 The Head of the enemies Bowsprit & Jib boom shot away by us

At 3.5 Shot away the enemies foremast by the board

At 3.15 Shot away The enemies Main Top mast just above the Cap

At 3.40 Shot away Gafft and Spunker boom

At 3.55 Shot his mizen mast nearly by the board

At 4.5 Having silenced the fire of the enemy completely and his colours in main Rigging being [down] Supposed he had Struck, Then hawl'd about the Courses to shoot ahead to repair our rigging, which was extremely cut, leaving the enemy a complete wreck, soon after discovered that The enemies flag was still flying hove too to repair Some of our damages.

At 4.20. The Enemies Main Mast went by the board.

At 4.50 [Wore] ship and stood for the Enemy

At 5.25 Got very close to the enemy in a very [effective] rakeing position athwart his bows & was at the very instance of rakeing him, when he most prudently Struck his Flag.

Had The Enemy Suffered the broadside to have raked him previously to strikeing, his additional loss must have been <u>extremely</u> great laying like a log upon the water, perfectly unmanageable, I could have continued rakeing him without being exposed to more than two of his Guns, (if even Them)

After The Enemy had struck, wore Ship and reefed the Top Sails, hoisted out one of the only two remaining boats we had left out of 8 & sent Lieut Parker 1st of the <u>Constitution</u> on board to take possession of her, which was done about 6. P.M, The Action continued from the commencement to the end of the Fire, 1 H 55 m our sails and Rigging were shot very much, and some of our spars injured—had 9 men Killed and 26 wounded. At 7 PM. The boat returned from the Prize with Lieut. Chads the 1st of the enemies Frigate (which I then learnt was the <u>Java</u> rated 38 - had 49 Guns mounted—)— and Lieut Genl Hislop – appointed to Command in the East Indies, – Major Walker and Capt Wood, belonging to his Staff. —Capt Lambert of the <u>Java</u> was too dangerously wounded to be removed immediately.

The Cutter returned on board the Prize for Prisoners, and brought Capt Marshall, Master & Commander of The British Navy, who was passenger on board, as also Several other Naval officers destined for ships in the East Indies. The <u>Java</u> had her whole number complete and nearly an hundred supernumeraries. The number she had on board at the commencement of the Action, The officers have not candour to say; from the different papers we collected, such as a muster book, Watch List and quarter Bills, she must have had upwards of 400 souls, she had one more man stationed at each of her Guns on both Decks than what we had The Enemy had 83 wounded & 57 Kill'd.

The <u>Java</u> was an important ship fitted out in the compleatest manner to [carry out] the Lieut. Genl & dispatches. She had Copper &c. on board for a 74 building at Bombay, and, I suspect a great many other valuables, but every thing was blown up, except the officers baggage when we set her on fire on the 1st of January 1813 at 3 P.M. Nautical Time.

Source: National Archives, Record Group 45, Captain's Letters, 1813, Vol.1, No.8 1/2.

APPENDIX B

LETTER FROM LIEUTENANT HENRY DUCIE CHADS, ROYAL NAVY, TO SECRETARY OF THE ADMIRALTY JOHN WILSON CROKER

United States Frigate <u>Constitution</u>
Off St Salvador
Decr 31st 1812

Sir,

It is with deep regret that I write you for the information of the Lords Commissioners of the Admiralty that His Majesty's Ship <u>Java</u> is no more, after sustaining an action on the 29th Inst for several hours with the American Frigate <u>Constitution</u> which resulted in the Capture and ultimate destruction of His Majestys Ship. Captain Lambert being dangerously wounded in the height of the Action, the melancholy task of writing the detail devolves on me.

On the morning of the 29th inst at 8 AM off St Salvador (Coast of Brazil) the wind at NE. we perceived a strange sail, made all sail in chace and soon made her out to be a large Frigate; at noon prepared for action the chace not answering our private Signals and backing towards us under easy sail; when about four miles distant she made a signal and immediately tacked and made all sail away upon the wind, we soon found we had the advantage of her in sailing and came up with her fast when she hoisted American Colours. she then bore about three Points on our lee bow at 1:50 PM the Enemy shortened Sail upon which we bore down upon her, at 2:10 when about half a mile distant she opened her fire giving us her larboard broad-side which was not returned till we were close on her weather bow; both Ships now manoeuvered to obtain advantageous positions; our opponent evidently avoiding close action and firing high to disable our masts in which he succeeded too well having shot away the head of our bowsprit with the Jib boom and our running rigging so much cut as to prevent our preserving the weather gage. At 3:50 finding the Enemys raking fire extreemly heavy Captain Lambert ordered the Ship to be laid on board, in which we should have succeeded had not our foremast been shot away at this moment, the remains of our bowsprit passing over his taffrail, shortly after this the main topmast went leaving the Ship totally unmanageable with most of our Starboard Guns rendered useless from the wreck laying over them At 3:30 our Gallant Captain received a dangerous wound in the breast and was carried below, from this time we could not fire more than two or three guns until 4:15 when our Mizen mast was shot away the Ship then fell off a little and brought many of our Starboard Guns to bear, the Enemy's rigging was so much cut that he could not now avoid shooting ahead which brought us fairly Broadside and Broadside. Our Main yard now went in the slings both ships continued engaged in this manner till 4:35 we frequently on fire in consequence of the wreck laying on the side engaged. Our opponent now made sail ahead out of Gun shot where he remained an hour repairing his damages leaving us an unmanageable wreck with only the mainmast left, and that toterring; Every exertion was made by us during this interval to place this Ship in a state to renew the action. We succeeded in clearing the wreck of our Masts from our Guns. A Sail was set on the stumps of the Foremast & Bowsprit the weather half of the Main Yard remaining aloft, the main tack was got forward in the hope of getting the Ship before the Wind, our helm being still perfect. The effort unfortunately proved ineffectual from the Main mast falling over the side from the heavy rolling of the Ship, which nearly covered the whole of our Starboard Guns. We still waited the attack of the Enemy, he now standing toward us for that purpose. On his coming nearly within hail of us & from his manouvre perceiving he intended a position a head where he could rake us without a possibility of our returning a shot. I then consulted the Officers who agreed with myself that on having a great part of our Crew killed & wounded our Bowsprit and three masts gone, several guns useless, we should not be justified in waisting the lives of more of those remaining whom I hope their Lordships & Country will think have bravely defended His Majestys Ship. Under these circumstances, however reluctantly at 5:50 our Colours were lowered from the Stump of the Mizen Mast and we were taken possession a little after 6. by the American Frigate <u>Constitution</u> commanded by Commodore Bainbridge who immediately after ascertaining the state of the Ship resolved on burning her which we had the satisfaction of seeing done as soon as the Wounded were removed. Annexed I send you a return of a killed and wounded and it is with pain I perceive it so numerous also a statement of the comparative force of the two Ships when I hope their Lordships will not think the British Flag tarnished although success has not attended us. It would be presumptive in me to speak of Captain Lamberts merit, who, though still in danger from his wound we still entertain the greatest hopes of his being restored to the service & his Country. It is most gratifying to my feelings to notice the general gallantry of every Officer, Seaman & Marine on board. In justice to the Officers I beg leave to mention them individually. I can never speak too highly of the able exertions of Lieuts. Herringham & Buchanan and also Mr. Robinson Master who was severely wounded and Lieuts Mercer and Davis [David Davies] of the Royal Marines the latter of whom was also severly wounded. To Capt Jn⁰ Marshall RN who was a passenger I am particularly obliged to for his exertions and advice throughout the action. To Lieutt Aplin who was on the Main Deck and Lieutt Sanders who commanded on the Forecastle, I also return my thanks. I cannot but notice the good conduct of the Mates, & Midshipmen, many of whom are killed & the greater part wounded. To Mr T. C. Jones, Surgeon, and his Assistants every praise is due for their unwearied assiduity in the care of the wounded. Lieutt General Hislop, Major Walker and Captain Wood of his Staff the latter of whom was severely wounded were solicitous to assist & remain on the quarter Deck. I cannot conclude this letter without expressing my grateful acknowledgement thus publicly for the generous treatment Captain Lambert and his Officers have experienced from our Gallant Enemy Commodore Bainbridge and his Officers. I have the honour to be [&c.]

H D Chads

1st Lieut of

His Majestys late Ship <u>Java</u>

PS. The <u>Constitution</u> has also suffered severely, both in her rigging and men having her Fore and Mizen masts, main topmast, both main topsailyards, Spanker boom, Gaff & trysail mast badly shot, and the greatest part of the standing rigging very much damaged with ten men killed. The Commodore, 5 Lieuts and 46 men wounded four of whom are since dead.

GLOSSARY

Aback. The situation of the sails when their surfaces are flattened against the masts by the force of the wind. This can be done on purpose, such as when tacking, or accidentally, as in the ship was **taken aback.**

Aloft. Up in the masts or the rigging.

Alow. On deck or below decks; opposite of aloft.

Avast. A command to stop doing something, as in "avast heaving."

Bells. Each day was divided up into watches which regulated what group of men and officers were on duty at any given time. Furthermore, most sailors had no personal time pieces nor were clocks placed around the ship; however, the time was publicly announced by the striking of the ship's bell which could be heard in many parts of the ship.

Number of Bells	Bell Pattern	Middle Watch	Morning Watch	Forenoon Watch	Afternoon Watch	First Dog-Watch	Second Dog-Watch	First Watch
One bell	.	0:30	4:30	8:30	12:30	16:30	18:30	20:30
Two bells	..	1:00	5:00	9:00	13:00	17:00	19:00	21:00
Three bells	.. .	1:30	5:30	9:30	13:30	17:30	19:30	21:30
Four bells	.. ..	2:00	6:00	10:00	14:00	18:00		22:00

Number of Bells	Bell Pattern	Middle Watch	Morn-ing Watch	Fore-noon Watch	After-noon Watch	First Dog-Watch	Second Dog-Watch	First Watch
Five bells	.. ... .	2:30	6:30	10:30	14:30			22:30
Six bells	.. .. ..	3:00	7:00	11:00	15:00			23:00
Seven bells	.. ..	3:30	7:30	11:30	15:30			23:30
Eight bells	.. ..	4:00	8:00	12:00	16:00		20:00	0:00

Bend. To affix a sail to its yard, to fasten a cable to its anchor, or to fasten one rope to another.

Boatswain, pronounced and often spelled "**bosun.**" A warrant officer in charge of a ship's rigging, anchors, cables, and deck crew. He is assisted by petty officers called bosun's mates.

Brig. A smaller square-rigged vessel, carrying only two masts rather than three. They can be both merchant ships or warships.

Bring-to. To check the course of a ship by bringing her head to the wind and arranging the sails in such a manner that they shall counteract each other. Similar to **heaving-to.**

Broad pennant or pendant. The distinguishing flag flown by a commodore.

Broadside. The virtually simultaneous firing of all of the guns from one side of a ship.

Cable. A large rope, usually in circumference ten inches or more around.

Cable's length. A nautical unit of length equivalent to about 600 feet.

Carronade. A lightweight, short-barreled cannon, usually of large caliber and usually mounted on the weather deck, which was only effective at short range. While carronades added greatly to a ship's firepower, they were not always taken into account when officially rating the number of guns. Named for the Carron Company in Scotland, which originally developed the weapon.

Cartel. Between wartime belligerents, an agreement for the exchange of prisoners. Also, a ship used for the exchange of prisoners, or used in carrying propositions to an enemy. Such a vessel would fly a flag of truce and would be privileged from capture.

Chearly, or cheerly. A word which usually implied heartily, cheerfully, or quickly, as "row chearly in the boats!" or "lower away chearly!" i.e. row heartily, lower speedily. The opposite of **handsomely.**

Colors. A ship's national ensign(s), which she "wore," while all other flags were "flown," as in "she was wearing French colors at the main."

Commodore. A temporary appointment for the senior of a group of captains whose ships were operating together. In effect it was a job title rather than a personal rank. In the early U.S. Navy, which did not carry the rank of admiral, it was the highest title to which an officer could aspire. Typically, in the U.S. Navy, once one had borne the title one continued to retain it even if no longer serving in that capacity. A commodore's ship flew a short "broad" pennant (rather than the usual long, narrow commissioning pennant) as a sign of distinction.

Coxswain, cockswain, or cox'n. The petty officer who was in charge of a captain's or admiral's barge or gig.

Come-to. Sometimes used similarly to bringing-to or heaving-to, but more usually it means coming to anchor, as in "she came-to in nine fathoms water."

Country ship. A merchant vessel chartered for local East Indies trade, by or for the Honourable East India Company.

Fathom. A unit of measurement equal to six feet.

First Lieutenant, First, First Luff, or Premier. On board ship, the senior commissioned officer under the captain, senior to the other lieutenants. In the modern U.S. Navy the position is known as the Executive Officer, or XO.

Forecastle or fo'c'sle. The forward part of the weather deck of a ship, particularly that part forward of the foremast.

Fore-reach. When one ship gains ground on another and overtakes her.

Frigate. During the eighteenth and early nineteenth centuries, a fast, square-rigged sailing vessel carrying 24 to 44 guns on a single gundeck. Frigates were employed by western naval powers as commerce raiders, cruisers, scouts, convoy escorts, and for blockade duty.

Gun-shot. A unit of measurement roughly equal to 1,000 yards.

Gunwale, (often pronounced **gunnel**). The upper edge of the side of a ship or boat.

Handsomely. Gradually, slowly. The opposite of **chearly.**

Heave-to. To stop a ship's forward motion, usually by bringing the head to the wind and trimming the sails so that they act against one another. This was often simply done by trimming the main or mizen topsail to push back against the mast (as opposed to the usual filling out forward ahead of the mast), and at times the command—instead of "heave-to"—was literally, "Lay the main/mizen topsail to the mast."

Hulled. To be hit in the hull by cannon fire.

In irons. See tacking.

John Company. A colloquial name for the **Honourable East India Company** (HEIC), the enormous and enormously powerful British joint-stock company, trading mainly in cotton, silk, indigo dye, saltpeter, tea, and opium.

Jury. A temporary replacement or improvisation, as in rigging a jury foremast. Alternatively jerry, as in jerry-rig.

Knot. A unit of measurement of speed; one nautical mile per hour. The knots on a log line were 48-feet apart, and timed using a 28-second glass.

Larboard. The left side, or to the left. Later in the nineteenth century this term was replaced with "port."

League. A unit of measurement equal to 3 minutes of latitude; approximately three miles.

Leeward, (pronounced loo'ard). The opposite side of a ship from which the wind is blowing.

Loblolly boys. Rudimentarily skilled laborers—usually men rather than boys—working in support of the surgeon in the sick berth or cockpit.

Luff. To sail the ship closer or nearer to the wind, which would take some wind out of the sails.

Master, or Sailing Master. The warrant officer responsible to the captain for navigation, advice on seamanship, and the stowage of stores (because stowage would affect the ship's trim, and therefore its sailing efficiency). Usually a long-serviced, highly experienced expert, often with both naval and merchant-marine background.

Midshipman. A naval rank of a class of boys or young men, who while actively serving as apprentice officers at sea, were preparing and hoping to earn a commission as a lieutenant.

Musket shot. As a measurement of distance, roughly 100 yards.

Overhead. In modern American usage, the top surface in an enclosed space of a ship; in modern non-nautical parlance, the ceiling of a room. In modern British nautical usage it would be the "deckhead."

Packet. A small vessel, appointed or hired by the government to carry dispatches, mail, packets, messengers, and/or expresses.

Pistol Shot. A measurement of distance equal to about 100 feet.

Pointing. Tapering the ends of lines to facilitate them passing more easily through blocks.

Puddening. A thick wreath, or circle of cordage, tapering from the middle towards the ends, taken up into the rigging and fastened about the mainmast and foremast of a ship. Thus, these things act as extra reinforcement to prevent the yards from falling down if the usual ropes by which the yards are suspended are shot away in battle.

Rake, or Raking. Maneuvering one's ship across the bow or stern of an enemy ship, firing the broadside guns down the length of the enemy ship for maximum effect, while the enemy is essentially able to return fire with only one or two bow or stern "chase" guns. One sought "to cannonade her on the stern, or head, so as that the balls shall scour the whole length of her decks; which is one of the most dangerous incidents that can happen in a naval action." Raking required extremely skillful shiphandling; it could easily go wrong, with the advantage then going to the opponent. It is sometimes referred to as "crossing the T," for obvious reasons.

Ratlines. Ropes fastened horizontally between the **shrouds** to create steps by which one can climb aloft.

Razee. A warship that has been cut down (*razeed*) to one with fewer decks. In the British Navy the operation was typically performed on a smaller two-decked 74- or 64-gun ship-of-the-line, effectively resulting in a large frigate which would be stronger than the usual run of frigates. The most successful and well-known razee in the Royal Navy during this period was the *Indefatigable*, which was commanded for several years by

Sir Edward Pellew—and was made even more famous in the fictional "Horatio Hornblower" series.

Ship, generally, a sailing vessel with three masts. Also, to install something in its proper place, as in "ship the tiller," or uninstall something, as in "unship the oars."

Ship-of-the-line, line-of-battle ship, battleship, or **liner.** A large, square-rigged warship, carrying from 70 to 120 guns on two or three gundecks. In the great naval wars of the 17th, 18th, and early 19th centuries, ships-of-the-line were the largest naval units employed, usually kept grouped in fleets or squadrons, formed into lines to do battle with the enemy fleets. The most common type was a two-decker carrying 74 guns. In the War of 1812, the Royal Navy had over 150 ships-of-the-line; the U.S. Navy had *none*.

Shivering. The state of a sail when it shakes or flutters in the wind.

Sound, sounding. To drop into the sea a weighted and marked line to ascertain the depth of the water.

Starboard. The right side, or to the right.

Strike. To take something and put it away, as in "strike the chest into the hold." More commonly, to haul down one's flag or colors, as a sign of surrender.

Studding sail, or stuns'l. A temporary square sail, set outboard of some of the principal sails using removable booms, to capture more wind and increase speed.

Spanker. On a square-rigged ship, the spanker is a gaff-rigged fore-and-aft sail set from and aft of the mizzen mast.

Surgeon. The medical officer—a warrant officer, rather than a commissioned officer—onboard ship. In 1812 most surgeons were *not* doctors in the sense of being university-educated physicians, though they might sometimes be addressed as "doctor" as a courtesy. They were aided by assistant surgeons, surgeon's mates, and loblolly boys.

Sweeps. Large, heavy oars once commonly used in galleys and galleasses. In the great age of sail, used mainly in barges and lighters, and in some smaller ships.

Tack or tacking. Maneuvering, somewhat laboriously, with a series of zig-zags, when proceeding to windward. When a ship changed tacks, tacking (zig to zag), she turned her bow through the "eye" of the wind by allowing the forward sails to come aback and then trimming them the other way. Occasionally, due to the strength of the wind or waves, or damage, or inefficient handling, a ship might find its turn stopped, failing in the maneuver halfway through, and thus find herself in the condition known as "in irons." It was often a chancy maneuver, particularly in bad weather or battle—to illustrate this, it's interesting to note that the French and Spanish orders for this maneuver were "adieu-va," and "vaya con dios," respectively. See also "wear."

Taffrail. The top railing around the stern of a ship's weather deck.

Top hamper. Upper sails, rigging, spars, tackle, and all other gear aloft above the weather deck.

Warp. To move a ship from one mooring to another, generally in a harbor, by heaving on warps (ropes or hawsers), which are attached to fixed objects (buoys, anchors, bollards, posts, trees, etc.) The pulling action can either be by hand or by a windlass or capstan.

Watch. See bells.

Wear, or wore. An alternative to tacking. A ship's stern, versus the bow, is put through the wind. It can be done in most conditions of wind and sea, where tacking requires a certain minimum of speed and reasonably smooth water. Its major disadvantage is that wearing requires more time and space than tacking.

Weather gage. To have the weather gage describes a favorable position of one ship relative to a second ship with respect to being upwind. The upwind vessel is able to maneuver at will toward any downwind point. A vessel downwind of another, however, in attempting to attack upwind is constrained to trim sail as the relative wind moves forward and cannot point too far into the wind for fear of being raked. A ship with the weather gage, turning downwind to attack, may alter course at will in order to bring either starboard or larboard guns to appropriate elevations.

Weather deck. The topmost level of decks, exposed to the weather.

Windward. The side of a ship upon which the wind is blowing.

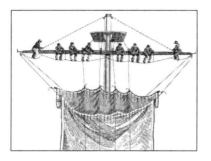

RECOMMENDED READING

Blake, Nicholas and Richard Lawrence. *The Illustrated Companion to Nelson's Navy*. Mechanicsburg, PA: Stackpole Books, 2000.

Barnes, James. *Naval Actions of the War of 1812*. New York: Harper & Brothers, 1896.

Bowditch, Nathaniel. *American Practical Navigator: An Epitome of Navigation and Nautical Astronomy, No. 9*. Washington: U.S. Navy Hydrographic Office, 1917.

Brodine, Charles, Jr., Michael J. Crawford, and Christine F. Hughes. *IRONSIDES! The Ship, the Men and the Wars of the USS Constitution*. Fireship Press, 2007.

Burrows, Montagu. *Memoir of Admiral Sir Henry Ducie Chads, G.C.B.* Portsea, England: Griffin, 1869.

Clowes, Willaim Laird. *The Royal Navy: A History from the Earliest Times to 1900*. Volume V. London: Chatham Publishing, 1997. Originally published, London: Sampson Low, Marston & Company, Ltd., 1900.

Colledge, J. J. *Ships of the Royal Navy: The Complete Record of all Fighting Ships of the Royal Navy from the Fifteenth Century to the Present*. Annapolis: Naval Institute Press, 1987.

Cook, Captain James, RN. *The Journals of Captain James Cook on His Voyages of Discovery: The Voyage of the* Endeavour, *1768-1771*. Ed. by J. C. Beaglehole. Cambridge: Cambridge University Press, 1955.

Cooper, James Fenimore. *The History of the Navy of the United States of America.* Vol. I. Philadelphia: Lea & Blanchard, 1839.

Dearborn, Brigadier General Henry A. S., USV. *The Life of William Bainbridge, Esq., of the United States Navy.* Originally pub. 1816. Ed. by James Barnes. Princeton: Princeton University Press, 1931.

Dudley, William S., and Michael J. Crawford, eds. *The Naval War of 1812: A Documentary History.* Vol. I: 1812. Washington: U.S. Naval Historical Center, 1985.

Evans, Surgeon Amos A., USN. "Journal Kept on Board the United States Frigate 'Constitution,' 1812." *The Pennsylvania Magazine of History and Biography*, Vol. 19, No. 2 (1895), pp. 152-169.

Farragut, Loyall. *The Life of David Glasgow Farragut, First Admiral of the United States Navy, Embodying His Journal and Letters.* New York: D. Appleton, 1879.

Forester, C. S. *The Age of Fighting Sail: The Story of the Naval War of 1812.* Garden City, NY: Doubleday, 1956.

Gardiner, Robert. *Frigates of the Napoleonic Wars.* Annapolis: Naval Institute Press, 2000.

Harland, John. *Seamanship in the Age of Sail: An Account of the Shiphandling of the Sailing Man-of-War 1600-1860, Based on Contemporary Sources.* Annapolis: Naval Institute Press, 1984.

Heidler, David S. and Jeanne T. Heidler, eds. *Encyclopedia of the War of 1812.* Santa Barbara: ABC-CLIO, 1997.

Henderson, James. *The Frigates: An Account of the Lesser Warships of the Wars from 1793 to 1815.* New York: Dodd, Mead & Co., 1970.

H.M. Frigate *Java. Master's Logbook*, August 1812—December 1812, Mr. Batty Robinson, Esq., Sailing Master. London: The National Archives.

James, William. *The Naval History of Great Britain, from the Declaration of War by France in 1793, to the Accession of George IV.* Volumes IV and VI. London: Richard Bentley, 1837.

Latimer, Jon. *1812: War with America.* Cambridge: Belknap Press of Harvard University Press, 2007.

Lavery, Brian. *Nelson's Navy: The Ships, Men, and Organization, 1793-1815.* Annapolis: Naval Institute Press, 1989.

Long, David F. *Ready to Hazard: A Biography of Commodore William Bainbridge, 1774-1833.* Hanover, NH and London: University Press of New England, 1981.

Maffeo, Captain Steven E., USNR, Ret. *Most Secret and Confidential: Intelligence in the Age of Nelson.* Annapolis: Naval Institute; London: Chatham, 2001.

Mahan, Rear Admiral Alfred T., USN. *Sea Power in its Relations to the War of 1812.* Vol. II. Boston: Little, Brown, and Co., 1905.

Marryat, Captain Frederick, RN. *Frank Mildmay (Book Two of the Marryat Cycle).* Fireship Press, 2007.

Marshall, Lieutenant John, RN. *Royal Navy Biography; or, Memoirs of the Services of all the Flag-Officers, Superannuated Rear-Admirals, Retired-Captains, Post-Captains, and Commanders, Whose Names Appeared on the Admiralty List of Sea-Officers at the Commencement of the Year 1823, or Who Have Since Been Promoted.* 4 vols. London: Longman, Rees, Orme, Brown, and Green, 1823-1835.

Marshall, Commander John William Phillips, RN. "Private Letter to William Phillips, 18 April 1813," unpublished; courtesy USS *Constitution* Museum.

Martin, Commander Tyrone G., USN, Ret. *A Most Fortunate Ship: A Narrative History of Old Ironsides.* Rev. ed. Annapolis: Naval Institute Press, 1997.

"Minutes Taken at a Court Martial Assembled on board His Majesty's Ship *Gladiator*, in Portsmouth Harbour, on the 23rd Day of April 1813." Additional title, "Proceedings of the Court Martial Held on the Officers and Crew of His Majesty's Ship the *Java*." 18 p. with a diagram entitled "Track of the Action." London [?], 1813.

O'Brian, Patrick. *The Fortune of War.* New York; London: W.W. Norton, 1991.

O'Brian, Patrick. *Men-of-War: Life in Nelson's Navy.* New York: W.W. Norton, 1995.

O'Byrne, William R. *A Naval Biographical Dictionary: Comprising the Life and Services of Every Living Officer in Her Majesty's Navy, from the Rank of Admiral of the Fleet to that of Lieutenant, Inclusive.* 2 vols. London: John Murray, 1849.

Pope, Dudley. *Life in Nelson's Navy*. London: Unwin Hyman, 1987.

Porter, Admiral David Dixon, USN. *Memoir of Commodore David Porter of the United States Navy*. Albany: J. Munsell, 1875.

Ray, Robert C. *The East Coast of South America, from Orinoco River to Cape Virgins*. Washington: United States Hydrographic Office, 1894.

Roach, Lieutenant j.g. John Charles, USNR. *The Art of Old Ironsides: An Essay in Sketches*. Fireship Press, 2007.

Roosevelt, Theodore. *The Naval War of 1812: The History of the United States Navy during the Last War with Great Britain, to which is Appended an Account of the Battle of New Orleans*. Vol. I. New York: G.P. Putnam's Sons, 1882.

Tuite, Peter T. *U.S. Naval Officers: Their Swords & Dirks, featuring the Collection of the United States Naval Academy Museum*. Lincoln, RI: Andrew Mowbray, 2004.

Turnbull, Archibald Douglas. Commodore David Porter, 1780-1843. New York: Century Co., 1929.

U.S. Department of the Navy. Naval Historical Center. Early History Branch. Old Ironsides' Battle Record: Documents of USS Constitution's Illustrious Deeds. Washington Navy Yard, Washington, D.C.
<http://www.history.navy.mil/docs/war1812/const1.htm>

U.S. Frigate *Constitution*. *Logbook*, September 1812—December 1812, William Bainbridge, Esq., Commanding. Microfilm. Record Group 45. Washington: U.S. National Archives and Records Administration.

U.S. Sloop-of-War *Hornet*. *Logbook*, December 1812—January 1813, James Lawrence, Esq., Commanding. Microfilm. Record Group 24. Washington: U.S. National Archives and Records Administration.

Wilkes, Lt. Charles, USN. *Narrative of the United States Exploring Expedition During the Years 1838-1842*. 5 vols. Philadelphia: Lea and Blanchard, 1845.

Woodman, Captain Richard, FRHistS, FNI. *The Sea Warriors: Fighting Captains and Frigate Warfare in the Age of Nelson*. London: Constable, 2001.

AUTHOR'S AFTERWORD

Upon laying this book down (or setting aside your e-reader), I'd like to think that you've been thoroughly entertained by a superb sea adventure. Regardless, there's no question that you now possess a solid knowledge of the real-life *Constitution/Java* story—a knowledge superior to that which you could obtain by reading *any* other historical *or* fictional account produced to date.

For anyone interested in the Great Age of Sail, the letters, reports, and statements of the very real Commodore Bainbridge, Lieutenant Chads, General Hislop, Surgeon Evans, Commander Marshall, &c are fascinating; as are the log books of the *Constitution*, *Java*, and *Hornet*; as are the Admiralty correspondence and orders; and as are the minutes of the British officers' court-martial. But, all of these are also (particularly for the early-nineteenth century) somewhat terse and to the point.

The same is true with various authorities of naval history, to include Alfred T. Mahan, James Fenimore Cooper, Theodore Roosevelt, William Laird Clowes, C. S. Forester, William M. James, Richard Woodman, Tyrone G. Martin, James Henderson, Edward Beach, and David F. Long—to name just a few—each of whom allows himself only three-to-four pages apiece to describe the *Java/Constitution* encounter. Even Patrick O'Brian, who fictionally fleshed it out with the coincidental presence and storyline of his major characters—Aubrey, Maturin, Killick, Bonden, Babbington—covered it with only 35 pages (and of those only 11 addressed the actual battle). And, while O'Brian masterfully made the battle come alive, he also altered a considerable number of facts to suit his particular agenda. I'm particularly concerned that he misrepresented Captain Lambert's tactical philosophy as well as tactical execution, and thus unfairly implied that Lambert mishandled the battle.

I've tried extremely hard to deliver to you solid historical truth, but at the same time bring the era to life and pull you into its time and place. As I mentioned in my "To the Reader" note at the beginning of the book, I began this story as traditional, formal non-fiction, but soon reworked it with a slightly fictional treatment. I thus hoped that such a process would colorize it and make it become more alive. I wanted the reader to sense to a greater degree what it was like to be standing on those decks amidst wind and spray and among those crews—and feel things beyond mere dry historical facts thrown upon a page. To quote Professor Lee Gutkind, the founding editor of the journal *Creative Nonfiction*, my goal was to present "reportage in a scenic, dramatic fashion," and communicate "information using the tools of the fiction writer while maintaining allegiance to fact." As I mentioned earlier, this has been a goal of such great authors as Stephen Crane and Michael Shaara in dealing with military history.

Thus, I've pursued a style that various scholars of literature, such as Gutkind, call "creative non-fiction." Literary critic Barbara Lounsberry further analyzes the nature of this *genre*: "Verifiable subject matter and exhaustive research guarantee the nonfiction side... ; the narrative form and structure disclose the writer's artistry; and finally, its polished language reveals that the goal all along has been literature."

I'm indebted to a large number of people who helped me on this voyage. Risking great chance of omission, my attempt at a fair list includes Tom Grundner and Jessica Knauss at Fireship Press (Tucson); Debbie Coffey, Betsy Muenger, Tom DiSilverio, Ed Scott, Karin Kaufman, Jeff Stotler, and Dolores Maffeo (Colorado); Hank Maher, Joe Troiani, and particularly Carl and Pen DauBach (Illinois); Terry Finnegan (California); Peter Colerico (Charlestown); Jim Dargan and Susan Smith-Petersen (Boston); Rich Whelan (Naval History and Heritage Command Detachment Boston); Kate Lennon, Matt McGrath, Gary Foreman, Dana Green, Laura O'Neill, Chris White, Jim Banfield, Burt Logan, Anne Grimes Rand, and—*particularly*—the awesome Matt Brenckle and Harrie Slootbeek (USS *Constitution* Museum, Charlestown Navy Yard); Lieutenant Joe Cooper, Commander Bill Bullard, Boatswain's Mates 1st Class Aaron Haney and Darrin Ritter, Seamen

William Crandell and Kiril Drozdov, Chief John Hutchinson, and
Master Chiefs Steve Brandt and Don Abele (USS *Constitution*);
Charles Brodine (Naval History and Heritage Command, Washington Navy Yard); Steve Phillips, Denis Clift, and *very particularly* John Rowland (Washington, D.C.); Stan Bryant and David
Keithly (Virginia); Leslie Carroll (New York City); and Andrew
Lambert (King's College, London). I gratefully salute—as always—my invaluable mentor and friend Richard Woodman (Har-
wich, Essex). Moreover, I owe an enormous debt to another English gentleman, Mr. David Chads (a direct descendant of the
Java's first lieutenant, the heroic Lt. Henry Ducie Chads), who enthusiastically supplied considerable public and family documents
and graphics—as well as cheerfully executed several crucial research forays on my behalf into the British National Archives. Another huge debt goes to military and adventure writer Steve
Coonts, who for over a dozen years has been a wonderful mentor,
critic, cheerleader, and sounding board—always remarkably generous with his time and advice. Finally, once again I virtually raise
my Number One scraper (my gold-laced hat) to my wife Rhonda,
my son Micah, and my father Eugene for their steadfast support
and interest. I'm very sad that my mother, June, didn't get to see
the completion of this book. She was intrigued with it as it began;
for a number of reasons I'm certain she would have loved it in its
final form.

June would have also liked the reference in the story—albeit
brief—to Royal Navy Hospital Haslar at Gosport. In February
1918, her father, Arthur Miller, was a soldier in the Wisconsin
Army National Guard, and survived being sunk by a German U-
boat while on board the British steamship *Tuscania*. Most of the
troops were saved (260 were lost out of 2,179), and they came
ashore along the north Irish coast. Many, including my grandfather, were shortly moved to Haslar. He spent considerable time
there trying to recover, and my mother told me that for the rest of
his life he often spoke about the wonderful care he received in
British hands. Thus, it goes without saying—but I'll say it anyway—if it weren't for the Royal Navy I wouldn't be here; they
pulled my grandfather out of the freezing North Atlantic and then
ensured his recovery at Haslar.

The lengthy passage I included concerning the actions in the
Indian Ocean around Madagascar and the Mauritius—which led to
the 1811 capture of the French national warship *Renommée* and
her transformation into the British frigate *Java*—is taken almost

word-for-word from William James' 1837 *magnum opus* entitled *The Naval History of Great Britain, from the Declaration of War by France in 1793, to the Accession of George IV*. I absolutely felt that the *Java*'s background had to be in this story, so I determined to have a major character tell it to other characters and thus also to you. My concern was not merely the facts but equally my ability to articulate them *at length* with the authentic tone and style of an expert early-19th-century British gentleman. I soon realized that James' construction, phrasing, and voice were perfect, exactly what was needed, and certainly beyond my ability to improve, so with little modification it's he who tells the story—through Capt. Lambert—and not I. (I'm hopeful that Mr. James wouldn't mind).

Likewise, and for the same reasons, I again borrowed heavily from Mr. James (as well as from William Laird Clowes, *The Royal Navy: A History from the Earliest Times to 1900*). These equally eloquent accounts of Lambert's 1804 and 1805 actions against the French vessel *Psyché*, as well as his 1810 actions while in command of the frigate *Iphigenia*, firmly establish his background as an experienced fighting captain—this time told through Lt. Chads.

I'm indebted to Lt. Charles Wilkes, USN, for his evocative descriptions of Madeira, the Canaries, and the Cape Verdes, found in his wonderful 1844 *Narrative of the United States Exploring Expedition During the Years 1838-1842*. Some of the iconic Capt. James Cook's place descriptions and hydrographic observations, taken from his journal on board H.M. Bark *Endeavour* in 1768, were also extremely helpful. Similarly, I owe Capt. Frederick Marryat, RN, (1792-1848), the ground-breaking sea-adventure novelist, for the lyrics to the Christmas song "Port Admiral, You be Damned," some dialog during the capture of the *William*, and much of the "Neptunus Rex" drama onboard the *Java*. As a brilliant storyteller with a particular eye for detail, having been a midshipman under the incredible Capt. Lord Cochrane, and having served as a lieutenant during the War of 1812, Marryat's given me some remarkable authenticity and insight. I recommend at least two of his books, *Frank Mildmay* (1829); and *Mr. Midshipman Easy* (1836). Lastly, I strongly recommend all of the publications of a former captain of the *Constitution*, Cmdr. Tyrone G. Martin, USN—and of those particularly *A Most Fortunate Ship: A Narrative History of Old Ironsides*.

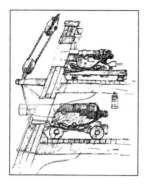

NOTES ON THE ILLUSTRATIONS

Some of the elegant drawings of masts and rigging (sometimes with slight modifications), were done by an Englishman named Darcy Lever and are taken from his remarkable book *The Young Sea Officer's Sheet Anchor, or a Key to the Leading of Rigging and to Practical Seamanship*, originally published in 1808. Some of the other evocative pen-and-ink sketches (again, sometimes with slight modifications) were done by Capt. John Charles Roach, USN and are taken from a mid-1970s U.S. Navy publication: *Old Ironsides, U.S. Frigate Constitution—An Essay in Sketches*. The beautiful sail plan of the *Constitution*, circa 1817, is taken from an image in the U.S. National Archives. The cutaway hull diagram of the ship (which I heavily modified) was originally done by the award-winning British illustrator John Batchelor, and published in a U.S. National Park Service Handbook entitled *Charlestown Navy Yard: Boston National Historic Park, Massachusetts* (1995). The chart of the Atlantic Ocean, again heavily modified, is from a copy of *Johnson's Map of the World on Mercator's Projection*, published in 1862 by Johnson and Browning.

The dramatic cover painting of the *Constitution* and the *Java* was done by the award-winning contemporary American artist Patrick O'Brien, who works in Baltimore (www.patrickobrien studio.com).

The illustrations at the beginning of each chapter are identified as follows:

Prologue

"Jonque Chinoise a Sincapour," from *Voyage au Polo Sud*, circa 1840.

Chapter 1

"U.S.F. *Constitution* Capturing H.B.M.F. *Guerrière*," by Thomas Birch (1779-1851), circa 1813.

Chapter 2

"Naval Engagement of 7 July 1777 between the American Continental Frigates *Hancock* and *Boston*; their Prize HMS *Fox*; and the British Frigates *Flora* and *Rainbow*," by Francis Holman (1729-1784), circa 1779. I could find no image of the *Essex* and the *Alert*, so I thought that this painting conveyed at least the essence of the situation.

Chapter 3

"Portsmouth, Rigging Hulk, and Frigate," by Edward W. Cooke (1811-1880), engraved by William Finden (1787-1852), circa 1842.

Chapter 4

"View of Bunker Hill, from the [Charlestown] Navy Yard [Commandant's House in the foreground]," date unknown (but prior to 1825), Boston National Historical Park.

Chapter 5

"[Boston] State Street, 1801," by James B. Marston (*fl.* 1803-1807).

Chapter 6

"View of the U.S. Navy Yard at Charlestown, Mass." In *Gleason's Pictorial Drawing Room Companion*, August 23, 1851 edition.

Chapter 7

"South View of Charlestown, Mass. ... A part of the buildings connected with the U.S. Navy Yard are seen on the extreme right." Postcard, circa 1840.

Chapter 8

"U.S.F. *United States* Capturing H.B.M.F. *Macedonian*," by Thomas Birch (1779-1851), circa 1815.

Chapter 9

"Portsmouth," by J.M.W. Turner (1775-1851), circa 1824.

Chapter 10

"Chart of Boston, its Environs and Harbour." Engraved and published by William Fadden, Charing Cross, London, 1777.

Chapter 11

"A Quiet Anchorage, 1795," by William Anderson (1757-1837).

Chapter 12

"View of Southsea Castle," as it appears from Spithead. Original drawing by Nicholas Pocock, engraved by Hall, circa 1806.

Chapter 13

"Sketch of the Sea and Seagulls," from *The Last Voyage*, by Lady Brassey, 1887.

Chapter 14

"Seamen Aloft," artist and date unknown—or, at least unknown to me despite considerable effort to identify.

Chapter 15

"Porto Praya, in the Island of St. Jago." Engraved by Hall, from a drawing by 'G.T,' published by Joyce Gold, 1811.

Chapter 16

"USS *Constitution*," USS *Constitution* Museum brochure, circa 2007.

Chapter 17

"San Salvador, Bahia," print published by Henry Colburn, Great Marlborough Street, London, 1839.

Chapter 18

"Crossing the Line," in *The Voyage of the Beagle*, by Charles Darwin, 1845.

Chapter 19

"Land... going for Bahia; Sight of the Capes W½N from Cape Salvador; Sight from Cape St. Antonio Fort," from *Voyage to New Holland* by William Dampier, 1699.

Chapter 20

"The Evening before the Battle of Copenhagen: the Wardroom of HMS *Elephant*," by Thomas Davidson (1863-1903). The great cabins of *Old Ironsides* and the *Java* would have looked quite similar during their Christmas dinners.

Chapter 21

"Action between USF *Constitution* and HMS *Java*," by Charles R. Patterson (1878-1958). Official U.S. Navy photograph, 80-G-K-9451 1948.

Chapter 22

"USF *Constitution* Defeats HMF *Java*," by Anton Otto Fischer (1882-1962). Official U.S. Navy Photograph, NH 85543-KN.

Epilogue

"Bahia de Todos los Santos, Town and Harbour," from *Voyage to New Holland* by William Dampier, 1699.

A TRIBUTE TO
THE KILLED AND
WOUNDED

Before we close this story completely, I respectfully ask the reader to join me in giving some recognition to the brave crews of the two ships of this story—and *in particular*—to those who gave their blood and lives for their respective countries. There is some evidence that the number of British killed was significantly larger than the list below admits—perhaps as many as thirty more; however, after cross-checking several sources—and thus to the best of my knowledge—in real life these men were as follows:

14 Killed on board the U. S. Frigate "Constitution"

John Aylwin, *Lieutenant* (mortally wounded)
Joseph Adams, *Able-bodied Seaman*
Jonas Angrau, *Able-bodied Seaman*
John Chevers, *Able-bodied Seaman*
Joseph Chevers, *Able-bodied Seaman* (mortally wounded)
Patrick Conner, *Able-bodied Seaman*
Peter Furnace, *Able-bodied Seaman* (mortally wounded)
Barney Hart, *Able-bodied Seaman*
Reuben Sanderline, *Able-bodied Seaman* (mortally wounded)
Stephen Webb, *Able-bodied Seaman* (mortally wounded)
John Allen, *Ordinary Seaman*
William Cooper, *Ordinary Seaman*
Mark Snow, *Ordinary Seaman*
Thomas Hanson, *Private of Marines*

25 Wounded on board the "Constitution"

William Bainbridge, *Commodore* (seriously, both legs)
Charles Waldo, *Master's Mate* (amputated thigh)
Lewis German, *Midshipman* (slightly)
Peter Woodbury, *Quartermaster* (severely)
Enos Bateman, *Able-bodied Seaman* (dangerously)
Phillip Brimblecomb, *Able-bodied Seaman* (amputated arm)
John Clements, *Able-bodied Seaman* (amputated leg)
Philip Cook, *Able-bodied Seaman* (slightly)
Abijah Eddy, *Able-bodied Seaman* (slightly)
James Hammond, *Able-bodied Seaman* (slightly)
William Long, *Able-bodied Seaman* (dangerously)
Stephen Sheppard, *Able-bodied Seaman* (slightly)
Joseph Ward, *Able-bodied Seaman* (amputated thigh)
William Weaden, *Able-bodied Seaman* (burns to legs)
Nicholas Wextram, *Able-bodied Seaman* (considerable burns)
Samuel Brown, *Ordinary Seaman* (severely, burns)
Daniel Hogan, *Ordinary Seaman* (severely, fingers lost on both
hands)
Thomas Williams 3rd, *Ordinary Seaman* (slightly)
John Vogel, *Ordinary Seaman* (severely)
Duncan MacDonald, *Ordinary Seaman* (seriously, burns)
Stephen Saunders, *[rate unclear]* (slightly)
John Brannon, *[rate unclear]* (contusion)
Michael Chesley, *Private of Marines* (slightly)
John Elwell, *Private of Marines* (slightly)
Anthony Reeves, *Private of Marines* (burns to legs)

24 Killed on board H.M. Frigate "Java"

Henry Lambert, *Captain* (mortally wounded)
Charles Jones, *Master's Mate*
Thomas Hammond, *Master's Mate*
William Gascoigne, *Master's Mate*
William Salmond, *Midshipman*
Edward Keele, *Midshipman* (mortally wounded)

William Hitchans, *Quartermaster*
James Fazan [Fagan], *Quartermaster*
William Weston, *Captain of the Afterguard*
D. Harraghan [Harrogan], *Bosun's Mate*
Jacob Bouch, *Able-bodied Seaman*
Thomas Card, *Able-bodied Seaman*
Charles Samuel, *Able-bodied Seaman*
Samuel Warren, *Able-bodied Seaman* (mortally wounded)
William Clarke, *Landman*
James Langford, *Landman*
George Woodward, *Landman*
John Doel, *Private of Marines*
Malcolm McClew, *Private of Marines*
Carl Schmidt, *Private of Marines*
George Taylor, *Private of Marines*
Thomas Mathias, *Supernumerary clerk*
William Clinton, *Supernumerary Able-bodied Seaman*
John Dunn, *Supernumerary Ordinary Seaman*

110 Wounded on board the *"Java"*

Royal Navy

Henry Chads, *Lieutenant* (slightly)
Batty Robinson, *Sailing master* (severe gunshot)
James Humble, *Boatswain* (dangerous amputation)
C. Keele, *Midshipman* (severe arm wound)
Martin Burke, *Midshipman* (severely)
Frederick Morton, *Midshipman* (severely)
James West, *Midshipman* (slightly)
James Hannans, *Armourer* (severe contusion)
William Roberts, *Quarter Gunner* (dangerously)
Robert Blackmore, *Quartermaster* (slightly)
Henry Blakey, *Captain of the Maintop* (severe gunshot)
Peter Saunders [Sanders], *Captain of the Foretop* (severe
face wound)
Charles Speedy [Speedz], *Captain of the Forecastle* (severe
leg wound)
J. Brennan, *Captain of the Afterguard* (severe hand wound)
John King, *Gunner's Mate* (leg wound)

M^t. Darby, *Bosun's Mate* (slightly)
Colin Hale [C. Kerr], *Carpenter's Mate* (slightly)
John "Barbeque" Smith, *Cook* (foot wound)
David Anderson, *Able-bodied Seaman* (slightly)
John Ansen, *Able-bodied Seaman* (severe gunshot)
Peter Bogarth, *Able-bodied Seaman* (severe arm wound)
Thomas Burnett, *Able-bodied [ordinary] Seaman* (severely)
George Fells, *Able-bodied [ordinary] Seaman* (dangerous
    arm wound)
A. Gullichson [Guilichsen], *Able-bodied Seaman* (slightly)
Joshua Harper, *Able-bodied Seaman* (slight arm wound)
Benjamin Leach [Leech], *Able-bodied Seaman* (slightly)
Martin Rain [Kain], *Able-bodied Seaman* (severely)
Thomas Platt, *Able-bodied Seaman* (contusion)
J. Sharp, *Able-bodied Seaman* (slightly)
Thomas Smith, *Able-bodied Seaman* (slight breast wound)
William Smith, *Able-bodied Seaman* (leg wound)
William Ansley, *Ordinary [Able-bodied] Seaman* (severe gunshot)
John Casey, *Ordinary Seaman* (slight lower jaw wound)
J. Cotterell, *Ordinary Seaman* (slightly)
Timothy Dayley [Dayly], *Ordinary Seaman* (severe arm wound)
Alexander Fowles, *Ordinary [able-bodied] Seaman* (severely)
Luigi [Luige, Luigne] Guilhard [Guethard, Guithard], *Ordinary
    Seaman* (dangerous arm amputation)
James Hooker, *Ordinary Seaman* (severe gunshot)
John Lafrette, *Ordinary Seaman* (severely)
Thomas Miles, *Ordinary Seaman* (slightly)
William Mooly [Woolfe], *Ordinary Seaman* (severely)
J. [I.] Murray [Murry], *Ordinary Seaman* (slightly)
William Robson, *Ordinary Seaman* (severely)
Pedro Rogrigues [Rodrigues], *Ordinary Seaman* (slightly)
James Russell, *Ordinary Seaman* (dangerous amputation)
Richard Sharey [Shaw], *Ordinary Seaman* (slightly)
James Smith (No. 2), *Ordinary Seaman* (severely)
James Smith (No. 3), *Ordinary Seaman* (severe gunshot)
John Smith (No. 1), *Ordinary Seaman* (slightly)
John Tregare [Tregear], *Landman [Ordinary Seaman]* (severely)
J. Williams (No. 1), *Ordinary Seaman* (severely)
Joseph Robinson, [*unknown*] (severe hand wound)
Thomas Roberts, [*unknown*] (leg wound)

Joshua Allen, *Landman* (fractured arm)
Anthony Cruize, *Ordinary Seaman [Landman]* (severely contused arm)
J. Debrie [Debnie], *Landman* (slightly)
John Kelly, *Landman* (severe gunshot)
Den^s. Harrington, *Landman [Ordinary Seaman]* (severely)
John Moore, *Landman* (leg wound)
H. Norton, *Landman* (slightly)
Thomas Porter [Portes], *Landman* (severe back and breast wounds]
Xars^T. [B.M.] Stanburgh [Stanhough], *Landman* (slightly)
Thomas Wallen [Waller], *Landman* (slightly)
J. Ward, *Landman* (slightly)
Richard Whittington, *Landman* (severely)
James Whybrows [Wybrow, Whybrow], *Landman* (severe gunshots)
Den^s. Handlin [Handling], *Landman* (slightly)
John Moriarty, *Second-class Boy* (slightly)
William Roberts, *Third-class Boy* (severe fracture)

Royal Marines

David Davis, *2nd Lieutenant of Marines* (several severe wounds)
Thomas Ellis, *Sergeant of Marines* (slightly)
Daniel Bennett, *Sergeant of Marines* (severe gunshot)
Benjamin Johnson, *Corporal of Marines* (severe head wound)
George Ketlow, *Corporal of Marines* (severe fractured clavicle)
George Rellocos, *Corporal of Marines* (fracture)
James Beuly, *Private of Marines* (amputation)
Benjamin Houlder, *Private of Marines* (slightly [severely])
William Dogmore, *Private of Marines* (severe [slight] neck wound)
D. Wood, *Private of Marines* (slightly [severely])
James Ford, *Private of Marines* (slightly)
Matthew Cook, *Private of Marines* (severe gunshot)
Charles Rankenburg, *Private of Marines* (slightly)
Thomas Lewis, *Private of Marines* (severe gunshot)
William Golightly, *Private of Marines* (several severe wounds)
Joseph Baxter, *Private of Marines* (severe arm wound)
Nathaniel Roberts, *Private of Marines* (foot wound)
John Williams, *Private of Marines* (slight leg wound)

George Wilson, *Private of Marines* (severe gunshot)
Thomas Powell, *Private of Marines* (slightly)
Thomas McHale, *Private of Marines* (slight arm wound
and gunshot)
Joshua Thompkins, *Private of Marines* (severe back wound)
William Read, *Private of Marines* (severe gunshot)
Samuel Bailey, *Private of Marines* (severely)

Supernumeraries

John Marshall, *Master and Commander* (slightly)
James Sanders, *Lieutenant* (slightly)
J. T. Wood, *Captain* (British Army), (serious head wound)
William Brown, *Master's Mate* (severely)
Samuel Swift, *Able-bodied Seaman* (slightly)
John Que, *Able-bodied Seaman* (slightly)
Robert Spence, *Able-bodied Seaman* (slightly)
William Dickson, *Able-bodied Seaman* (slightly [severely])
Daniel Hayes, *Able-bodied Seaman* (severely)
Samuel Clarke, *Ordinary Seaman* (severely)
John Fletcher, *Ordinary Seaman* (severely)
Henry Assea, *Seaman* (slightly)
Antony Francisco, *Landman* (amputation)
Benjamin Pauling, *Second-class Boy* (slightly)
George Herue, *Third-class Boy* (slightly)
William Corman, *Private of Marines* (severely)

ABOUT THE
AUTHOR

STEVEN E. MAFFEO

Steve Maffeo is the Associate Library Director at the U.S. Air Force Academy. He was born and grew up in Denver. He holds a B.A. (English) from the University of Colorado; an M.A. (library science) from the University of Denver; and an M.S. (Strategic Intelligence) from the Joint Military Intelligence College. His civilian career's mostly been as a line librarian and as a library administrator at the University of Northern Colorado (Greeley); the U.S. Naval War College (Newport, R.I.); the Aurora (Colo.) Public Library; and the Air Force Academy.

In 2008, Steve retired as a navy Captain after 30 years' service (both enlisted and commissioned) in the Colorado Army National Guard, the U.S. Navy, and the U.S. Naval Reserve. He had many assignments with many organizations; the last were Commanding Officer, Office of Naval Intelligence Reserve Unit 0287 in Salt Lake City; Director, Joint Intelligence Center Pacific Detachment Denver; and Reserve Director, National Defense Intelligence College Part-Time Programs, Washington D.C. His military decorations include the Legion of Merit, the Defense Meritorious Service Medal, and three Navy and Marine Corps Commendation Medals.

For the past nine years he's also been a visiting history lecturer / tour-guide instructor for the "age-of-sail" frigate USS Constitution ("Old Ironsides") in Charlestown, Mass. Steve's other major interests are military/naval history in general, the history of secret intelligence, the Boy Scouts of America, and old cars (he has a '69 Chevelle Malibu coupe and a '67 Corvette Stingray convertible).

He lives in Colorado Springs with his wife Rhonda (a computer programmer/analyst) and his son Micah (an Eagle Scout and 2nd-degree Karate Black Belt).

Please visit Steve's website at www.StevenMaffeo.com.

Two unforgetable books about
OLD IRONSIDES